Who Should Melissa Marry?

Who Should Melissa Marry?

Created by Bill Adler
Written by Doris Cassiday

A BIRCH LANE PRESS BOOK
Published by Carol Publishing Group

A Birch Lane Press Book
Published by Carol Publishing Group
Birch Lane Press is a registered trademark of Carol Communications, Inc.
Editorial Offices: 600 Madison Avenue, New York, N. Y. 10022
Sales & Distribution Offices: 120 Enterprise Avenue, Secaucus, N.J. 07094
In Canada: Canadian Manda Group, P.O. Box 920 Station U, Toronto, Ontario M8Z 5P9
Queries regarding rights and permissions should be addressed to Carol Publishing Group,
600 Madison Avenue, New York, N.Y. 10022

Carol Publishing Group books are available at special discounts for bulk purchases,
sales promotions, fund-raising, or educational purposes. Special editions can be created
to specifications. For details contact: Special Sales Department, Carol Publishing Group,
120 Enterprise Avenue, Secaucus, N.J. 07094

Manufactured in the United States of America
10 9 8 7 6 5 4 3 2 1

Library of Congress Cataloging-in-Publication Data

Cassiday, Doris.
    Who should Melissa marry? / created by Bill Adler : written by
Doris Cassiday.
        p.   cm.
    "A Birch Lane Press book."
    ISBN 1-55972-259-2
    I. Adler, Bill. II. Title.
PS3553.A79555W48   1994
813'.54—dc20

94-12616
CIP

We are most grateful to Bruce Cassiday for his
creative assistance

Contest Rules

Reading this book will qualify you to enter a $10,000 contest for the best answer to this question: *Who Should Melissa Marry?*

Follow these simple rules: Use plain or lined white paper, with your name and address clearly printed at the top of each page. Select your candidate from these three men: Barry Ford, Jonathan Stark, and Andrew Royce. Then write an essay of up to 750 words, printed or typed, telling why you believe him to be the best one for Melissa to marry.

In writing your essay, be sure to tell why you have made your judgments, using material that is in the book and facts that can be determined or assumed from reading this book. The clarity of your reasoning, the rationale for your decision, and the literary craftsmanship of your writing will be the determining factors in our judgment of the winner.

All entries must be postmarked no later than March 31, 1995. Mail to Carol Publishing Group/Melissa, P.O. Box 2516, Secaucus, N.J. 07094. No entry form or entry fee is necessary. You can enter as many times as you wish, with one entry per envelope. All entries will become the property of the publisher.

The winner of the $10,000 prize will be notified by mail on or before May 15, 1995. No substitutions for the prize will be allowed. Any and all applicable taxes are the responsibility of the winner. The winner may be asked to sign a stagement of eligibility and the winner's name and likeness may be used for publicity purposes. Entries are the property of Carol Publishing Group. This contest is open to residents of the United States and Canada.

Contest entries will be judged by the author, the creator, the editor, and the publisher, with the final decision at the sole discretion of the judges. Employees (and their families) of Carol Pub-

Contents

WHO SHOULD MELISSA MARRY?
A romance novel without an ending— and the reader whose ending is selected will win $10,000!

Melissa Bonner is a successful young sports reporter working at a Seattle television station. During a crucial phase of her young life, she is faced with the decision that will dramatically affect every moment of her future: she must decide which of three men to marry.

Barry Ford, 28, the star quarterback for the Seattle Sea Lions. He is a charismatic figure with an almost legendary aura about him.

Jonathan Stark is the president of the University of Seattle. A divorced man in his late forties, Stark is elegant and aristocratic.

Andrew Royce, at 33, is a solid, straightforward man who is Melissa's bodyguard when she begins to receive threatening letters.

One of these three men is perfect for Melissa. The reader is asked to help Melissa select the right man to be her husband and the reader with the winning entry will collect $10,000.

Who Should Melissa Marry?

One

Superstar

In the third row of Channel 8's screening room Melissa Bonner turned to Al Griswold, her cameraman, to see if he was ready; he was. Then she waved to Takeo Kubo, her soundman, who as usual was slumped down in the back row where it was quiet and conducive to nodding off.

"Ready?"

"Ready when you are, M.B.," Kubo called in a mock reprise of the oldest gag in show business.

She really had an eclectic crew, she thought as she signaled the projectionist in the rear booth. Kubo, the most talkative nisei on the West Coast, perhaps in America; and Griswold, the most reticent if not mute cameraman in television.

As for Melissa herself, Channel 8's sportscaster was already, at the age of twenty-five, a TV news personality in her own right. Even more beautiful in person than on the screen, she projected electronically the perfect image of integrity and authenticity. Her light brown hair was delicately coiffed, appearing almost as if it were windblown into place and not carefully sculpted by a studio stylist. She had honey-colored eyes and a way of smiling quirkily that lit up her whole face. Her demeanor was of a soft and personable nature. And yet playing against her appearance was an impish sense of humor that occasionally surfaced to cause visible discomfort to sports figures she interviewed.

She was dressed now in her on-camera wardrobe: a loosely fitting yellow jacket and skirt, a white scoop-neck knit tank top, and a faux pearl choker. Incongruously, she wore running shoes to navigate the variety of surfaces she encountered on her daily field excursions. Slim and well-proportioned, she was one of the most listened-to and talked-about sports reporters in the Northwest.

Melissa Bonner had always prided herself on doing her homework. That was the reason for this preliminary screening of every bit of film and tape Channel 8 had on Barry Ford in action. She would be facing the Seattle Sea Lions' new quarterback on Monday morning at a press conference in the Kingdome. She wanted a good, solid, in-depth look at him before she prepared her questions. Background searches sometimes dug up interesting angles on people she interviewed. She wanted to see *everything* available.

The room lights dimmed and the screen lit up. The clips had been arranged in no particular order. There were snippets from games. There were bits and pieces of interviews with the quarterback. There were shots of Ford on the field and off.

Melissa had been at the Kingdome and had seen Barry Ford play three years ago. That was before he had sustained a bad knee injury that put him on the sidelines for eighteen months. With the departure of Reggie Brown, Seattle's quarterback, who had been leading the Sea Lions in a lemminglike rush into the waters of Puget Sound, the team's owner had prevailed on Miami to trade Barry Ford in return for two draft choices. By now Ford was rumored to be back at full strength.

Time would tell.

He looked great in the action clips Melissa was watching. He had joined the Dolphins in 1987 and hit his peak in 1992, just before his injury. There were a number of slow-motion shots, and in them Ford came across as almost a balletic genius—a man who was the personification of grace under pressure. He moved quickly and surely, like a dancer, perhaps, but without the nuances and flourishes that put a dancer in another world from a football player.

The screening-room door opened. Melissa was spellbound as Barry Ford dodged three tacklers and delivered a long pass into the end zone for a score. She turned her head. It was Luanne Doty.

"Sorry I'm late."

Melissa accepted her excuse with a nod of the head. Luanne was Melissa's assistant—actually her writer. She prepared the text that Melissa read on camera during the sportscasts. Twenty-three and blond and perky, she had cool blue eyes and a bee-stung mouth that struck some males as very sexy. She was no easygoing pushover, however. In fact, she was in it for no one else but Luanne.

The clips rolled on. Luanne was staring at the screen in total enchantment. "Look at that marvelous hunk!" She sighed. "He's magnificent!"

Luanne was looking at him as a man—a masculine body, a macho personality, a force of nature. Melissa was viewing him as a veteran Pro Bowl quarterback who might be the answer to Seattle's quest for a winning season.

Melissa Bonner had come onto the sports scene honestly. Her father had been a longtime linebacker for the Chicago Bears after a distinguished football career at the University of Iowa. He had even scouted for the Bears on a part-time basis after retiring. Melissa was assessing Barry Ford through the eyes of her father, Brad Bonner.

She felt that queasy little twinge of despair as her thoughts settled on him. The deaths of both parents—even though six years in the past—were still on her mind. The way of their going was part of the miserable irony of fate: their house in Sioux City, Iowa, had blown up because of a gas furnace leak.

Luanne gasped.

Melissa shook off her moment of despondence and stared at the screen. It was a close-up of Barry Ford, stripped to the waist, grinning into the camera and chatting with an off-camera interviewer. He was headed for the showers, but that didn't matter to him.

"Look at those pecs!" Luanne sighed. "And the nipples!"

Ford turned and the camera caught him moving away.

"What a tush!" Luanne whistled. "Those beautiful, absolutely ravishing—buns!"

Kubo was laughing in the rear row. "They call him Supertush down in Miami," he cried out to Luanne.

"Super, super, Supertush!" Luanne crowed. "I could nibble those buns!" She noticed the silence emanating from Melissa Bonner. "What about you?"

Melissa was watching an in-your-face shot of Ford talking. The sound wasn't on. But she was studying him. He had laughing, dancing, mischievous eyes. And a mobile mouth—quick to laugh, quick to bark out orders, quick to shut tight. Here was a man who was in full control of himself and the people around him.

A quiver of excitement quickened Melissa's breathing. "Damned good quarterback," she said, half aloud.

"Oh, that. Sure." Luanne sank back in her chair.

The rest of the clips went by in silence. When the lights came on, Melissa signaled to Kubo and Griswold to join them. They huddled around her.

She said, "The word is that the Sea Lions are going to put Barry Ford to work immediately, without any easing into the job."

"With Reggie Brown gone, they've got to," Kubo noted.

"They've still got Jack Adams—Back-Up Jack," Melissa said. "That's what I'm going to ask. 'What about a rotating two-quarterback system? You know, one set of downs by Ford, the next set by Adams.'"

Kubo groaned. "Horrible idea."

"But it's a damned good *question*," Griswold offered.

"The old one-two punch," Luanne observed. "That's the way to do it."

Melissa looked at her notes. "I've got to alert Elmer Layden to dig up some clips from the archives on Back-Up Jack." Layden was the film editor. Melissa looked around. "Otherwise, are you guys all ready for Monday?"

"Steady on!"

Two

Chaos at the Kingdome

The Kingdome was a madhouse. Television crews, radio teams, journalists, and sports freelancers swarmed the area. The security was absolutely unbreakable. The parking lot had cops three deep directing the mob of reporters into the proper slots.

Melissa drove the Channel 8 van into a side area under the watchful eye of one of Seattle's officers. She led Kubo and Griswold across the lot, in through the tunnels, and laterally to the big, well-lighted press room.

The din was awesome. Melissa imagined that being sealed inside a bass drum with a drummer beating on the sides with giant-sized sticks felt exactly like this. Lights flashed, bulbs popped, voices bellowed over amplifiers. Bedlam.

Finally, about fifteen minutes after the time set for the press conference had elapsed, a door opened at the far end of the huge room. A shambling, slouched-over, sixty-five-year-old Slats Montgomery entered to make his way toward the center. He stopped where the microphones were taped, tied, locked, and braced against a podium that looked as if it might collapse from sheer electronics overweight.

"Hey, guys," the owner of the Sea Lions began in as uncharismatic a way as possible, "let's get this show on the road." He had a tight-fisted Alabama accent that he cherished to this day, even though he had gone to Yale and received an M.B.A. at Harvard.

He lauded the "great acquisition" by the Sea Lions, told how difficult it was to persuade the "great quarterback" to leave Miami to come to the Northwest, and noted how marvelous it was going to be with a tested, "great qualified athlete" of his dimensions leading the Sea Lions. Finally he mentioned the great name: "Ladies and gentlemen, Barry Ford!"

Applause. It was like the Academy Awards. The media were cheering this guy because he had all the right moves. The same door opened again and Barry Ford, in loose sweatshirt and jeans, began to walk the gauntlet to the microphone tree. He was grinning, ear-to-ear, like a jack-o'-lantern.

Melissa could not take her eyes from him. He seemed bigger than he had appeared on the football field and in the tapes and films. The lights shone directly on him, and he exuded charisma, good health, and ability. That was the only way she could describe it to herself. He was a charmer. Breathtaking.

Again, it was his eyes that caught her immediate interest. They were a lot bluer than they looked when he was photographed in his football helmet. His hair was curly and cut short, with a kind of golden sheen to it. He had a gap between his two front teeth. They gave his grin a kind of smart-ass, cocky look. Wrong words, she thought. It was a welcoming grin, a brotherly-love grin. It was affable, wise, and tolerant. This was the guy who was going to take the Sea Lions to the playoffs. Maybe to the Super Bowl. Hello, Barry Ford.

He got behind the formidable bank of microphones and looked around. He was actually blinded by the light pouring onto him, but he pretended to look everyone straight in the eye.

"I'm Barry Ford," he said. "Pleasure to meet you."

Wild applause again.

"Thank you," he said. "If that's all, I'll be out of here."

"No!" yelled the room in unison.

He laughed at them. He was having them on. Somehow, nobody cared. Hands immediately began waving in the air. Ford pointed, squinting into the light. "You. Channel 7?"

"Yeah. Uh, how long will it take you to get back your cutting edge after being on the sidelines for eighteen months?"

Ford looked into the light. "How'd you know I'd been out eighteen months?" he asked innocently.

Laughter.

"I heal good," he said. "I feel great." He glanced at Coach Ed Hatchett, who was standing next to Slats Montgomery. "I think I'll be able to suit up in maybe four months' time."

There were shouts.

Quickly Ford turned to Hatchett. "That's a joke, Coach."

Hatchett waved. He did not smile. It was not his nature to smile. Nor to be humorous, nor to be humored. He continued to stand like a slash pine in the middle of a threatened forest.

Hands waved in the air. Ford spotted someone in the back row. He enjoyed finding people in the back row. It seemed to be a part of his eagle-eye routine. Besides, he liked to work the underdog concept. He got good mileage out of it from the press.

"You in the back there. The guy with the field pack. *Seattle Times?*"

"How long do you think it'll take you to get used to Coach Hatchett's system?"

"What I can't memorize by next Sunday I'll write out on my shirt cuff," Ford said. "I've got long arms." He pointed from his wrist to his shoulder.

Coach Hatchett appeared to have left the group. Montgomery was grinning. Melissa wanted to get in her zinger to Ford before this whole press conference degenerated into a mob scene.

"Mr. Ford!" she kept yelling, waving her arm and pushing forward. Griswold continued to shoot everything that happened. "Mr. Ford—here! Please!"

He chose someone else. The questions droned on. Griswold continued shooting. Kubo glanced at Melissa and shrugged. He motioned her forward. She surged ahead and waved her arms.

Two more questions. Finally the blue eyes moved to Melissa. "Mr. Ford!" she shouted.

"Don't I know you from somewhere?" Ford asked, shading his eyes against the glare of the overheads.

"No, sir," said Melissa honestly.

"You seem familiar." He was puzzled. He frowned.

"Mr. Ford—"

"I've got it. I remember your picture."

"You've watched Channel 8?" Melissa asked in astonishment. "But you've just come to Seattle."

"The picture was on a man's desk," Ford said. His eyes were sparkling now. The ghost of a grin appeared on his lips. "The man was Brad Bonner, an ex-linebacker, who was scouting for the Chicago Bears at that time."

Melissa was momentarily stunned. "Yes, sir."

Ford looked at Melissa, a mischievous look in his eyes. He gazed out over the crowd. He had them. "It was my big chance. I was trying to break into the National Football League."

There was a pause. "What happened?" someone yelled.

"The son of a bitch turned me down!" Ford shouted, like a cornball comic delivering a punch line.

Melissa stared. Tears of anger started in her eyes. He was talking about her father—who had been killed in a terrible accident. What a bastard! "Your question?" Ford called out. "Ms. Bonner?"

She could not get hold of her tongue. She backed away in the crowd, clutching the microphone and melting down into the ground in a tiny heap of humiliation.

Someone gripped her by the elbow. It was Kubo. "Hey, Bonner, you haven't got your question out."

"I can't, Tak," she said in distress, shaking her head. "Let's get out of here."

"But—"

Melissa turned to Griswold. "Have you got enough for us?"

"I've been shooting from the beginning."

"Let's go," Melissa snapped.

"Hey, you can't do this!" Kubo warned in a low voice. "Hobbs will have your head on a plate!"

She willed herself to stand straight and move quickly through the crowd and out the door. Her eyes were moist but she did not break down. She would tell Hobbs to use the general stuff Griswold had shot. They could always pick up the extras from other stations.

They got out to the parking lot and Kubo shook his head. "I think you've made a bad mistake."

"I don't. I think the mistake was made by that—that—that—"

"—A-Number-One quarterback," Kubo supplied.

"He shamed me. He shamed the memory of my father."

Griswold laced his hands behind his head in the backseat of the van as she started it up. "He shamed himself."

Three

The Red Taurus

If it had not been for the nonstop prattle of her soundman, Takeo Kubo, Melissa Bonner would have noticed the red Taurus in her rearview mirror sooner.

"Know anybody who owns a red Taurus—last-year's model?" Melissa asked in the middle of one of Kubo's long Samuel Johnsonian turns. He was apparently trying to get Melissa's mind off the disastrous outcome of the Barry Ford confrontation.

"Huh?" Kubo grunted, turning to stare at her.

"Behind us." She indicated the rear of the company van she was driving.

Kubo turned to look out the back window. So did Griswold, who was in his usual mute funk following any bit of work in the field. Griswold shrugged quickly. Kubo gave a long, squint-eyed look at the Taurus and shook his head.

"Sun's on the windshield. Can't make out who's inside driving it," Kubo said briefly. "You getting paranoid?"

In point of fact, she was just a bit. Certain phone calls with no one on the other end had begun to erode her normal self-confidence. She had even seen what looked like that same red Taurus a week or so before, behind her for more than a few blocks. And there were those odd news stories that she had been getting in her in-basket about assaults on women. Or was it just careless misrouting of news clips?

So far she had told no one about the red Taurus, the news stories, or the phone calls, which seemed to have stopped lately. Perhaps, after all, they were just coincidences—wrong numbers or misdialings.

She knew that if she projected these things as threats of some kind she would appear to be building a façade of glamour around herself. After all, she was in the public eye and consequently subject to just such threats.

"Maybe one of your fans really fancies you," Kubo grinned. "You stick with us, kid," he continued, doing his Humphrey Bogart bit, "we'll protect you from a fate worse than death."

Her elbow jabbed him sharply in the chest.

In the rear of the van Griswold, sitting next to his precious shoulder camera, sighed.

By now Kubo had lapsed into silence himself. Melissa drove grimly on. Certainly she had blown the assignment. Darryl Hobbs, head of the news department at Channel 8, was a stickler for follow-through. She would have to face him when she was back in the office.

They pulled into the basement garage and were up in the studio unloading their equipment in minutes. Melissa went to the newsroom and spilled her notes on her desk. Then she sat down wearily, half hiding out and half waiting for the inevitable.

Thirty minutes later it happened. The door opened. Darryl Hobbs was slouching in the entrance. He was big-bellied, graying, and teddy-bear cuddly. She had once been asked what she thought of Hobbs, who was her hard-nosed, slave-driving, and yet essentially fair boss. "I adore him," she admitted.

She still adored him. But she could tell that at this point he no longer adored her. Obviously he had been screening the stuff Griswold had shot.

"We've got a problem, luv," he told Melissa.

"And its name is Melissa," she responded bleakly.

Hobbs began pacing. "I screened the material, waiting for your key question to come up. I continued screening, but the question never surfaced."

"I know it, Mr. Hobbs," Melissa said defensively.

"I then call in Kubo and Griswold. I find that you just walked out of there after Ford went for your father."

Luanne Doty entered the office without knocking.

"You gave up right then and there, luv," Hobbs went on, facing Melissa without losing a beat. Luanne realized that she had invaded a no-man's-land. She started to exit, but Hobbs motioned her to stay.

"Not if we're the only ones in town who *don't* run anything on the great Mr. Ford!" snapped Melissa.

"We've *got* to run Ford!"

"Let's run the Back-Up Jack stuff in the archives *instead*," Melissa said, with a glint in her eye.

Hobbs threw up his hands. "Then we'd be backing the loser in the quarterback game."

Melissa was biting her lip. "I did it wrong, didn't I?"

Hobbs turned to her directly, controlling his ire with difficulty. "Of course you did it wrong, luv! You had him! You had him by the short hairs!"

"I don't think I quite see how *I* had *him*," Melissa murmured.

"This is the way you had him," Hobbs explained. "The man was getting back at someone who had done him a bad turn a few years ago—your father. Here he is in Seattle playing the brand-new star quarterback, the savior of the city. You had a surefire put-down question to ask him. Were he and Jack Adams, Mr. Number Two, going to *share* the quarterback spot by alternating quarters or ball possessions? It seems to me by asking *that* question after his gauche put-down of your father you would have put him down in turn."

Melissa stared at him, unable to speak.

"Besides, he didn't know your dad was dead. Don't you see?"

Melissa's eyes opened wide. "You think he didn't know?"

"I'd bet on it. He's not an insensitive man."

"I hate him." Melissa smoldered.

"I've got an idea," Luanne said suddenly.

Hobbs turned to her. "What?"

"Let me see if I can get something out of him."

"No!" Melissa said.

Luanne stared at her. "Why not?" Luanne wondered, putting on her hurt-little-girl look.

Melissa glared at her. Then she turned to Hobbs. "I feel it would be better if we just played it straight. We use the footage Griswold got and the Q-and-A's the rest of the group provided. We'll pretend the remark about my father never occurred."

Hobbs was pinching his lower lip between his thumb and forefinger. "That may be the best way at that."

"Say Ford loses the game next week," Melissa went on. "*Then* we come in with our archive stuff on Back-Up Jack and go with that. 'Look who *might* have been a hero Sunday afternoon.' That kind of angle."

"And if he wins?" Hobbs asked.

"Just hang on to it. He's going to lose sometime!"

Hobbs shrugged. "Maybe you're right. We pretend the Ford attack on your father never happened. And we ride with what we have and the press conference boilerplate."

"I goofed up!" Melissa sighed. "But I was furious. I had to get out of there."

Hobbs was thinking. "Maybe we should run exactly what you asked and his reply. Then we let you face the camera and explain that your father died six years ago and that you're glad he isn't around to hear what Barry Ford thought about him."

Luanne's eyes lit up. "That's a kick in the ass. I like it!"

"No!" Melissa cried. "It's a gratuitous insult—exactly what prompted Barry Ford to go on about my father. Let's play it straight and forget the comment. Nobody else's going to use it."

Takeo Kubo came hurrying into Melissa's office. "He apologized!" Kubo said quickly, standing there with his hands on his hips.

"Who?" Luanne wanted to know.

"Barry Ford! He apologized to Melissa Bonner!" Kubo explained with a grin. "It's on the radio. A radio reporter called him on his lack of taste in telling that anecdote about Brad Bonner, and Ford simply rolled over on his back. 'I sincerely apologize to Ms. Bonner,'" he said. "They've got it on tape."

Melissa stood up, outraged. "Now we can't use anything at all! That man should have apologized to me! And if he had apologized to me, we would have had our story."

Hobbs frowned. "There's still a way to get around this. He snapped his fingers. "An open letter to Barry Ford. 'Dear Sir, I was so appalled when you insulted the memory of my father who has been dead for six years that I resisted the impulse to call you on it.' And so on. 'Now, to have you apologize to me through an intermediary—an intermediary who is in direct competition with

Channel 8 and with me—I cannot but believe that you have absolutely no regard for any kind of propriety or dignity. You should have apologized directly to me! I was the one who suffered the most. I loved my father dearly . . .' and so forth and so on. Luv?" Melissa felt a broad smile breaking out on her face. "Okay. And I quietly castigate him after we run the full exchange, with me looking at first very upbeat, then slowly approaching meltdown, and finally the walk-out that Griswold so realistically filmed."

Hobbs nodded. "He's got to respond somehow. And then we use his response—and add in our own counterresponse!" Hobbs turned to Luanne. "Write up a draft of the thing, bracketing it around the live stuff Griswold got, and let me see it. Quick now. At least we'll have an exclusive on the rebuttal, if not on the remark itself."

"Six o'clock?"

"You bet your ass. Six *and* ten. Get on it!"

Four

Open Letter

Barry Ford sat slumped on the couch of his suite at the Seattle Sheraton Hotel and Towers on Sixth Avenue in downtown Seattle. He watched in horror as the tape of Melissa Bonner's question was played on the huge television set. His own response came over as clear as a bell.

He could not imagine why the station had chosen to air the gratuitous insult to Brad Bonner that he had given that afternoon. If he had known Brad Bonner was dead, he never would have replied in such a manner, especially to the daughter of the man himself.

Ford felt again like the worst lummox in the universe. In a field of competitors who proclaimed their professionalism and their love of football as a game and not as personal aggrandizement, he was being made to look like a first-class klutz.

He closed his eyes as his own words snapped out of the set. There was a quick flash of Melissa Bonner's face: the horror there, the quick blinking of the eyes as the tears started, her withdrawal and the tension around her. He shook his head. If only—

The camera quickly closed in on Melissa. She was now in the television station's studio, sitting relaxed and controlled at the news desk. Ford could not take his eyes off her. She was a lovely young woman. To realize that Brad Bonner's daughter was as unlike him as it was possible to be did not make Ford feel any better. Brad Bonner had deserved Ford's rebuke. His daughter, however, had not—all things considered.

"An open letter to Barry Ford," Melissa Bonner said slowly, her eyes soft and appealing. "My dear sir, I was so surprised at your lack of taste in mentioning my father at today's press conference that I did not feel it appropriate to ask you for an apology for your rudeness."

"However, since you have already apologized to me indirectly through an intermediary—an intermediary in competition with us here at Channel 8—I must bring it to your attention that such an apology is not at all acceptable."

"Perhaps I am being overly sensitive on this issue, but I feel that you should have made your apology directly to me. I suffered the most from your crass reference to my father, whom I loved very much."

Ford felt himself sinking down farther and farther into the couch, biting his lips and cursing himself for his stupidity.

"I can only hope," Melissa Bonner was saying, "that your ability to get along with your fellow athletes on the Sea Lions will prove to be greater than your ability to get along with those of us who report your deeds on the playing fields of the Northwest. Melissa Bonner, Channel 8."

She faded from view.

Jesus! thought Ford. It was an absolutely hideous public relations snafu. He had come to town like a conquering hero, had spread his charismatic persona far and wide, and had assumed he was participating in a P. R. blockbuster. Sure, Channel 8 was a struggling channel, not the biggest in the area. But this woman was well liked by the sports fraternity. Also, she came from a bloodline that included a sportsman known far and wide in his own right— the late Brad Bonner. What had ever possessed him to come on like that, even if Bonner had been alive?

He knew. He had loved to cite the fact that the great Bonner had decided against him when he was scouting for the Chicago Bears. Well, there wasn't much he could do about it now. He was in that part of the sports game that was the trickiest to navigate: the public relations pit.

The crawls were moving down the television screen now, and Ford jumped to his feet and began pacing the main room of his suite. He moved to the west and looked out over the water. He had a panoramic view of Seattle, Elliott Bay, Puget Sound, and the islands in the distance. Even late at night the lights were shining everywhere.

He picked up the phone immediately when it rang. "Ford."

"It's Nick," said the voice. He recognized the Long Island accent of Nick Franz, who ran the public relations department of the Sea Lions. "I guess you saw it too."

"Uh huh," Ford said.

"My fault," Nick continued. "We should have done just what she said."

"What do I have to do?"

"I guess, apologize."

"Get me her number, will you?"

Nick read off the number of Channel 8.

"She may have left now," Ford said. "Do you have her private number?"

"Here it is." Nick read off another number. "Hey, sorry as shit about this, buddy. This is a hell of a thing when you're in a brand new place and everybody's looking you over to see how you add up. Or *if* you add up."

"The publicity game is harder to play than the football game." Ford sighed. "About the woman, Melissa Bonner. Is she like her father?"

"I never knew Brad Bonner," Nick said. "Melissa is well received in the area here. She won the 'Best Sportscaster in the Northwest' award last year."

"Who gave her that?" Ford asked.

"Now that you mention it, I don't really know. Look. It won't be easy for you to get on her good side. She's objective and fair when she's reporting. At the same time, the reason the viewers like her is that she'll ask the questions no one else wants to—embarrassing things, tricky ploys, inside stuff."

"Oh, boy," Ford groaned.

"So it's up to you to strike just the right note." There was a pause. "I'd suppose the direct approach might work better than anything. Just a standard apology. Then, if that doesn't work, I suppose you'll have to play it by ear."

"She's a very good-looking woman," Ford said softly. "Is she involved?"

"There was—" Nick hesitated. "I think she was seen around town with some guy, a basketball coach or whatever, but they broke up some months ago. She's not a real publicity hound like some of the TV performers. She keeps to herself." Nick came on again, his voice half-amused. "Why? You interested?"

"Never in a million years!" Ford said. "I just didn't want to walk into some kind of buzz saw if I approached her."

"Phone her up and see what happens," Nick suggested.

Ford waited a few minutes and then telephoned the station. Ms. Bonner, the operator said, had left the station. Was there a message? No, there was no particular message, Ford said. Thank you very much.

A half hour later he tried her home number.

The answering machine came on. "This is Melissa Bonner. I am not able to get to the phone at the present moment. Please leave your name and the approximate time you made your call. I'll try to get back to you as soon as possible." Beep.

Ford gave his name and telephone number and a message asking her to call.

Five

The Sound of Silence

There was no red Taurus behind her as Melissa Bonner drove her Range Rover home that night. She parked it in its special slot in the underground garage and took the elevator to her fifth-floor apartment.

As she slipped the key in the lock she could hear her dog, Danny, inside, barking his friendly greeting to her through the door. She pushed it open and there he was, jumping up at her, his heavy golden retriever body almost bowling her over and backward out into the hallway again.

"Ssh!" she warned him. "Quiet, Danny!"

As usual, Danny paid no attention to her shushes and continued to bark. He was four years old. Melissa's sister, Denise, had given him to her for a birthday present. He had been a staggering, loose-limbed, comically inept puppy then. She had fallen in love with him the very first week she had him.

And now that he was full grown—a good mature twenty-eight years old in human time—he was just as lovable and as forgivable as he had been as a puppy. If anything, her love for him had increased exponentially as the months and years had gone by.

She slipped his leash on quickly, took him downstairs, and walked him around the block. This was his nightly routine, always carried out the moment Melissa got home from work. She wished she had a better schedule to care for him in a more normal fashion, but she knew she would not change her career and her working routine even for Danny's sake.

When she and Danny returned to the front of the apartment, they met George Murphy, the building manager, on the front steps.

"Evening, Ms. Bonner," George said with an exaggerated bow. His brogue was going full tilt and his eyes glowed with whatever beverage he had been drinking. "Nice night out." He leaned down and patted Danny on the head. Danny swung his tail. "Hello, Danny Boy!"

Danny Boy slobbered and twisted, bobbed and licked. He was in ecstasy. "How is Denise?" the custodian wanted to know. For a brief half year Denise Bonner had lived with her sister in the apartment. That was shortly after her messy divorce, when Denise needed emotional as well as financial support.

"She's fine." George was waiting for more. "Always asks after you, George," Melissa lied gracefully.

"Nice woman," George said. Melissa looked at him sharply, for the words were odd, coming from him in just that manner. But George did not seem to mean anything other than the words he had uttered.

Danny wanted to wag his tail at George all night, but Melissa dragged his protesting body up the steps and into the elevator.

Once in the apartment she fixed Danny's meal and put fresh water in the bowl. Hurrying into the bedroom, she changed into her sleepshirt. When she came out again Danny was still slurping down his food in the kitchenette. She went into the room she used for a home office—it was the second bedroom—and glanced at her answering machine. The red light was on.

She pushed the playback button and listened.

The voice was male, expressive, and forthright. She recognized the intonation immediately.

"This is Barry Ford here. I'd like to speak to you, Ms. Bonner, if that's at all possible. Could you please call me?"

And he gave his telephone number.

She was immediately of two minds. With the sound of his voice she felt a surge of excitement, of triumph, even, that he should bother to call her. Yet almost at the same moment she was turned in another emotional direction. She could feel the warmth rising in her neck and cheeks, the result of a rush of anger over which she had no control.

Her next impulse was to call him up right at that moment and tell him what she thought of him for maligning the memory of her dead father. Then she remembered that Hobbs had assured that it was a mistake on Ford's part to mention her father at all in what he supposed to be an amusing anecdote. It would do no good to punish a man who was simply too stupid to know any better.

She blinked her eyes in surprise. Already she was pacing up and down, hands clasped grimly behind her. There was something about this man that set her teeth on edge, that made her come all loose inside, that made her fuss and fume.

The rage, she decided on closer analysis, was directed at herself, not at Barry Ford. She was angry that she had violated all tenets of her profession, that she had walked out on a good story to the shame of the television channel she worked for. To her dismay, she discovered that her hands were doubled up into fists and her cheeks were pink with anger.

Well, to hell with him, she thought, and to her astonishment realized that she was speaking out loud. Look out for the person who talks when she's alone, her mother had always warned her. And look! She was doing it!

She groaned aloud. With that she determined that she would watch television before going to bed. Quickly she moved into her bedroom and turned on the set. For a few minutes she watched the news on the NBC channel and then decided she had had a very long day. It was time to pack it in.

The phone rang.

She reached over and lifted the bedroom extension. So! He *had* decided to try to reach her again! Good! She could now tell him just what she thought of him.

"Hello!" she snapped in her decisive, business-as-usual manner.

For a moment she listened carefully, and then realized that no one had said anything at all on the other end of the line.

"Hello!" This time she shouted the word.

She was just about to slam down the handset when she felt a cold chill shoot up her spine. In what seemed a split second, perspiration covered the surface of her skin.

"Who is this?" she asked, her voice suddenly hushed and hoarse.

That damned phantom caller! she thought, putting a label to her suspicions.

"Answer me!" she cried.

There was just the suggestion of an amused chuckle somewhere in the distance, a chuckle that was swallowed up by miles and miles of wire between the caller and the listener.

Then, quite firmly, the caller hung up.

Almost, she thought, as if to prove that there *was* someone on the other end of the line. Almost as if to *remind* her of other previous empty calls of the same kind. To make her *think*. To make her *suffer*.

She was trembling. Here she had been innocently waiting to lash out at Barry Ford for what he had done to her—and instead she encountered the phantom caller who had telephoned her before.

Closing her eyes tightly, she tried to remember when she had received the first phantom call. It must have been at least two weeks ago. Interestingly enough, the first sighting of the red Taurus had been at just about the same time. She remembered clearly that she had dismissed the sight of the car instantly—at least, it hadn't seemed to be following her. Or had it? And there were those stories.

As if to torment her, the phone jangled again. She reached for it and almost instantly withdrew her hand. No! She wouldn't give this annoying caller a chance to frighten her again.

She waited until the answering machine had given her electronic spiel. There was no response from the caller. The beeper sounded and everything was quiet once again.

Now a sudden warmth washed over her. What if that had been Barry Ford trying to get in touch with her—twice in the same evening?

She was still angry at Ford and at herself for her reaction to his tactless anecdote. She wasn't going to chase him breathlessly. That would only make him look good!

She sat there blinking back the tears of anger that had surfaced momentarily. And then, as she knuckled the tears away and dried her eyes, a broad smile, lit up her face.

She knew exactly what to do to Barry Ford!

And she would do it tomorrow!

After all, it was the perfect answer to his plea for forgiveness.

Six

Back-Up Jack

Jack Adams, the Sea Lions' back-up quarterback, was in the slot trying to guess how Stan Brewster would free himself from his persistent coverage when he saw the big number **8** on the shoulder camera and equipment coming through the tunnel of the King-dome. Brewster, of course, zagged when he should have zigged and the ball Adams had tossed, spiral-perfect, hit the turf harmlessly. A moment later Adams was leveled by the onrushing defensive line.

"Take ten," the offensive coordinator yelled. He pointed to Melissa Bonner and her TV crew heading laterally across the field toward the north goalposts. "Jack!"

Adams pulled himself awkwardly to his feet. He shook his head, trying to get rid of the cobwebs, while he started jogging toward Melissa.

As the cameraman and soundman began sorting out their equipment, Jack Adams could see that Melissa Bonner was studying him carefully. He had the distinct impression that she was laughing at him. She had seen him clobbered by the defense. But she had the good breeding not to let her amusement show. She knew the game. She knew the players. So did he. Had the sight of her arrival thrown him off-stride? Perhaps. Or perhaps it was his usual clumsiness.

She was leaning against the goalpost, arms folded across her chest, giving him a smile of greeting. They knew each other well. He had been back-up quarterback for some years now, first for Reggie Brown and now for Barry Ford. Even Nick Franz had agreed to Melissa Bonner's request that day. It might be fun for some cross-dressing in the media this week: that is, interview the back-up guy and get some good publicity for the support team.

"Hi, Ms. Bonner," he said.

"Mr. Adams." Melissa unfolded her arms and stepped forward.

"Hatchett told me you were coming."

She nodded. "Yeah. It's a whole new ball game, you know."

He couldn't help but stare at her. She was always beautiful in person, but she looked *great* today.

"How have *you* been?" she inquired. She made it seem as if she were really interested, not just asking to fill up the time while her crew got set up.

"I've been better," he said with a shrug. "No. I'm tip-top!"

She squinted. "I must say, you don't look too down."

"Should I play it that way?" he asked, mock-serious.

"Up to you," she said.

"I've been briefed not to."

"By the Ford in your future?" She was digging a little.

"By Nick Franz, our P.R. guy."

"Figures," she said with a smile. "Where's Ford?"

"Looking at the tapes."

"Ah, yes, I'm a slave to tapes myself."

"Or the lack of them," he said, smiling gently, watching her closely.

Not much escaped her. "Touché," she said, pointing her finger like a pistol at him. "I didn't handle that too well."

"Neither did he."

"All set, Melissa," Kubo said. Griswold nodded.

"Okay, Mr. Adams," Melissa told him. "I'll just ask questions now. The introductory stuff will be written in the studio."

After testing the sound and measuring the distance for the camera, Melissa Bonner took a deep breath and immediately metamorphosed into her professional persona.

"What was your immediate reaction on hearing that Barry Ford of the Miami Dolphins had been traded to the Seattle Sea Lions?"

"I was gratified that we had a replacement for the departed Reggie Brown."

Melissa smiled. "That's all well and good. But didn't you hope *you* would be selected to be the first-string quarterback?"

Adams found himself beginning to perspire. "Of course," he said quietly. "But in life—in the real world—things don't always turn out the way you want them to."

"But this isn't the real world at all, is it?"

"It's the world of games. Sports. Entertainment."

She laughed. "What is your assessment of Barry Ford? I mean, what kind of quarterback do you think he will prove to be?"

"Ford is one of the best in the field," Adams said steadily.

"But he hasn't scored a point in two years," Melissa Bonner shot back. "Do you think he's back to strength again after all that—well—rest?"

"If anyone can get back quick, he can."

"Still," Melissa said slowly, "you'd think Coach Hatchett and Slats Montgomery would have considered making you the lead-in quarterback when Brown left."

Adams shrugged, smiling. When you do not know exactly how to answer a question or how to follow up a new line of thought, you keep your mouth shut. Adams knew that number-one public relations precept.

"You won the pre-season game against the San Francisco Forty-Niners last week," she went on. "Don't you think that victory should have qualified you for consideration?"

Adams forced a benevolent smile. "I'm not running the club, Ms. Bonner."

"No," Melissa admitted. "But doesn't that term 'Back-Up Jack' bother you just a little bit?"

Well, for God's sake, what did she *think*? Of *course* it bothered him! He was a full-fledged pro. And he was still good. He could scramble and pass and hand off and hang in the pocket with the best of them. Back-Up Jack! He even heard Melissa's tone in his wife's voice sometimes when she was trying to get him to mow the overgrown grass.

"You get used to it," Adams said roughly, his voice unexpectedly harsh.

"After all these years, I guess you should," Melissa said softly.

Adams responded with surprising alacrity. "It hasn't been all *that* long!" he snapped. "I'm not over the hill yet!"

"Although Reggie Brown is?" Melissa cut in smoothly, one eyebrow cocked suggestively.

"Absolutely not!" Adams said. It was up to him to cut down a bit on the speed of the Q and A. Fast talk—that was the trap the media set. He cut through the rising hostility with a laid-back smile. "Hey, Ms. Bonner," he said slowly. "What's wrong with just being a member of the National Football League? Your father was satisfied with that. And he was a good one."

"Thank you," Melissa said with a faint smile.

"A lot of football players don't get even *that* far," Adams went on. He was watching her closely. He had put out the fire that she was fanning alive. If she tried to stoke it again, he'd hit her with a new change of pace. He felt, however, that she would not try now. She had her piece.

Adams was right. Her next question put paid to a possible negative confrontation.

"Then you look forward to the leadership of Barry Ford?"

"Certainly."

"And no 'quarterback problem' will surface in Seattle here?"

"No ma'am."

"When you were with the Kansas City Chiefs five years ago, you and José Striker almost split the team into warring factions—along with the fans."

"That was five years ago, Ms. Bonner."

"Sure." She hesitated. "Well, good luck to you, Mr. Adams. It's been a pleasure."

Adams nodded silently.

"Melissa Bonner, Channel 8, Seattle."

Adams walked away, turning over in his mind the various ways in which Melissa Bonner had handled him. She had made him out to be some kind of second-rater—a back-up jock—because he wouldn't fight for the start-up job, because he wouldn't put Barry Ford down. Then she had had the gall to remind him of those bad years in Kansas City when he had really been in a battle of survival with José Striker, the so-called fastest gun in Chihuahua.

He'd learned something from that encounter. He knew he couldn't win every fight he started. And now here he was losing the game even before he started to play in it. One thing about her, she was smart enough to cover up the fact that she was trying to rile him. And she had made him say things he had not wanted to talk about in the first place. But not enough to drop him into the slop pit.

He turned. She was waving to Mo Sandusky, the Sea Lion linebacker.

Adams thought, lots of luck, Mo.

Seven

Quarterback Sneak

They called Barry Ford out of the showers to catch Melissa Bonner's interview with Jack Adams during the six-o'clock newscast that evening. Wrapped in a bath towel and dripping on the floor of the clubhouse room, Ford watched the last half of the interview.

He was particularly interested in the fact that Melissa brought out into the open a "quarterback problem"—although there had been no suggestion of one up to that point.

"It'll be on the ten o'clock news at Channel 8," Nick Franz told him. "You can see the whole thing then."

"As if I'd *want* to!" Ford snapped. "By saying there's no quarterback problem, she establishes the fact that there *could* be one, therefore, there *is* one. I know those media tricks!"

"Actually," Nick argued, "she let you two guys off the hook easy. It could have been a bloodbath."

"I've got a call in to her. She hasn't answered."

"Put in another one," Nick said quickly.

"Bowl her off her feet?" Ford suggested sarcastically.

"Something like that."

He stood there with his hands on his hips, dripping water in a ring around his bare feet. "What's she after, anyway?"

"I guess she's after you, friend," Nick said with a chuckle.

"That stupid gaffe about her father," Ford sighed.

"I suspect that."

Ford shook his head. "How did Jack take this?"

"Back-Up Jack?" Nick repeated.

"Yeah."

"He knows her. He says she was digging for this one just a little. I thought he handled it well."

"I'd better talk to him tonight."

"We don't want the quarterback problem to surface."

Ford frowned. "It already has! That mention of Jack and the Kansas City Chiefs will remind other sportscasters."

Nick agreed.

"What can I *do*?" Ford asked.

"Stay in the pocket, kid," Nick said with a wide grin. "Then, if the pocket breaks down, scramble a little. You'll find a way."

Ford made a face.

"You always have, haven't you?"

Ford thought about that.

"After all," Nick sang out, "she's a woman, isn't she?"

"Yeah. But she's just a little different."

Nick stared hard as Ford turned and plodded back into the showers.

Ford ate dinner with the team and got back to his hotel suite in time to review Melissa's ten-o'clock sportscast.

He could see where she was coming from at the beginning of the Q and A with Jack Adams. The first give-and-takes were routine, of course. By the time Melissa got to the question about Ford's competency—the fact that he hadn't scored a point on the field in two years—Ford was beginning to squirm just a little. Equating eighteen months of therapy and getting back to normal with a "rest" period really bugged him.

When she began to unload on Back-Up Jack with that question reminding him that he had won the pre-season game against the Forty-Niners, Ford was getting angry. She didn't mention it, but Jack had *lost* three other pre-season games.

When she put the needle in about whether Jack was annoyed at being called "Back-Up Jack," Ford was steaming. He almost cheered when Adams came back at her about not being over the hill yet. And he was nodding happily by the time Adams had turned it around and had complimented Melissa's father on being content and happy in the National Football League too.

But the reminder of Adams's feud with José Striker got his dander up again. He snapped off the set as he began building another head of steam. She had done all she could to start a fight between the two quarterbacks, it seemed to him. He knew controversy was an old media tool used to create news—since journalism *is* controversy—but it bothered him that it had almost worked.

He had played enough football to know that irritations like petty jealousies could fester and turn into angry battles. And a team of men had to work *together.* Even the reminder of a past conflict was enough to start it raging again. He didn't want anything like that flaring up on the field.

Whatever had happened between them was already past history. What she did in the future would matter all the more. Had he turned her into a permanent enemy of the Sea Lions? He was pacing now. There had to be *some* way—

His mind returned to his brief conversation with Nick Franz in the clubhouse room. He knew what Franz was telling him: You're in control of the team. All you've got to do is exert control over the media, specifically in the person of Melissa Bonner.

Nick was laying the cards on the table. To exert control, you get in there and you *pitch.* If it's a man, you play him soft and easy, with strokes that count. If it's a woman, you play her soft and sweet. After all, Nick was reminding him, you don't do badly with women. What's the matter with you this time? She's beautiful. Get busy.

Shit!

Ford strode to the telephone. He would compliment her on the broadcast. It was a great piece of imaginative journalism, he would say. He liked the way she handled Jack Adams, a really wonderful person to play ball with. He dialed her number.

And got the electronic buzz-off.

This time he played the no-nonsense male. The businessman in charge of his underlings and his staff and his right-hand lieutenants.

"This is Barry Ford again." He threw the "again" in because he did not want to let her think he was in the *habit* of calling again and again when he was getting absolutely no response. "I'd appreciate it if you did call me back." He said it that way because he was just a little annoyed—and he had every right to be—that she had *not* yet returned his first call.

"I do have something important to tell you." He hung up and stood there a long moment, trying to clarify his thoughts and the direction they were taking. He remembered Adams at that point.

If he had been Adams, with all that stuff about being over the hill, and so on, he'd be mad as hell. Not especially at Melissa Bonner, but—and that was the bad news—at Barry Ford! Because Ford had quite simply taken his job away from him.

Dialing Adams's number, he waited patiently until someone picked up the phone. It was Jack's wife. "You did great on the Channel 8 thing," Ford said when Jack took the phone. "It's not an easy thing to take all that guff."

"Thanks, Barry."

"This Bonner woman. She isn't really against us, is she?"

"No, no. That's just the way she is. How do you say it? Contentious?"

"So *I'm* the one that screwed up here."

"You said it, not me."

"My problem is communication. I can't establish it with her. I mean, reestablish it."

"You're not married, you know," Adams laughed. "This happens all the time whenever there's any kind of ruckus."

"I'm supposed to be glad that's true, huh?"

"Just keep trying," Adams said.

"And you're *sure* she doesn't really have anything against us?"

"Far as I know."

"I didn't want to get into any kind of quarterback problem when I came out here," Ford said wistfully. "But I guess it's there, isn't it?"

"Doesn't have to be," Adams said.

"Thanks. I'll see you tomorrow. I just needed a little personal assessment of Melissa Bonner."

"Lots of luck."

Ford hung up and stared at the huge television set in the corner of the suite. He had the sound turned way down. Some horror show was on, with enormous bats swooping down out of a ruined Mexican belfry. A woman screamed. A cat howled into the night. A curdled voice began laughing in a maniacal manner.

Ford muttered to himself, "Welcome to Seattle, *amigo*."

Eight

Rip-and-Read

On Wednesday Melissa Bonner used the second interview she had taped Tuesday—the one with Mo Sandusky, the Sea Lion linebacker—for her center piece. The rest of the sportscast was read off the prompter—a group of sports items from all over the country that she rehearsed beforehand. These included clips from teams sent by their public relations flack. For the six-o'clock newscast, Melissa used wire service flashes instead of the baseball scores that would appear during the ten-o'clock show.

Between the evening and night broadcasts she sat in her office and sifted through the junk in her in-basket. As usual she flipped most of the stuff into the circular file at her feet. There were letters from fans, which she saved, a bill the station had forgotten to pay, and a number of pieces of junk mail.

At the bottom of the basket there was a rip-and-read from the newswire someone had pulled off the machine and routed to her desk. She glanced at it and then began reading.

SUTCLIFFE, MARYLAND—BETTY DANFORTH, A TV COMMENTATOR FOR CHANNEL 7 IN BALTIMORE, NARROWLY ESCAPED DEATH LAST NIGHT WHEN HER CAR WAS INVOLVED IN A COLLISION WITH A TREE JUST OFF HIGHWAY 1.

MS. DANFORTH SAID THAT SHE HAD BEEN FORCED OFF THE ROAD BY ANOTHER VEHICLE WHICH HAD CUT IN FRONT OF HER, JAMMED ON THE BRAKES, AND BLOCKED HER WAY.

SHE HAD BEEN ABLE TO SWING HER CAR AROUND THE ONE IN HER WAY, BUT THE VEHICLE LEFT THE ROAD AND SMASHED INTO THE TREE.

SHE SAID THE ACCIDENT HAD HAPPENED TOO FAST FOR HER TO NOTICE THE MAKE OR CONDITION OF THE OTHER

CAR. NOR HAD SHE BEEN ABLE TO SEE THE LICENSE PLATE.
MS. DANFORTH IS AN OUTSPOKEN COMMENTATOR IN
THE BALTIMORE AREA AND HAS HAD NUMEROUS CON-
FRONTATIONS WITH POLITICAL FIGURES HEREABOUTS.
WHEN ASKED IF SHE THOUGHT THE ACCIDENT WAS AN AT-
TEMPT TO DO HER BODILY HARM, SHE LAUGHED OFF THE
IDEA.
"THERE IS NO TRUTH TO THAT SPECULATION AT ALL. I AM
CONFIDENT THAT THIS WAS PURELY AN ACCIDENT."

Melissa's heart was beating faster when she finished reading the
story. She looked around her almost fearfully. Then she opened
the desk drawer and removed a manila folder. She glanced at the
papers inside and added the rip-and-read to the top of the pile.
She shivered as the sight of the red Taurus reappeared as if en-
graved on her memory. A feeling of horror gripped her again as
she imagined hearing that distant chuckle on the phantom telephone call.

She looked at the file again and flipped through the sheaf of
newswire stories. All concerned serious criminal acts that had been
perpetrated against women.

One of the stories, only two weeks old, involved a woman who
had been shopping at a large supermarket on her day off. As she
got back in her car with her bags of groceries, two armed young
men demanded the keys to her car. But the young woman had
refused to give up her keys. She was then beaten by the armed
men, shot once in the upper arm, and left lying wounded in the
parking lot near the supermarket after they stole her keys. Luckily
another shopper had seen her car being driven off and called 911.

In New York a woman was jogging in the morning through a
large park in the city when she was set upon by some teenagers.
They dragged her off into the woods.

Her screams alerted other joggers, who found and rescued her.
One of the youths had been shot in the melee. Once again that
familiar frisson of fear traveled up Melissa's backbone. Were these
stories simple accidents of the station's routing system, or were they
some kind of warning to her? This current one was, after all about

a TV newscaster—just like Melissa Bonner. Things seemed to be closing in on her. Was someone envious of her position at Channel 8, or of her popularity on Seattle television, or simply of her?

She stood up, trying to shake off her misgivings. It was nonsensical that she should become anxious about something she could not do anything about. If these stories meant she was being threatened, who was the culprit? And did someone really want to harm her?

Danny was barking when Melissa finally opened her apartment door later that night. She quickly leashed him and took him around the block for a fast walk. On their return he bounded about the apartment as she prepared his evening meal. When she had it ready, he calmed down and attacked the bowls of water and food.

Melissa yawned and stretched. She had had a busy day. She glanced at her answering machine and discovered a new message on it. She flipped on the MESSAGE button. It was Barry Ford again. For the third time that week! And this message was delivered with no more than a modicum of panache. In fact, if anything, it sounded like a farewell, as if he didn't really care whether she returned his call or not.

"Barry Ford again," the message said laconically. "Hope to hear from you. 'Bye."

She particularly loved that "'bye." Not "goodbye." Just " 'bye." Yet she did not allow herself to laugh at anything Ford said or did. He had become a kind of rock of Sisyphus to her—she kept pushing the rock to the top of the hill to dispose of it only to have it roll right back down again for her to push back up.

Mostly, she was annoyed at her subconscious, or whatever part of her it was that determined her dreams. Monday night she had dreamed of Barry Ford. It was one of those hazy romantic encounters that seemed so very real but was exactly the opposite—with just the suggestion of physical involvement. Tuesday night the dream had differed: this one took place in a brightly lighted Kingdome, with Melissa standing next to Ford as he executed a dropback pass into the end zone. The dream ended in an almost passionate embrace between them right in the middle of the playing field in front of thousands of people. Melissa was naked.

Hopefully, tonight, she would fall asleep and get through the whole night without a thought of him.

As she went into the kitchenette to wash Danny's bowls, she opened the cabinet door, glancing at the cans of dog food inside.

Two left.

She would have to replenish her supply. Funny, she thought. Four cans were there this morning. Or was that yesterday morning? Something didn't seem right. She counted back. One a day. She'd been to the pet store last week. She began touching her fingers. Monday, Tuesday—

Danny was slopping up his water now. He made more noise than the dishwasher. She laughed and shook her head, reaching down to grab Danny's neck and shake it.

"You silly old thing!" she said, and put her arm around his neck.

He slobbered on her, getting her shoes wet.

She passed the waste basket on the way out of the kitchenette. The sight of the two empty cans of dog food there seemed to mock her.

Nine

Blue Boxers

Every morning when she did her daily jog, Melissa followed the same route. Her course described a simple horizontal rectangle superimposed on the map of Seattle Northwest: north to the park, east to the campus, south to the playing field, and then west toward the sound and back to the apartment.

She had long ago calculated the distance by driving her Range Rover over the route. Her mind was the kind that demanded accuracy in data: it was two miles by the odometer of her four-wheeler.

Her jogging exercise was always preceded by a romp around the block with Danny. Thursday morning she hooked up his leash, got into her warm-ups quickly, and took him out into the street for her preliminary run. It was a beautiful day in Seattle. She could see the sound to the west sparkling in the distance, with the sun to the east rising behind the higher buildings of the city.

She rarely met people while walking the dog at six-o'clock in the morning. Everybody was driving somewhere then—usually to work, or home from an all-night job perhaps. The sidewalk around the block was empty. Nor was it much different when she jogged along her regular two-mile route.

Today, with Danny safely back in the apartment, Melissa descended once again and began her route north to the park. As she got into sync with her body, she let her mind drift as she began to feel weightless and trouble-free.

Her jogging routine was a relatively new thing for her.

Melissa had been enrolled in an aerobics class for several years. There was nothing wrong with aerobics, actually. It was just that she realized now that she felt freer going her own way without the constant yammer of other people at her side. She needed that time alone to wrestle with the problems caused by others.

As usual lately, Melissa's mind focused on the problem of Barry Ford. Somehow she had allowed him to become an incubus on her back, like some hideous growth out of a medieval German horror tale—one that simply appeared there and was impossible to excise. As hard as she tried to dismiss him from her mind, he always managed to crawl right back into it.

Just as he was now!

What did she want of him? She simply did not know. Her reactions to him were hopelessly ambivalent, confused, and unfathomable.

Melissa thought about the Jack Adams interview, wondering if she had erred as badly as Ford had done in his original putdown of her father. She had considered it a brilliant ploy to dramatize the original question she had failed to ask Barry Ford during the press conference—by playing it out in an interview with Back-Up Jack himself.

As she had done once or twice already, she decided that she had acted capriciously, trying to drive a wedge between Jack Adams and Barry Ford. It actually was up to her to get in touch with Ford *and* Adams and apologize to them both!

Damn that Ford! He *was* an incubus!

And she was *not* going to apologize to him! Or, for that matter, let him apologize to her. Any bridge that might have been built between them was an impossibility now.

Melissa turned at the park and began jogging to the east. Out of the corner of her eye she saw movement down the street she had just left. She slowed momentarily and squinted to get the entire scene in focus. Yes! There was another jogger there—a lean, almost skinny man in bright blue boxers and a gray tank top, wearing black reflecting shades. He was way back there, but obviously following the pattern that Melissa had established for her jogging course.

Following?

As she jogged from the park to the campus she kept looking back behind her to see whether the man in the blue boxers was catching up with her.

He was not. It was with a vast sense of relief that she turned south at the campus and continued all the way to the playing field without spotting him. She was beginning to get her breath back. Her heart was definitely slowed down to its usual running rate by then. She even felt better.

She wondered if she should call Barry Ford today. He had been trying to reach her since Monday night. Perhaps by playing the silent act she was being willful and childish.

She was thinking of the way his hair curled around his ears, the way his eyebrows tilted, the way his mouth turned in that funny smile. She doubled her hands into fists and shook them at the still air around her.

She jogged to the apartment and entered the underground garage. She was up to speed. She had caught her second wind. She felt marvelous.

She trotted over to the elevator bank, past her Range Rover, and pushed the UP button. Still jogging in place, she turned slightly and glanced back over the parked cars.

My God! She felt her heart zoom into her throat.

There he was!

The slight man in the blue boxers! The man who had seemed to be following her. How had he beaten her back to the apartment building?

Of course. He had followed her part way only and had then cut back to intercept her at the garage. And there he was waiting to—

The elevator doors opened. She fell in, pushing the FIVE button frantically. The doors closed and the last thing she saw was the man in the blue boxers and gray tank top peering through the gloom of the garage at her.

She sank back against the elevator wall.

There was something about that figure that reminded her of someone she knew. Someone from college? Someone at Channel 8? Someone in the sports world of Seattle? She had a nodding acquaintance with so many different people. Especially men.

He *was* someone she knew. She was positive of that. But who? And why hadn't he come up to her to speak to her? She was perspiring freely when she let herself into the apartment and peeled off her warm-ups. In a moment she was in the shower, trying to wash off the fear that now seemed to enshroud her.

Ten

The Evaluators

Darryl Hobbs settled back in his swivel chair and read the fax again. The communication came from the London offices of Global Communications, a firm owned by a British publications tycoon second only to Rupert Murdoch in international holdings. During the greedy eighties, Global had begun a long and prosperous acquisitions career, which had ended with the beginning of the nineties.

The gist of the message Hobbs was holding in his hands was that a team of experts would be arriving in Seattle to assess the standards and practices of Channel 8's staff. Hobbs had received one copy of the letter; so had the other department heads.

The team was a part of Simmons and Lockwood, well known in the television business for its acumen in advising stations on management and—especially—on programming.

Hobbs's news department, of course, was the most vulnerable one at Channel 8. Network stations were network controlled. Independents functioned on some specialized gimmick: old films; game shows; syndicated reruns; religious stuff. Channel 8 was striving to be big in its news programs. But the networks were ahead of Channel 8, a problem that Hobbs always had to face.

Hobbs knew who paid the bills at Channel 8. On the surface, this planned exercise was simply a brush-up-on-your-Shakespeare routine. Hobbs was an old hand at the game. He knew something had been cooking beneath the surface for some time now. It did not bode well for Channel 8 or any of the people in it.

Actually, Hobbs had come from the world of print news. But the twentieth century in the sixties through the eighties had not been happy days for newsprint. Only a skeleton representation of big newspapers remained after painful mergings, foldings, and outright zappings.

When the *Los Angeles Record* had gone under and Hobbs had lost his position as managing editor, he had swallowed his pride and gone to work for a supermarket tabloid edited and printed in Miami. Most of the reporters were British, since the paper was owned by Global Communications. The British tycoon had recognized Hobbs's worth early on and took him to England to develop a news program for a newly acquired television channel.

The British learned from Hobbs; Hobbs learned as much from the Brits. He married Verna Oates in England and appeared set there for life. But in the late 1980s Global Communications had bought Channel 8, along with a number of other U.S. channels, and Hobbs was sent to Seattle to get the station on a paying basis.

The bad times in the early nineties had not helped Channel 8 find its way. Although Hobbs continued to be well liked and respected by Global, the station barely broke even.

And now the assessment team from Simmons and Lockwood would be arriving in two days to observe and advise. Hobbs crushed the fax in his hand. It was 4:00 P.M. He punched his intercom alive and said:

"Attention, all staff. There will be a meeting in the conference room at four-thirty. Please be prompt."

Then he sank back in his chair, wondering what he could do about improving the news-gathering abilities of his staff. The real problem, of course, was the low pay and heavy work loads. Channel 8 was a place to start out—not a place to stay.

A half hour later he sat at the head of the big conference table and waited for everyone to assemble. He observed the apprehension, fear, and occasional sardonic curl of the lip on the faces of his staff members as they came in and sat down. Hobbs noticed that Pam Morton and Rick Jones, the news co-anchors, both looked haggard and put-upon—almost as if they had guessed what the meeting was going to be about. They were good newscasters, but they were over the hill, and everybody knew it. Yet Hobbs believed in loyalty. And he would stick with them as long as he could.

The only one who seemed relaxed and confident was Melissa Bonner. Of them all, Hobbs knew, she had the potential for success. The way she had bounced back from the Barry Ford affair showed her resilience and professionalism.

Melissa had no self-doubts. She could draw people out. She was often aggressive and sympathetic by turns, using the shifting technique to disarm the people she interviewed. He would soon lose her. He was going to miss her charisma, her talent, and, yes, her sheer beauty, when she left.

"Simmons and Lockwood will be arriving next week for a look at our operation here at Channel 8. Simmons and Lockwood is a prestigious firm of television practices evaluators. That is, they move from station to station to assess each channel's present accomplishments and then make up a report of suggested improvements before leaving.

"Management needs higher ratings," Hobbs went on without shifting gears. "I'm afraid we have gotten sloppy. We've missed stories we could have gotten."

"Such as?" Ian Chambers, head of political news, asked.

"The Barry Ford case."

"I thought we came out of that one with bells on," Rick Jones remarked in his slow, thoughtful, on-camera way.

"Still, it did give us a black eye from our opposition," Hobbs retorted.

"So management—and I assume that means Global Communications—wants the *usual* rather than the *imaginative* or the intriguing," Melissa said.

Hobbs relented. "I'm not saying you haven't been doing well. I'm saying we have to do better. There's no perfect method for getting high ratings. If there was, there wouldn't be any guesswork at all."

"What do we do when this probe starts?" Ian Chambers asked.

"Come on, guys," Hobbs pleaded. "You know what to do. Just pay close attention to your p's and q's and everything will be all right."

"We're already doing that," Pam Morton objected. As usual, she was the voice of common sense.

"Most of us." Hobbs let his eyes slide around the table. Several faces turned downward or avoided his gaze as he went by them.

"That's it?" Chambers asked hopefully.

"Yes," Hobbs said. "Oh, and let's not make it obvious, shall we? I mean, if you're running off copies of your resumés, do it on your own time, please."

No one knew whether to laugh.

Hobbs picked up his folder, clutched it to his chest, and retreated quickly from the room.

Eleven

Big Sister Night

The Tavern in the Town, just north of Green Lake, was a nice quiet place to sit and talk. Melissa's sister, Denise Bonner, sat nursing a Dewar's and soda at a table for two not too far from the long bar across the opposite side of the room. She liked the informal, friendly, almost funky atmosphere of the place.

Every Thursday night she and Melissa would have something to eat and drink to celebrate the previous week and tell each other about what had happened to them.

Denise Bonner liked to think of Thursday as the last day of the week. In that way, she would feel the work week was over and she had nothing more to do. By clearing her mind of everything, she could enjoy Friday more when it came the next day.

Denise's married name was Enright—but she had been divorced from Mark Enright for seven years. And so she had become a Bonner again.

It was about eleven o'clock when Melissa arrived. Dressed now in fawn-colored slacks, cotton-mesh tunic, and midnight black shades, she was hardly recognizable as the Channel 8 sportscaster. Still, a few male eyes followed her as she moved smoothly through the packed-in tables to join Denise in the corner.

Denise tried to keep all expression out of her face. Her kid sister could read her only too well. It had always been Melissa who got the honors, the dates, the accolades. For Denise there were only the droppings.

But Denise had to admit that her sister was an elegant sight. With her hair tied back tightly in a bun with a gold ribbon around it and her face devoid of stage makeup, she resembled a superstar from a Hollywood of another era on a coffee break—a kind of Norma Desmond caught in a time warp.

"Hi, Ellie," Denise said in her husky voice. Melissa was a dumb name, Denise had always thought. The nearest she could come to a nickname was "Ellie," which was probably all right for Elizabeth, but hardly for Melissa. She simply didn't like the "Lissa."

Melissa Bonner slid into the seat opposite her sister with a faint smile. "Big day today. Hobbs had us in for a meeting."

"Oh, Jesus," Denise said.

"Nothing important." Melissa turned to give her order to the waiter. Denise ordered a refill and then selected a salad for the main course.

"Was it about the Barry Ford interview?" Denise asked, leaning forward expectantly.

"Not exactly," Melissa said. She closed her eyes, her mouth stiffened, and an uncharacteristic tic tugged at her upper lip. She folded her glasses and slipped them into her purse.

"God, it's been an *awful* week!" Melissa groaned. "That silly jock made me look like a dumb fool."

Denise could feel a rush of adrenaline as she took in her sister's momentary anguish over her professional gaffe. Then immediately she felt a pang of guilt over her surge of schadenfreude at Melissa's misstep.

"I'm sorry it turned out so bad," she said, somewhat disingenuously. Melissa glanced at her suspiciously and shrugged. "And it was tasteless of that airhead to go after our dad."

Melissa looked up. "He didn't know Dad was dead."

"Doesn't he read the papers?"

"Apparently he missed that item."

"I don't believe it!"

"Come on. He *makes* news. He doesn't *read* it."

"That's no excuse. Dad *was* a football star."

"Sure. Long ago. But he retired to be a scout. Scouts aren't famous like coaches or managers. Besides, maybe the Miami papers didn't have the story about Dad's death."

"Ellie, give me *all* of it."

"Nothing much to give. I delivered the 'open letter' on air Monday night right after the press conference. And Tuesday I interviewed Back-Up Jack. That was *it*."

"The open letter was a demand for an apology. Did he deliver?"

"There were some telephone calls."

"What did he *say*?"

"I never answered them."

Denise's mouth hung open. "You didn't?"

"No. And I don't intend to."

Denise shook her head sadly. "You demand an apology and yet you won't permit him to give it?"

"He didn't try very hard to get it to me.'

"So that's it!" Denise cried in triumph.

"So that's *what*?" Melissa wondered.

"You don't even know what you've been doing, Ellie. It's the oldest trick in the book. You like him. You want him. So you test him to see if he's interested enough to come on to you. By forcing him to apologize. He tries to."

Melissa flushed.

"But you don't let him reach you because you don't answer his calls. And you go one step further. You try to force him to move with that Jack Adams interview. That was a shabby come-on if there ever was one. Overkill, you know."

"Thanks for the free analysis, Dr. Bonner," Melissa snapped. Then she forced herself to relax and smile. "Hey, how have *you* been?"

"Good. Well, fairly good."

Melissa's eyebrow lifted.

"It's Scott O'Hara again." Denise found herself unconsciously biting her lower lip.

"He's had a great year. What's bothering him now?" Melissa asked impatiently.

"Nothing at all," Denise confessed. "But—" She had been fingering her cocktail napkin. Suddenly the paper tore apart, and she was stunned at the fury that must have been at work inside her to shred it like that.

"But what?"

"Dr. Stark has heard it on the grapevine. Apparently Scott has been badgering the alumni for help in getting more money channeled into the basketball program."

Melissa nodded. "Makes sense. They won their conference for

the first time in history under Coach O'Hara. So they get more backing."

"They want a new gymnasium." Denise sighed.

"And Dr. Stark doesn't want to give it to them." Melissa nodded thoughtfully. "And you're in the middle."

Denise worked for Dr. Jonathan Stark, the president of the University of Seattle. Four years ago, Stark had been head of the English department at Seattle and had been promoted from department head to president in a rapid and radical restructuring, the purpose of which was to upgrade the academic standards of the college.

Melissa had been in several of Stark's classes during her college years. He had been her favorite professor. And, indeed, she was his favorite student.

It was during Denise's most traumatic months, when she was staying with Melissa in Seattle, that Melissa had suggested she answer an ad in the newspaper for a job in the Admissions Office at the university. And she had been hired as a processing technician. Just three months ago, Stark's executive secretary had left, and Denise had immediately applied for the job. She was smart and aware, had a good appearance, and Stark had hired her immediately—not entirely overlooking her ties to Melissa.

In his four years in office, Stark had succeeded in his appointed mission by hiring some of the best names in the humanities and sciences and making them heads of departments. It cost money. By channeling money into academic excellence rather than athletic excellence, he had become a target for the powerful alumni group that preferred athletic clout to academic clout.

And Scott O'Hara, the well-liked basketball coach—because of his winning basketball season this year with the Seattle Timberwolves—had been coming on strong in pushing for more athletic money at the expense of the academic budget.

"It's almost a case of conflict of interest," said Denise with a wan smile. "I mean, my going with Scott."

"I'm sure Dr. Stark will know what to do about any problem you might have," Melissa said quietly.

Denise gazed at Melissa thoughtfully. Melissa had been in several classes that Stark taught before his precipitous rise to president of the university. She had once confessed to having a mild crush on him when he was her English professor.

"I hope so," Denise said.

"Is Scott coming on to you about this?"

Denise felt her eyes filling with tears. "He says he isn't, Ellie, but he's been pumping me for information about how the academics feel about this new direction Seattle has been taking since Stark's promotion to president."

Melissa studied her sister. Denise could guess what was going through her mind. Ironically, Denise was now involved with Scott O'Hara. She had been involved ever since Melissa's affair with Scott had ended about six months ago, just at the beginning of Scott's great basketball year. When Denise had been assured by Melissa that it was all over—that it was simply a matter of easy come, easy go with Melissa and Scott—she had become Scott's "significant other."

"Just don't tell him anything," Melissa said, leaning back. "There's nothing dishonest about Scott. He's straight. He'll write it off as par for the course. Don't you worry about it."

"I can't help it."

"I suppose not." Melissa reached over and patted Denise's hand on the table.

With an effort Denise sat up straighter and tried to put on a cheerful look. "So it's Barry Ford now, is it?"

Melissa sat back and laughed. "I'd hardly say that!"

Denise leaned forward. "I would. You know where you put all your interest in men, don't you?"

"What are you talking about?"

"You worship muscle, don't you?" Denise asked, her eyes narrowed on her sister.

"I don't worship it. I know what it is. I know where it belongs."

Denise pressed her lips together. "You were always just like Dad."

Melissa flushed. The waiter appeared and delivered their salads. They watched in silence as he arranged the tableware. When the waiter was out of earshot, they continued.

"It's true, isn't it?" Denise persisted.

"Nonsense!"

"I always thought he acted like a macho male toward Mom."

"I *never* saw him that way."

"No. You always saw him as a kind of football star."

"Well, he was good at football. And people did like him."

"Sure. The football jocks!" Denise frowned. "Just what is it you see in a man? I mean—what's your ideal?"

"Let me be frank about it, Denny. I just don't spend twenty-four hours of the day thinking about men."

"No, but you *like* men. What kind would you prefer—if you had your druthers?"

Instantly a very clear picture of Barry Ford flashed into Melissa's mind. She could see his humorous eyes, his mouth twisted in a grin, his curly hair, his erect stance, his fluid body movements. She bit her lip.

"I suppose a decent, hard-working male with a sense of humor and a feeling for integrity."

"No, no! I mean—physically."

"I like a man who adds up right," Melissa said softly. "Not muscle-bound. Not scrawny. Anyway, what is it about 'physical' that excites you so much?"

" 'Physical' doesn't *excite* me."

"No? You brought it up," Melissa reminded Denise, "when you talked about worshiping muscle." Melissa thought for a moment. "I think I'd settle for a man without a lot of psychological hang-ups."

There was a long silence. Melissa sampled her food. Then she looked up again.

"I guess neither one of us is a genius at picking out men."

"Certainly not I!"

"Do you ever hear from Mark?"

"No. And I hope I never do." Denise chopped savagely at her salad. "Whatever made you ask about him?"

Melissa frowned. "I don't know. It just came to me out of the blue."

"Well, put it back. That man was all trouble."

Denise's marriage to Mark Enright had been a disaster from the beginning. Once married, her cover-up of his physical abuse became a day-to-day horror story.

Denise with a black eye: "I stumbled into the door last night." Denise with bruised shoulders: "I fell getting out of the car." Denise with a broken tooth: "I'm going to sue my dentist!"

Her father, Brad Bonner, had finally rescued Denise. The newlyweds lived in Sioux City. Somehow Bonner found out about what Denise was going through. One night in a Sioux City barroom he confronted his son-in-law and warned him never to touch Denise again.

When he did—by his very nature, he was bound to—Denise stumbled into her parents' home bloodied and sobbing and collapsed. Brad Bonner stalked across town to the apartment and told Enright it was all over. Denise was filing for divorce. And Enright would leave Sioux City. He had come from Arkansas originally. Bonner financed his one-way train trip back to Little Rock.

And that was all it took. Enright left. Denise got her divorce on the grounds of desertion. She never saw him again. Shortly after that she flew out to Seattle, where she stayed with Melissa for several years and then got a job at the University of Seattle.

She blotted Mark Enright out of her mind.

Melissa, who was busily eating, glanced up. "How is Jonathan?" What had prompted her to ask about Jonathan Stark was a question she herself could not answer. In fact, the name when it came out of her mouth had startled her so much that she could just sit there saying nothing more.

"Dr. Stark is fine," Denise said quietly. "It's been two years since his divorce, and I think he's quite recovered." She looked up at Melissa. "He even asks about you. In fact, he was mentioning you today. Because of the Barry Ford thing."

Melissa laughed. "He always wondered why I liked sports so much. He's a real unreconstructed literary man, you know. I don't think he feels I'm really doing myself any favors in the job I have."

"He needs help, Ellie."

"Help?"

"Yeah. Confidential help. On the Scott O'Hara thing."

"I see," Melissa said.

"Drop by after lunch tomorrow. Can you? I know my boss would like to see you."

"It depends on the way things work out. Actually sometime next week would be better. I'll call you."

Suddenly Melissa looked up. Denise was puzzled at the expression on her sister's face. It was as if Melissa had remembered something she did not want to talk about. For a moment, Denise tried to guess what was on her sister's mind, but could not.

"Something's up, Ellie," Denise said. "What is it?"

"Nothing," Melissa said, looking away.

"Yes, there is!" Now Denise was positive her sister was hiding something. What?

Melissa smiled brightly. Too brightly. Quickly she changed the subject. "I told you Hobbs had us in for a conference tonight."

"Yes. What was it about?"

"We're having an outside firm come in to evaluate our television image."

Denise's mouth sagged open. "You're what?"

"Honest to God. We're going to be assayed."

"How do they do that?"

"It's something like a thoroughgoing proctoscopy."

Twelve

Play Misty for Me

Sunday was a beautiful day, the sky bright blue, the few clouds riding high, scudding eastward happily and blissfully. Melissa sat in the press box with a group of sports reporters. Channel 5, the NBC station, had the contract for the local coverage, but Melissa liked to see the game at the Kingdome so she would have the proper feel for it when she reported on it later.

The first half was a disaster for the Sea Lions. They were playing the San Diego Chargers, and the score was 21 to 0. Although Barry Ford was pinpoint accurate in his throws, his receivers seemed to be dropping all the passes he threw them. And the running game simply did not get off the ground.

In addition, the defense was awful. The Chargers were all over the field. It was luck that the score only tallied 21.

Like almost everyone else in the stands, Melissa found herself focusing on Barry Ford. When he was on the field, he was in complete control—even if the team didn't make points. Off the field he was walking up and down, talking seriously to his receivers and chatting with the runners and blockers.

At one point Hank Rambeau dropped a pass that would have been a sure six points. The team left the field. Instantly, Ford was standing next to Rambeau, smiling easily, chatting in a friendly fashion, and making signs in the air as if to indicate to Rambeau how the pass had been intended.

After the half it became apparent that something had happened. Almost at once the Sea Lion defense forced a fumble and the Chargers gave up the ball.

Rambeau ran out and up on the first play, dodged his defender, turned him around completely, caught the ball and was down to the five-yard line before being tackled. It took three tries, a penalty, and two more downs before they scored, but the Sea Lions did score.

Then the offensive coordinator called for a two-point conversion, and Ford tossed a pass near the end zone on the right, and that was eight points going in.

It was then that the game turned around. Even though the next Sea Lion touchdown did not occur until well into the third quarter, the teams seemed much more evenly matched. Ford connected again with another wide receiver who made a beautiful seventy-yard lope across the goal line for six points.

But then the Sea Lions bogged down. The two-point conversion failed. It wasn't until the end of the third quarter that a fumble gave the Sea Lions a chance to try a field goal. They made it. It was now Chargers 21, Sea Lions 17. The fourth quarter was a stand-off. With only two minutes to go in the game, the Chargers failed on fourth down to make it to the Sea Lion forty. Ford jogged out into the field with a faint grin. The players formed a huddle. Ford seemed to be talking to them in a low, conversational tone.

They came out. A twelve-yard run. A bobbled pass. A line drive. A tricky end-around. Another pass. Two more line drives. A fake reverse and a touchdown way out toward the left in the end zone. The Kingdome went wild.

Melissa realized she was yelling with all the rest of the fans. That was unusual for her. She watched the players depart the field for the locker rooms and wondered what Barry Ford would be saying down there. It wasn't up to her to interview him. Owly Metz handled all the weekend newscasts and after-game one-on-ones.

All the way home in her Range Rover she kept looking in the rearview mirror to see if the red Taurus was following her. All she could see was Barry Ford's laughing face.

She turned the mirror so she couldn't look out the back window. It got Barry Ford out of the Range Rover at last.

She went back to her apartment and was greeted in the usual fashion by Danny. She took him out for a walk around the block. Then she fixed herself a light dinner and curled up with Sara Maitland's *Ancestral Truths*. She watched Owly Metz do the ten-o'-clock news. He had a few words with Barry Ford.

METZ: How did you turn that game around?
FORD: Things came together for us in the third.
METZ: I beg to differ. You took charge. How did you do it?
FORD: This is a good lineup. It just takes teamwork.
METZ: I think you've got a lot to do with making it come off that way.
FORD: That's what I get paid for.

Melissa leaned back. He was a fascinating person—Barry Ford. There was just a jot of quirkiness about him, something that set him off from the crowd. She liked that smile that kept flitting ghost-like across his face. She liked the way he looked straight into the eyes of anyone he talked to. She liked the tensile strength of his slender but steel-tough body.

Good Lord, she thought. That's the guy I've made my own personal enemy. Or, rather, that's the guy who's decided I'm *his* personal enemy.

She sank into bed and went right to sleep. In the morning she discovered that Seattle had provided her with a weather special for Monday: a dense, London-like pea-soup fog.

The fog did not depress her too much, but it did put a damper on her schedule. As she looked out the window of her apartment she could barely see the street five stories below.

Danny was waiting for her, thumping his tail on the bathroom floor as she staggered in to splash water on her face. She pulled on her jeans and T-shirt and took him out through the back way. They ran around the block and returned, Danny huffing and puffing and enjoying himself.

Melissa slipped into her warm-ups, with the drooping shirt that had the Channel 8 logo on it, as she always did. Then she took the elevator to the basement and started her run going up the ramp to the street. George Murphy happened to be standing by the entrance to the garage.

"Morning, Ms. Bonner." He nodded to her.

"Hi, George."

"You watch those cars, now," he said with a big Irish grin.

"I'll have to listen for them today, won't I?"

He waved her on.

The mist was everywhere. It made the air heavy about her. It always amazed her that physics did not completely follow the rules of logic. For example, when the air seemed heaviest—that is, when it was full of moisture like a dense fog—the atmosphere was actually lighter than when the air was clear.

After a couple of blocks she began to hit her stride. Her breathing slowed and deepened, and her muscles started to relax. Miraculously, her head cleared. Jogging was pure ecstasy when she was in tune with her body. It was the time of day when she could let her mind dwell on details that were not nice, on complexities that arose to be solved, on contradictions that could be explored and neutralized. Jogging was the very best way to spend her quality time—like this early Monday morning in Seattle.

Melissa was about one-fourth of her way through the course when she came to the park, where she jogged along a row of hedges. There was no one out this morning. The trees dripped with moisture. The mist was thicker than she had ever seen it. Even the echo of her Reeboks seemed muted and somehow just a bit strange to the ear.

She paused a moment, listening intently. And then she heard it again. Another jogger? Probably. But where was the other runner? In front of her? Behind her?

She stopped, marking time with her feet. Then she started up again, skirting the hedge and making her way toward the campus, which formed the second corner of the rectangle that was her jogging route.

And the echoes persisted. But they could be the echoes of her own shoes—distorted by the heaviness of the mist, refracted from the sidewalk. As always she was all alone.

One thing had become quite clear over the past few days. Melissa was arriving at a point where she had to seize hold of herself and determine what the future would hold for her. She was fast approaching decision time.

The problem was with her work situation, not with herself. She had been in this job for two years, working her way up from sports writer, the job she was hired to do four years ago. Channel 8 was small-time—even in relation to the other Seattle television stations. She had to get on with her career.

New York or Los Angeles? These were the meccas of the communications industry. A place in either city could mean a job on one of the big networks.

But she must plan her moves carefully.

Her thoughts returned to Luanne Doty. Luanne was ambitious, and she was trying to move up to Melissa's level. Let her. She was a reminder to Melissa that her own days at Channel 8 should be carefully measured. To remain too long on one level would create a pattern that was unacceptable to her own ambitions.

How could she make herself important to the people who counted in the big networks, in the big centers of communication?

She suddenly stopped. The University Administration Building loomed to her right. There was rolling grassland to her left. Someone was coming up behind her. She listened, her breath steaming out into the mist.

She started up again, moving quickly and smoothly. She could hear nothing but her own heart pumping. For two blocks she trotted, and then she stopped once again.

There *were* steps behind her. Someone was jogging the same route she was taking. But who was it? She had never met anyone else.

The mist swirled as she stood there, and then she saw a figure coming toward her. Her heart jumped into her throat. She plunged forward, running hard now, all thought of jogging and pacing herself gone. She had to get away from whoever was following her.

Was it the man in the blue boxers and gray tank top? Had he come to search her out in the thick mist that shrouded the streets? She ran, faster and faster. She knew she would eventually wind herself, but for now she was at least getting ahead of him, making it harder for him to gain on her. Sooner than she thought she had reached the third corner of the rectangular course. In instants she was on her way down the last lap toward the apartment building.

She was sobbing now. The mist closed in on her. Lights burned dimly in the mist, the electric rays refracted and distilled in the wet air. And because she could not see clearly where she was stepping, she missed a curb and sprawled flat on the concrete sidewalk in front of her.

Her knee. She was too exhausted even to cry out. And as she lay there, panting and trying to crawl ahead, she could hear the inexorable pattern of footsteps coming up on her. She turned her head, trying to see over her shoulder.

With the last resources of her body, she drew herself together and crawled to her feet, staggering blindly forward. Her outstretched hands smashed into the side of a building. Disoriented, she collapsed against the wall, her palms pushed against the rough plaster and brick surface.

She sensed him directly behind her. When she turned her head she could see his bulk there, right next to her face. He had his hands out, reaching for her. She cried out, not knowing what she said or what she intended to say.

"Are you hurt?" It was a familiar male voice. But she could not place it.

"No," she said, struggling to free herself from his grip. Yet she knew now that the grip was not one of menace or hostility; it was a sustaining grip. She sagged and closed her eyes, trying to get her breath back.

"These curbs are difficult in the fog," the voice continued.

She pulled herself together and looked at the big man who had come up to help her. And now a fresh course of adrenaline surged through her body. This time it was not panic but anger that she felt.

"You!" she shouted.

Barry Ford was much bigger close up than he had seemed on the football field. Big even in his jogging gear, which made his body difficult to distinguish.

"What do you mean chasing me in the fog?" she shouted at him in rage. "You scared the life out of me. I could have killed myself trying to get away from you!"

"The story of my life," Ford said softly, a wry grin surfacing.

She shoved his hands away. As she did so, she somehow wished that he had fought her, had left them there gripping her arms. But now he was polite and thoughtful. Sensitive, even.

"What on earth are you doing on my jogging patch?" she asked, more in surprise than in anger now.

"I had no idea it was private property," Ford responded, his face innocent of guile.

"It isn't," she admitted. "Oh—what are you doing here anyway?"

"Trying to apologize directly for last Monday," Ford said with a straight face.

She wilted. All the anger and terror and emotion drained out of her. She sagged against the facade of the building. "Oh," she said in a small voice.

"I tried the phone."

"I know." She sighed.

"You didn't call back. Look. I'm sorry. I'm sorry I said anything that hurt you. Your father was a great sports figure, in spite of what I said."

"Thank you." She faced him, her heart slowing somewhat and her breathing returning to a more normal pattern. "You mean you found out where you could intercept me? Where you could scare me to death?"

Her anger seemed to be beginning to build again but somehow she could not restrain the smile that curved her lips.

Ford held both hands up in front of him in patty-cake position. "If I scared you, I'm sorry for that, too!"

"I could kill you!" She laughed. "I was terrified!"

"Walk you home?" he asked, taking her arm casually.

This time she did not yank herself away from him, but submitted and the two of them began to walk side by side through the fog. Her knee was stiffening up, but she did not mention it.

"We get Mondays off," he said with a grin, looking into her face. She could almost feel his self-assurance and his masculinity envelop her. "How about dinner tonight?"

Well, she thought.

Why not?

"Sure. I get off at ten-thirty."

He whistled. "Late date." He looked her over, his eyes approving. "Better late than never," he observed with a grin that was crooked, quirky, and very, very appealing.

Thirteen

Chief Inspector Hobbs

Darryl Hobbs was fuming. The Simmons and Lockwood evaluation group had been underfoot all Monday morning, ever since they had arrived in Seattle. And just before noon Hobbs had walked by the screening room and was surprised to see Tim Harrison, the lead member of the team, screening Melissa Bonner's Barry Ford interview from the previous Monday and her Jack Adams interview from Tuesday.

By asking a few judicious questions here and there, he had discovered from Elmer Layden that Harrison was putting together a profile of Melissa Bonner—a kind of Guy Fawkes replica to set afire with his critical opinions.

Hobbs could do nothing about heading him off. But he could warn Melissa about what was coming. He typed a note to her. *See me. H.* Then he moved into her office to leave it on her desk. She would be there in minutes—but Hobbs wanted this one right now. He didn't want her intimidated by any remarks or accusations Tim Harrison might make.

Hobbs placed the torn piece of copy paper in the center of her desk and turned to leave. As he did so his eye caught sight of a newly shorn rip-and-read in her in-basket. The word "wounded" surfaced instantly. He wondered who had forwarded this item to Melissa Bonner. Some sports figure involved in a deeper game? Hobbs wondered sardonically.

He picked up the wire service fragment and read it.

LOS ANGELES—JODIE POWELL, AN ACTRESS WHO PLAYS THE "OTHER WOMAN" ON TELEVISION'S DAILY SOAP OPERA "A SENSE OF QUALITY," WAS WOUNDED IN THE SHOULDER THIS MORNING IN A BIZARRE SHOOTING INCI-

DENT IN THE FOYER OF MS. POWELL'S CONDOMINIUM ON WILSHIRE BOULEVARD.
SHE WAS NOT SERIOUSLY HURT AND WAS RELEASED FROM U.C.L.A. MEDICAL CENTER AFTER BEING EXAMINED.
DON HAMMILL, AN UNEMPLOYED COMPUTER PROGRAM-MER, WAS ARRESTED AND CHARGED WITH ASSAULT, CARRYING A CONCEALED UNLICENSED WEAPON, RESIS-TING ARREST, AND MALICIOUS MISCHIEF.
A SPOKESPERSON FOR CALUMET PRODUCTIONS, WHICH PRODUCES THE SHOW, SAID THAT MS. POWELL HAD BEEN RECEIVING THREATENING LETTERS MADE UP OF NEWSPA-PER HEADLINES PASTED ON SCRATCH PAPER.
SHE SAID CALUMET WAS ASSUMING THAT HAMMILL'S ATTACK ON MS. POWELL WAS A CLEAR CASE OF "PSYCHOTIC OBSESSION."
HAMMILL INSISTED THAT MS. POWELL WAS HIS LOVER AND THAT THEY HAD QUARRELED. MS. POWELL SAID SHE HAD NEVER SEEN THE MAN BEFORE.

Hobbs replaced the story carefully, wondering why it had ap-peared in Melissa Bonner's in-basket. Was she gathering back-ground material for an editorial of some kind? It did not sound like her at all. Besides, she was always up-front and aboveboard about everything she was working on. He had no idea what her interest might be in this particular area. That was something the two of them would have to discuss.

But it had to wait. The fact of the matter was that Melissa did not arrive at the office within minutes to read Hobbs's note and report to him. She was involved in a brief but exciting negotiation with Madame Chang, the most exclusive couturier in Seattle. Mel-issa had never visited Madame Chang before. But Madame Chang, who rarely greeted newcomers, recognized her from her broadcasts on Channel 8, and hurried out to take care of her in person.

"I need something tonight," Melissa said. "I want to look good."

"Ms. Bonner always look good," Madame Chang said.

"Better, then. What's the 'in' color this year?"

Madame Chang shrugged her shoulders. The trivia of the fashion experts in the newspapers and on television never fazed her. She had her own standards. Instead of answering, she went to a wall-to-wall closet in her private office and returned with a very simple jet-black dress.

"Ms. Bonner will try this on, please?"

Ms. Bonner did. Ms. Bonner was pleased. Ms. Bonner thanked Madame Chang and Madame Chang hoped that Ms. Bonner would visit her shop again in the future.

"He will like you in that," she said by way of parting.

"He?" Melissa repeated with an air of mystification.

"One does not dress for one's luncheon companions," Madame Chang said.

And Melissa retreated, with visions of Barry Ford's laughing eyes and curly hair dancing in her head.

When Melissa appeared at the station somewhat tardily, she hurried across the newsroom to her office. Hobbs was watching her carefully, worried not only about the problem of Tim Harrison but the problem of the wire service story on the actress's assault.

However, she seemed to be in an excellent mood, and he did not want to put it in any jeopardy. Dressed in slacks and sweater, she had her hair tied tightly in the back. She wore no makeup, but her skin was glowing and alive.

Must be the mist, thought Hobbs, little guessing that the reason for Melissa's euphoric appearance was hanging safely in her Range Rover.

She smiled at him in passing and disappeared in her own office. A few minutes later she emerged and waved the paper. He held up his hand: five minutes. She nodded and went back to her work space.

"What's up?" she asked as she came into his big glassed-in office a few minutes later.

Hobbs studied her intently. "You seem to have had a wonderful weekend, luv."

She laughed, showing her teeth and throwing back her head archly. "But I'm always in good spirits, Mr. Hobbs."

"Never lose that nice edge you have, luv," he said sternly.

"Why the note?"

"Oh. Well." He abandoned the original reason he had wanted to speak to her: to reassure her that Tim Harrison's assessment of her would not be all that important. Instead he concentrated on the weird story on the rip-and-read. "Look. Are you working on something I don't know about?"

Her eyes widened. Hobbs realized that her expression belonged to someone who might be hiding something—or at the very least might know something that he did not know.

"No."

"A story about harassing and injuring women?" Hobbs persisted.

She flushed. "Ah," she said.

"So you *are* working on a story?"

She shook her head. "No."

"But why order up those tear sheets?"

"I didn't order up any tear sheets." She looked him in the eye. "They just came."

"They? There's more? How many?"

"Five or six."

Hobbs sat up straight. "That many?"

"Yes."

"All unrequested?"

"Yes, sir."

"But why?"

Melissa looked out the window. "I don't know."

"Get them."

She came back with the manila folder and opened it on Hobbs's desk.

While she sat there quietly, he read the stories through one by one, going back from the present to almost three weeks.

"What do you think?" Melissa asked.

"It's obviously not the stories that are important. It's the intent of the person sending them to you."

"And what might that intent be?"

Hobbs shook his head. "It seems to me it's an attempt to soften you up." Hobbs frowned. "Have you been having any—problem lately?"

"Only Barry Ford!" Melissa said with a laugh.

Hobbs nodded. "I mean, anything personal?"

"I broke up with a boyfriend some months ago."

Hobbs snapped his fingers. "I remember. Scott O'Hara."

Melissa sat up straight. "You've got a great memory."

"Only the talents of a professional voyeur, luv," he admitted ruefully. "Could he be a threat? I mean, was he devastated at the breakup or—?"

"I thought he made out rather well," Melissa said. "My sister got him on the rebound."

Hobbs laughed. "I take it you don't fear him at all."

She shrugged.

"Anything else?"

"Well," said Melissa. "I did think—" She hesitated.

"You thought what?"

"I was being followed. In a car."

"This morning?" Hobbs persisted.

"No. Last week."

Hobbs considered. "These facts, added to the stories, make me nervous."

"Me, too."

Hobbs frowned and thought out something as he sat there. "I'll find out who instructed the wire service woman to route these stories to you. Meanwhile, pretend nothing has happened."

"Well, it hasn't, really—has it?"

"No."

After Melissa left, Hobbs called in Mrs. Alita Sanchez. She was a plump, middle-aged woman with a head of gleaming black hair, and an ankle-length cotton knit dress. She always had a pleasant smile.

"As I understand it," Hobbs began, "you've been clipping out stories about harassed and injured women for Ms. Bonner."

"Melissa? Yes, sir. She told me to."

Hobbs stared. "She *told* you to?"

"I mean, sir, she sent me a note asking me to clip certain stories."

"Do you have the note?"

"Yes, sir." In a moment she returned with it. Hobbs studied it. Obviously, *someone* had put Mrs. Sanchez on the track of such stories. The note of instruction was typed without a single scratch of pencil or pen on it. It could have come from any one of the station's printers.

As Hobbs looked at it he was reminded of any number of British television series about Scotland Yard operatives working a puzzling case. He could see the kind of thing those chief inspectors were up against when they came across a puzzler like this one. For the life of him he could not figure out exactly what to do next.

"What should I do, Mr. Hobbs?"

"No need to keep it up." Hobbs handed back the note. "Thank you very much."

"I have been doing something wrong?"

"Not at all."

"I mean, with the evaluators around, and everything." Mrs. Sanchez was worried.

"Nothing to worry about," Hobbs reassured her. But it did appear as if someone was trying to shake Melissa Bonner's tree.

Fourteen

What's in a Name

 B oth the six-o'-clock and the ten-o'-clock newscasts went well, and Melissa Bonner was out of the station just after her close. In minutes she was parked in the apartment basement. When she got to her apartment door, she found a huge bouquet of long-stemmed red roses leaning against it. There was a note inside. She removed it and then opened it.

Barry Ford, the note was signed.

She unlocked the door, carrying in the bouquet. Danny began barking and running up and down the living room. He jumped up on her and slopped his big tongue all over her face.

"Danny!" she cried, although she was not thinking of Danny at all. She was thinking of Barry Ford.

Patting Danny on the head, she sank onto the couch and stared at the big bouquet. Where could she put the flowers? As she sat there, thinking, she realized that she had to take Danny out and return with him before her guest arrived. She quickly hooked him to his leash and led him out the door. They were back in ten minutes, and, after a quick shower, Melissa was slipping into Madame Chang's black dress.

She had only a few minutes to put on her makeup before the doorbell rang and he was there, waiting. She had loosened her hair and it fell softly to her shoulders. She was looking very good.

So was Barry Ford. He was in a nicely tailored charcoal-gray suit, with a striped tie and white shirt. He was a big man and had a walk that resembled a sure-footed jungle cat. She remembered studying those clips of him in the screening room before she had ever met him. In person he certainly lived up to all advance billing.

"Hi," he said, and extended a single white rose to her from behind his back.

"That's number twelve," he explained. "In case you didn't like red."

"I love red!"

By now Danny had discovered the new friend he had to make welcome. He romped about, wrinkling up the carpets and throwing the room into a furor. Ford was not intimidated by the dog's antics and began wrestling with him in the middle of the floor. It was obvious he liked dogs.

Then he was down with him, hugging him and scratching him behind the ears, at which point Danny gave up all thought of propriety and rolled over on his back with his legs kicking ecstatically into the air.

When Ford rose, Danny turned over and crouched at his feet, thoroughly befriended, tamed, and mastered by his new conqueror, who was glancing about the apartment.

"You've got a beautiful place," he told Melissa.

She smiled her thanks.

He glanced out the window. "Nice view of the harbor."

"Sound," she corrected him. "Where are you living?"

"A suite at the Seattle Sheraton Hotel and Towers. Temporarily, of course. They're trying to get me a place in north Seattle."

She took the white rose he had given her and fastened it to her black clutch bag with a pin.

"Unless you prefer the red?" he said.

"No. White for—hope?"

"You know Cucina! Cucina!?" he asked.

"Mine, or the restaurant?" she teased him.

"Your what?"

"Kitchen."

"Is that what it means? I didn't know."

"I've heard it's a fun place," she said.

"Then let's get going."

"My car or yours?"

"Oh, I've got wheels," he said with a grin. "I'm parked in your garage. A nice old Irish geezer told me just where to park."

"That's George Murphy. The building manager."

"He seems to think you're something very special," Ford said.

"Well, of course. That's because I give him something at Christmas, you know." She looked at him through slanted eyes.

"That's not the way I got it," Ford said.

She giggled. "Let's go. I'm hungry."

"Me, too."

"I'll put the roses in water when we get back."

They rode the elevator down. Ford took her hand and led her across the garage to the guest parking places. A uniformed chauffeur sat in the driver's seat of a white stretch limo. "This is it," Ford said.

She looked at him, her eyes wide.

"All the amenities." Ford laughed.

"One of your perks with the Sea Lions?" Melissa asked.

"Sorry. Strictly cash and carry."

"A rent-a-limo," she noted as she surveyed it.

The chauffeur opened the rear door for her. She slid across to the far side. Ford followed her in and signaled the chauffeur. "Let's go, Harry."

He turned to Melissa. "Champagne?"

"Well, sure," she said. "At dinner?"

"On the road." Ford pushed a button, revealing a backseat bar. He took a bottle of chilled champagne from an ice bucket and began working out the cork as the limo backed out of its parking space and ascended the garage ramp. In a moment they were out in the open air and driving in the direction of Lake Union, on which Cucina! Cucina! was located.

"So," said Barry Ford after removing the champagne cork and pouring the glasses nearly full. "To the best sportscaster in the Northwest," he said with a smile.

"Please! I'm embarrassed."

"Don't be. You're very good, you know." He held his glass high, and she touched it with hers.

"Thank you."

They drank.

Now she lifted her glass. "To the new Sea Lion star."

He laughed. "I thank *you*."

They drank.

He looked over at her. "You're not as mad at me as you were."

"No," she admitted. "Consider yourself lucky. Don't tempt me."

"No way." He sighed.

"I saw you play yesterday."

"Oh?"

"I think the Sea Lions made a good choice when they selected you."

"It was a trade," Ford said.

"You know what I mean."

"Another drink?"

He filled her glass again. "I don't want to get tipsy before we eat," she warned him.

"We'll be all right."

Soon they were at Cucina! Cucina! Melissa stepped out and Ford climbed out after her. The two of them went into the restaurant while Harry took the limousine out to the parking lot.

It was late, and Melissa could see that although there were people still eating, many of them were almost through. She noted several diners looking at her as she went by, and she realized that she had been spotted as a well-known Seattle television performer. The long looks and the popping eyes, however, were focused on her escort.

As they followed the maître d' to the deck, she could hear tiny bursts of whispers behind them. She felt a tingling frisson of amusement at the stir their entrance had caused.

The scene from the deck overlooking Lake Union, Seattle's downtown lake, was spectacular. Lights sparkled everywhere—across the lake and on the distant slopes of the city. It was a mild night, luckily, and they were not blown flat by the sometimes waggish September winds. Even on the deck they were noticed. The whispers began again, and then soon died down.

"This is lovely," Melissa told Ford. She had gone to college in Seattle, and had lived in the city ever since, but she had never been to Cucina! Cucina! even though she had heard about it.

"I thought you'd know what to order," Ford teased her.

"You're on your own, sir."

"Barry."

"That's a somewhat odd name. What's it short for?"

"It's not short for raspberry—I hope." Ford grinned. "I don't know what it's short for." He was looking at the menu. "What's Melissa mean?"

Melissa was studying the menu herself. The dishes were Italian. " 'Mel' is short for 'meli'—'honey' in Greek. I guess you could call me 'Little Honey.' "

"I'd opt for 'Little Honey-Bee.' You've got the stinger."

She laughed. "I'm putting you on. Melissa doesn't mean anything at all. It's a name made up by some medieval writer."

"Which one?" Ford asked. "I'm bluffing, you understand, because I don't know *any*."

"Ariosto."

"Oh, right on," said Ford blankly. "Sam Ariosto, the Notre Dame cornerback."

"Melissa was a prophetess in *Orlando Furioso*, Ariosto's masterpiece. She lived in Merlin's cave."

"Merlin? Not Merlin Olson, the ex-Ram of FTG fame?" Ford said.

She ignored him. "And there was *another* Melissa in Spenser's *Faerie Queene*—Pastorella's handmaid."

"Great. That Spenser guy. He's the detective on television. The guy who is always doing the bench press."

She looked at him a moment, wondering if he was putting her on. That was the trouble with kidding. You never knew how far you could go and still be on dry land.

"Yeah, as played by Robert Urich."

"I'm glad you keep up on literature," Ford said. "You want

those clams as a starter? The ones 'broiled on the half shell' because I can't pronounce the Italian." The waiter was hovering. Ford turned to him. "Those are razor clams, aren't they?"

"Yes, sir, Mr. Ford."

Ford glanced at him and then returned to the menu. "What would you like, Melissa?"

"The same as you, please."

Ford gave the order and added a carafe of the house's white wine. "I watched your show every night," Ford said suddenly, leaning back in his chair.

"As atonement of some kind?"

"For my inexcusable lapse of taste last Monday."

"I shouldn't have been so infuriated. I lost my temper. It was obvious to me later that you didn't know my father was dead."

"Still, it was a gaffe." He looked at her. "You didn't cover the game Sunday."

"The weekend sportscaster handled that. But I did see you play."

The clams came and they ate. The food was excellent, and for the next half hour they were absorbed mostly in eating and indulging in small talk that just drifted over the surface of things and then disappeared like melting snowflakes. They ordered coffee and no dessert.

"I researched you enough to find out you jogged every morning," Ford said finally, stirring the sugar into his coffee. "But that was as far as I got."

"So?"

"I never found out what I really wanted to know."

"Which is exactly what?"

"Whom do you date?"

She laughed. "Whoever asks."

"You're kidding."

"Nope. Did I have to check in my date book when you asked me out for dinner tonight?"

Ford shrugged. "A lucky break."

"I'm a professional sportscaster, Mr. Ford. I—"

"Barry, for God's sake."

"Barry, for God's sake."

He laughed.

"I don't usually have the time to date excessively."

"You're stuck on Seattle?"

"Career-wise? Not at all."

"The Big Apple?"

"Maybe."

"I've been there. It's highly overrated. So is the Jersey Meadowlands. I lost a few there myself." He made a face. She knew he was talking about the Giants or the Jets.

"All right. Let's get down to brass tacks. Every time you play in Los Angeles you're always squiring that up-and-coming movie actress around town. Anne Whittaker?"

"She's a bright kid."

"And you fancy bright kids."

"You're getting a little close to the heart of things, Ms. Bonner."

"I'm just doing what we call basic research."

He leaned back chuckling. His coffee cup was empty. So was Melissa's. "I've got a rough week ahead of me. Shall we call it a night?"

"Call it whatever you like. It's been lovely for me."

"Say 'Barry,' please."

"Barry, please."

"Me, too, Melissa." He hesitated. Then: "I hear tell things are not going too smoothly at Channel 8 these days. There are all kinds of rumors afloat."

"I'm sure there are."

"Tell them you put out the fire that started last Monday. Tell them that everything is back to normal. Tell them that you wowed Barry Ford and have him in the palm of your hand."

Melissa looked at him calculatingly.

"Because you do, you know." He picked up his credit card and stuffed it into his wallet before signing the check and helping her out of her chair.

He ordered Harry to pull up in front of her apartment building. Ford helped Melissa out, opening her door from the sidewalk side.

"It was fun, Melissa," he said, but made no move to kiss her.

She waved good-bye and the door swung open to reveal a smiling George Murphy just inside the foyer. He was grinning at Barry Ford as he got back in the limo.

"Real nice guy," he told Melissa.

Fifteen

Bay Area Blueblood

Before dipping into the more weighty articles in the *Chronicle of Higher Education*, Jonathan Stark loved to read the "Marginalia" column on one of the first inside pages of the publication. Today's bloopers were up to standard. The column skewered typographical errors, unintentional double meanings, non sequiturs, and oxymorons of all kinds in college periodicals—a kind of roundup of idiocy for future generations to laugh at.

"From a statement printed on an essay folder at East Texas State University," one began today. " 'Plagiarism and academic creating will not be tolerated in the Department of Literature and Languages.' "

And the laconic comment: "That's the spirit!"

It took sharp eyes and a sense of the ridiculous to spot the humor—in this case, of course, the unintentional typographical substitution of "creating" for "cheating."

Stark then went on to the in-depth academic data in the more serious section of the paper.

In a moment he was absorbed in reading a story about the football program controversy at a Southeastern college. It was surprisingly similar to the one that had quite suddenly erupted like Mauna Loa on his own campus. The football team there had been put on probation for improper recruitment of players.

A group of faculty members had organized a petition to drop all sports at the university. In turn, the athletic department, through the help of a powerful alumni association, had taken an opposite stance. Now the students were out demonstrating—half on one side, half on the other.

Of course at Seattle no team had been put on probation. But a philosophical division had appeared in the student body and administration. It was becoming a case of athletic excellence pitted against academic excellence.

Stark shook the paper, trying to let off some steam. The problem in its many ramifications had become a persistent one in modern university circles. The brains wanted college out of the athletics business; the brawn wanted college out of the academic business. And, by the looks of it, both sides were waging battles to the death.

He placed the paper in front of him and stood up, wandering over to the window, which looked out over one of the many lakes in Seattle. In the distance he could imagine Rainier, cloud-covered but in part shining in the bright sunlight. A beautiful sight. He loved it here in Seattle, even though he had spent only a part of his life in the West.

In his forties, Jonathan Stark was in excellent physical shape, the picture of good health. He was an anomaly. He did not jog every day. He did not do aerobics. He did not play golf. He did, however, sail, as his ancestors did. It was all a matter of genes. He had come from a slim, muscular, bright, low-key, emotionally contained ancestral stock. Not only that, but he had been extremely lucky in economics, in social contacts, and in status given him by his birthright.

Stark was a true blueblood, of the type that had at one time inundated the Boston area. With Stark's generation, much of the blueblood stock had left the Northeast, to proliferate elsewhere. Stark himself had followed in his uncle's footsteps. He graduated from Amherst like his uncle, earned a doctorate at Harvard, and then moved to the University of Seattle as a young teacher.

Rising almost immediately to department head, he had been on call when the board of regents made a vital decision: to upgrade the university's academic status by hiring prestigious teachers, by tightening up on academic procedures, and by making Seattle the image of up-market academe.

Stark was the college's ace in the hole. With an excellent high-profile background plus impeccable personal credentials, he had become the obvious choice to head the college. And overnight he became the youngest college president of the decade.

Everything he did won accolades for the college: two Nobel Prize winners on the faculty, a gaggle of scholars of international fame, and a quick rise in student performance.

His triumphs in academic endeavors led to a diminishing of the school's athletic allure. The current situation—with Seattle winning the basketball conference—put the spotlight on Coach Scott O'Hara, a charismatic and interesting showman with great leadership qualities. And so now the rift between athletics and academics was apt to widen.

At the same time, Stark had faced personal problems. What had not worked well was his marriage to Cornelia Bascomb; they had no children and everything fell apart with the divorce finalized two years ago. He still liked her. She apparently liked him. But their lives had not paralleled well.

Stark's eyes moved down the long flight of steps that led to the Administration Building's entrance just below him. Students were coming back from lunch and others were grabbing a coffee across the street.

He watched idly, and then saw a familiar face. He took a sudden breath. It *was* Melissa Bonner. He could see that the film crew that usually accompanied her was not present. Perhaps she was visiting her sister, Denise.

He felt elated. Of all the coeds who had been in his classes when he was teaching, Melissa Bonner had been the one he remembered the most. He had been on the verge of breaking up with Cornelia at the time. With difficulty he had forced himself to adhere to his own high ethics, let alone university regulations—that is, not to try to date Melissa Bonner.

He had followed her career after she left college. It had been easy—every night she appeared on Channel 8. He simply tuned in, and there she was.

In a way, of course, it was a disappointment to Stark that Melissa had chosen to direct her talents to the sports news area, rather than to ordinary hard news. She would have made a first-class anchorperson. Instead, here she was laboring in the somewhat questionable vineyards of professional sports in a second-tier city.

And Stark meant no disparagement of Seattle when he categorized the city that way. It was a marvelous place to live. But for the really successful people in communications it was hardly the site for a career peak.

He had seen her problem with Barry Ford and had found himself smiling as he thought about it. Melissa had handled the matter theatrically and successfully. Although Stark would have ignored the matter entirely, he knew that communications situations were different from his own preference. Perhaps it had been the television station's bosses who had advised her. Or directed her.

As he stood there he could hear low-voiced conversation coming from Denise's office just outside his own. Someone laughed. It was Melissa. He could remember her laugh even though he had not talked to her for months. He felt a quickening of his pulse.

Unable to restrain himself, he crossed to the heavy oak office door and thrust it open. He saw Denise seated at her desk, with Melissa hip-seated sideways on its edge. They were smiling at one another in complete conversational rapport.

Now Melissa slid off the desk top and stood. She was wearing a loose-fitting sweater and a short skirt that showed off her legs. As she faced him, the corners of her mouth turned up in a pretty, heart-stopping smile.

"Hello, Dr. Stark," she said. She held out her hand. "How are you?"

He took her hand. "Fine, fine. I see you're doing very well yourself."

"Thank you."

He took a deep breath. "Denise, do you mind if I steal your guest for a few minutes?"

"Certainly not, Dr. Stark."

Melissa looked at Stark for a moment, and then decided to enter the office ahead of him. He sat at his desk and indicated the chair opposite. Melissa sank into the easy chair and looked at him.

"I saw you do the Barry Ford interview," he said with a smile.

"So did everybody else." She didn't sound too happy about it.

"I always thought you should have gone in for straight news," he observed judiciously. "But I can understand your interest in sports because of your father."

She sat there wondering where the conversation was headed.

"Actually, I'm glad you chose to come here today to see your sister. It's one of those coincidences, but I'm beginning to find myself in the midst of an athlete-versus-academic battle."

Her face lit up. "Oh?"

He gave her a brief rundown on the situation, naming no names, but outlining the problem and pointing out the fact that as yet no opposing sides had formed on the Seattle campus.

"Do you think they will?" Melissa asked. "I mean, has anyone made an overt move? It's Scott O'Hara we're talking about, isn't it?"

He stared at her. "Of course. I don't know what he's done. That doesn't matter. The problem I face is how to handle a possible pro-athlete and pro-academic confrontation."

"You're in favor of dropping sports?"

"Absolutely not! I can't really be, in my position. I represent both sides. But I came in here to increase our academic visibility. And I've done it. What I'm trying to do is figure out the proper stance to take if things suddenly get out of hand." He frowned. "There was a similar confrontation between coach and president recently."

"Who won?" Melissa asked.

"They were both fired!"

They both laughed briefly. Melissa leaned forward to underline her interest. "Consider me an ally, Dr. Stark. If you need anything in the way of a public statement—an interview, a Q and A, a panel—let me know. I can't promise anything, but I am in the business."

He nodded.

"And my interviews don't all come out like the Barry Ford mess." She laughed. She stood and he rose after her, realizing that she had developed an amazingly clear head for timing, for protocol, for the right way to proceed no matter on what level of the power structure she was operating. He opened the door for her.

"It's nice seeing you again. You always were my favorite professor here." She held out her hand again.

He took it in his and started to squeeze it. Then he thought better of it. "Do you have an hour or so?"

She hesitated a moment. "Yes, I do."

"Would you like to have lunch with me?"

"I'd love to."

"I'll have Denise phone ahead for a table for us."

It was just a bit cool that noon as the two of them strolled across campus to the commissary building. The sight of Dr. Stark with his attractive guest—someone who had been seen by any number of students on Channel 8—drew surprised glances their way. An occasional greeting of "Hello" or "How are you today, Dr. Stark?" floated across to them as they moved on.

They entered the commissary building and climbed the steps to the faculty dining room on the second floor. It was a bit early yet for the big surge of diners, but there were small groups forming along the wall tables.

The head waiter—no maitre d' here; the University of Seattle was a very democratic institution—took charge of the two of them and seated them in a prize spot at a window overlooking the campus. In the distance they could see the waters of Puget Sound and the tip of one of the islands.

Melissa gazed out the window at the spectacular panorama looking across Seattle and commented on the clearness of the air. They finally decided on salads. And a glass of white wine. Stark leaned back in the chair and smiled.

There was a moment of silence—not in any way strained, but perfectly relaxed and quite comfortable. When Melissa looked up she saw that Jonathan was studying her closely. She felt her cheeks suddenly warm up.

"How is life treating you these days, Melissa?" he asked with a smile.

Fleetingly, all her troubles flashed through her mind. What would he do if she really told him what was happening? She suppressed any thought of letting it all hang out and simply matched his smile with a neutral one of her own.

"Fine, fine," she said. She looked directly at him. "And you? How is life treating you?"

"Very well," he said easily. "I've never been better."

"But divorces are always messy, aren't they?"

"I've had better experiences," he admitted. "But it's all over now."

"I always liked Cornelia," Melissa said, taking the bold approach. "She was energetic, caring, and interested in people."

"True," Jonathan replied. "She was a dedicated volunteer. If she'd had her way, she would have been running every nonprofit service west of the Rockies." They both laughed. "And, yes, I'd have to agree with you. She *is* very likable. We're still friends."

"Things just didn't work out?" Melissa asked slowly.

"We were going our separate ways without quite realizing it," Jonathan said. "Suddenly there was nothing at all between us. No kind of connection at all." He spread his hands out.

Melissa suddenly felt like her alternate journalistic persona conducting an interview. "And is there anyone in whom *you* are interested now?"

He stared at her uncertainly. "Sorry. I don't seem to be the adventurous type. That is, if you're measuring romance on the Richter Scale." He was watching her closely.

She flushed. "I didn't mean to turn into Barbara Walters."

He chuckled easily. "And you. Are you—I don't know quite how to say this—are you romantically inclined with anyone these days?"

"It *is* dumb the way we speak about love and sex and intimate things, isn't it?" She adjusted her thoughts. "A significant other? Not really."

"I remember you were interested in Scott O'Hara."

"The basketball coach? You've got a memory like an elephant." Her eyes moved to his. "That just didn't work out, but we are still friends."

He nodded. "And there's no one else?" He was probing. Melissa wondered what he had heard. Was it all over town about her and Barry Ford? Was that what he was trying to find out? Well, she thought. What the hell.

"I was out with the football player Barry Ford one night. That was after our dust-up over his press conference. I doubt that is going to be a longtime thing. He's much too active in the romance department."

"He's very personable," Jonathan said.

"Oh, he's that."

"Do you like your job at Channel 8?" Jonathan frowned. "Or perhaps I should say, how much do you like your job at Channel 8?"

"I love it!" she said quickly, without thought.

"You were an English major. It's an anomaly: an English major speaking sports jargon. I had always considered that you might be perfect for a straight newscaster."

"The chance hasn't come up," Melissa said. Her eyes gleamed. It would be the best thing that ever happened to her—if it would happen.

He reached across and grasped her hand. "Maybe you'll get your chance sometime."

She blinked suddenly. He was close and vital and she was vulnerable to his warmth and consideration. Well, she had to admit, it wasn't like the feeling she got from Barry Ford. But it was real. She had to change the subject. Things were getting a bit out of hand.

"If you need me," she said with a shy smile, "call the station. I think I can help if you want to go public on this athlete-academic problem you have."

He smiled. "You may be hearing from me."

"I'd like that. You're the kind of person I wouldn't mind being lost in a jungle with," she said, startling herself by the wide-ranging implications of the statement.

He laughed. "Depends on the jungle, doesn't it?"

Sixteen

The Good Times Past

After leaving Jonathan Stark and saying good-bye to Denise, Melissa wandered out onto the campus. It was two o'clock. The campus was in a somnolent state. She remembered her own days as a student—focusing especially on that dreamlike state in which she usually took her early afternoon classes.

She had always loved the Gothic motif of the campus architecture. The buildings might have been copied from ancient churches in England or France. In appearance they were gray and steel-colored.

The windows were composites of tiny panes of glass leaded in place in larger expanses of window. The thin spires spider-webbed into the sky, where they seemed always to be leaning this way and that as the clouds drifted by.

She stopped at the campus bookstore. It was a quiet nook on a grassy slope, almost deserted at this time. She poked about, picking up volumes and laying them down. Occasionally one of the students would recognize her and would covertly watch her and then pretend not to have noticed her at all.

She was surprised at how glad she had been to see Jonathan Stark again. She had gone through four years of college knowing that she had a teenage crush on him, but now that she had seen him, she was beginning to feel just a little mushy. Of course he was out of her generation—one ahead of it, at least. And yet she saw him as a very attractive, definitely interesting male animal.

Now that he was finally on his own again, he was a different man. Melissa could see the qualities that had always attracted her before, shining out of him more strongly now. That absolutely marvelous aristocratic WASP persona simply was too real to be overshadowed and obscured in any way.

But more than that, he was always the obviously perceptible

intellectual—*the* academic paradigm. She could hear his accent once again, that almost automatic, precise, perfect pronunciation of each word, the self-assured manner in which he plunged into any sentence of explication he was about to make.

Lucky Denise, she thought. And yet she still had Scott O'Hara, who was anybody's catch. Yet she wondered why Denise didn't try to go for broke with Jonathan Stark. Melissa was glad somehow that neither Denise nor Stark had seen anything romantic in the other. As for Melissa, she could still see the perfect man in Stark—and the image he projected now was much clearer and firmer than it had ever been in the past.

She headed for the parking lot. As she ascended the steps to the lot she could hear someone hurrying behind her.

"Melissa!" she heard a voice cry out.

She turned quickly. It was Scott O'Hara!

"Hi, Scotty!" She went into his open arms and he hugged her. Then he held her away from him and looked her over. "How've you been?"

"Great!" she said. "You?"

"Couldn't be better!"

"Hey, what a team you guys had this spring!" She had not seen him for a good six months.

He beamed. Scott O'Hara was a sharp-featured man, with greenish eyes and straight brown hair that had a touch of red in it. He was not tall, but managed to look sturdy. He always wore slacks and a nonmatching jacket. His ties were uniform and ultraconservative. But in the long run he was the perfect image of the explosive, gesticulating, shouting basketball coach.

And yet much of the time he spent sitting placidly on the sidelines, chin cupped in hand, watching the moves of his stellar performers.

He was energetic, generally outpacing anyone with whom he was walking. He was quick to speak, quick to think, quick to act. And Melissa knew something else. He was fun to be with.

"Have you got a minute?" he asked.

She didn't have, really, but she said, "Okay." After all, it was Scott O'Hara.

"Let's sit down." He indicated a bench under a sycamore.
She followed him and sat beside him. The bench was not designed for comfort of any kind; in fact, it was built to discourage
any lengthy occupation in order to keep the place free of idlers.
She shifted about until she got comfortable.

"Saw your open letter to Barry Ford."

"You liked it?"

"Loved it! He made a mistake and he paid for it. Not a bad guy,
really. I think he's going to make the Sea Lions into a championship
team."

"I hope so."

"Even if he did make you flaming mad?" O'Hara was grinning.

"Why not?"

"Didn't I see you going across the lawn to the commissary this
noon with El Presidente?"

"That you did."

"You always did like him, didn't you?"

She smiled. "Maybe I did and maybe I didn't."

"I know one thing, Melissa. You and I had a ball, didn't we?"

"We did," she agreed, and had a warm feeling while she said it.

He looked at her closely. "They were the best of times."

"They were, Scotty."

He looked away. "We need that basketball gymnasium," he said
in a lower tone. "We are the champs, you know." He swung around
on her suddenly and stared into her eyes.

"You're pushing, Scotty! You said you'd never do that with me
again."

"Just a suggestion, Melissa. Just a suggestion." He grinned.
"Now, I don't really mind getting all hot about academic johns
who are in the encyclopedias and that kind of thing. But don't
forget about us poor jocks. Will you?"

"No. I won't." She laughed.

He could always make her laugh. And yet he could always get
under her skin. Actually, their breakup was very clean. Neither had
gotten hurt by it.

"And don't forget the academics, either, Scotty."

"I'm sure you won't. I appreciated that interview you gave us when we started out this year," he said. "I think it gave us a jump-start."

"Glad to be of service."

"I've got a meeting this afternoon with the alums." He stuck his hand out. "Planning some kind of underhanded mischief, I'm sure." He laughed. "So long, Melissa. It's good seeing you again. If I didn't say it already, you're looking just great." He thought about that. "*The* greatest."

He waved at her and went swiftly down the path to the parking lot. Melissa smiled and thought about their days together. Never a dull moment, she recalled. It was odd what had happened. One day there just wasn't anything there between them.

Wasn't that what it was all about anyway? You looked around until you found someone you could be happy with. On a permanent basis. Always.

She sauntered up the path after O'Hara.

Seventeen

Luanne

On Wednesday one of the former Seattle Seafarers—the city's professional baseball team—died of an embolism, and even though he had not been on the team for several years, his death was a big sports story. Melissa with Luanne Doty gathered the loose ends of tape they had on him to create a fitting tribute. It was all scut work and Melissa was glad when she and Luanne finally got it under control for Elmer Layden.

Running through the extant footage of the ballplayer's exploits was a fatiguing job. Moreover, Melissa found herself much less sweet-tempered than she usually was at the end of the day. She knew, however, that she must at all times do her job on a businesslike level. Holding in her temper as best she could, she went through the material twice before she was satisfied and by nine-thirty had it mastered.

Then, when she came to read the final edited copy on the prompter at ten, she found herself wading through material that she had not previously encountered. She was a good sight reader. She made just two bloopers and only had to clear her throat twice, but it was inexcusable that she had been given cold copy to read without being informed beforehand.

Once off camera she searched out Luanne Doty.

"What are you trying to do to me?" Melissa snapped, her eyes flashing. "Don't pretend you don't know what I'm talking about! That paragraph about the ballplayer's father."

When she realized that Melissa was coming at her, Luanne stiffened.

"But honey," she said wheedlingly. "It was one of those things that came up from the print file."

"All you had to do was *tell* me!" Melissa stormed on.

"There wasn't time! Mr. Hobbs instructed me to go ahead if I felt it was important."

"I'll handle Mr. Hobbs. You should have told *me.*"

"You were in makeup," Luanne said stiffly.

"Where the hell should I have been?" Melissa exclaimed.

Luanne's expression shifted. She was immediately remote, moving into a defensive position. "It was a judgment call," she said. "At least that was the way I felt."

"It's done. There's no going back." Melissa watched Luanne warily. "See that it doesn't happen again."

"I thought you handled it well," Luanne said softly.

Oh sure, thought Melissa angrily. But she was cooler now. "Just be sure to run it by me before I find myself stumbling through another raw item."

"Yeah," Luanne said, her blue eyes watching Melissa carefully. After all, she was lower on the totem pole than Melissa. She knew it. Melissa knew it. So did the rest of the crew.

The tension suddenly evaporated. Melissa waved a hand. "I'm out of here."

As she strode across the newsroom for the elevator, she found herself reviewing her nasty exchange with Luanne in a highly critical manner. What had ever possessed her to come unraveled? She understood Luanne and knew how to handle her. What, then, had caused her to break all precedent and go for the jugular?

It was as if she was unable to concentrate anymore. Her mind would drift away from what it was supposed to be focusing on. Barry Ford seemed everywhere. She could hear him laughing, could see him ducking his head and grinning, the gap between his two front teeth giving him a very special look.

She shook herself. It still didn't help. As the elevator sank, she felt dizzy. For the first time she understood exactly what the word *queasy* meant.

She dismissed him from her mind. One, two, three. He was gone!

In the underground garage Melissa found her Range Rover immediately, but before going over to it, she glanced about her at the other parked vehicles. She saw no red Taurus among them, nor did she see anyone sitting in any of the cars watching her.

On the road she continued her surveillance by means of the rearview mirror, but did not catch a glimpse of anything that seemed unusual. She was becoming totally paranoid, she thought. But then again, she only had to fasten her mind on that manila folder loaded with wire service stories to feel a cold chill settling in her backbone.

She pulled into her own car slot in the apartment building's garage. Still no stalkers in sight. She turned out the lights, locked the door, and hurried to the elevator. In less than a minute she was opening the door to her apartment and bracing herself against the assault by Danny.

He barked. She hugged him. He banged her thighs with his tail as he twirled around her. She talked to him. She fed him. He held himself right to the task of eating and drinking and then he was at the front door, looking back at her and wondering why she was taking so much time.

Laughing, she went over to him, slipped on the leash, and took him out and around the block. When they were back in the apartment, he looked at her and then slumped down on the living room carpet.

She switched on the television and watched the opposition as she undressed. She was very tired, as she always was at the end of a hard day. The opposition station was a lot bigger than Channel 8, but the news seemed no fresher and actually was no different from 8's. The news team comprised a male and a female coanchor, a male sportscaster, and a female weatherperson.

The woman coanchor was a Jane Pauley type—blond, cool, laid-back, understated. The one flaw in her speech was her main attraction. She lisped just slightly over certain keywords. Her green eyes tended to drill right into the viewer's. But her diction was excellent, with the exception of the lisp.

Melissa knew her history. She had been rising more like a rocket than a steady climber, and San Diego was about to lose her to New York when a catastrophe occurred that ruined her. A police raid on a nightclub revealed her in the company of a rock singer. That fact in itself added to her aura of glamour. Unfortunately, the two of them were discovered in the possession of controlled substances.

New York cooled on her. San Diego worried about its own future. Within nine months she was out. Seattle's NBC station, Channel 5, picked her up for the late-night slot. She was on her way down now, not even in a leveling-off mode. Within two years, Melissa knew, she would be out of the business entirely.

Melissa shivered. With the lights out, she wandered over to the window overlooking the sound and gazed at the lights. It was a beautiful night, the stars out, the artificial lights gleaming through the night air, the flickering red lamps of cars rushing away from her on the highway. She loved Seattle.

And suddenly she was humming "A Wink and a Smile" to herself.

Danny Boy was thumping his tail on the carpet keeping the beat for her.

"We could use you at the station to review the motion pictures!" she said, bending down to hug him.

"A Wink and a Smile" was what did it. She brushed her teeth, looked at her hair, and frowned as she removed her makeup. Then she thought of Barry Ford and a wink and a smile.

It was Barry Ford's image that climbed into bed with her, and, when she turned over to will herself to sleep, that was the imp that crawled out of the covers and sat on her forehead grinning down into her eyes. She didn't get to sleep until 1:00 A.M. That was when Barry Ford finally gave up and left the apartment.

Eighteen

Break and Enter

Melissa was awakened from that most delicious of deep sleeps—that first hour or so after falling into bed exhausted and eventually drifting off—and it was difficult for her to focus her mind on the details of reality around her. Dominating all sounds was a loud screeching of a bell, then silence, and then the loud screeching of the bell once again.

Telephone, she thought drowsily, trying to pry her eyes open. It was pitch dark in her bedroom and she almost knocked over her clock radio when she reached out to snap on the bedside lamp. By the time the light was on, she could see the phone and lifted the handset.

"Ellie!" cried a voice excitedly. "Thank God you're there! Oh, Ellie! Someone broke into my apartment! There are cops all over the place!"

"What *is* it?" Melissa asked, trying to clear her head. "You've been burglarized?"

"That's it!" Denise sighed. "I woke up in the middle of the night. There was a noise in the other room. I got up and saw a man going through my things. He—he heard me." She was beginning to sniffle. "He hit me, Ellie!"

"I'll be right over," Melissa said. "You say the police are there?"

"Yes, yes. You don't need to bother about me, Ellie. I'll be all right on my own. I just wanted you to know."

"Nonsense! I'll bring my things. You've still got that spare cot, haven't you?"

"Of course. But I don't *need* you."

Within minutes Melissa had dressed and pulled on her shirt, slacks, and heavy sweater. Danny was up and around, barking now, and she had to pat him on the head and tell him she would be back in time for his walk next morning.

Quickly she drove her car up out of the garage and headed for her sister's apartment building.

She could see the patrol cars in front of the place, their car-top lights flashing dizzily. She parked on the street near the corner and stepped out of the car, running across the street and entering the foyer of the building. There were two patrolmen inside.

"Ms. Bonner," one of them said, recognizing her.

"I'm Denise's sister," Melissa said to identify herself.

"I know. Come with me. She said you'd be here."

Denise's apartment was on the ground floor in the rear. The patrolman led her through the hallway and opened the door to the apartment. Several uniformed men were inside the room, concerned mostly with a window under which there lay a small clutter of glass shards.

"Ellie! I'm so glad you're here!" Denise said, getting out her handkerchief and blowing her nose.

Melissa wrapped her sister in her arms and squeezed her reassuringly. When she released her she saw the bloodied cut on her left temple.

"Is that where he hit you?" Melissa asked.

"Yes," Denise said, her voice steadier now.

"Don't you think you should have it looked at?"

"I'm all right," Denise replied.

"Are you? No. We're going to take a run down to Ballard General Hospital. Officer," Melissa said to the nearest uniformed man. "we're going to the hospital to have a doctor look at my sister's head wound."

"Yes, ma'am." The officer, a young man with a pencil-thin mustache, nodded. "We don't know how hard the perpetrator hit her. It's always best to be sure everything is all right."

"We'll leave right now," Melissa said. She took Denise in hand and led her out to the Range Rover across the street. They drove to the back entrance of the hospital and pulled up at the emergency room door. In a very short time the intern working emergency that night had made an examination of the wound, determined it not to be serious, and instructed a nurse to put on a butterfly bandage.

While Denise filled out the forms and handed over her health plan I.D. card, Melissa waited for her at the desk. In a very short time they were on their way back to Denise's apartment. It was in the Range Rover that Denise found her voice, and, once started, went on nonstop.

"It was awful!" she told Melissa. "I was sound asleep, and something woke me up. I lay there trying to find out what had disturbed me. Then I heard someone moving around in the other room. I was terrified, but I got up anyway and opened the door. There was a man there with a flashlight, and he was pawing over my things."

Denise tried to hold back her tears, blew her nose, and went on.

"I should have been smart and ducked back into my bedroom and locked the door against him. But I wasn't. I was so darned mad that someone should pick on me that way. I went toward him instead of away from him."

She dabbed at her face again.

"He saw me and lunged. He was too fast for me to duck. He hit me on the forehead with the edge of the flashlight. I went down fast. I didn't get a chance to see what he looked like! He had on one of those ski masks. I don't think I passed out at all, but I just collapsed. He ran over and yanked open my front door. He was gone before I could even shout out."

Denise straightened.

"I called 911 right away. In moments the cops were there. Then more came. Pretty soon they told me the prowler had entered by the back window. I could see the broken glass. No one needed to tell me that!" Denise was getting annoyed now.

"Then I called you. And—and—"

"Enough, Denny!" Melissa said. "Do you want to go to work tomorrow? Or do you want to take a sick day?"

Denise leaned back. "I hadn't even thought about that. Well, I don't see why I shouldn't go to work. Nothing's missing." She glowered. "Except my faith in my fellow man, maybe!"

Melissa laughed. "You're recovering already. You'll survive!"

"Why me?" Denise wondered. "I don't have anything anybody'd want! And I looked around already. There was nothing."

Melissa glanced hard at Denise. Why, indeed? Wasn't that what she had been wondering for the past few weeks after hearing those phantom calls, seeing that red Taurus, reading those stories, and discovering the man in blue boxers in her garage?

She turned into the nearest side street from the apartment after Denise told her that would be the best place to park. They got out, Melissa locked up the car, and the two of them went back into the apartment building.

The policemen who remained were getting ready to leave. The officer with the pencil-thin mustache was the last to go.

"We're all through, ma'am," he told Denise. "I've alerted the super about the broken window. He'll be here as soon as he can to board it up."

"Will that be enough to keep people out?" Denise asked nervously.

"The perp won't be back tonight." The officer smiled knowledgeably. "Don't worry about him. You need protection against any small night animals."

Denise shuddered. "Goodness," she said.

When the sisters were alone, Denise went over to the window through which the intruder had entered and leaned over to inspect it. Melissa could see that the prowler had simply smashed the bottom of the glass pane and reached up inside to unlock the double-hung window. Then he had raised it and crawled in.

"He must have put a towel around his fist," said Melissa thoughtfully.

"A towel?" Denise was puzzled.

"To break the glass. You didn't hear the noise of the glass breaking, did you?"

"Not at all. I see what you mean. The towel would muffle the sound." She stood there and stared around the room. "I don't understand what he wanted."

"Maybe he didn't know either."

"Now, what do you mean by that?"

"It's just deep psychological insight," Melissa said with a laugh.

There was a discreet knock on the door. Denise opened it. The super, a lean, tall man in his sixties wearing light-blue glasses, was standing there holding a piece of plywood in his hands.

"Took a long time to find this thing. The basement's such a mess." He nodded to Melissa. "Evening, ma'am." Then he turned back to Denise. "I'll nail this over the broken window and let you get to bed."

"Thank you," Denise said.

It took him longer than expected. He had to saw the piece so it would fit properly inside the window frame. Then he had to drill holes for the wood screws that finally fastened the plywood in place. He was sweating and cursing when he finally got it secured. After apologizing several times he left the apartment.

"Whew!" Denise said.

"You'll have to get new glass put in that window tomorrow," Melissa reminded Denise.

"Don't I know it!" Denise sighed. "Well, we'd better get to bed. I'll have a hell of a time getting to sleep with all this on my mind."

Melissa shook her head. "Two aspirins for you, Denny."

"I won't fight that," Denise admitted.

As she made up the cot, Melissa was struggling with her own thoughts. She did not intend to tell her sister about the various intrusions in her own life. But she was wondering if it was right to ignore the possibility that the assaults on the two sisters might be linked in some way. And that her own life could be in jeopardy.

Perhaps the perpetrator—as the police called him—had simply followed Melissa to her sister's office the day before and was now visiting on her the same odd disruptions he had inflicted on Melissa Bonner.

"A penny for your thoughts," Denise said, as she noted Melissa's abstracted look.

"Go to bed," Melissa replied. "Get some rest. After all, you've got to go to work tomorrow."

Denise giggled. "You're all heart, Ellie," she told her sister, padding off into her bedroom. "Night."

Nineteen

Fantasy Island

Sunday's game with the Denver Broncos was a no-contest shoo-in for the Seattle Sea Lions. The defense held their ground against Denver's first assaults. The offense got the ground game going almost from the start. When they had softened up Denver enough, the offense shifted gears into its run-and-shoot phase, with Ford's passing racking up a score of 30 to 7 in the first half. Ford was able to convert two of the four touches for eight-point scores by pretending he was bluffing.

Melissa, who sat in the press box watching, felt that this was simply a matter of bravura on the quarterback's part. The Sea Lions really didn't need to rub it in so much.

The second half opened with a quick turnaround, giving the Sea Lions a momentary scare. Even the sale of hot dogs in the Kingdome fell off for fifteen minutes. It was only a short-term fright. The two seven-point touchdowns in that period were the Broncos' final effort. Soon enough the Seattle defense tightened up and the offense was able to add a field goal for a final score of 33 to 21.

Melissa hung around the locker room trying to catch Barry Ford's eye while Owly Metz, the weekend jock, interviewed Coach Hatchett. At one point she thought she had got it, and she had—but in moments Ford demonstrated by his actions and talk that he was out for a night on the town with his offensive unit. In fact, he gave her a wink as he saw her leave the locker room.

On Monday morning, as Melissa rounded the corner to start in on the first leg of her jogging course, she found that she was not alone in the street.

"Hi," said Barry Ford, immaculate and cheerful in his jogging gear.

"Hi, yourself." A kind of pleasant heat radiated through her body. She studied him. He was smiling at her, admiring her physical condition. "A night out with the boys?" She tried to make her tone light and not at all pointed.

He laughed. "A little bit of political maneuvering."

"Soft-soap for the masses."

"For the masses of muscle that protect me, Melissa."

"Where'd you go? Or is that some deep, dark secret?"

"It's deep and dark, but it's no secret. We went to The Mermaid Tavern."

"Back-Up Jack's place?" Melissa knew that Jack Adams had bought into a nightclub on the south side of Seattle during his early days on the team. "I'm sure the dialogue sparkled with classic literary allusions." She smiled.

"Sure. We even discussed the new two-point conversion rule. Decided it was tough on the coaches as well as the players."

"You won handily yesterday."

"Yeah. Everybody did what was expected of him."

"Including you."

"Oh, sure. Hey, last Monday was fun. Can't we do it again tonight?"

"Why not?" Melissa asked. She looked up at him. "Only how about making it today? Say, a picnic on an island retreat. A fantasy island kind of thing."

"I thought you worked," Ford said offhandedly.

"I'm loaded with sick days I haven't taken."

"I'm all for it! I've got all day."

"We'll go exploring on Bainbridge Island."

"Okay. What is it?"

She laughed. "It's an island in Puget Sound. Takes a half-hour ferry ride to get there. We'll go in my car. It's my date."

"If you let me supply the picnic basket."

And so it was agreed.

Melissa picked up Barry Ford at the Seattle Sheraton Hotel and Towers at ten o'clock; then she drove over to the ferry terminal at Colman Dock where they pulled up to wait in line at Pier 52. They sat there laughing and watching the antics of the other ferry-goers. The weather was warm and brilliant—a lucky break for them that late in September.

"Why go to this island, anyway?" Ford asked her.

"It's a beautiful day. I thought we could ride through the countryside and find a good spot to eat."

Soon enough they were loaded onto the ferry and whistles began blowing. They got out of the car and climbed onto the deck, where they found a place at the railing and leaned over to watch the boat maneuver into the sound. The seagulls circled overhead looking for food while the craft got up to speed on its outward swing.

Soon they found a seat and watched the receding skyline. Ford closed his eyes and laced his hands behind his head. "This is the life," he said.

"Are you a yachtsman?" Melissa asked. She really knew very little about this man—except for his football feats.

"The ocean isn't in my blood. I was born in Fresno, California, and if you know your map, you know that's miles from the sea. My dad was a farmer."

Melissa smiled. "Most city people don't know there *are* farmers anymore."

He grinned. "Oh, there are. They don't wear red suspenders and they don't slap their thighs when they get off a 'good un.' "

"What *do* they wear?"

"My dad was partial to five-hundred-dollar ensembles—when everybody else was wearing fifty-dollar suits off the rack."

"Rich?"

"He didn't flaunt it. Mom was a housewife." He glanced aside at her. "That's a historical term, Ms. Bonner, referring to a chattel of the nineteenth century. Somebody who stayed at home and kept the place running, cooked, sewed, paid the bills, and otherwise made everything look easy."

She nodded thoughtfully. "I *heard* somewhere that you weren't a male chauvinist."

"One week I'm not. The next I am. Just call me 'fair game' for the media." He smiled. "As you should surely know by now."

"How'd you like Stanford?"

"Fine. The competition wasn't all that tough, and I got to be the quarterback. In my senior year we won the Pac Ten—and went to the Rose Bowl."

"You win there?"

"We beat Michigan. And on national television. I just got a good break, you know."

"No. You were good. Weren't you up for the Heisman Trophy?"

"Oh, yeah. Up for it. But I didn't win."

"Who did?"

He grinned. "You know, I can't remember."

"Are your parents still in Fresno?"

"Nope. They bought a marvelous little villa in Carmel."

Melissa blinked. "Oh, what a lovely place to live!"

"Not many places better on the West Coast," Ford admitted.

"No more hayseed in your father's hair, huh?"

"Not a blade. And none in mine, either, Ms. Bonner," Ford said, reaching into his pocket for his wallet, from which he extracted a small plastic card. "Here's my credentials."

Puzzled, Melissa took what he handed her. It was a copy of an H.I.V. medical report, stamped "negative." The name on the card was Barry Ford's.

"I read an article in the *New York Times* some months ago. A man gave his bride-to-be a copy of his H.I.V.–negative report for her engagement present. I thought it was appropriate for our current era. And so I got myself one."

Melissa giggled. "Well, I don't know why you're showing it to *me*."

"Oh, well, I show it to everybody."

They looked at one another a long time in silence.

The seagulls began circling the ferry, and Melissa stood up. "We're coming in to port. We'd better get down to the car."

Soon the ferry ground to a halt, the hawsers were looped over the bollards, and the craft started to waffle in the tide. They drove off onto dry land, and Melissa headed up the road, bypassing Winslow, which lay off to their right, and headed for the open country.

Within twenty minutes they had found an ideal place for a picnic and pulled over. There was an overspreading copse of trees, some sward, and a tiny pond in the distance. They unloaded the picnic basket, which Ford had carried in through the trees to a sunlit spot by the small pond.

The Sheraton chefs had catered a picnic basket for Ford, and he unpacked it slowly, oohing and ahing at each item he came to. Melissa was amused. He seemed like a small child enjoying a very special treat. She wondered about that. Sometimes sports figures were simply kids who had never grown up.

They munched their crab salad sandwiches contentedly and drank ice-cold Coca-Colas straight out of the bottle. Some ducks patrolled the opposite side of the pond, keeping their eyes constantly on the two strangers who had invaded their territory. One quacked and then another replied. When she was finished, Melissa lay down on the grass, putting her shades on to protect her eyes from the sun directly overhead.

Suddenly a shadow loomed over her. She opened her eyes. Ford was bending down, looking at her. "Now it's your turn."

She blinked. What was he talking about?

"What about your past?"

"I don't have a past." Melissa laughed. "Only a future."

"Your parents are both gone?"

"Yes. I come from Sioux City, Iowa. Dad actually came from a long line of blue-collar working-class he-men. Even if he did spend his life in the National Football League, he was really always—in his own mind, anyway—just another working stiff. Work was his pride and joy."

Ford said nothing. He was looking into the stand of trees beyond the pond. "Why do you persist in putting him down?"

"Do I? I thought I built him up too much."

"You're right. I was the one who put him down." Ford smiled crookedly. "How'd you get into TV?"

"I worked at it—right here at the University of Seattle. I was majoring in English, but switched to communications in my junior year. That summer I was lucky enough to intern at Channel 8. After I graduated, I got a steady job at the station writing sports."

"How come you didn't go into news?"

"Sports was a natural, since I grew up with sports all around me. Besides, I was offered a job in sports writing at Channel 8 and I took it."

"The future?" Ford asked, lying back himself and looking up at the sky where tiny puffy clouds drifted eastward.

"I'm perfectly happy being a sportscaster," she said with a smile.

"You were made for better things," Ford said shortly.

She turned to look at him. For a moment she thought he was teasing her, and then she realized that he was serious. She sat up.

"What *better* things?" She pulled off her shades and stared at him.

"A big career in communications. Television. News anchor. The big time."

She relaxed and lay back. She had thought she might be heading into a slugfest about feminism and antifeminism. But seemingly Ford had no such intention.

"I'm a practical person," she said. "There's room for everybody in this world. I don't mind the place I've been allocated."

"It's no good. You've got to fight for something better."

She lay there silently. Somehow, both Ford and Jonathan Stark seemed to be coming from the same place she was: that she should be going on to something more challenging. She knew her own thoughts were in the right place.

Ford turned over and lay on his stomach, bracing himself on his elbows. He turned toward her. "You're a beautiful woman. You come across like a golden glow on the television set. Your coloring is marvelous. Big eyes. High cheekbones. Lovely mouth."

He was watching her.

She glanced at him. His eyes were unmoving. He was chewing a blade of grass. He thought about something. It brought amusement to his eyes.

"There's a scene in an old movie between a fight trainer and an aristocratic woman. She's a blueblood. He's a dis-and-dat sleaze. As she stalks off after some argument, he turns to his sidekick: 'There ain't much meat there, but what's there is cherce.' "

"Hepburn and Tracy." She giggled.

There was a long silence. She was aware of his penetrating gaze. She turned slightly. And found herself looking at him in a critical fashion too. He had a strong face, the face of an intelligent, self-confident man. He was tall and commanding. His movements were precise, unwasted. She had studied him from afar, and she had studied him close up. She could feel the heat begin to rise in her lower body. She was going soft at the thought of him so close to her.

"Let's go for a walk," Ford said to her.

"You don't believe in goofing off?"

"Yeah, but I'm afraid to stay here so close to you. And I don't want to spoil it."

"Who says you'd spoil it—whatever you did?" Melissa responded. But she rolled over obediently and patted the grass off her slacks and blouse.

He reached over and took her hand as he helped her up. He did not release his hold. Together they strolled through the trees and into the fields beyond, just looking around and letting the warmth of the sun flow into their bodies.

"And you?" Melissa asked, as they were about to return to pick up the picnic basket and load the remnants into the car. "What do you have in mind for your future?"

"I'll opt out of an answer along those lines. I'm too happy enjoying the present. At this point I'll just go along with the good things I've got."

"That's not an intelligent man's answer."

He shrugged. They loaded the car.

"I have a philosophy of life," Ford told her. "You get one chance at the gold ring. Take it. If you get the gold ring, well and good. If you don't, do without it. But never pull back from the big chance."

The rest of the day passed as in a kind of dream—a fantasy, actually. They drove about the island and explored various nooks and crannies. They went into Winslow and walked hand-in-hand past the shops. They drove around some more, lined up at the ferry dock, caught the ferry, drove off in Seattle, and wound up back in Melissa's apartment, where she cooked a light dinner for the two of them.

Then they took Danny for a walk. He was in ecstasy that the two of them were playing with him.

They settled down to coffee on the couch when they got back, and finished their cups slowly and thoughtfully. Danny, thoroughly exercised, fell asleep in the middle of the carpet. Ford reached out and cupped the back of Melissa's neck in his hand, drawing her face close to his. He brushed his lips over hers in a slow, sensuous way. She responded almost immediately by opening her lips. He kissed her slowly and surely.

She could feel the warmth flow through her body, touching parts of her she had forgotten existed. He did not let her lips rest for long. When he moved back to kiss her again she found she was breathing hard and fast.

"Oh, Barry."

"Don't talk."

He opened her blouse, letting her breasts come free. She had worn no bra—he had been aware of that all along. He touched a nipple and it came erect and hard. He pinched it smartly. She felt a tremor all through her body. Even her stomach was jolted. Then he cupped her other breast in his hand and squeezed tenderly.

They lay on the couch against each other. Melissa found her body arching itself to his in a kind of automatic response. It was as if her body had an existence all its own, and was now making its desires and needs known to her through its own independent movements.

But there was more than her body expressing itself. His own body had taken over and was expressing itself as well. She relaxed and let herself move in concert with him. It was almost as if she were outside herself watching from close range as she performed to achieve what she wanted and needed.

He was kissing her breasts, and kneading the nipples until she could hardly stand it. She could feel his hand moving down her waist to her hip. Then his fingers sought and found her buttocks, sliding around slowly to her inner thigh. She shivered and pressed herself against him. His hand continued its caresses and she could feel the warmth and moistness on her sensitized skin.

She pulled away from him and then locked herself tightly to him, twining her legs around his and bracing her heels against his legs. The couch pillows shifted. He was nibbling on her ear, his tongue entering it. She moved against him, a flow of warmth pervading her now.

Then in a smooth, sensual movement, his body penetrated hers. She could feel herself opening to receive him. And in harmonious union their bodies began to move rhythmically together. Her head pushed back into the cushions of the couch as her body arched spasmodically against his.

Soon, although never too soon, she felt her body shimmer and quake as they reached climax, with the aftershocks permeating her as the two of them lay there immobilized and spent.

She opened one eye and saw Danny on the carpet, looking up at them. He gave a doglike sigh and slumped down flat, curling up as if waiting for an eternity to pass before anyone noticed *him* again.

And now, when it was all over, she was conscious of the fact that somehow Barry had managed to prepare himself and herself for safe sex with a condom even though she could not quite figure out how he had done it without disturbing her.

She vaguely remembered something she had told Denise once about sex in one of their talks together. "If it's going to happen, it's going to happen."

Well, it *had* happened.

Twenty

Danny Boy

Melissa Bonner awoke the next morning thinking of Vivian Leigh stretched out voluptuously in bed the morning after Clark Gable had finally broken through her reserves and made love to her. Of course, Leigh was an actress and was *acting* out her satisfaction. Yet somehow Melissa felt she was going through exactly the same experience, but for real.

Danny was there to help her celebrate her newly discovered body with all its special parts deep within her, and as he continued to bark and she continued to shush him, she got into her jogging clothes and took him downstairs for his turn around the block.

Then she was on her way herself, exulting in the expansive feeling of running in the outdoors as she did only when she was in top condition and perfect health. She returned, refreshed and on top of the world, ate breakfast, and drove over to the station. She waved at Hobbs as she passed his glassed-in office.

Two minutes later, as she settled into her chair and began to look over the stuff in her in-basket, she discovered her boss hovering in the doorway.

"Everything okay?" he asked, genuinely worried.

"Couldn't be better," Melissa said. "Why?"

"Well, it's not like you to phone in for a sick day. Are you all right now?"

She almost flushed as she realized that she had taken advantage of the system she worked under. "I'm fine! Just one of those things." She frowned. "Something must be going around."

Like love, she thought ironically.

"Probably," Hobbs agreed. "I instructed Luanne to read your sportscast."

"Oh," said Melissa.

"She did very well."

"She's a bright girl," Melissa said absently.

Still he persisted. "I've told Mrs. Sanchez not to clip any more of those stories for you."

"Right. I haven't gotten any lately."

"None today?"

Melissa fumbled through her in-basket. "No. None here."

"Good. I thought whoever it was might distribute them himself—or herself—if Mrs. Sanchez stopped doing it."

"Maybe we've seen the last of them."

"We'll find out what's behind all this," Hobbs said. "Don't you worry." He left.

About an hour later Luanne looked in. "Mr. Hobbs had me read the sports thing last night."

"So I hear," Melissa said with a smile. "Thanks."

"No. Thank *you*. It's something I've always wanted to do."

"How did it go?"

"Great. I think. I did the best I could."

"I'm sure it was fine."

"Are you doing a field interview today?"

"Yes, but we haven't decided where yet."

"Good luck." Luanne started to leave. "Oh. Are you feeling better?"

"Better than what?" Melissa said testily. "Oh. You mean—Yes. I'm fine."

It was just after she had eaten lunch that Melissa dialed her sister's number at the University of Seattle. "Dr. Stark's office," Denise announced clearly.

"Denny. It's me."

"Ellie! What's up? You never call me."

"I took a sick day yesterday. I went to Bainbridge Island."

"Ye gods—why? What's gotten into you?"

"Barry Ford and I went there on a picnic."

Denise's voice cooled down. "Oh. Well, how was it?"

"It was *won*derful!" Melissa was surprised to hear herself stress the "n" in "won." She did not usually—if ever—go in for that kind of exaggerated ham-actory intonation.

"You must be brain dead, Ellie! Have you lost all sense of proportion?"

"He's something else, Denny. I *like* him."

"If that means what I think it means, I'm surprised at you!"

"I wanted you to be the first to know."

"Know what? I don't know anything!"

"I think I do."

"What *is* this? Some new kind of electronics communication without electronics?"

Melissa burst out laughing. "You're cute, Denny."

"You aren't!" Denise snapped. "Now get off the wire. I've got an incoming call."

" 'Bye."

She hung up, smiling at the wall in front of her. She took a deep breath and tried to get her mind back on her work. In a minute she would have to go see Hobbs to find out what had been decided about the day's scheduling.

The phone rang. She thought it was her sister again.

"Yeah?"

It wasn't Denise. It was a small, childish voice—probably that of a boy or a girl about twelve or so years old. Melissa had fans of all sizes and shapes. And she treated them all the same—with respect and kindness.

"Is this Miss Melissa Bonner?" the youthful voice wanted to know.

"Yes, it is," she said.

"Your dog is here, Miss Bonner."

Melissa sat up straight. "You mean Danny is there?"

"Yes. That's what it says on his collar."

It didn't make sense. "Where are you? Are you in my apartment?"

"No," said the young voice. "I don't know where your apartment is."

"Where are you calling from?" Melissa asked.

"I'm at the lake, Miss Bonner."

"And my Danny is there?"

"Yes, ma'am. He's sleeping."

A chill went down Melissa's spine. "He's sleeping?"

"Yes. Can you come and get him?" The boy—she was sure it was a boy speaking to her now—was obviously upset. He was on the verge of crying.

"Of course! What part of the lake?"

"I'm near the Pitch and Putt."

"What lake, please?" Now Melissa was becoming frantic herself. Could she believe this kind of nonsense?

"Green Lake."

That was near her jogging route. It made sense. Perhaps Danny had somehow broken loose from the apartment and—

"You stay right there. I'll be over as soon as I can. The Pitch and Putt, you say."

"Yes, ma'am. Hurry, Miss Bonner."

Melissa went through the newsroom to Hobbs's office. "My dog, Danny," she said in a breathless voice. "Something's happened to him. He must have gotten out of the apartment. I have to pick him up."

"Where is he?" Hobbs asked.

"Green Lake."

"But how do you know?"

"A young boy. He called me here. Must have seen my number on the collar. Knew who I was, too."

"Go. When you get back I'll line up your stories."

She hurried out to the elevator, pushed the basement button, and a minute later was on her way in the Range Rover. It did not take her long to get to Green Lake. Luckily she was not driving during the rush hour.

There was a parking lot near the Pitch and Putt. Melissa drove quickly into it and stopped. She tore the key out of the slot and slammed the door shut after her. Then she headed for the lake, where she could see a small knot of people in a tight circle on the edge of the grassy embankment.

She was running by the time she crossed the grass. As she came up she heard someone talking to the crowd, and distinguished a man in a police uniform. He turned around and saw her coming up.

"It's your dog, Miss Bonner. Danny. Excuse me, ma'am, but I recognize you from your sportscasts. I'm—I'm sorry about this."

Sorry?

The people gathered around Danny had moved back. Lying in the center of the group was the golden retriever on his side, soaked with water. He was not moving at all.

"We have to assume he drowned, miss," the police officer told her patiently. "It was Tony Mann here who found him in the water."

A youth—whose voice on the telephone was a perfect match for him—came walking up to Melissa. "I was the one who telephoned you," he told her proudly. "I couldn't wake him up."

Melissa sank onto the grass beside Danny's body. She felt suddenly dizzy. She reached out and touched his side. He was as cold as the water he had apparently been in. Had he drowned? It didn't make sense. She had never heard of a dog drowning. Especially a dog like Danny who knew how to dog-paddle.

"I don't understand," she said helplessly, turning to the police officer standing above her. "What can I do?"

"He's dead, miss. Do you have transportation?"

"Yes. I've got my car. It's a four-wheeler."

"I'll help you get him to the car. You do have a veterinarian, don't you?"

"Of course."

And it was at that point that Melissa Bonner broke down. She leaned over Danny, put her arms around his cold, stiff body, and began to weep. Her body was wracked with long, shuddering sobs. She could barely catch her breath. She touched him and fondled his muzzle. He was as cold as ice. Not a muscle stirred.

Finally she was able to regain control over herself. She led the police officer, the boy, and several men from the crowd to her Range Rover and opened the back. They lifted Danny in and laid him on the floor of the car.

Melissa climbed in the driver's seat and started the engine.

"Thank you, Tony, for calling me," she told the boy. "Thank you—so very much." Her eyes filled with tears again.

She backed the four-wheeler out of the parking lot and headed downtown for Dr. Houseman's animal clinic. As she turned into the small parking lot and shut off the engine she was crying steadily, tears streaming down her cheeks, unable to stop.

What had happened to Danny? How could this be?

Finally she roused herself and plunged into the clinic, where a startled receptionist leaped up to help her into a seat against the wall.

"What is it, Ms. Bonner? Can I help you? Would you please—"

Dr. Houseman came and stood over her. "What *is* it?"

She sobbed out meaningless words.

"The car," the receptionist said. "Something about her car."

She followed Melissa into the lot. Melissa unlocked the back. On the floor lay Danny's body, still wet. "He's dead," Melissa explained needlessly.

The receptionist was all efficiency. "You wait right here, Ms. Bonner. I'll get the boys to carry him inside."

"How did it happen?" Dr. Houseman asked.

"I don't know," Melissa said, finally calming herself. "A young boy called me at the station. He'd found Danny's body at Green Lake."

Dr. Houseman nodded. "I'll try to find out what happened. I'll be in touch with you. Can you give me your number at work?"

She did.

Back at the station, Hobbs was briefing his staff on the night's news. When he saw the ashen face of Melissa Bonner, he waved her off to her own office. Five minutes later he was inside, with the door closed behind him.

"What on earth is the matter?" Hobbs asked. "Are you sick again?"

"I wasn't sick before. But I am now. It's—Danny. He drowned in the lake."

Melissa's phone rang. It was Dr. Houseman.

"It's very strange," he said. "There's no sign of any wound. But I did find a pinprick in him. I assume you didn't give him a shot of anything."

"No, sir."

"Then I can only guess that someone gave him an injection of something that slowed his system down. He simply went to sleep, after someone dumped him in the lake."

Melissa stiffened herself to keep from crying out.

"Thank you, Dr. Houseman."

Hobbs was right there, looking into her eyes. "What?"

"Somebody—somebody killed Danny."

"Killed him?" Hobbs whispered.

"Put him to sleep—and dumped him in the lake."

Hobbs gripped her shoulder with a strong, firm hand. "I'm so sorry, Melissa. So very sorry. I think you should take some time off. This situation seems suddenly to be turning serious."

"No. I'm staying. I'll do my job. It's the least I can do."

"Whatever you want," Hobbs said, leaving her alone.

Twenty-one

Late Supper

Melissa reached for the telephone. She had to call Barry. He
would be at practice in the Kingdome, most likely. She glanced at
her wristwatch to confirm the time. Actually, practice was probably
over. Perhaps she should ring the hotel and either find him there
or leave a message for him.

The hotel operator rang his room number several times. Then
she came on the line. "Mr. Ford is not in his suite," she said.
"Could I take a message?"

"Yes. Please tell him Melissa Bonner wants to speak to him as
soon as possible."

She hung up and, as she did so, it all came back to her. The Sea
Lions would be out of town all week, finishing up with their away
game in Los Angeles on Sunday. How could she have forgotten
that?

Melissa sighed softly. She had been counting on Barry's vitality,
his concern for her, his presence to give her the lift she so badly
needed. Of course, she could always ring him in L.A., but he might
not even be there yet. Or, if there, he might be settling in at the
hotel or even eating dinner with the team.

She dialed the president's office at the University and was connected with Denise. Quickly she filled her in on Danny's death.
Denise was shocked at first, and then worried.

"You watch out for yourself," she said slowly. Only then did she
realize that less than a week before, Melissa had been telling Denise
exactly the same thing! "Ellie, what's *happening* to us?"

"I don't know," Melissa answered flatly. "What's happening to
Seattle?"

"This is unbelievable! In six days one of us is burglarized and
hit on the head, and the other has her dog killed."

Melissa was about to mention the other things that had been bothering her—the car following her, the man in the blue boxers, the phantom phone calls, the disturbing stories from the rip-and-read—but she quickly shut it all out of her mind.

"We'll just have to look out for ourselves better," she said lamely.

"Did you tell Barry Ford about this?" Denise asked suddenly.

"No."

"Why not?"

"He's in Los Angeles," Melissa explained. "The team's away this weekend."

Then Denise echoed exactly the first thought that Melissa had had when she heard of Denise's break-in. "You want me to come over tonight?"

"No. I'll be working through the evening on my usual schedule," Melissa told her.

"Perhaps that's the best way to handle the problem," Denise said offhandedly. "Work."

They chatted for a moment and then Denise hung up.

About eight o'clock in the evening Melissa was called to the phone from the editing room and found herself talking to Jonathan Stark. Unaccountably, her spirits lifted. "It's good to hear your voice!"

"I'm calling for a special reason. Would you like to have a late supper with me after you finish your ten-o'-clock newscast tonight?"

"I'd love it." She was feeling better already.

His voice lowered. "Denise told me about what happened to Danny. I'm terribly sorry. I know how you worshiped that dog. He was such a loyal companion."

"Thank you," she said, realizing that her eyes were suddenly full of tears.

"You and your sister seem to have both struck a bit of bad luck in your lives. I don't want you to let it get you down."

"Furthest thing from my mind," Melissa said resolutely.

"Glad to hear it."

"And I can certainly use that shoulder of yours tonight. Thank you for offering it."

"I'll pick you up at your place. About eleven. I know a little late-night restaurant near the waterfront."

"Lovely," Melissa said. "You know, I think you've given me just what I needed to get me through the rest of a difficult evening."

"See you, then."

In spite of her cheerful words, she went through the motions for the ten-o'-clock broadcast, and in a state of numbness drove to her apartment. She gazed about the empty rooms, steeling herself against thinking of Danny's welcoming barks, his adoring gaze, and his thumping tail. Quickly she changed into a sweater and skirt.

The place Jonathan had selected for their late supper was just right for Melissa's mood. It was secluded and quiet, and catered to people who were low-key, somewhat intellectual, and sober-sided. Jonathan seemed to know exactly how she felt and laid on a great deal of academic small talk. It took her mind off the sports world and television and in minutes he had her laughing and sipping away at her white wine.

Slowly he mesmerized her away from her inner turmoil and the ordeal of Danny's death. When they had finished, Melissa could not remember any details of the brief meal they had eaten, but she felt relaxed now and glad to be alive. It was amazing how Jonathan knew exactly what buttons to push to lift her gloom.

He drove her back to the apartment and accompanied her upstairs. Once in the living room, Melissa started to ask him if he would like a nightcap—when it suddenly struck her how empty the apartment seemed without Danny. He would be leaping in the air, barking, licking her hand, slapping his tail excitedly at her, jumping up at Jonathan, slurping at his wrist. And now there was just silence.

She burst into tears. Jonathan instantly wrapped his arms about her and held her closely to him. She was suddenly furious with herself for losing control. She, so poised, so absolutely cool. And he was there, holding her together.

He led her over to the couch and the two of them sat down

together. She began to cry, deep, racking sobs that reached down into the bottom of her being. He smoothed her hair back, took out a handkerchief, wiped her face dry of the tears streaming down her cheeks, and pressed her close to him.

Calmer now, she realized that she had always pictured a scene something like this in her mind's eye. Back then, in the old days, she had thought it was a crush, but she knew now that her feelings for him must have been far stronger than she had realized. Their eyes met, his glowing with—well, what was it?—love?

He leaned forward and kissed her lips, softly and deeply. He held her firmly and with tenderness. She lay there in his arms, opening her eyes once to see his very concerned face close to hers.

This was certainly not like the inner heat she had felt when Barry Ford had made love to her, but there was something serene and extremely important about his touch. There was, underlying it, a great deal of sexuality. She could feel that in all its intensity. If he made the slightest move to cross that invisible line he so respected, she would surrender to him wholeheartedly, body and soul. She knew that.

So real. So deep. So powerful. Yes, she could love this man with as much fervor and passion as when she had made love to Barry Ford. It was there, just beyond reach. If he moved—

He stood up. "It's late," he said. "You'll need your rest." And he again told her how sorry he was about Danny. "I hope I've given you a little strength to cope with his death," he said. He leaned over and kissed her on the lips, fully and straightforwardly. "Good night, Melissa."

And he was gone.

Later, trying to get to sleep, she felt again the surging emotion she had felt when he was close to her. There were different facets of love, she realized. Jonathan's feeling for her was quite different from Barry Ford's.

But it was just as real. Just as powerful.

And it meant just as much to her as Ford's unbridled sexual drive.

She shuddered. Her body, she realized, was struggling with conflicting reactions. She would have to think things out more carefully. Think! That was the key word. Without thought, without a conscious notion of what direction she was going in, she would find herself drowning in a crosscurrent of emotional tides.

Deliberately, she forced herself to close her eyes and sleep.

Twenty-two

It's All or Nothing

With the menacing exultation of Scarpia's *Te Deum* resonating in his ears, Darryl Hobbs strolled with his wife, Verna, out into the upper lobby of the Opera House at Seattle Center, glancing about to see if he could recognize any familiar face in the crowd. Verna touched his arm, indicating that she would rejoin him later, and made her way to the crowded rest room.

Hobbs was debating with himself over whether to indulge in a glass of wine when he realized that he was being addressed by someone he knew. It was Curtis Mitchell, the commissioner of the Seattle police.

He was a powerful man with a swarthy complexion and the hulking presence of someone on the winning side of any argument he might choose to take up. Yet Mitchell was a contradiction in himself; with all his muscular and political clout, he was a man who delighted in a good book as well as a good opera.

"Enjoying the show?" he asked Hobbs. Mitchell still retained the distinct accent of his Long Island upbringing. He had never made any deliberate attempt to neutralize it, even though he had earned his undergraduate degree at Notre Dame and later attended Columbia University for his doctorate.

"Not a good night for law and order," Hobbs said with a smile, referring, of course, to the libretto of *Tosca* with its menacing undertone of political chicanery.

"It's those blasted hangups all Italian librettists have with the Roman *polizia!*" Mitchell sighed. "Scarpia's good, don't you think?"

"Excellent."

"I like Tosca, too," Mitchell observed. "A lot of depth there."

"Funny I should run into you tonight, Curtis. I've got something just a bit criminous on my mind."

A ghost of a smile crossed Mitchell's face. "There's nothing 'just a bit' about crime, Darryl," he said carefully. "It's like being pregnant. It's all or nothing."

Hobbs steered the two of them into a kind of alcove near the curving staircase and moved close to Mitchell. He pitched his voice on a confidential level.

"I've uncovered a curious problem in my staff," he told Mitchell.

"Oh?" Mitchell frowned. "I haven't heard about that one."

"I'm sure you haven't. It's in an early stage of development."

"Go on."

"I've an on-camera interviewer and news reader. She's been getting weird notes through office distribution. Stories off the wire service teletype about women in jeopardy."

"What kind of stories?" Mitchell was interested. The gleam in his dark eyes showed it.

"Harassment stories, mostly. Car hijackings. Attempted rape. Shootings."

"You're suggesting that these might be warnings of some kind?"

"Exactly. There's more."

"Has to be."

"She thought she was being followed by someone in a car recently."

"A stalker," Mitchell mused. "Copycat crime from television. Lots of stalkers on the little screen. Second only to serial killers."

"Today she was in tears."

Mitchell frowned.

"Somebody found her golden retriever drowned in Green Lake."

Mitchell shrugged. "Dogs do get in the water and go down."

"But the veterinarian told her somebody had jabbed the dog with a hypodermic needle."

"Put him to sleep," Mitchell mused. He rubbed the sides of his chin with the thumb and forefinger. "Then let him drown."

"I'd guess."

"Trouble is, we can't do anything about that. There's been no crime yet. I mean, even the fact that the dog seems to have been killed doesn't count."

"I know. I'm not asking you to get Seattle's cops on this. What I'm trying to determine is the best course of action for us at the station to take."

"It's that pretty woman, isn't it?"

"Melissa Bonner." Hobbs nodded. "How'd you guess?"

"She's very attractive. Just the type to trigger off stalkers. The dog thing, though—that's a lot more worrisome. The next thing that happens is a, you know, 'You're next' note." He stood there in deep thought.

"I can't figure out anybody who might want to scare her."

"It has psychopathic overtones. The killing of the dog. The stalking in the car. Heavy stuff."

"But there's no motivation!"

"But it's obvious somebody out there has a deep interest in her. Envies her? Fears her? Hates her?"

"What can we do at Channel 8?"

"Put a bodyguard on her," Mitchell said quickly.

"A bodyguard!" Hobbs was appalled. "She'd never stand still for that! Besides—that costs a lot of money, doesn't it?"

"You wanted free advice. The service comes higher." Mitchell smiled.

"Is a bodyguard necessary?"

"Darryl, our world is a bit more complicated than it was a few years ago. People are kidnapped and held for ransom on all levels of society. People are stalked and beaten. Celebrities are killed by snipers. Politicians are ambushed and assassinated for no known reason—except politics as usual. You asked me for advice. I've given it. I know it isn't the be-all or the end-all. It's a stopgap measure. But it protects her—which I sense is your primary objective."

"It is that."

"Wasn't she the one involved in that confrontation with Barry Ford, the Sea Lions' new quarterback?"

Hobbs nodded. "Do you think there's a connection?"

"Not necessarily. As I recall, she tends to be a bit sharp-tongued in public at times. Has she made any other—I hate to say it—*enemies* lately?"

"No. And I think she's patched up the Barry Ford thing."

"Get her a bodyguard, Darryl. Before it's too late. I've got just the proper one, if you're interested."

Hobbs took down the pertinent facts on the back of an envelope he pulled out of his pocket. The lights went down, twice, and he saw his wife coming toward him. He shook hands with Mitchell and joined Verna in the walk back to their box seats.

Twenty-three

Midnight Oil

Melissa Bonner walked in through the newsroom, making a concerted effort to appear absolutely composed and normal in spite of what she had been through in the past twenty-four hours. Hobbs waved her over and she stood in front of him without a word.

"You don't need to come in today, Melissa," he said slowly. "We're all sorry about Danny. Don't you think you should take some time off? You've got days coming."

"No, sir," she said stiffly. She realized that her voice did not seem normal at all. She was cruelly conscious of the fact that her attempts at normalcy had turned sour. But she had made up her mind and she was not going to go into seclusion. She might never come out of it again. It was too easy to go down and out.

"All right, then," Hobbs said. "I had an idea you might do exactly as you're doing. I want you and your camera crew to go out to one of the high schools. They're having a race for the handicapped." He told her which school.

Melissa nodded.

"Do the usual. Interview some of the kids. It's a departure from what we've been doing, but it's perfect human interest stuff."

"Kubo and Griswold know this yet?"

"Yeah. They should be loading their stuff in the company van right now."

"I'll get on it." Melissa allowed herself a small smile. "What if I hadn't come in today?" she asked.

"I knew you would." Hobbs smiled.

"Soft on the outside, tough on the inside," Melissa noted.

"Don't go all muscular on me," Hobbs warned her.

She waved at him as she went into her office to gather up her papers. In the basement garage she found Takeo Kubo and Al Griswold exactly where Hobbs had said they would be, in the back of the van, packing their equipment.

"Hey, Melissa," said Kubo. "Sorry to hear about Danny."

"Thank you, Tak."

"Me, too," said Griswold.

"You ready to go?"

"Pretty much so."

"Then let's do it."

She climbed in the van and started it up. In moments they were in mainstream traffic, headed for the high school. Melissa drove carefully, trying to focus her attention strictly on the driving. It was a difficult proposition. She was thinking about a thousand other things, particularly about what had happened to Danny.

"So what's the boss up to?" Kubo said idly.

"You mean assigning us to this handicapped story?"

"No, no," Kubo retorted. "I mean all this long-distance telephoning, the lights burning well into the morning, the headaches and the aspirin swallowed in fours and sixes. I mean—the heavy business at Channel 8."

Melissa blinked. "What are you talking about?"

Kubo shrugged. "What I hear. You, Grizzy?"

Griswold nodded. "Big secret stuff going on."

"Right. Hobbs at the opera. Then at the office. He's long-distancing New York. Burning the midnight oil, as the cliché has it. What is this all about?"

"I haven't the slightest idea."

Kubo threw up his hands. "You see. Nobody ever tells me anything!"

They turned into the parking lot at the high school and unloaded their equipment. They could see the teachers and the coaches preparing the field for the race, with the kids in wheelchairs and on their feet waiting around in their usual noisy fashion.

Soon enough the races began, and Melissa moved in quietly and efficiently with Kubo and Griswold to get everything they could for that night. Melissa talked to one of the coaches at length; he was articulate and enthusiastic—two pluses that made it inevitable that his comments would appear on the show.

The kids were reticent at first, but once they got into the swing of the thing, they were hard to shut off. By midafternoon they had enough for a full take-out, and left for the station.

Twenty-four

"Hello Means Goodbye!"

D arryl Hobbs signaled Melissa Bonner when she returned to the newsroom and she went over to him.

"How was it?"

"Great! We got plenty," Takeo Kubo answered for her.

"Take it up to the editing room," Hobbs said. "Melissa, you wait here." As Kubo and Griswold went off he fiddled with papers on his desk. It was obvious to Melissa that he was unnerved about something. Finally he looked up at her squarely. "There's a guy sitting in your office."

"What's he want?" Melissa wondered, turning around and looking across the bull pen. She could not make him out. He had his back to her and was seated across from where she usually sat.

"His name is Andrew Royce."

"Okay. I still would like to know what he wants."

"It's not exactly what he wants, but what we want." Now Hobbs was beginning to squirm in his chair.

Melissa sensed trouble.

"He's one of the best in the business," Hobbs said.

"What's his business?" Melissa asked, her voice rising slightly. She had cried her eyes out the night before. She had tried to think her way clear of Danny's death. She had tried to reach a point where she could get back in harness without any more trouble. Unhappily, she had found that she was not able to recover so easily from the death of her beloved dog.

"He worked for a big company in New York."

"I see," said Melissa. "At what?"

"Well, he was on their security team."

"Okay. He knows about locks and picks and keys and safes. And he keeps his eyes on things. And now what does he want here?"

"He's actually working here."

"But we don't have any security—"

"We do now. He's it."

She looked startled "Wait a minute! What's he doing in my office?" Melissa could feel the banked coals of anger quickly coming ablaze. "Are you saying—?"

"I'm saying that we hired him for security purposes."

"All right. What has that to do with *me?*"

"I'm worried about those harassment stories you've been getting. I'm also worried about the car you think is following you. And, for God's sake—I'm more worried now that Danny's dead."

"Don't blame this on Danny!" Melissa snapped.

"Royce is your bodyguard," Hobbs said finally. He stared at her, waiting for the outburst.

"What?" Melissa leaned forward, her palms flat on Hobbs's desk, her head thrust out toward him. "You've hired a bodyguard for me?"

"Yes. It was a quick decision. He just flew in from New York. Go in and—"

"How come I had no knowledge of this?"

"The decision was made overnight."

She was pacing back and forth now. Hobbs stood stolidly there, watching her. He knew she was angry, but he knew he wasn't going to back down either.

"Calm down, Melissa. We're all worried about you. Too much has been happening. It's obvious to me—and to the station manager—that you're in some kind of danger. We did the only thing we could do." He rose. "Come on." Hobbs was pleading now. "Take a deep breath and follow me. I'll introduce you to him."

"No bodyguard for me!" she said. "I'll go with you to meet him. Hello means goodbye. I'll volunteer to take him down to the airport myself. And be glad to get him on the plane for New York."

They trooped out of his office and headed across the bullpen. Every eye in the newsroom followed her. She tore open the door to her office. Hobbs followed her inside. The man in the chair opposite her desk glanced around. When he saw who it was, he rose. Not hurriedly or nervously, but politely. Respectfully.

"It's all off!" Melissa declared. "I've just talked to Mr. Hobbs—"

The man's face was expressionless. As he stared at her, she got her first good look at him. He was a strong, athletic, muscular man, thirty or so. He appeared larger than life. He was strictly muscle and bone. He had a triangular face, with high brows, strong nose, and a narrow mouth. His hair was curly and uncombed.

There was a flicker of amusement in his eyes, although it did not spread to any other part of his face. If anything, his face and body seemed hewn from a rough grade of absolutely unbreakable granite. He was like one of the Gutzon Borglum stone faces at Mount Rushmore.

He smiled. That made his face entirely different. It was broken up now. A human face.

"Yes, ma'am," he said softly. He had a very low voice that did not go with his bulk at all. It was almost difficult to distinguish what he was saying. The smile did not last long. As immediately as it had appeared, it vanished.

"We've agreed this is all a mistake," Melissa went on.

"We've decided that you can"—she waved her hand in the air—"fly back to New York."

"I see." He made no move to go.

"I mean it!" she exclaimed. "Out!"

He smiled. "Certainly, ma'am." He moved quickly and was outside the door to the office in seconds.

The door closed gently. Melissa turned. Andrew Royce was standing with his back to her, arms folded across his chest, guarding the doorway.

"No!" cried Melissa in a strangled voice. She crossed to the door and yanked it open. "You!"

Royce turned and looked at her. "Yes, ma'am?"

"I said you can go back to New York."

"In due time, ma'am."

"I mean, now. This instant!"

He nodded, then turned, placed his back against the glass wall, and folded his arms across his chest.

"What are you doing there?" She realized that everyone in the newsroom was staring at her, waiting.

"I am doing my job," he said softly. "Allow me to elaborate. The people I work for are a diverse and varied lot. They come in all shapes and sizes. Some want me to disguise myself as a well-dressed executive type. Some want me to wear a gun riding on my hip, Wild West style. Some want me in a uniform to resemble a police officer." He shrugged. "Whatever you want, that's what you get."

"I want you gone."

"And so consider me gone, ma'am. The game I always play is to be agreeable to the client I am guarding. One client had me carry a portable chessboard and set of chessmen all over London. We would play in the limo, at board meetings, at the theater. An American had me brush her Maine Coon cat regularly. A stand-up comedienne wanted me to laugh at her jokes."

She slammed the door shut. The glass shivered. But Andrew Royce did not move. Hobbs was still watching Melissa.

"Andrew Royce is very good," he said. "I have that on the best authority. The Seattle Police Department has been alerted to assist him."

Melissa shook her head sadly.

She sank into the chair behind her desk and held her head in her hands.

"What is happening to me? Who is doing this to me?"

Hobbs leaned over and squeezed her shoulder affectionately. "You're in good hands," he said as he left her office.

There was a knock on her door some five minutes later. It was Andrew Royce, looking in through the glass at her. He made signs that he wanted to speak to her.

She stalked to the door and opened it. "Yes?"

"Sit down, please. I'd like to talk with you a moment."

She shrugged and sat. He pulled up the chair opposite her desk. "As I understand it, Ms. Bonner, you are being troubled either by a stalker or an avenger. Isn't that correct?"

She nodded.

"At least someone is a threat to you. Who it is we do not know.

There are two ways to combat this situation. One. We can find out who it is and try to stop him—or her. Or two. We can teach you martial arts tricks to protect yourself, or show you how to handle your own defense weapon."

She shivered. "I have an natural abhorrence of guns, Mr. Royce. And for some reason I do not trust myself as a potential martial arts student."

He smiled. "I had assumed as much when I took the job. I am a substitute for the second option, providing the expertise in weaponry and the weapon. And, at the same time, I work on the first, trying to I.D. the person who is bothering you."

"Oh, I know why you're here."

"But you make it very hard for me to function. Understand me. I have a good idea why you resent my presence. In a way it reminds you that you have been unsuccessful at drawing out and ridding yourself of this stalker."

She bit her lip.

"I would request one favor. Could you allow me twenty-four hours in your presence to prove to you that I am perhaps the most invisible, unencounterable nonentity in the security world? Then, if at the end of twenty-four hours you have decided that you just can't stand me anyway, I'll get myself my favorite seat on the old red-eye and be out of your hair forever."

"Well, I suppose I could gamble twenty-four hours of my time."

"It's all I ask," Royce said softly.

She was looking directly into his eyes now. She realized that they were brown and penetrating, with tiny flecks of gold in them. And always, even when he was at his most sober, there was a sparkle of life, of humor, of zaniness that was ready to flare into life.

He put his forefinger against his lips in the hush-hush position. "Then we're not in a war zone any longer. At least, for twenty-four hours. Agreed?"

"Agreed."

"Relax. It'll all be over soon. I promise."

Twenty-five

Rent-a-Cop Royce

At Hobbs's instruction, the maintenance crew brought in a small table and swivel chair for Andrew Royce and set them up in the far corner of Melissa's office. She had only to look across the way to see him; he had his back to her, was facing a blank wall, and had to turn all the way around to view her.

Almost contritely, Melissa accepted the addition of the bodyguard to her work space. She felt that she had already made enough noise about him. If management insisted, she would go along with the new arrangement. But she was not going to give anybody the impression that she was pleased.

When Hobbs called for the daily news conference, Royce stood obediently to follow Melissa into the conference room at the end of the newsroom. Hobbs shook his head. "We'll be all right. It's secure in there."

Although he was in the mood to argue, Royce did not open his mouth. He watched Melissa as she marched out of the office and closed the door behind her. He noted, however, that she gave just a tiny glance over her shoulder at him, exposing an amused curl of the lip. When she saw he was watching her the smile vanished.

Royce slid out of his jacket and placed it over the back of the chair. Then he hung up his shoulder holster and Colt .45 automatic. He sat down again, with a sigh and a brief yawn.

Actually, he was absolutely pooped. His rush to the red-eye in New York, his flight out, his cab ride in from the airport—all that had exhausted him. And then, the tension between him and his client—although not unexpected—provided another blow that tired him more. He had another ten hours to go before he could decently hit the sack.

He reached for the folder Hobbs had given him. It contained a memo he had written and handed to Royce when he had first arrived. He began studying it carefully. It consisted of three parts: one outlining the deliberate forwarding of rip-and-read stories about harassing women to Melissa Bonner in her in-basket; another outlining the known facts about the death of her golden retriever, Danny; and a third mentioning the fact that she thought she was being followed by a car.

The door to the office opened. Royce turned, prepared to greet Melissa with a smile. It wasn't Melissa at all. Standing in the doorway was a young woman with blond hair and an attractive bosomy stance. She was grinning at Royce. Royce immediately read the look as a come-on. The look seemed appropriate for her.

"I'm Luanne Doty." She strolled toward him, her hips sliding sensuously inside her tight-fitting skirt. "I know who you are. You're Andrew Royce."

"What can I say?" Royce responded.

"Just say hello." She giggled.

"Hello."

"I work for Melissa."

Royce nodded. "I see. In what capacity?"

Luanne frowned. "I'm her writer."

"Ah," Royce said. "Now that's a surprise to me. I thought *she* wrote all those words she delivers so expertly."

"You've heard her?"

"No. But I've talked to people who have." He let his mouth tilt in a slanted grin.

"She writes her own questions," Luanne admitted dutifully.

"Then she is not totally without imaginative resources herself."

She smiled widely, showing her teeth. They were perfect. "You talk funny."

"If I were a comic, I would thank you. However, I am not a comic."

Her mouth dropped open. He could see her tongue sliding along the tips of her upper teeth. It was a sexually arousing routine, one he was sure she had worked on in front of a mirror.

"You're a rent-a-cop?" She leaned against the table, her hip sinking onto its sharp edge. She was so close he could feel the heat of her body.

"I'm a security agent," he said.

"That means that Ms. Bonner is insecure, is that it?"

"You're playing with words, Ms. Doty. Ms. Bonner is not *insecure*. The death of Ms. Bonner's dog is of concern to Mr. Hobbs and to the management of this television station."

"There is a contract out on her?" Luanne asked, her eyes wide.

Royce leaned back in the chair, the .45 Colt jabbing into his back. How many times had he gone through this exercise with smart alecks? It flashed into his mind that it might be she who was routing those stories to Melissa. He studied her. This was a typical *All About Eve* woman.

"The death of her dog leads us to believe that she may be in danger. It signals psychotic aberrations in someone."

"Her dog died yesterday. You're very fast."

"Not I. It is the air transport that is very fast. The red-eye zipped me out from New York last night."

She let her tongue trip along the tips of her upper teeth again. And laughed. "He's gone, you know."

"He?"

"Barry Ford."

"The quarterback?" Royce felt he was being put through some kind of intelligence test, with all the questions in code.

"Right. He's in Los Angeles this week. They're playing the Raiders Sunday."

"What's that got to do with Ms. Bonner?"

"She and him. They're having—you know—an affair. It's brand new."

"How can you be sure of that?" Royce asked, knowing damned well that if anyone had the facts, it would be this street-smart young woman.

"Monday night last, I'd guess," Luanne said softly. "Two days before you came."

Royce stared at her. He did that when he wanted more information. Nine times out of ten people continued to talk when he said nothing.

"I saw her in the morning. Tuesday A.M. There was a big difference in her."

Royce raised an eyebrow. "In what way?"

"Oh, you know." Luanne almost reached out to touch him. But instead she began tracing a circle on her upper thigh—the thigh attached to the hip that was dented by the edge of the table. He could feel his skin crawl. "She was—oh—bed damp," she said, reaching for the proper phrase.

They gazed at one another in silence. He understood perfectly. Yet her motive in giving him all this information was as yet unclear. Certainly to point out that Melissa Bonner was having an affair with Barry Ford did not put Melissa down in his eyes; Luanne knew that as well.

She opened her mouth to say something. At that moment one of the writers on the news staff signaled her from the bull pen outside. She slid off the table, smoothed her skirt over her hips, and gave the bottom of her bra a little jerk, all the time looking deep into Royce's eyes. "Got to run."

He nodded, and tried not to watch her too carefully as she moved across the office, opened the door, and went out into the newsroom.

He settled down once again with the report Hobbs had written for him, and finished reading it. There was no question about it, Royce thought. Someone was trying to terrorize Melissa Bonner— or bother her so much it would make her fearful.

As he sat there he reviewed exactly what Luanne Doty had told him. The affair with Barry Ford—if it was true—might be fueling these strong actions. But no. The stories had begun arriving before Barry Ford. Still, someone might have had advance knowledge of Ford's arrival. Someone in the know.

Royce looked at Hobbs's report once again. One paragraph referred to the police commissioner of the Seattle Police Department. It seemed that Curtis Mitchell was planning to set up a liaison between Andrew Royce and August Simms, of the Detective Division, to investigate the Melissa Bonner situation as soon as Royce arrived in Seattle.

Royce knew there were strange crosscurrents here. He was anxious to get in touch with Simms. But he knew he had to wait until he had checked the Bonner apartment for security leaks before meeting Simms to discuss the case with him. He glanced at his wristwatch. It was getting late.

Then he wondered where he would stay. He would have to be somewhere close to her. In her apartment? How big was it? Royce rose from his cramped corner and began pacing the office. He was running out of time! He had to move—and quickly.

Twenty-six

Zone of Danger

Almost as soon as Darryl Hobbs was settled in his office after
the news conference, his phone rang. It was Andrew Royce. He
had only known the man for an hour or so, and yet he recognized
his voice immediately.

"We've got to talk," Royce said in that no-nonsense voice of his.

"Right." Hobbs replied "Come into my office."

Royce hung up without another word and as Hobbs instructed
the operator to hold all his incoming calls he watched the security
man lope across the newsroom.

"Two things," Royce said after settling in the chair facing
Hobbs's big desk. "I've got to inspect Ms. Bonner's apartment. It
sounds like a security disaster."

Hobbs nodded. "I'll give her the afternoon off. You can go out
with her and look things over now."

"What about her job here?"

"She'll read the news," Hobbs said, surprised that Royce should
be concerned over the details of the television operation. "There's
a baseball game at the Kingdome this afternoon. We can pick up
clips from the team's public relations department. On camera, she's
mostly reading clips, anyway."

"Two, I need accommodations."

"But I thought—" Hobbs interrupted himself. "Oh, I see what
you mean."

"Right." Royce nodded. "This is a twenty-four-hour surveillance.
I have to be with her when she's here, when she's on the road, and
when she's home."

"Don't you guys camp out in the living room or something like
that?" Hobbs asked with a half-smile, to take the edge off the
words.

"Us guys do that in the event the client is wealthy enough to have half a dozen bedrooms attached to an enormous living area," Royce said, imitating Hobbs's half-smile and touch of wry humor. "Besides," he went on in a normal voice, "I have my own way of doing things. I do not believe in encroaching on anyone's space." He looked directly into Hobbs's eyes. "And vice versa."

"Fair enough," Hobbs said.

His assessment of Andrew Royce rose just a bit after their brief exchange. Melissa was not the easiest person to get along with, particularly in a close, one-on-one relationship. In fact, it was almost impossible to deal with her in any way without ruffling some of her feathers.

It flashed through Hobbs's mind that the last time he had seen the two of them together they were both squared off and lashing out at one another. He wondered how Royce had managed to calm her down—if indeed he had soothed her at all.

"I don't like to bring up any more problems than I have to," he said hesitantly, "but I am wondering how you and Melissa are getting along now."

"She's given me twenty-four hours in which to prove my worth." Royce looked up at the ceiling. "No. That's not right. I have given her twenty-four hours in which to get used to me. Then, if I prove to be too upsetting, she fires me and you get yourself another boy."

Hobbs sighed. "Well, that doesn't bode at all well, does it?" Without waiting for a reply, he asked, "How are you going to maintain guard over her during the hours when she's by herself in her own apartment?"

"I'll need a place close to hers."

"You two had better get out to her apartment. I want you to get your security arrangements under way. While you're gone, I'll work something out with the apartment management—or provide you with accommodations myself."

Hobbs lifted the handset and said, "Get me Melissa."

When she answered he told her to pack up for the rest of the afternoon. She would be with her bodyguard, looking over her apartment for security leaks.

"You'll still read the six- and ten-o'-clock shows," he told her.

Royce could not hear her answer.

"Well, that didn't make her sound any better than she was this morning."

"I'll bet not," Royce said softly.

Melissa Bonner seemed determined not to break the truce that had been decided on, although her expression warned Royce that if he so much as overstepped that invisible line they had drawn between them she would erupt.

She drove through town to her apartment without saying much at all. Royce maintained a neutral silence that was neither sullen nor superimposed. If anything, he gave the impression that everything was normal between them and would remain so.

As they crossed the George Washington Memorial Bridge, he looked out into the waters of the Lake Washington Ship Channel now sparkling in the afternoon sunshine.

"Beautiful view," he said.

"It's a lovely city," Melissa responded, her voice sounding impersonal.

They parked in the apartment's underground garage.

"No lock on the entrance?" Royce asked as she drove down the ramp and pulled into her own slot.

"Of course not." She turned to him with a frown. "There's a building manager. He keeps things in order. No cars stolen yet."

Royce lifted an eyebrow. "Amazing."

They got out of her Range Rover and crossed the garage to the elevator. Melissa pushed the button and they quickly ascended to the fifth floor. When the elevator stopped they walked out, Royce glancing up and down the hallway to note the number of doors opening out into the corridor.

Melissa opened the door to her apartment. Royce looked at the doorjamb and studied the lock's strike plate. Then he examined the face plate in the door. His face was blank. The jamb was set improperly. A husky man could give the door a kick or shoulder roll and break right through the badly set jamb.

Royce sighed.

"You don't approve?" Melissa asked with a frown.

"The apartment's lovely. It's the lock that's ugly."

She smiled vaguely.

The phone rang. Royce saw the quick stiffening of Melissa Bonner's neck. Her face was suddenly pale, eyes darkening with fear. Then, seemingly overcoming her reluctance or fear, she strode across the living room and swept up the handset.

"Hello!"

It was Hobbs. He explained something to Melissa at length and finally, after she heard what Hobbs had to say, she turned and handed the phone to Royce.

"It's all set," Hobbs told Royce. "There's an extra room across the hall. Funny thing. The manager has been using it because of a leaky tap in his own proper place on the ground floor. It's been fixed. The room up here was originally part of a larger apartment. It's got a kitchenette and bath. Motel modern."

"Good," Royce said. "We'll get to work on the locks and window and door alarms."

Melissa was looking at him. "He told me everything. You'll be across the hall." She was not too pleased about it, but she did not make any further comment.

He nodded. "Let's get busy with your security system. Or, I should say, let's start building one. Frankly, you don't have any."

Twenty-seven

The Safety Beeper

Melissa Bonner glanced again at her answering machine. No one had called. Somehow she felt betrayed by her whole elaborate electronics system—and by the telephone company as well. Jonathan Stark had called her and taken her out to sympathize over her loss of Danny. Where was Barry Ford? Why hadn't *he* called?

Of course, he did not know about Danny's death. But wouldn't you think that he could have picked up the phone last night to call her and ask her how she was? After all, he and she had made love the night before. Was he so busy down in Los Angeles that he couldn't phone? Had he lost her telephone number? Or had he lost interest all that quickly?

Or perhaps that was just his way. Casual. Laid-back. Careless.

Before she knew it, she was pacing the floor. She wanted to talk to him. It would be an easy thing to call the hotel where the team was staying and leave a message for him. Then he could call her when he was free to do so.

She *should* be watching her security man. She had to confer with him at every turn. Now, she realized, Andrew Royce was looking all around at the interior of her apartment. She followed him as he went into her bedroom and gazed at the window. It was an ordinary double-hung window that slid up from the bottom and down from the top—just like Denise's. But who was going to come in a fifth-floor window? she wondered.

She watched him. He unlatched the bottom half and slid it up. Then, as Melissa gawked, he leaned his upper body out, twisted at the waist, and looked up along the outside wall. When he came back inside, she stared at him.

"Who's going to come in there? Count Dracula?" she asked in disbelief.

"Fifth floor," Royce answered. "You're on the top floor."

"That's dangerous?"

"For windows it is. All somebody has to do is hit the roof, climb down a rope, break a pane of glass, reach inside and unlock the window, and he's inside your apartment."

"Hanging on a rope?"

"Sure. Rappel yourself down. It's an old mountain climber's trick."

"Burglars are mountain climbers now?"

The moment she said it, she knew she was playing this thing way too dumb. Of *course* burglars came into places. It had often been said that if anyone wanted to get in *any* house or apartment, it could be done. After all, Denise's break-in had been a frighteningly simple operation. But who—?

"We've got to secure this place," Royce was saying softly. "You need perimeter coverage. That is, strip foil across every window. Sensors across doors and windows. Magnetic switches on doors and windows. All that so whenever a door or window is interfered with, the alarm goes off at security headquarters. Heat and motion sensors, too."

"Why?" Melissa asked wildly. "Who's trying to get in?"

"Somebody did get in already," Royce advised her.

He was right. She closed her eyes. Somebody got in and took Danny out.

Beckoning, Royce led her to the apartment door. "Here's where he got in. A set of lock picks or a slim jimmy—even a credit card in the hands of a skillful operator—could get you in through this archaic system. With the naked eye I can make out scratches."

"What'll we do?" Melissa asked in sudden panic.

"This lock will have to be changed. And we have to fortify the lock with a dead bolt. You've been inviting in anyone who might want to see what you've got!"

He walked back through the apartment, scribbling on a three-by-five card he had pulled out of his pocket. "New locks on the front door," he said. "Strip foil on all the windows and the front door as well. We need a control panel for the connections. Plus a siren that sounds immediately—both on the site and at the security station. This place, as it is now, is a break-in disaster area."

Melissa was watching him in disbelief. "But it'll cost a fortune!"

"Channel 8 is paying for this, just like it's paying for me," Royce said quickly. "Not to worry."

The buzzer sounded.

Melissa opened the door. George Murphy was standing outside. "Hello, Ms. Bonner," he said. "I'm told we have someone moving in the room across the hall. I've removed my stuff. He can move in anytime now."

Andrew Royce pushed past Melissa. "Yes," he said. "I'm the new man. I'll be using those rooms. Will you show me?"

"Right," Murphy said, waving to Melissa as he handed a key to Royce and led him across the way.

Melissa waited a few minutes for Royce to reappear. When he did so he stared at her sympathetically. "You did that all wrong, you know."

"I did *what* all wrong?"

"You've got a peephole in that door!"

"I never use it."

"You should. How do you know who's out there?"

"I don't *need* to know!" She bit her lip. "Okay. I see what you mean." She shrugged her shoulders. "I know that peephole's there, but it seems so stupid to peer out whenever there's a buzzer. It's as if I didn't trust anyone I've invited over."

"It's not the invited you should distrust. It's the uninvited!"

She lifted an eyebrow. "I suppose you're right."

"Of course I'm right." Royce led her over to the front door. "I'm going out. I'm going to ring the buzzer. I want you to look out and see if you can see me."

Royce walked into the corridor and closed the door. In a moment she heard the buzzer sound. Obeying his instructions, she put her eye close to the tiny clear-marble sphere and tried to make out what she could.

She saw him, distorted in a fun-house way, but plainly visible— especially his face. Then she opened the door and he came in.

"You saw me?"

"Plainly."

"Don't let anybody in unless you can make him or her out."

She nodded meekly.

He beckoned her to the living room couch. "I want to explain something to you," he said. "Sit down beside me."

She did so.

"I've marked everything here that needs doing. But there's one last thing you and I have to face. When I'm across the hall, I'm not actually by your side. Right?"

She nodded, annoyed at being treated like a child. And yet she had not been able to protect even her own dog before. She determined not to let her annoyance show.

Royce took a small round, hand-held circular device out of his pocket and gave it to her.

"Hold it in your palm. You feel that button in the middle?"

Her thumb immediately moved to the button. "Press the button," Royce said, standing up and moving to the opposite side of the room.

She pressed it. Immediately there was a strong beep from his pants pocket.

He took out the beeper and showed it to her. As he did so, it beeped again. And a third time.

"Now press your button again."

She did so.

The beeping stopped.

"This gadget works at least a hundred yards away. That's a good long distance. I'll never be over a hundred yards from you when I'm in that room across the hall. If anything happens here that you don't like—I mean in the way of somebody getting in—press that button. I'll be here in seconds."

"But what if the door is locked?"

"Oh, I'll have a key to that!" He came over and sat beside her. "You keep that on your person at all times."

"Good God." She sighed. "I feel like such a fool!"

"Why?"

"Because I never used to worry about prowlers. Or burglars. Or people coming after me."

"Of course you didn't. Because no one was after you then."

"But now—?"

"That's what we have to defend against," Royce said.

"You really think I'm in some kind of—of danger?"

"Oh, yes," Royce said. He looked at her with a smile. "That's why I'm here. To keep the danger from getting to you."

Twenty-eight

The Stalker

After she had finished her stint on the six-o'-clock news, Melissa Bonner sank down into her chair and closed her eyes. She was bushed! It had been a bad day from the start. First, waking up and realizing Danny was dead. Second, finding out she had another problem to face at the station: the employment of a bodyguard. And third, walking around her apartment to inaugurate a klutzy but essential security system.

She knew that Royce was looking at her from across the office. She had almost forgotten that he was there—like an anchor hung around her neck. Proved how tired she was.

"I'm hungry," Royce said. "I'm still on New York time, you know."

"So eat," Melissa said shortly.

He was standing now, walking over to her desk, looking down at her. "I can't leave you here. If you'll come with me, I could grab a sandwich downstairs at that coffee shop on the first floor." He stared at her. "My treat."

"Gee whiz boy howdy golly gee," said Melissa Bonner in a mock country-Western accent.

"There's something we've got to discuss." He worked at his lower lip as he spoke.

She shrugged. "Let's go. I've got a lot of hang time till ten o'clock."

It was an hour past peak service at Coffee Bar Number 8 and they found a table for two by the back wall. The front windows looked out onto a busy street. But the noise inside was at a minimum.

He ordered a hamburger, California style, and she, not to be outdone, ordered a Western omelet, Seattle style. The waitress wandered away, her expression revealing that she did not think it was amusing to give funny orders to someone trying to do a good job.

"The twenty-four-hour deadline is up," Melissa said as they waited for their food to arrive.

"I assume I've passed your rigid tests?"

"Some of them. I still reserve the right to terminate any time I get fed up."

Royce looked at her. "Excellent," he said. "And now that that's settled, let's move on to some details that have not yet been cleared up."

"And they are—?"

"I know pretty much about what happened to Danny and about what you call the rip-and-reads. I also know you suspect you've been followed by a mystery car. But I don't know anything else that's been happening."

She shrugged. "Nothing else *has* been happening."

He stared at her. She was not allowing him to see her eyes. They were moving around gazing at the interior of the coffee shop and the few patrons still there.

"I see," he said. He meant he did not see why she should be covering up anything now that they were on a more professional basis with one another.

"Then let's talk about something else." She smiled at him, not meaning it. "This afternoon when the phone rang in your apartment I noticed something that struck me as odd."

She glanced quickly at him, then away. "Oh?"

"You were scared to death."

Her eyes were steady. Now she was looking at him. "I do not scare that easily," she told him.

"Maybe not. But you were frightened."

"Frightened, perhaps." She studied him. "You pick up on things, don't you?" she observed.

The waitress arrived and placed the hamburger and the omelet in front of them. Royce ordered coffee; Melissa, tea. The waitress hurried off.

"Have you been getting obscene telephone calls?" Royce asked suddenly as he bit into the large, juicy burger.

"No," Melissa said softly, going after her omelet.

"But there's something about that telephone call—" Royce said softly. "Look! Your dog is dead. Somebody's trying to frighten you by sending you stories about women victims of harassment. A car is surveilling you. There's a phone connection, too, isn't there?"

She kept her eyes on her plate. "I've gotten several telephone calls. And there's nobody there. It's probably a coincidence."

"In my business, there's no such thing as a coincidence," Royce said. "When did these telephone calls start?"

"Oh, maybe four weeks ago."

"Fairly recent, then."

She nodded. "I place absolutely no value on them," she said airily.

"The mind that plans and executes the killing of a dog is a mind that works anonymously and surreptitiously on a telephone in exactly the manner you describe."

Her face paled. She fussed with her omelet. "You mean it?"

"Yes!" he said, leaning forward. "It's all part of the syndrome."

"What syndrome?" She looked up, puzzled.

"The stalker syndrome."

Her eyes widened. "Good lord!" she whispered.

"There's more?" His eyes narrowed. He was almost angry now. Her dog was dead. Someone was trying to wreak psychological damage by sending her poison pen stories. She'd gotten a number of phantom phone calls. What else was this woman covering up?

"No, no, no," she said defiantly, shaking her head. "It can't be! It's just a coincidence."

"Tell me!" he said in that soft, yet penetrating, voice of his.

"My sister. A burglar broke into her apartment one night last week."

He sucked in his breath to control his agitation. "What did the intruder take?"

"Not a damned thing," Melissa said in a hoarse voice.

"It gets worse and worse," Royce said, staring at her.

"Worse? She *wasn't* robbed! It was just one of those things! I can't *believe* this!"

"You don't want to believe it, but you do believe it," Royce said doggedly. "There *is* a connection. Look at you. You're as pale as a ghost. You've been hiding all this, keeping it from everyone you know. You couldn't fool your boss. He discovered those assault stories. And he extracted from you the fact that you'd been followed by a car. Now your dog—that couldn't be covered up. But you've buried the telephone calls and your sister's break-and-enter."

She blinked her eyes, trying not to look at him at all.

"What else are you hiding, Ms. Bonner?" He stared at her, trying to mesmerize her into telling him the whole truth. Why was it that people who were strong and blessed with willpower were their own worst enemies when it came to covering up very real dangers?

Melissa was sipping at her tea, trying to hide from him. He could sense it, if she could not. It did no good. He was watching every move she made. He knew there was more—but he was afraid to push her too hard. It had to come out. And that was the reason he was easing off just a bit.

He went back to munching his hamburger, but his eyes did not leave her face.

Her eyes moved desperately about the interior of the coffee bar, pretending to herself that he was not there, that whatever had happened had not occurred. Finally she set her teacup down in the saucer and looked directly at him. Her face was suddenly relaxed and calm.

"I jog every morning," she told him with a smile. "Do you jog?"

"Ms. Bonner!" he growled. "Don't play with me this way. I have to know the truth. I'm trying to help you, but you're not giving me any cooperation at all."

"I like it because I can get out early in the morning before the streets are too crowded and it's hard to run across a busy intersection."

He leaned back, irritated.

"I rarely meet anyone out jogging, probably because of my timing. A few days before Danny was killed I did see a man on the jogging route."

Royce's eyes widened. He looked at Melissa's face again. She was half-smiling now.

"He wore blue boxers and a gray tank top. He wasn't following me. He vanished. But then, just as I came back into the garage and was waiting for the elevator, I saw him in the basement garage."

"What happened?"

"I got in the elevator and went to my apartment." She said it calmly. Royce could see the artery in her throat. It was throbbing.

"Did you ever see him again?"

"No. He made no attempt to follow me upstairs." She smiled. "I thought it was just something I dreamed up. A casual encounter in the street. And yet, I thought he looked familiar, somehow. But I couldn't place him. Not with the biker's reflecting shades he wore. I still can't."

"Keep trying," Royce urged her.

She looked at him steadily. "The car was a red Taurus."

"There are lots of red Tauruses," Royce said.

"And then there were the empty cans of dog food."

Royce straightened up. "Tell me."

She told him how she thought she had made a mistake by not counting the cans of dog food properly. "But then, after Danny was killed, I had a feeling that those extra empties might have meant something."

"That's a burglar's trick," Royce told her matter-of-factly. "You break into a house. You feed the dog. He's your friend. He helps you rob the place."

She went white. "But this time he made friends with Danny. And then he came, got him and killed him!" She began to sob.

He reached over and held her hand. "Get hold of yourself," he said sternly. "You're absolutely right. That's what the killer did. He made friends with Danny so he could kill him later on."

"I—I should have guessed. Maybe I could have saved Danny."

"In no way could you have correctly guessed what was going to happen. Don't blame yourself."

Royce drank his coffee. Melissa wiped at the tears with a handkerchief. She was feeling better already. Her face had regained its natural color. She sat there looking at Royce and then she said: "My forte is asking sportspeople questions and getting answers. Your forte is asking potential victims questions and getting answers to prevent crimes from occurring. I think we're both good professional interrogators."

Royce nodded absently. He wondered where she was going with this line of thought.

"But we haven't found out much *about* one another, at least not on a personal level, have we?"

"No," Royce admitted. "Is that necessary?"

"Well, I think it is. So I suggest we reverse the process of the Q and A, and make it an A and Q affair. That is, instead of asking questions, we'll give answers. The person being answered will score the answers true or false."

Royce smiled. "It's a deal. Who starts?"

"You do. After all, I thought this game up."

"What questions do you want me to answer?"

"Tell me what kind of person you think I am."

"You're a thoroughly professional woman. You're intelligent, you're sharp, you're not afraid of taking a chance now and then."

"That's one true answer. Now. What about my *private* life?" Her eyes were shining.

"You're not one to commit yourself to a man. Not yet, anyway. Perhaps you haven't met the right person. Perhaps you never intend to make such a commitment. Time will tell."

"That's another true statement."

"I haven't finished. You need your independence. The men who usually attract you are men of action. You fancy someone who is in control of not only his destiny but the destinies of others about him."

She was laughing in his face. "Someone *told* you." Mentally he finished her sentence with the words: "About Barry Ford."

"Possibly. Your relationship with the one you are thinking about is an active one. Your problem is that you are fascinated by men of action but you need your freedom. You like controllers, but you do not want to be controlled."

She stared at him thoughtfully. "Just because I once dated the basketball coach at the University of Seattle, don't think I'm mad for *all* men of action! Besides, my relationship with Scott O'Hara is none of your damned business!"

"In addition, you are conflicted in another way," Royce went on, ignoring her outburst. "Your love of action-oriented people is balanced by your love of intellectually oriented people."

She shook her head. "My *sister* works for Dr. Jonathan Stark.

And I'll admit he was my favorite professor when I went to college. But that doesn't mean anything *deeper* occurred."

She was breathing hard now, and restrained herself with some difficulty. "How do you know all *that*?"

He straightened up in his chair. "That's enough for me. Now you. How do you assess me?"

"You're a bit of a rock, you know. There's a lot of you there, no questions about it. And it's solid. But I'm damned if anybody can figure out exactly what it all means. Every time anything comes up that's at all personal, or on an intimate level, you become an impenetrable wall."

He laughed. "That's true. But it's just the way I am."

"Let's go further. Now it gets tricky. You seem like a happily married man, and I have no way of telling you how I guessed that. Probably with at least two children." She sank back. "Am I right?"

"Thoroughly wrong. I'm not married. Never have been. I have no children."

"Well, at least I know now that you aren't married. But I'll bet you've lived with a woman."

"Is that your answer?" Royce smiled.

"Yes. That's a definite answer."

"You got that right."

"But no commitment—at this time."

"Again, true."

"You keep your personal life definitely segregated from your professional life. Right?"

"Oh, yes."

"I win," Melissa said.

"You lose," Royce objected. "I got all trues. You got two falses. And important falses at that."

Royce reached over and picked up the check.

"But the loser pays!" Melissa said.

"No. The winner wins the right to choose. Pay. Or not to pay. I choose to pay." He smiled. "Besides, I got you down here on the pretext of a free meal. I'm not a man who goes back on his word." He looked into her eyes. "Ever."

She smiled and shook her head, trying to unsnarl the intriguing line of reasoning he had taken to arrive at his conclusion.

As they walked out of Coffee Bar Number 8, Royce said, "I do want to thank you for answering all my serious questions earlier. At least now we have some kind of pattern to look at. It may even lead us to who is doing all these things to you."

He knew that by getting her to tell him those mysterious little details he had made her feel just a bit better about the troubles she had been carrying around with her.

"We'll get him!" Royce assured her.

Oh yeah? he thought.

Twenty-nine

All the Usual Suspects

Augustus Simms was a round black man, a dead ringer for James Earl Jones, right down to the rich baritone voice that was both impressive and mesmerizing. Behind the twinkling eyes lurked a prodigious sense of humor that was waiting to break out into the open on the slightest pretext.

Simms was a fashion plate. He wore only what he considered to be the best. Most of his income went into clothes. Looking good made him feel good. No one could say that Augie Simms did not usually feel good.

He had numerous friends from every sphere he moved in, from his professional life as a detective to his personal life as a married man with two small kids who were carbon copies of their father.

He arrived at Andrew Royce's one-room apartment at about midnight Wednesday, flashing his badge and I.D. with a wide grin that showed off his perfect teeth. Royce shook hands and gestured him into his new one-roomer. As he did so, he stifled a yawn. "Sorry!"

Simms grinned. "Hope it's not me, although I do have a narcotic effect on some people I meet."

Royce shook his head. "I'm into my thirty-sixth hour without a wink of sleep," he said. "Sit down, sit down!"

"Bad scheduling."

"Couldn't be helped."

Simms looked around. Royce had not even unpacked his case, which was thrown onto the bed waiting for him to open it. "You travel light," Simms observed.

Royce took a chair opposite the big man. "You've read Hobbs's memo?"

"Oh, sure."

"What do you think?"

"I think we've got hold of a live one. Nobody kills a dog unless there's a reason. Even if it is a psychotic one."

"There's more."

"It's the dog, the telephone caller, and the following car—plus?" Simms said with surprise.

Quickly Royce led Simms through Melissa's discovery of the empty dog-food cans.

Simms raised a finger. "That's how he was able to lead the dog out of the apartment. The old 'killer's best-friend' gambit."

"Exactly. Incidentally, her place is a security disaster. I've got workmen coming tomorrow to wire the windows and doors, plus redo the locks."

"Any idea who's after her?"

"No."

Simms nodded.

"But there's definitely a stalker," said Royce.

Simms pursed his lips into a whistling position. "Oh ho."

"She's had a visual of him. Skinny guy in blue boxers and gray tank."

"Bad taste dude." Simms grimaced.

"He's obviously the one who's following her in a red Taurus."

"Taste in cars is better," Simms rumbled.

"There's also the fact that her sister's apartment was broken into last week."

Simms frowned. "Her sister?"

"Denise Bonner. Lives not far from her."

"You think it's connected?" Simms's eyes narrowed.

"I can't believe for the moment that it is *not* connected."

"Go on." Simms grinned. "I mean, say that's all there is. Please."

Royce shook his head. Then he quickly briefed him on all the details of the case he could remember. At the end of his recital, the two men looked at one another. "How do you read it?" Royce asked.

"Oh, it's a psychotic all right. And I wouldn't want to frighten the woman—she's a good sportscaster—but I think she's next in line."

Simms leaned forward and clasped his hands together between his thighs. "What can SPD do for you?"

"I have discovered no motive of any kind. But somebody hates or fears Melissa Bonner. We know that."

Simms pursed his lips and squinted into the distance. "I'll need a list of people. You know, the usual suspects. I'll run a cross-check on those names. If any one of them appears anywhere else in the records, I'll tell you and get to work on it." He paused and frowned. "If we don't get any cross-checks—as we probably won't—we'll have to round them up and begin work on all the suspects."

"I've made a partial list," Royce said. "Let me run these down with you. First there's Melissa Bonner's sister. I'll be meeting her tomorrow night. I doubt that she has anything to do with the stalker. But she might have."

Simms took out a notebook and began writing.

"Then there's that basketball coach named Scott O'Hara. He was having it on with Melissa, and then he switched to Denise."

"Reason?"

Royce shrugged. "He likes variety." Pause. "And don't forget Barry Ford."

"Of course not."

"The problem with Ford is that the red Taurus and the telephone caller predate his arrival in Seattle. Also the news wire clips."

"But there may be a connection," Simms said.

"Yes." Royce pondered. "She's eyeballed the stalker only once. She's got a description of him—but it's vague. The kicker is that she thinks she's seen him before somewhere."

Simms grunted.

"I'd suggest we go through all her known associates at college. She graduated from the University of Seattle. Plus all her known associates at Channel 8, where she works. And let's not forget the manager at her apartment."

"Here?" Simms's voice rose slightly in surprise.

"His apartment is on the ground floor. But he's been using this room here. Some excuse about a leaky tap in his basement digs."

"Have you seen him?"

"He's in his sixties. He's a rumpot. Just hanging in there. But who knows? Maybe somebody's pulling his strings."

"That's the complete list?"

"There's one more. I understand that Ms. Bonner is fairly close to the president of the University of Seattle."

Simms whistled this time. "My, oh, my. Her credentials do escalate."

"A father figure, I guess," Royce said. "Jonathan Stark had a fast rise to president, from head of the English Department. He was Bonner's teacher when she went to college. So there might be something there."

Simms nodded. "Anybody else?"

"Not on my list," Royce said, glancing at the paper in his hand. "That doesn't mean we've zeroed in on him yet, though. He could be anybody out there."

"When you say 'he' you do mean 'he' or 'she,' don't you?"

"Goes without saying."

"By the way," Simms rumbled on after a brief hesitation. "Are there parents around in the area? Other siblings?"

"Both parents are dead."

Simms leaned forward. "How did they die?"

"Gas explosion."

"Gasoline?" Simms asked, puzzled.

"Natural gas. One of those household tragedies."

"I see," Simms said slowly. "Any other siblings?"

"Just the two sisters."

Royce yawned again. He apologized to Simms. "Look," he said. "We should meet every night if possible, until we get this thing in the bag."

"I'm on nights," Simms said. "Midnight?"

"I think so. Bonner keeps irregular hours because of her weird job schedule."

"Meet here? You and I?" Simms asked.

"Has to be. I can't let her out of range of my safety beeper. That's how I keep her on a leash."

Simms got up to leave. At the door he turned. "Always wanted to work New York," he said.

"Highly overrated place," Royce said. "Still, there's only one Big Apple."

Simms grinned. "So I hear."

They shook hands and Simms left.

Royce didn't even bother to shower. He unpacked his case and sank into bed as soon as he took off his clothes. In seconds he was out for the count.

Thirty

The American Dream Inverted

Melissa was just starting to make her breakfast on Thursday morning when she heard the quick tap on the door. For some reason Royce did not subscribe to the usual method of using the buzzer. She rose and peered obediently through the peephole at him. He looked surprisingly alert for the tired man she had said good night to seven hours before.

He was standing there in his familiar uniform—jacket, tie, and shirt, comfortable slacks, and running shoes. The shoes were the only incongruous item of his attire—at least they were when he was dressed for "work."

She opened the door for him and he came into the apartment.

"You're up early," she said in a voice clearly unused to speech so soon in the day.

"Tricks of the trade." He waved a hand.

"I'm not ready yet." She tried to keep the petulance out of her voice and failed miserably.

"I'll wait here," Royce said, staking out the living-room couch.

"Care for coffee?" she asked, not wanting him to acquiesce.

"Don't mind if I do." He smiled that rare smile that transformed him almost instantly into another person. She led him into the kitchenette, where he pulled out the chair opposite hers. With that he got two cups out of the cupboard, measured out two instant coffee units, and set the kettle on to boil. In minutes, while she poured orange juice for herself, he filled both cups with hot water and stirred them.

She was watching him. She had been noticing that Andrew Royce was not at all like most of the muscular, tough-bodied males she knew. His movements were different from those of an athlete, too. Even when he poured the hot water for the coffee she was attracted to his swift fluid motions. He never had to backtrack or correct an inadvertent misstep. Clearly, he had perfect and complete control over every muscle in his body.

Nor had she ever seen him overcome by an occurrence or event that happened unexpectedly. He had a way of instantly correcting his own movements to conform to or escape from sudden disaster. By being in such solid control of himself, he was able to meet, read, and triumph over almost any obstacle in his path.

Now, as she saw that he was watching her closely, she felt a tingle in the middle of her body. He was a cipher in that he could not be viewed, seen through, or analyzed with any clarity of vision. But he was no cipher when it came to emotional connection. She could feel a sudden wave of warmth rising in her viscera.

It was his eyes. Usually he kept them on whatever he was holding, or viewing, or studying. Now they were locked on hers. She lowered her lids, trying vainly to break the connection between the two of them. She was shaken. Somehow this was the most incredible thing of all—that she could be feeling so much toward this man. She hated guns. She hated violence. Here were guns and violence personified in one man. And she was being swept away by him.

"Thanks for making the coffee," she said after a moment. She did not look up. "I like a man who shares the work."

"I'm good at instant."

She smiled faintly. "I'll bet you're good at everything."

"It all depends on what you mean by 'everything.' "

She laughed out loud. "How in the world did you ever become a security agent?" She hesitated. "I guess that's what you call a bodyguard. Right?"

"It was a shortage of cash," he explained.

"Ah. The American Dream turned inside out."

"I didn't have enough to get through college," Royce said. "My dad ran a hardware store in Bowling Green. That's where I come from—the one in Ohio. Anyway, we were white-collar middle-class strapped. Barely enough to live a life of ease, but nothing for the frills. So I worked."

"What did you work at?"

"Anything I could find after high school. A supermarket. A gas station. The usual. I wanted a degree."

"In what?"

"Law." Royce smiled. "Sounds kind of dumb, doesn't it? Like 'L. A. Law Revisited.' But lawyers were the cream of the crop in the eighties. Anyway, I signed up for the National Guard so I could make a little extra money."

He spread his hands.

"I finally went to N.Y.U. in New York, got my law degree, and eventually passed the New York bar exam."

"Into a job?"

"No. In 1990 things began to fall apart—not only for me, but for a lot of others, too. My National Guard unit was called up to take part in Operation Desert Storm in Iraq."

She was fascinated. "That was hardly the reason you signed up for the National Guard?"

"Hardly. I was assigned to a headquarters unit in Riyadh. One day a group of us were strolling around the compound wondering when the action was going to start—nothing had happened yet, you understand—when suddenly an old guy in a desert camouflage outfit came out and pointed to the six of us."

Royce got a twang in his voice. " 'Hey, soldiers,' the guy called to us, 'you, you, you, you, you, and you. What unit you in?' We told him. 'Got a job for you.' "

"What was the job?" Melissa asked curiously.

"Guarding General Stormin' Norman Schwartzkopf."

She burst out laughing. "You're kidding me."

"Nope. The general had gotten upset by the last group he had—too much smoking, he said. We went in and replaced them. Our records were transferred. I spent the duration of the emergency right at his shoulder. Big shoulder, too."

"But when you came back home—"

"That wasn't for another year. Kept an eye on the general."

She took another sip of coffee.

"Short story. When I got home in 1991, the Guard called me back almost immediately in the summer. I went to Norway with a politician who needed someone to watch over him. Then I was transferred to London, where one of our ambassadorial staff needed me. And so on."

He continued. "I've got a law degree—and a good one, too—but I've never really been able to do a nine-to-five. I always get called up to save somebody's life."

She was laughing with genuine amusement. It was such an odd story—and yet, it was the kind of thing that happened to people all the time.

"How did you like growing up in Bowling Green?"

"I loved it. All these other places—they're nice. But they're not home. Incidentally, it's time to be going, isn't it?"

She nodded.

"You know," he said, "you haven't told me today's program yet."

"I have no idea. It's up to Hobbs."

Royce was stirring his coffee. She watched in fascination. The same effortless movements, the same concentration, the same—

"Nice guy, your boss."

"Of course," she said.

His eyes drifted slightly. He was looking at her sweatshirt—the white one without any lettering. She could feel the sudden rise of her chest as she began breathing just a bit more quickly. Damn him! she thought. She could feel her nipples hardening against her bra. One glance like that from him, and her insides began to melt. Her face hardened.

She flounced up, although she had not yet finished her coffee, and started out of the kitchenette. Her warm-up pants clung to her backside. She could feel him looking at her hips and thighs. Critically. Assessingly. Lasciviously.

She spun around to face him. He was just rising. "You like the view?" she taunted him.

He froze. The total professional was being called by his client on a display of obvious unprofessionalism.

"Love the view," he said, his face purposely blank.

"The view is forbidden," she announced. "No more ogling the goodies!"

His eyes narrowed just slightly. There was a silver glint in them. Instead of speaking he smiled. "I can't imagine that you've never been glanced at in your life," he said in a new and silky soft voice. "Why do I bother you so much?"

"I just dislike people who stare at the cleavage and the legs— even when there isn't any cleavage." She could feel the blood rushing to her face. Why was her body playing tricks on her?

"No offense," he said, and turned his eyes from her to look out the window. "Nice day outside," he observed.

They went out the door, which he locked carefully behind them.

"This is the jogging part?" he asked again, to be sure.

"This is the jog. We come back. Then we go to the grocery store. Then to the office."

"And that's the program," he said with satisfaction.

She nodded.

"I think I can handle that," he said.

Thirty-one

Poison Pen

Andrew Royce sat at his table in the corner of Melissa Bonner's office. She was attending her daily meeting with Hobbs and the rest of the news staff. In front of Royce lay the stripped parts of his Colt .45, which he was cleaning with his usual meticulous attention to detail.

This was his second day on the job. It was time to begin fine-tuning the details of the assignment. After talking to Melissa at some length the previous day about the things that had been happening to her, Royce realized that she had good reason to be thinking about something other than her day-to-day duties and chores.

She was in deep trouble; of that he was positive. She knew it, too. It was frightening her, although she would be the last to admit it. Royce was more determined than ever to get to the bottom of the problems that were enmeshing her and destroying her sense of well-being.

That morning she had jogged while he followed in her car. She spoke little as they went shopping for groceries. Her mind was still concentrated on something far beyond his ken.

Now that he was able to reason with a clearer head, he realized that Melissa was traversing the same course millions of men and women did every time they fell in love.

What a dummy he had been not to have spotted her inattention for what it was: the far-off glaze in the eyes; the aimless wandering about; the lack of conversation; the inability to focus on details.

This was no easy client to service, Royce thought again. She was smart and she was astute. She was opinionated, self-centered, and, at the same time, self-assured. The reason for her self-assurance was undoubtedly her superior intelligence and her ability to read motivations and emotional fluctuations in others. It was no surprise to Royce that someone should be after her—that is, after her in the sense of trying to avenge some injustice, prepare for a final showdown for some unguessed reason, or simply to hurt her for reasons unknown.

What it was really about was still unclear. But he would find out, especially with the help of Augie Simms, that very good SPD homicide detective.

Royce did not realize it, but as he was handling his Colt .45 automatic, he had begun whistling softly to himself. It was a habit he had only lately gotten into.

"Begin the Beguine"—an odd tune to whistle. He tried to suppress it, but it continued to return to his mind and to his lips. He began to whistle the countertheme in minor.

"What *is* that?" Melissa Bonner asked, coming up behind him unexpectedly.

"It's a Colt .45," he said equably, turning to face toward her. He had hoped to get it all back together again before she returned from her meeting.

"Why are all the pieces spread out on your table?"

"I'm cleaning it," he said, "so it'll work."

She frowned slightly. "I've got to confess that I don't like firearms of any kind." She watched him a moment as he continued to reassemble the parts of the gun. "Is it necessary to take it apart like that to get it in working order?"

"Not all the time. But if you don't keep all the pieces oiled they'll rust together."

She was standing over his shoulder now, staring down at the metallic pieces he was working with. In spite of herself, he noted, she seemed to be absorbed. Apparently he had managed to come to a sort of working arrangement with her; the two of them seemed to have gotten it together.

The fittings slipped into place and in a very short time he had the Colt assembled, loaded, safetied, and in his shoulder holster.

Melissa was still watching him. "Do you think you should wear that in the office?" she asked. "I mean, someone might get hurt."

"I need to be armed," Royce said simply.

She conceded that. "I never asked you, but did you ever have to use a weapon in your guard duties?"

Royce looked up. "Yes, I did."

She blinked. "How many times?"

"Only once, thank God." Royce grinned.

"What happened?" she asked, genuinely interested but acting as if she might not want to hear the answer.

"I was working for a state senator in New Jersey," Royce said. "Somebody had been threatening him over the phone. We had no idea who it was. The election was coming up and things were getting hot. On the podium one day I spotted a man moving toward the front row from the back during my client's speech. Then I saw him draw a gun out of his belt. I was running and snapped off a shot just as he took aim." Royce nodded. "Shot the weapon right out of his hand."

Melissa tried to smile, but some of the blood had left her face.

"Got a conviction, too," Royce said.

"I just hope nothing like that happens here," she said unsteadily.

"It's my job to see that it doesn't."

As she turned to leave him her eyes happened to fall on the newspaper he had spread out on the table where he was cleaning his Colt. Before he could collect the oil rags, she had snatched the newspaper up from the table and was holding it in front of her, reading with wide-eyed disbelief.

"Well, I'll be damned," she said in sudden understanding. "So that's where he was."

Royce tried to see over her shoulder, but he could not make out the article she was staring at.

"I can't believe this," she said to herself as she threw down the paper and moved across to her desk. As soon as she was seated, she began sifting noisily through the items in her in-basket.

Royce picked up the paper. It was yesterday's. His eye made out the item immediately. It was about Barry Ford. He had been seen at some Hollywood night spot on the Sunset Strip with a starlet named Anne Whittaker. Luanne was right. Royce laid the paper down and threw the cleaning rags into the wastebasket.

No one he had talked to knew anything detrimental about Barry Ford's background. Ford was twenty-eight years old, and some telltale weather stains should have developed around him during all those years. Yet maybe he was exactly what he seemed to be— a really nice guy who could also play football.

On the other hand, nothing was ever quite that simple in the world of sports. That was an area where all kinds of nasty little things came crawling out of the walls: harassing callers, stalking men, pursuing cars, dog drowners—the whole lot of them.

And sick stories from the rip-and-read.

Royce could sense exactly what Melissa Bonner was doing at her desk. She was going through the in-basket items one by one to see if she found any more of those wire service stories about women victims of harassment.

He had already sifted through everything there. Nothing today, nothing yesterday. Nothing at all.

It meant to him that whoever had been trying to upset Melissa Bonner had discovered that the sender of the stories was being sought. And it meant also that there probably would not be any more items from the rip-and-read.

He could hear her give a sigh of relief and dump most of the junk in the out-basket. Then she reached for the mail. Royce knew that there were only three letters there. Two were junk mail, and the third a typed letter.

"My God!" Melissa gasped. Quickly Royce jumped up and was at her shoulder, reading the typed message on a sheet of paper.

"Danny was only Act II. Are you ready for Act III?"

"Let me," Royce said quickly. He picked up the letter by the corner and placed it carefully in a glassine bag he removed from his pocket. The envelope followed. "These go to the police," he explained.

She was too astonished to object. "But, you see," she said, "the point is it didn't come through the office. It came from outside."

Royce nodded. "I looked through your in-basket myself. But I didn't open your mail."

"You went through my things?"

"Just a job," he said. He whisked the glassine bag into a brown envelope, sealed it, and scrawled the name *Augie Simms* on the cover.

Melissa was standing behind her desk now, staring across the office at him.

"What's that all about?"

"What's *what* all about?"

"That envelope. That glassine bag in it. That letter."

"I'm sending the letter over to the Seattle Police Department. You'd be surprised what can be picked up from a simple thing like a letter."

She looked dubious.

"Incidentally, your analysis of where that envelope came from is moot."

"I beg your pardon?"

"You said it didn't really come from the office."

"It didn't. It came in the U.S. mail."

"How do we know that?" Royce asked her. "Somebody in the office could have mailed it. Or someone could have picked up an old envelope of yours and put that note in it and dropped it on your desk."

"But who'd be that devious?"

"Probably more people than you think." He played with the brown envelope. "I said there may be a clue on the letter. But don't count on it too much. Nine times out of ten the police lab can't pick anything up."

Melissa looked pale. "If you think you're making me feel better, I'd like to tell you that you aren't succeeding."

"I'm trying to give you the facts."

"Melissa."

She turned toward the doorway.

Hobbs was standing there, smiling at her. "There's a chance the Seattle Seafarers can trade two of their people for Sam Bains, the Dodger twenty-game winner. You get your gang up there right away. There's a press conference at two."

Melissa glanced at Royce and Royce glanced at Hobbs.

"Hurry up," Hobbs said. "Kubo and Griswold are loading up the van."

Thirty-two

Advice From an Expert

Denise Bonner sat waiting for her sister to appear at the Tavern in the Town that Thursday night. She could understand why Channel 8 wanted to protect her sister, but somehow she could not imagine Melissa allowing anyone to follow her around so closely.

She pictured a bulky, overweight, middle-aged fud, who had been a heavy-breathing and doddering cop on the force for forty years. He would have hair growing out of his ears and would look like a recycled android.

Yet of course Denise could understand that her sister needed some support after the death of Danny. Even Denise had felt a wrenching agony when Melissa had telephoned her on Tuesday afternoon to tell her the story. The news about the bodyguard—Melissa had phoned again Wednesday—had not surprised her as much as Melissa had thought it might. In fact, Denise sensed that Melissa was in danger and hoped she would be doing something about protecting herself.

Melissa was right on time tonight. Denise saw her come in, glance around, and then turn to wait for someone behind her. A fit, no-nonsense man in his thirties came up. Denise suspected he was a man of few words. But no man like that needed words. He leaned down to hear what Melissa had to say to him. Denise watched as the two of them came over to her table.

"Mr. Royce," Melissa said, "this is Denise Bonner, my sister."

"How do you do, Ms. Bonner," Royce said softly. He leaned over ever so slightly, almost as if he might be bowing to her.

"Pleased to meet you," Denise said with a smile.

"I'll just take a seat at the end of the bar," Royce said politely. "I'm sure you two would like to be alone."

"Thank you," Denise said effusively.

Royce strolled over to the last bar stool where he hunched over as the bartender came up to him for his order.

Melissa sat down.

"That's him?" Denise asked. "He's gorgeous!"

Melissa straightened with a frown. "Come on, now! He's a frozen lump of suet. Don't believe what your eyes tell you!"

"I thought he'd be some over-the-hill ex-flatfoot."

"No. He was in the service. The Gulf War. Not a cop." She tilted her head up. "Not that I care what he was."

"Of course you don't," Denise agreed, her ironic tone skewing her meaning in the opposite direction. Her expression softened. "I'm so very sorry about Danny!"

"That's what brought all this on," Melissa said, blinking rapidly. She would not cry! She would not!

"Is there anything new on Danny's death?"

"Nothing," Melissa said sadly. She reached across the table and gripped her sister's hand. "Thanks for the support," she said. "I mean, thanks for telling Jonathan what happened. He was so damned decent. Took me out for a late supper. He was so marvelously civilized about it." She shook herself so as not to burst into tears.

"It was the least I could do," Denise said stiffly. "What do you think a sister is for, anyway?"

The waiter came and they ordered drinks. Denise was seated so that she could glance over at the man on the last stool at the bar without giving herself away. She saw that he was actually able to keep his eye on Melissa at all times. He was drinking and ordering something to eat now. Someone had come to sit beside him, and the two of them exchanged a few words.

"He's very good," Denise told Melissa.

"Who?" Melissa frowned.

"Your—you know—guard."

"Oh, him." She dismissed him with a grimace. Then she thought better of it. She leaned forward. "He says someone did break into the apartment, took Danny, drugged him with a hypodermic injection, and then led him to Green Lake."

"And nobody saw it?"

Melissa shook her head. "It was apparently timed just right. Danny was still OK when he was walking beside the lake embankment. When he went down, he slid into the water. At least they think so."

Denise made a face. "How gruesome!"

"They're after me," Melissa told her sister. "It was just another way of getting me pissed."

"Is this your new on-air persona, Ellie?" Denise grinned.

Melissa ignored the comment. "I got some hate mail, too."

Denise's eyes widened. "What kind?"

"The 'you're next' kind."

"Really?"

They ordered salad and Denise changed the subject. "If it wasn't Thursday I'd have called you. There's a very good reason I wanted to see you tonight. The athlete-academic controversy has taken a serious turn."

Melissa's eyes gleamed at the thought of a story. "In what direction? Tell me."

"All the talk about more money for a basketball stadium did just what Dr. Stark was afraid it would do. It aroused some members of the faculty to action."

"What action?"

"The action started out as an idea by a faculty group to petition the administration to allocate more money for academic excellence—that is, for hiring more well-known professors. And that's what Dr. Stark has been doing ever since he became president."

"So?"

"I'm just beginning. Another faculty group heard about this move and got the bright idea to petition the administration immediately to *drop football*."

"Drop football! But why?"

"You can easily guess why. The football team hasn't won a game this year. It's a beautiful target. And a lot of the faculty members don't like *any* sports."

"Anything else?"

"There's already talk among the alums about promoting Scott O'Hara's call for the new stadium. And if that happens, it's all-out war—and it could mean curtains for Stark's entire academic excellence program. You know how those things go."

"What is Jonathan going to do?"

"He won't go completely against the alums and Coach Scott O'Hara. If he did, he'd become the public's whipping boy. Every sports-minded fan would hate him. In fact, he really wants to remain completely neutral—that is, maintain the status quo."

Melissa nodded. "Put the fires out before they burn down the forest. When I saw Jonathan the other day, I told him I'd be happy to arrange air time for him."

"I know."

"You think he's ready?"

"I do, Ellie," Denise said. "What do you think?"

"If I know Jonathan," Melissa said thoughtfully, "he'll come out with an intelligent, well-balanced exposition of the situation. In that way, he might be able to defuse both sides."

"I think you're right."

"He might blame me, though, if the story only built up momentum for controversy," Melissa said cautiously. "I wouldn't want that to happen."

Denise considered her words. "No matter *what* you do, Jonathan will back you."

"Are you sure? I *am* a media person."

"You're a damned fool," Denise snapped. "I can read that man. Don't you know? He's got *more* than a crush on you."

Melissa Bonner studied her sister for a long time. "Nah."

"Don't be such an ass. He still talks about you whenever your name comes up. Good God, I think he even *watches* Channel 8. Dr. Stark. Can you imagine that?" She burst out laughing. "He's in love with you—if you want it flat out."

Melissa blinked. "But he's so much older than I am."

"You're a fool, Melissa. You don't understand men."

She shrugged. "I'll go after the story anyway."

"I had a feeling you would." Denise looked at her a little longer. "You think I'm doing wrong?"

"No. I think you'll do whatever you want to in any case."

"You're trying to be my conscience now. I thought you were here to advise me." Melissa was smiling.

"I advise you, but what good does it do? You always do something else."

"That's my nature." Melissa laughed.

"I thought I'd be hearing all about Barry Ford tonight."

Melissa made a face. "He's out of town. Playing in Los Angeles." Denise looked up. "Playing football? Or playing beddy-bye?" That was a low blow, Melissa thought. Or maybe Denise hadn't seen that item in the paper. It occurred to Melissa that she had not talked to Denise about Barry Ford since the day he and she had gone on that idyllic picnic on Bainbridge Island. *Everything* had happened since that time—Danny's death, Jonathan's unexpected invitation to supper, and that gossip item about Barry and Anne Whittaker.

Melissa had been in a swirl ever since. Danny, Barry, and Jonathan all spun about her, drawing her down into a vortex of conflicting emotions. She had been having trouble getting to sleep each night. Wherever she went in the apartment, she could sense the presence of Danny there, the aura of Barry Ford's personality, the inimitable influence of Jonathan's cool intellect.

Even that morning, as she made breakfast, she had felt the presence of all three in the place around her. And she remembered how she had blundered about, trying to put the milk back in the cabinet rather than in the refrigerator. She knew she was being silly about this—but there was nothing she could *do*. She was hopelessly confused and mixed up about her true feelings.

"You like Barry?"

There was a pause. Melissa began picking at her salad. She wondered when it had arrived. She had been thinking too hard to notice.

"Of course I like him."

"Love him?"

Melissa dropped her fork and took her time in picking it up. "How do I know that? How does anybody know that?"

She told Denise about the way he had announced his health qualifications by showing her his H.I.V.-negative card. She told her about his family and his way of joking with her. She told her everything she could and then suddenly she went silent.

"I for one have absolutely no sympathy for you," Denise said.

"Here you are, running around with a marvelous hunk following you everywhere you go—even to the ladies' room, I'm sure—and you totally ignore him. And you're on all kinds of excellent terms with the greatest quarterback in the N.F.L.—bodywise, certainly. There's a college president who wants to get you into bed at the first opportunity—"

"Denny!" Melissa yowled, although she knew how close to the target her sister's words had struck.

"It's the damned truth, you stupid woman," Denise said, jamming her fork into her lettuce and radicchio.

"I've got a message you can forward for me, Denny."

"To Jonathan?"

"Yes. Tell him I'll probably be in touch with him about an interview."

Thirty-three

At Ada's

Ada's was located across the street from the Channel 8 building. It was a typical hole-in-the-wall bar. Because Channel 8 functioned as a twenty-four-hour operation, Ada did too. The clientele was generally supportive of the overall policy of "live and let live." That is, if someone from Channel 8 was in a conversation that appeared private, no one would butt in. If, however, someone was alone and seemed in need of company, anyone would join in immediately without waiting to be asked.

At a table in the corner of Ada's Darryl Hobbs and Police Commissioner Curtis Mitchell were seated on that same Thursday at midnight in what was obviously a private conversation for two. It was plain to see that they wanted to be left alone. And no one made a move to bother them.

Yet, on closer observation, the conversation was not all that deep or heavy—at least at its inception.

"Who's Ada?" the police commissioner wondered aloud.

"Ada from Decatur," Hobbs responded.

Mitchell frowned. "I'm sorry?"

"You never shot craps?" Hobbs asked in astonishment.

"Sure I've shot craps." Mitchell's eyes widened. "Eight-er from Decatur! Eight-er is Ada. Ada's! For Channel 8." The big man chuckled. "I like it."

"Her name really is Cecilia, but she's called Sicily by her family because her parents came from Sicily." Hobbs smiled. "But she's Ada to us around here."

"Anyway, I've got some updating for you."

Hobbs nodded. "Royce reported yesterday. He looks good."

"How's he getting along with Melissa Bonner?"

"They seem to have hammered out a working arrangement," Hobbs said cautiously.

Mitchell laughed. "Royce is as tough as they come."

"Melissa is, too."

"So I've heard," the police commissioner said.

Hobbs leaned back. He seemed relaxed and rested for a change. "He's been at her side two days now."

"Establishing the modus operandi of any security system is the hardest part."

"This one was not without its glitches."

"I'm sure."

"We were lucky. I was able to cut a deal with the apartment house management where Melissa lives. There's a vacant single on her floor. Royce has already moved in. That way he can guard her from across the hall when she's in the apartment."

The commissioner nodded. "Standard operational procedure."

"Any other arrangement—like holing him up in her guest room—seemed likely to create more problems than it would solve." Hobbs shrugged. "And there was Melissa's situation to think about, too."

"What are the overall specs?"

"He rides shotgun in the car wherever she goes out in the area. He waits for her in the office and goes out on assignment with her. So, he accompanies her wherever she is—discreetly, of course."

"Okay." Mitchell hunched over his beer. "I looked over the list of odd things that have been happening. Something's cooking, Darryl. You know it and I know it. No use scaring the young lady, but she's in danger." He paused, gathering his thoughts. "Here's what I did. I've alerted one of my top homicide detectives to the details of the case. He's already had a brief conversation with Royce."

"When?"

"Late Wednesday night. At Royce's room. My man's on the night shift. They've compared notes on the killing of the dog, on the car following Ms. Bonner, and on anything else that might provide a clue as to what's going on."

"Good."

"Royce is not bad at digging up evidence. And he also knows

how to put disparate facts together. He's got a good imagination. Incidentally, you didn't tell me about the missing dog food."

Hobbs spread his hands. "I didn't know."

"Royce knows. He dug it out of Melissa last night when they were talking. In the past two or three weeks Melissa had noticed that Danny was fed an extra can or two of dog food."

Hobbs frowned. "And exactly what does that mean?"

"It means that someone got into that apartment and made friends with him. Then, on the day he was found by the lake, he was obviously taken out of the apartment and put to sleep before being led to the lake water."

"But how—?"

"Lax security at the apartment building. Whoever did it simply drove in the back, parked, and got it done in a very slick fashion. "Royce has already taken care of the security problems. He's had all the locks changed and tapes put on the windows. And he's rigged up an alarm system in the Bonner apartment. If she signals him, his beeper sounds, and he's in there in seconds."

Hobbs shuddered. "Even with all those safety precautions, I'm still nervous about Melissa."

"I would be too, if I were you," Mitchell said ominously.

"So far, the death of the dog is the most important link in the chain of events, isn't it?" Hobbs asked. "I mean, the other things are minor compared to what happened to Danny."

"True. But in all the excitement and the visual focus on Melissa Bonner, we had been unaware of one important factor. There was a burglary last week at Denise Bonner's apartment. Royce dug that out of Melissa yesterday."

Hobbs shrugged. "I knew nothing about it."

Mitchell gave him a brief rundown, and then went on: "My guy is wrestling with that one. It doesn't really compute—unless it is some kind of spillover from the Melissa Bonner affair. I mean, there's always the idea somewhere in the back of our minds that since Melissa is the enemy, or the feared one, Denise, by extension, is also the enemy, or the feared one. Thus *both* sisters are potential victims."

"There's more to it than that," Hobbs said dismally.

"What do you mean?"

"There's another connection. It was Denise who gave Danny to Melissa."

Mitchell's eyes widened. "I didn't know that!"

"It's true. There's also a poison pen letter she got today."

"I'll let my guy know all that tonight—if he doesn't know it already." Mitchell lifted his beer glass. "This is an in-depth operation, Darryl. I've instructed my man to dig as deeply as he can into the backgrounds of all the people connected with the targeted victim."

Hobbs closed his eyes. "Targeted victim," he repeated. "I *hate* that!"

"That's what she is." The police commissioner looked up at Hobbs and kept his voice level. "There's somebody who worries me in this affair. 'Affair' in its generic sense. Although, come to think of it, I don't know if it *is* strictly generic."

Hobbs nodded thoughtfully. "I guess you're talking about Barry Ford."

"It strikes me that all these things started happening just at the time Barry Ford arrived in town."

"Actually both before and after."

"I don't know how to phrase this, Darryl, but I need to know. How intimate are they?"

Hobbs shrugged. "Since we don't know for sure, let's assume they are sleeping together."

"There's a lot of pride, a lot of ego, in the man. That kind of thing." Mitchell shook his head. "I've told Royce. He passes it off as just another minor problem. 'Don't worry about it,' he tells me with that expressionless face."

"You think Ford may be involved?" Hobbs found it hard to articulate his suspicions.

"Even if he's involved only with *her* and not with the chain of events, he's a powder keg. The slightest spark can set him off. And your star sportscaster could be hurt."

"She's hurt already," Hobbs said sadly.

"Isn't Ford going to be out of town this coming weekend?"

"Yeah," said Hobbs. "The Sea Lions had two games at home. This week they're on the road—Los Angeles, I think."

"The L.A. Raiders. It'll be a tight game. The Sea Lions may win. Ford is doing a lot to make that team a valuable property for its owners."

"More power to him," Hobbs murmured.

"Oh? Think about the people who were making out when the team was losing."

Hobbs glanced up, startled. "The big money bettors?"

"Exactly. Now, you could have a scenario where the people who were winning bets with the Sea Lions rolling over dead every Sunday are becoming anxious about losing money. If the Sea Lions continue to win under Ford—these people are out big bucks."

Hobbs was puzzled. "Wouldn't the big money simply bet on the Sea Lions to win?"

"Sure. But there's really no such thing as a sure winner. *Anything* can happen on the field. But there *is* such a thing as a sure loser. And the Sea Lions have had that with Reggie Brown as their quarterback."

Hobbs traced through the story line. "Then they might be interested in ruining the chances of the Sea Lions—say, by unnerving Barry Ford, the fair-haired boy, through harassing Melissa Bonner."

"Something like that, Darryl. Just speculation." Mitchell waved his hand in the air.

There was a short silence as the commissioner worked at his beer. When he leaned forward, Hobbs instinctively leaned forward, too.

"I hear it from the grapevine that there are important figures in the city here who don't thoroughly approve of Ms. Bonner's method of operation either. I mean, she likes to make waves."

"It's a newscaster's job to make waves, Curtis."

"Oh, I know it. And the people I'm talking about know it, too. That doesn't mean they *like* it. It doesn't mean that they won't try to put a stop to it—if it continues to bother them."

Hobbs considered. "You're talking big money. You're talking muscle. You're talking enforcement."

The police commissioner nodded. "These guys don't fool around. I don't want you to get into too much of a swivet over this, but if I were you, I'd watch out where your star sportscaster is poking her nose these days."

"Point taken," Hobbs said. He finished his beer. "Another, Curtis?" He pointed to his empty glass.

"Thank you, no." He got up and shook hands with Hobbs. "I'll be in touch."

Hobbs nodded and called for the check.

Thirty-four

Sound Bites

At Friday afternoon's newsroom meeting in the conference room, Melissa Bonner raised her hand at the beginning of the session. Hobbs pointed to her.

"The University of Seattle Timberwolves won the Northwest Basketball Conference this year for the first time, prompting the college's athletic association to request funds from the administration to build a new basketball stadium.

"In a strategic countermove, an anti-sports group of faculty members have decided to petition the administration to drop its football program and put all its money into academic programs.

"I can get an interview with Dr. Jonathan Stark, the president of the university. I think we can get an exclusive. I want to know if you think it'll work out for us. The athletic-academic controversy has been raging for some time on the American college campus. This looks like a good deal to me. Dr. Stark has raised the academic standards at Seattle and is no enemy of the sports program. I'm sure we'll get a balanced viewpoint from him."

"I like it," Hobbs said, scribbling on his note pad. "It looks like the kind of thing the public will eat up. There's plenty of money in college sports."

One by one the staff members voiced approval of the story. In the end, Hobbs waved Melissa out. "Go with it."

In minutes Melissa was on the phone to Denise, who put her through to her boss immediately. Melissa told Jonathan what was in the works. He thanked her for arranging the interview and invited her to bring her crew around as soon as possible. He agreed to let her shoot the interview inside his office.

Royce was waiting around, listening to one side of the phone conversation. "We're off," Melissa told him joyfully.

Royce rose to his feet. "Let's go."

He helped Kubo and Griswold stash the heavy equipment in the back of the station van and they all got in. In no time at all they were barreling into the campus parking lot. After they removed the equipment from the van the four of them were trooping across the campus to the Administration Building.

Denise let them in the office, where Dr. Stark was standing by the window. He said hello to Melissa and waited while the crew set up the lights and sound equipment.

"Who's that?" Stark asked Melissa, indicating Royce.

"He's my bodyguard," she told him. Stark was not one to over-react. He simply looked briefly at Melissa, to see how she had intended the explanation, and then shifted his gaze to Andrew Royce.

"I understand. The break-in at Denise's. The death of Danny."

"Yes," Melissa said. "Mr. Royce," she went on, "I'd like you to meet Dr. Stark." She flushed slightly. "We go back a long way. I guess you could put it like that."

"I do put it that way," Stark said, shaking hands with a smile. His eyes continued to assess Royce. What he found there appeared to satisfy him, although he seemed to be searching for something over and above the man himself.

"And he works with the crew when I'm with the crew," Melissa was saying.

"You seem to be a very fit person," Stark said to Royce. "You keep your eye on Melissa. She's a particular favorite of mine."

Melissa was surprised to see the glint in Royce's eyes. It was such a brief thing, she did not know if she had actually *seen* a glint. But something transformed his face for a split second.

"I'll do that, Dr. Stark," Royce said with the shadow of a smile.

Then it was work as usual. Melissa got her crew going and the president of the University of Seattle watched in fascination as the lights were set up, the reflectors mounted, and the sound equipment carefully monitored and tested. There was discussion over what Dr. Stark would be doing as he spoke, and it was decided he would be sitting at his desk, with his back to the window that looked out over the campus. It was a pretty sight.

There were no flubs or glitches and the crew was ready in fifteen minutes. Melissa had discussed the sequence of events with Stark: he would open with a statement of his own; then she would ask him several questions in a face-to-face interview. Afterward she and the crew would get random comments from campus figures outside the office.

As planned, he began his statement with a list of the typical sports almost any college in the country indulged in: football, basketball, baseball, soccer, lacrosse, tennis, track and field, swimming, and so on. The main attractions, of course, were football and basketball, with very little competition from the others.

He acknowledged that the public got its perception of the universities from their sports programs and that sports revenues generally went to finance athletic scholarships, stadiums, and other allied programs. Also, it was usual for alumni groups to support most generously those universities with the more high-profile sports programs.

On the other hand, funds were equally necessary to enhance the academic image of universities and to support merit scholarships, the acquisition of renowned teachers, and the development of strong academic libraries. The main purpose of a college was to educate the students who spent their four years there.

In struggling with each other for public attention and support, both sides of the academic entity—athletics and scholarship—only harmed one another, and did simultaneous and irreparable damage to the full-bodied educational system. Both could exist, he said, in a yin-and-yang balance, a synergism in which each could support, nourish, and strengthen the other.

When Stark had finished, Melissa moved in for a Q and A.

"In your statement, Dr. Stark, you hinted that there are some people who do not like campus sports. Are you one of those people?"

"In no way," Stark said. "I love sports, particularly football. It is a contact sport that is exciting and real. I enjoy the combination of complex strategy and physical skill."

"I see," Melissa said. "Isn't it also true that the universities make a great deal of money through their sports programs? Don't you feel that to drop sports from a college's activities would be depriving the school of revenue? I mean, of course, that without the sports program, don't you think the price of tuition would go up?"

"Of course it could," Jonathan Stark answered. "But some of my faculty believe that if the University of Seattle dropped its sports program, it might leave openings for students who are more interested in academic achievement than in sports records—and that quite possibly the price of tuition might go down, not up." He paused. "After all, sports programs do cost money. Big money. The stadium, for example. The locker rooms. The equipment. However, we simply cannot be sure what would happen. But as I said before, sports programs do bring in money."

"Do you see the move by this faculty group to ban football as a number one step in a drive to drop all competitive sports from Seattle's athletic program?"

"I do not. I feel that those on our faculty who have an anti-sports bias have selected football as a target because of the team's so-far unfortunate season."

"That leads to my next question. If your faculty committee manages its aim and does drop football, will basketball be the next target?"

Stark smiled. "I doubt that with the sudden popularity of basketball this year they would have a chance to do so. A winning season does a lot to enhance the particular sport involved. That is the reason I believe the best way to approach the problem is to leave our sports program exactly as it is now."

"That's all well and good, Dr. Stark. However, I understand that an action committee has been formed already, and that if the administration—you—refuses to listen to and act upon their petition to drop football, they are prepared to demonstrate in public for their stand."

"We have made our intentions clear. You must understand, the demonstrations envisioned are not at all like the many campus demonstrations of the 1960s. We envision no trouble here at the University of Seattle. Yet, as I have continually said, I regret the disruption in our general program of studies."

"Thank you, Dr. Jonathan Stark."

Melissa turned to her crew. "That's a wrap."

She thanked Stark and shook hands with him. The two of them chatted briefly while Royce helped Kubo and Griswold pack up their heavy equipment. In five minutes they were out of the office.

"We're going to walk through the campus to get student reaction," Melissa told her crew. She turned to Kubo. "Tak, you and Grizzy with me?"

Kubo nodded.

Once outside the Administration Building they encountered a dark-haired, blue-eyed coed who seemed outgoing and anxious to speak. Griswold shouldered his camera and Kubo waved the microphone wand over her head.

Melissa confronted her. "There's a move afoot on campus to drop football from the university's activities. How does that strike you?"

The coed smiled. "I think that's cool. Maybe then there will be more money for women's basketball!"

A muscular jock followed the brunette.

MELISSA: A group of faculty members wants to banish football from the university. How do you feel about that?

THE JOCK: Bad call. We need both. What's wrong with having football *and* serious studies? After all, the two are not actively competitive with one another. Let's leave things the way they are.

Two others:

MELISSA: What will happen if the university should decide to abandon sports and turn itself into a study machine?

MALE STUDENT: It'll sink to the bottom of Puget Sound.

MELISSA: What do you think about dropping football from the university's program? Are you for it or against it? And why?

FEMALE STUDENT: I'm against it, even though I could never be considered a football fan. It is my belief that sports of all kinds are a very positive thing in college life.

The answers, pro and con, were about evenly matched.

Once back in the Channel 8 building, Melissa turned the material over to Elmer Layden to cull into a workable film segment for the evening news.

When he finished, Melissa was surprised at how tight the whole thing looked. Dr. Stark's statement had been pared down and his answers to Melissa's questions were edited down to sound bites. With those changes, it was a good story—the perfect kind of initial presentation that might be the prelude to a major, interesting campus confrontation.

Thirty-five

The Joggers

Although Barry Ford really did not need to wield any magic tricks to win the game between the Sea Lions and the Raiders that Sunday afternoon, he was there not only in spirit but in the flesh—quick and sharp and in total control of the team. And of the game itself.

Melissa watched him on her television screen. At one point she found herself waving her arms and cheering Ford while he successfully evaded a crushing linebacker whom he sent face-first into the turf.

Then she wondered sheepishly if Andrew Royce, across the hall, had heard her cheering away for her prize quarterback. Somehow the thought of that embarrassed her and she dug her fists into her thighs. But her excitement surfaced again anyway. In the end, she was glad the Sea Lions won the game for Ford.

Her relationship with Andrew Royce had improved over the days he had been serving as her safety net. Once she had slipped and called him "Andy." Usually she confined herself to a stilted "Mr. Royce." Or "you."

At least he practiced what he preached. He was in some ways an invisible, unencounterable, nonentity. But in other ways, he was hardly that. He was flesh and blood, male, and solidly dependable.

She felt rested, relaxed, and ready to take on the world Monday morning. Royce picked her up right on schedule and they rode down in the elevator together. They spoke little. She was bright in her warm-ups. He was natty in his usual white-collar uniform.

In the garage she jogged in place, waiting for him to get her Range Rover going, and then ran across the floor to the ramp up into the street. She was ahead of him when she came out into the sunlight.

As she started the second leg of her jogging course, she realized someone was coming along behind her. She turned. Barry Ford, in his own warm-up gear, waved at her. He had a big grin on his face. She waved back, forgetting for the moment that she was angry at him for being linked with Anne Whittaker in last week's newspaper and for not having called her during his week in L.A.

Ford was a half block away, and he jogged faster to catch up to her while she slowed down. Suddenly, from out of nowhere, Melissa saw her Range Rover slam around the corner, pull over to the curb beside her, and screech to a grinding stop. Instantly Andrew Royce was out of the four-wheeler, crouched in a tense arc, and aiming his .45 at Barry Ford in the traditional two-handed grip.

"Back off, mister," snapped Royce in a menacing whisper.

Barry Ford was stunned. He stopped. His hands were up, his face a mixture of comic astonishment, actual fear, and strained puzzlement.

"Jesus Christ!" Melissa shouted. "Put that goddamned gun down, Andy!"

Barry Ford was standing with his hands up, unable to figure out what was happening.

"Your I.D.?" Royce ordered, holding out one hand as he rapidly approached Ford.

"What the hell do you think I'm doing? I'm out jogging. I don't carry a goddamned I.D. every time I go out for a walk!"

"Who are you?" It was obvious Royce knew who he was. It was also obvious that Royce was covering up a huge grin that might break out at any moment.

"I'm Barry Ford, goddamn it! Who are you—that's the question of the moment!"

"He's my fucking bodyguard," Melissa said, letting all her irritability out in one gush of steam. She turned to Royce and advanced on him. "Well, that's just great, Mr. Royce! You've finally saved my life from a demented mugger! How does it feel? You're a hero—how's that? Put that ridiculous gun down and get back in the car! This is a friend of mine! Can't you see that?"

Royce did not smile. He lowered the automatic, but continued to face Ford, who was still wondering whether to go toward Melissa.

She was next to Royce now, and she smashed her fist into his upper left arm. "It's all over, stupid. Mr. Ford and I are going to jog together—can you get that through your thick head? I want you to follow us. I'm sure the neighborhood is full of dangerous bandits."

Andrew Royce reholstered the automatic, turned, and looked at Melissa. "Anything you say, Ms. Bonner." He glanced back at Ford, gave just the slightest suggestion of a smile, and strode around the Range Rover and got into the driver's seat. He started it up with a flare of exhaust.

Ford was beside himself. "What's this all about?"

Melissa was staring at him without smiling. "Things have changed, Barry," she said. "You've been out of town for a week. Danny was drowned." Tears appeared in her eyes. "Somebody killed my dog!"

Ford's face drained of color. "Danny!" He reached out to take her in his arms. She slapped him away. "I'm sorry." He frowned at her rejection, looking puzzled.

"The station hired a bodyguard for me. I've been threatened."

"Threatened?" Ford repeated, truly stunned.

"You know," she said. "Message: Your dog is dead. You're next!"

"Does this moron who's guarding you suspect me?" Ford asked in astonishment.

"Of course not," she shot back. "I don't know, though. Maybe—"

"Why are you mad at me?" Ford asked, a hurt look on his face.

"Nothing, really," Melissa said, her tone somewhat lofty. "I know you *had* to see Ms. Anne Whittaker down in Los Angeles. I read all about that, of course, in the gossip column."

Ford blinked and looked away. "God. I had a feeling—"

The door to the Range Rover opened and Royce got out, approaching the two of them on the sidewalk. "Excuse me, ma'am," he said directly to Melissa. "Are you two going to continue your conversation on the sidewalk here, or are you going to jog?"

Melissa stared at Royce for a moment, and then turned to Ford. "Shall we jog?" she asked him.

"But of course," Ford said.

Melissa dismissed Royce with her hand. He got back in the Range Rover and, as Melissa and Ford began to run along the sidewalk, he started to follow them at a short distance.

"There's nothing between Anne and me," Ford said after a moment.

"I believe you. I believe you." Melissa said it twice to make it obvious that she did not believe him.

"What can I say, then?" Ford looked grim. "I was going to ask you out to dinner tonight."

"Then ask."

"How about dinner tonight?" Ford asked.

"No."

"Because you're angry at me for seeing Anne?"

"Maybe. Mostly because I can't imagine what it would be like to be alone with you with my bodyguard sitting within ten feet."

"Ten feet? Is that part of the contract?"

"Yes." Melissa said, stone-faced. "It's no fun being a target, I can tell you that."

They jogged along in silence for a few minutes.

"You like this guy, huh?" Ford asked, with a side glance at Melissa.

"I hate him!" Melissa said. "He thinks I feel safe because he's hovering around me all the time. Actually, I'm sick of the sight of him."

Ford grinned. "He seems to take the job seriously. I thought for sure I was at the end of the line when he zeroed in on me."

"Don't try to be funny, Barry," Melissa said. "And look, call me later in the week."

When they arrived at Melissa's apartment, Melissa waved to Royce to stop the Range Rover and come to her.

"Andrew Royce," she said, "I'd like you to meet Barry Ford." Royce nodded. "Sorry I had to come on so strong."

Ford looked Royce up and down. "You seem to know your business."

"Yeah," Royce said.

"Nice meeting you," Ford said.

"That Anne Whittaker," Royce said in a low voice. "She as sexy as she looks on the big screen?"

The temperature dropped forty degrees around the three of them. Barry Ford glared at Royce. Melissa glared at Barry Ford. And Andrew Royce got in the Range Rover and headed it toward the garage entrance.

"*Ciao,*" he called out to Ford as he swerved into the down ramp.

Thirty-six

The New Look

T im Harrison was in Hobbs's office, trying to patch up some of the wounds that had been opened at Channel 8. The bulk of the assessment team had departed Friday after work; Harrison was staying in Seattle to confer with Hobbs this Monday and to turn in his report by the end of the week.

"Assessment is a nasty little game," Harrison was saying now. "You and I have not always seen eye to eye. But I trust our little differences have not made our visit any more difficult than the normal visit of good friends." Harrison beamed. "I have already begun to write up the report. All the issues are decided. My conversation this morning with you is simply to apprise you of where we have gone and what conclusions we have arrived at during our work here."

"I appreciate it," Hobbs said quietly.

"As I believe you are aware," Harrison went on, "the entire exercise was originally conceived to strengthen Channel 8's news department."

Hobbs had not known that management had instructed Simmons and Lockwood to take that tack. Indeed it was the news department—Hobbs's baby—that actually gave the channel its image and provided it with its competitive edge.

"We began our assessment by screening all the newscasts for the preceding two weeks and analyzing each, detail by detail. Then we took each of the newscasters one by one and examined them minutely: weather, local news, national news, sports, home improvement, gourmet cooking, women's features, children, and so on. The details of those assessments have been noted in our daily meetings in the screening room. And you have typed transcripts of what I said during all of them." He drew up his chair closer to the desk and leaned toward Hobbs. "Now comes the gist of the assessment—what hasn't as yet been reported."

Hobbs took a deep breath and closed his eyes. "Let's get on with it."

"The main point is that Channel 8, for all its vigor and energy, just doesn't seem to have a proper team of co-anchors."

Of course Pam Morton and Rick Jones were not Dan Rather and Connie Chung, but did it matter all that much? Apparently, yes.

"It seemed obvious to all of us on the team that the present co-anchors had to go," Harrison went on. "Or, perhaps, be moved into another slot somewhere. The team then looked over the possibilities of replacing the two of them with members already on the staff. But the only contenders did not quite seem up to it. I refer, of course, to Ian Chambers and Jill Jamison." Harrison took a deep breath.

"Ian Chambers is certainly a mature and charming man. But he's still caught up in a time warp of the campus demonstrations and the anti–Vietnam War movement. It's as if he never grew out of it.

"As for Jill Jamison, she's an excellent women's features announcer. She looks like the most comfortable housewife in the world." Harrison cleared his throat.

"Because of the deficiency of potential anchorpersons on your staff, Simmons and Lockwood proposes that Channel 8 bring in one or two outside anchors."

Hobbs glared at Harrison. "And that's it? Look here, Harrison! I've been working for months on the problem of replacing Morton and Jones with someone here. Don't forget our ace in the hole. She's the best thing that's happened to this station since I've been here."

Harrison's eyes glazed. "You're talking about Melissa Bonner."

"I sure as hell am," Hobbs said. "She's interesting. She's sharp. She's beautiful. She dresses well. She speaks like an angel—although not all the time. She's our top-drawing newscaster and right now she's in the sports department. All we have to do is move her over to news and she's our number-one anchorperson. And she doesn't need a co-anchor there with her to keep her from drifting."

"Mr. Hobbs, a true anchor personality must be a totally objective individual. Ms. Bonner is in no way totally objective. Everything she does, every word she says, every move she makes, bespeaks Ms. Bonner herself. Her ego sticks out a mile."

"I like the sight of it," Hobbs murmured, "no matter how big it is."

"In my own opinion she could never be trusted to read a purely unbiased report of a news event. She would certainly twist it into a personal connection of some kind." Harrison's face was struggling to retain its good nature. His forehead was wrinkling dangerously. His eyes were glaring in spite of his attempts to keep them focused neutrally.

"She blew that assignment at the Kingdome," Harrison went on.

"She made a mistake," Hobbs said blithely.

"But the mistake underlined her key vulnerability. She simply cannot view things about her dispassionately. More than being simply objective, a good news anchor has to be able to distance herself from the story she is reporting so that he or she can present it without personal or political bias."

"Tell some of our famous co-anchors that little white lie," Hobbs said.

"There's a great deal of interest in news anchors today," Harrison said briefly. "Are they as biased politically as you say they are?"

"Sure they are!"

"I doubt it. The very fact that both major political parties in the U.S. claim to be misrepresented by the media proves to me at least that most of the media are not particularly on one side or the other."

Hobbs spread his hands in front of him. "Besides, Melissa and I went over her mistake that day very carefully. I know she will not make the same error again."

"Mr. Hobbs, people are always saying, 'I'll never make *that* mistake again.' And yet people—almost without exception—continue to make the same mistakes over and over every day of their lives."

Tim Harrison rose. "Actually, I've said all I came in to say. It's been a pleasure doing business with you, and I can say it's been instructive as well."

Hobbs laughed. "Seattle has that effect on some people."

Harrison shook Hobbs's hand turned to leave. At the door he paused.

He smiled at Hobbs. "I *love* Seattle."

Thirty-seven

"Old Devil Moon"

The sight of the yellow Jaguar XKE parked near the down ramp into Melissa's underground garage alerted her to the fact that the clientele of the apartment was visibly improving. In fact, the owner, Barry Ford, was seated under the wheel of the Jag, his head back on the seat rest, listening to the car radio.

As she pulled into her own parking space, she glanced over her shoulder and saw him. He was eyeing her without expression. "Oh, oh," said Melissa under her breath. She had told him on Monday morning she would call *him* sometime during the week. And here he was, as usual, doing it *his* way. Not hers.

Royce was looking across her at the Jag. "You've got a guest."

She said, "I'll fix him," and climbed out of the Range Rover.

"I'll bet," Royce said, mostly to himself.

She was striding purposefully across the concrete floor toward the Jag. "What are you doing here?" she demanded.

"I'm visiting Ms. Bonner," Ford said with a grin.

"Does Ms. Bonner know this?" Melissa asked.

"I haven't told her yet."

"You feel she will be thrilled to hear the news?"

"Not necessarily."

Melissa leaned against the Jag. "Get that car out of that parking space or I'll have to call the manager. He'll throw you out."

"But Mr. Murphy is an old friend."

She stared at him.

"We just signed a lifelong pact. *Amicitia aeterna.* Eternal friendship." Ford gave a big wide grin. "You'd be surprised what two tickets to the Kingdome can do in Seattle!"

"You're a bloody extortionist," she observed.

"Just an opportunistic sportsman."

"Why are you really here?"

"To ask Ms. Bonner out on a date."

Melissa looked at Royce, who was standing right behind her. "Does part of your job include shooting people who are bothering me?"

"Such contingencies are covered in the contract," Royce said.

"Then, at the count of three, if you are not out of this garage, Mr. Ford, I have authorized—nay, demanded—that Mr. Royce exercise his prerogative to defend my peace and tranquillity."

"Does Ms. Bonner like jazz?" Ford asked quietly.

"She may." The man, she thought irritably, was absolutely incorrigible.

"I have reserved a table at Herriman's," Ford went on.

Melissa blinked. Herriman's was a funky little jazz joint in the middle of the city. She knew that Freddie Cole, Nat King Cole's younger brother and Natalie Cole's uncle, was appearing there that week with his backups. And Freddie was one of her very favorite jazz pianists.

"Cole is there." He was looking directly into her eyes, not missing a beat.

"I see."

"There's dancing."

"I know."

"There's good food."

Melissa sighed. "I can't go without Mr. Royce."

"Oh, I've provided for Mr. Royce!"

"Aha!" Melissa's face lighted up.

"He'll eat in the kitchen."

Melissa stared at Royce. Royce's face was absolutely expressionless.

"A B.L.T. on toast for you, Mr. Royce," Ford said, looking at Royce with a faint smile. "I figured that was about your speed. *We'll* be having fresh Pacific halibut."

"How does that suit you, Mr. Royce?" Melissa asked, looking at him with amusement.

"As long as the B.L.T. isn't microwaved," Royce said.

"That can be arranged."

"I need to change," Melissa told Ford.

"I'll give you twenty minutes," Ford said offhandedly, as if timing, the absolute quintessence of the game of football, meant little when applied to the comfort and welfare of a woman.

She leaned closer to him. "How sportsmanlike of you," she said carefully.

They hit Herriman's about eleven fifteen. It was quiet and intimate, with the Cole trio on a break. Royce had been promoted from the kitchen to a place in the back corner. The table at which Ford and Melissa sat was visible to him.

"You're still mad at me," Ford said after the waiter had seated them and hastened off to bring the menus.

"Flaming mad," Melissa agreed. She glanced around to see who was in the place—if she knew anybody. There were several people who recognized Barry Ford. Some were whispering.

"Because of that gossipy little news item?" Ford looked annoyed. "I heard about it!"

"Now you're claiming that the news was wrong. That you never saw her while you were in Los Angeles."

"I saw her." He shrugged his shoulders.

"Close up, I'll bet."

"We ate together."

"You took her out."

"I took her out."

"And you bedded her down too, didn't you?" Her voice was low, but fierce.

"I broke off with her," said Ford steadily, tearing a roll in two and reaching for a pat of butter.

"How come there was nothing about *that* in the newspaper?" Melissa wondered.

"I have no idea. It did happen," Ford said pleadingly.

"You're a fast talker, Mr. Ford," Melissa replied. "How can I believe anything you say?"

"I may be a fast talker, but I'm not a liar."

"Now that's a contradiction in terms!"

Ford chewed on his French roll. "I tell you. I was going to call you, but I never did. If I had, I'd have heard about Danny." He looked down apologetically.

"That's right," Melissa said.

"You didn't call me," Ford came right back at her.

"At first I forgot you were going to be away last week."

"I figured if you didn't call, I didn't have to call either." Ford shook his head. "No, no. That sounds as lame as your excuse."

The waiter came and took their orders. Then he returned with the white wine. Freddie Cole and his two sidemen appeared and the music began. Melissa and Ford drank in silence, listening to the trio. So did everyone else in the place. The jazz created absolutely the right mood. Melissa felt herself being carried away. She was even feeling benevolent toward Barry Ford.

There was a postage-stamp-sized dance floor, but it didn't seem to get very crowded. When they had finished eating, Ford reached across to Melissa and gestured toward the dance floor.

At that very moment Freddie Cole started to play his arrangement of "Old Devil Moon," the E. Y. Harburg and Burton Lane love duet from *Finian's Rainbow*.

They did not speak. He held her lightly and moved across the dance floor with a kind of natural authority. She found it absolutely enchanting to follow his movements, even though they did not in any way resemble the one-two-three-four movements she had painstakingly learned in dancing class.

Instead, she found herself instinctively moving her body with his across the floor to the beat of the jazz. She seemed to be in a dream world all her own as she circled and floated through the air with him.

The solo ended. They sat down. The number wound up the set and Cole and his sidemen disappeared.

Melissa was transfixed by the romance of the moment. Why was she angry with Barry Ford? She had forgotten the details. It was stupid to dislike someone for an unknown reason. She felt herself being drawn more and more to him.

She found herself playing with her dessert. It was a mocha parfait. And then Barry Ford began talking.

"I lived in Fresno when I was in high school. We were not in the middle of the city at all. We had a lot of acreage where the farm was located. I got my dog, Jason, when I was in the eighth grade. He went everywhere with me. Jason was one of those old-fashioned collie dogs—a male Lassie. And I loved him."

Ford sipped at his coffee and leaned back.

"There was a spindly woods near the farm. Jason and I would walk over there in the afternoons and stroll under the trees. When the leaves were full in the spring and summer it was always shady and cool. You could go for a long ways without seeing anybody at all."

The waiter brought more coffee. Melissa happened to glance across the room and was surprised and interested to see that Royce was looking right at her. He dropped his eyes from her as she spotted him.

"I didn't have as much time to spend with Jason when I got into high school. Anyway, I was just getting interested in football. And I'd work out in the afternoons with the other guys. If I do say so myself, I was pretty good at it."

Cole and his sidemen came back on and began playing again. Ford continued talking.

"I saved up what money I could when I worked during the summer at a local market. I stacked cans on the shelves and did a turn at the cash register every so often. The management of the store was very good to me."

Ford leaned back again. He listened to the piano solo Cole was playing, a familiar Cole Porter tune.

"I was saving up my money to buy a secondhand car. I was in my senior year now and I thought I needed wheels to get dates." Ford thought about that. "I was right, you know. As soon as I got my car, I began going out to dances, to parties, and that kind of thing. Jason and I didn't have that much time to be together in the afternoons. Besides, now I was a football star. But he stuck by me and whenever I was around he was there for me."

The horn man did a solo with Freddie Cole backing him up.

"I came in late one night from a dance. I usually parked my car in the backyard next to the garage. We had two cars in the garage, in addition to my Chevy. That night my cousin from Visalia was visiting us and she had her car where mine was usually parked. I backed up in the driveway in the dark, figuring I would leave mine on the other side of the garage."

Ford looked down at his coffee cup and lifted it for another sip. "Jason was there in the dark. He was waiting for me to jump out and grab him in my arms. The wheels caught him, crushed his chest. He was dead when I got to him."

"My God!" Melissa whispered. She could feel the hot tears starting up in her eyes.

"Hey!" Ford said, turning to the trio. " 'My Funny Valentine.' Let's—"

They danced to it, Melissa shifting weightlessly in his arms.

When she sat down again, Melissa felt starry-eyed, wondering curiously if she looked that way. It really didn't matter. She felt soggy with romance. She had argued with Barry Ford, and he had argued with her. Then they had listened to the music and he had told her about his dog, Jason. And that had turned her soft and gooey inside.

The horrible fact that Barry Ford had accidentally killed his own very much loved dog was almost too much for her to absorb. What he was telling her was that at least she had not been responsible for her pet's death—the way he had been.

Yet in the long run, Melissa realized that Barry Ford had made a very important connection between himself and Melissa Bonner. Each had a beloved dog that died under pathetic circumstances.

At Melissa's apartment door the three of them stood awkwardly while Melissa fumbled for her key. Then she turned to Royce and reached inside her purse, removing the signaler with the button in the middle. She gestured with it toward his room.

He nodded. "Gotcha."

Then she led Ford into her own apartment. "How about a nightcap?" she asked him as she closed the door.

Outside, Royce checked that the door was locked and went into his own room.

It was about one in the morning when Royce heard Barry Ford say, "Good night."

He couldn't hear what Melissa said in return. Royce opened his door and watched as Ford disappeared down the hall and into the elevator.

Thirty-eight

September Song

He had told her it was simply a way of paying her back for the interview she had conducted on Friday. And now here she was, seated with Jonathan Stark in a well-placed box at the Moore Theater. They were listening to the Northwest Chamber Orchestra. Andrew Royce sat about eight feet away to their rear.

It was Bach Festival time. For years Melissa had loved the musical genius that had made Johann Sebastian Bach the most influential composer of the Western world.

For her, his work bubbled with the excitement of life and a kind of personal warmth. Bach's emotional power, dramatic sense, and melodic inspiration were qualities that were universally recognized.

Now, with the Partita in B Minor nearing its close, there was absolute silence from the concertgoers as they became enraptured by the sounds of the harpsichord. She sensed that Jonathan was as caught up in the performance as she was.

When the Partita in B Minor concluded the audience gave a standing ovation to the woman at the harpsichord who had performed the piece.

"Brava!" the audience shouted. "Brava!"

The next number was the concluding one for the evening and as soon as the performers had stood and bowed to the audience, people began to rise, gather up their things, and depart up the crowded aisles. Melissa saw that Andrew Royce was on his feet, concentrating on the movement around him. It occurred to her that a moment of almost universal stirring would be the obvious time for someone bent on assault to act and escape in the shifting crowd.

Royce followed Melissa and Jonathan out of the theater, keeping everyone nearby under close surveillance as they moved along the crowded corridors. When the three of them stood outside, Jonathan turned to Melissa and suggested that they stop down the street for some cappuccino. She nodded agreement and they turned and began walking down the sidewalk in the midst of the other departing concertgoers.

The evening was cool and Melissa put on the stole she had brought along just in case. Behind them, about ten feet back, Andrew Royce followed, still checking everyone as the crowd thinned about them, his eyes scanning each individual carefully.

Once in the après-musique café, Royce headed for the bar while Jonathan escorted Melissa to a small table beside the back wall. The place was not crowded, even with other concertgoers walking by and entering sporadically in small groups.

Jonathan said, "You've helped me immeasurably by arranging that interview about the football situation at Seattle."

"It was a good story," Melissa replied. "Thank *you*."

"I had hoped the faculty members would withdraw their petition to drop football. As yet, even though I've requested it, they haven't done so."

"How do the students feel about this?"

Jonathan shrugged. "The students are pretty levelheaded about the whole thing. I'm afraid in this instance it's the public that is more concerned. No one wants to lose a football program."

"True. Even with a losing team."

"On the other hand, sports recruitment is a very volatile situation on the American campus."

"And that's what makes it a good story."

She saw that Jonathan glanced at her quickly, with a half-smile forming.

"And a bad problem," she concluded.

"These are odd times, Melissa. And the times they are a-changing. We'll just have to wait and see what happens—if anything does."

The waiter brought their cappuccinos and left. Jonathan was staring down at the tablecloth.

"I've got to say that I'm concerned about you." His eyes rose to hers.

"Me?"

"Yes. Danny's death. Denise's break-in. And whatever else it is you're worried about."

Melissa debated a moment over how much she should reveal to him. He was more than an old friend. He was important to her. She thought she was important to him. But did he need to know *all* that was going on around her? No, she thought.

He looked up at her. "When I first saw that bodyguard in my office I realized that things were much worse than I had thought. No one is going to hire a permanent bodyguard for someone who isn't in danger."

"It'll all be settled soon," Melissa said softly.

"I'm sure it will be—somehow. But, meanwhile—"

"Meanwhile?"

"I'm glad you're in Mr. Royce's hands. I trust him."

"So do I," Melissa said.

There was a pause in the conversation. Then they both spoke at once:

"Melissa—"

"Jonathan—"

There was laughter. Jonathan said quickly, "You first."

"It was just a random thought. A pleasurable one."

"Oh?"

"About you. I'll always remember that wonderful cruise on your sailboat when you took our Literature of the Sea class out into Puget Sound. You've probably forgotten it, but it was a very special moment for us."

Jonathan smiled. "It was my way of showing you the sociological and physical effects of the sea's environment and its connection with the writings of Conrad, Smollett, and Melville."

"I remember we had just finished reading Hemingway's *The Old Man and the Sea*. Sailing really highlighted what you called the dramatic power that is a large part of the ocean's mystique."

"That's what I miss in this job—the classroom rapport between teacher and student."

"Have you ever taken a cruise in Canadian waters?" Melissa asked.

"Many times. But it's the longer voyages that give you the feel of the age-old challenge of the sea. The trip I really remember was the summer I sailed all the way to Washington, D.C."

"How can you do that?"

"You go south to the Panama Canal. You go through the canal and then you make your way up the east coast of Mexico. Tampico. Matamoros. From New Orleans you go down to Key West and up the east coast to Norfolk. There are miles and miles of protected water there, called the Intercoastal Waterway. From Norfolk you sail into Chesapeake Bay to the Potomac. And from there to Washington."

Melissa found herself staring at Jonathan with new interest. "I never knew all that."

"It's something every sailor learns."

"I mean, I never knew all that about you—oh, *adventuring* like that."

"Nothing to be shocked about."

"Certainly not. I'm impressed."

"By what?"

"Your—versatility."

He seemed uncharacteristically pleased. "Maybe we could go out sailing again sometime."

"I'd like that."

Jonathan picked up the check and they left the café, with Royce following. The bodyguard climbed in the back of Stark's BMW and they drove down to Melissa's apartment. As the three of them gathered at Melissa's door, Jonathan turned to Royce.

"Melissa and I will be talking for a short time. Thank you for your help tonight, Mr. Royce." He put out his hand and shook Royce's. Royce nodded to Melissa and unlocked his own door, while Melissa fumbled in her bag for her key.

Once inside Melissa turned to Jonathan. "Liqueur?"

"Excellent," he said. He sat on her couch, listening to her moving about in the kitchenette. Soon she brought out glasses and a bottle of Grand Marnier and joined him on the couch. After pouring the liqueur she looked over at him.

"I never let you have your say at the cappuccino bar," Melissa observed. "You remember—when we both spoke at once."

He shrugged. "That's why I'm here now. I've got to tell someone." Suddenly he seemed nervous. She stared at him. In no way was he the nervous type. "I've been closeted with a headhunter for several weeks now. And I think I've finally made up my mind."

She simply stared at him.

"Melissa, I'm going to make a change."

"Out of academe?" Melissa asked curiously. Somehow, it did not compute.

"Out of Seattle."

"Oh, no!" It was a heartfelt cry. There had always been a strong tie to the university there and to the man who had been first her favorite professor and then her favorite college president. Without him there— She dreaded what the future might hold. It was as if this was simply one more trial to add to the tribulations that were following her these days.

"The decision has been made," he said. She could see a sheen of perspiration on his upper forehead, just at the hairline. She was shocked. Never before had he ever appeared anxious. Was she affecting him? What was the decision he had made?

"Then what's the problem?"

"None, actually." He looked up, his eyes clear and watchful. "I'll be leaving next summer," he said. "I'm finishing out this year. And that's it."

"And you're going where?"

"New York," he said.

"But that's marvelous! It's a move up, then? You'll be president—"

"Actually, I'll be a vice president of one of the greater universities there. But the move is being made so I'll be in place when the present president steps down."

Melissa leaned forward. "I want an exclusive on this. When are you announcing?"

"Not until the spring."

She leaned back. "Damn."

"What do you think of the move?" He was watching her carefully.

"It's marvelous! And they came here to get you?"

He grinned. "Seattle isn't the backwash everybody thinks it is.

After all, it's the home of the grunge look, isn't it? And grunge rock?"

She giggled. "I wish it was true in the communications business."

"But it's a learning place," Jonathan said. "And you've learned here—both in school and in television. I have been wondering how to bring this up, but I have simply kept postponing it again and again. You're too good for Channel 8, Melissa. You're too good for the sports scene. You were made for better things."

She laughed. "Such as what?"

"Hard news, Melissa. The job of anchorperson for one of the big networks."

She leaned forward, teasingly. "You'd be surprised where I heard those very same words not ten days ago."

He seemed baffled.

"Barry Ford, the sports jock, told me that."

"You've been seeing him quite a bit."

She felt the blood rising from her neck into her face. "Yes." She glanced up. "It's really nothing," she said soberly, wondering how she could lie so glibly.

"He's right." Jonathan looked away. His composure seemed shaken. Then, briefly, he took a deep breath and looked at her for a moment. "I can't wait any longer. I've got to find out how you feel."

About Barry? she wondered.

"How would you like to come along with me?"

She was so stunned she could think of nothing to say. He was asking her to go along with him, she realized—but what did that really mean?

"As my wife," he said finally, looking across at her.

She blinked. Here was a wonderful friend who had become much more to her than a friend—and could certainly become *the* man in her life—with a marriage proposal.

She closed her eyes momentarily, trying to sort her way through her feelings. It would be so easy to make a decision—and, at the same time, so very difficult. She was suffused with an inability to see where she was going, a kind of psychological impasse.

"There's more," he said with a half smile.

She was staring at him. She was still unable to get her voice going. Now she found herself waiting to hear more.

"These have been weeks of long conversations," Jonathan said. "I've been thinking of you all along, too. I have a very good contact in one of the major television networks in New York. My contact works in the newsroom of the network. Actually, he runs the newsroom. In fact, he's my cousin. I've arranged for you to have an audition with him—if and when you feel up to it."

Melissa slumped back, almost unable to keep from going limp all over. A move to the top had always been part of her plans for the future—and now here all those wishes seemed to be coming true. In shadowy form, at least, they *had* come true. The big chance was there. If she blew an important opportunity like that, what did *anything* matter?

It was as if she was floating around somewhere under the ceiling of her apartment. And she was looking down on a distraught young woman whom she knew only slightly. And what the young woman was saying did not synchronize with her thoughts.

"I'll have to think about it," Melissa said. "This is all—pretty sudden."

"I understand." Jonathan smiled again. He was his own cool self once more. All his patrician bearing was in full control. "Take your time."

Melissa found herself thinking about what Denise had told her. And now she knew that Denise had been right. Jonathan *was* in love with her. Stupidly, she had not known. She had only half-dreamed it.

Jonathan reached for a package she had seen him bring in from the car. "I forgot to give you this."

She unwrapped the package and found a book, *Reel Women: Pioneers of the Cinema*, by Ally Acker. "You remembered my interest in women filmmakers," she said as she leafed through the pages quickly. "Thank you!"

She put the book down, leaned across the couch, and put her arms around him, kissing him on the cheek. Then she could feel his arms around her, holding her tightly to him as he kissed her tenderly and thoroughly on the mouth.

She was immediately shaken by the strength of her own passion as he held her. Then suddenly he lifted her from the couch and stood with her in his arms. Slowly he let her go and stood eyeing her fondly.

Did she love him? The answer seemed obvious and instantaneous. She would not allow her mind to reach out to grapple with whatever thoughts and feelings she might have about Barry Ford.

"I'll—I'll think about it," she stammered.

"Good." He reached out and took her chin, lifting her head just slightly and kissing her warmly once again. She was shaking when he moved away.

Then he was gone.

She sat slumped on the couch for a long time as all sorts of emotions swirled through her. Passion. Joy. Sensuality. Desire. Calm. Wonder. Need.

Thirty-nine

Pleading the Cause

Barry Ford parked his Jaguar in the visitor's slot in the garage under the Channel 8 building and got out. He knew the newsroom was on the eighth floor, and in less than a minute he was stepping out of the elevators and looking across a sea of faces and computer terminals. It was two o'clock in the afternoon.

Ford had on a sports shirt open at the collar, jeans, and loafers. He opened the door that said CHANNEL 8 NEWSROOM and noticed that all conversation immediately came to a halt. It was obvious that everyone there recognized him.

"Help you, Mr. Ford?" asked a young man in his late teens.

Ford nodded. "I'm looking for Ms. Bonner."

"Follow me," the teenager said. He led Ford through the desks and computer monitors to her glassed-in portion of the room.

Melissa was seated at her desk, and Ford could see Andrew Royce at a little table in the corner. When the teenager knocked on her door, Melissa waved him inside, and then she saw Ford. She looked surprised.

As Ford entered he saw that Royce was about to leave the office. "Hi, Melissa," Ford said to her, and waved Royce back to his desk. "Stick around, Royce."

Melissa was looking up at Ford with a crooked smile. "To what do we owe this unexpected honor?"

"I've got a proposition for you, Melissa."

"I'm not in the mood today. Unless, of course, you've come to deliver proof that you've broken up with Anne Whittaker."

"That's not quite the reason I'm here."

Melissa smiled. "Why is it that I'm not at all surprised?"

Ford sat down in the chair facing Melissa's desk. "Perhaps it's because you're a most difficult person to fool."

"I do pride myself on my journalistic acumen."

"And I am here to test your journalistic acumen. I'd like to offer my services to the sports world—specifically the world of football."

"In what way?"

"By helping keep football at the University of Seattle."

Melissa leaned forward. There was a brightness in her eyes, as if she sensed a good story in the making.

"How would you go about that?"

"I want to plead its cause on your television station."

"There's an attention-grabbing headline: 'Football star comes out for football.' "

Royce and Ford laughed.

"Come on, I'm kidding. I like the idea. Keep on talking."

"I'd just like to get in a few points. Woo the public, sort of. I'd hate to see my fellow football players at Seattle lose their chance at the game."

"An interview?" Melissa asked, studying Ford intently.

"However you want to set it up. Friday night Dr. Stark gave a well-balanced and intelligent overview of football—and of sports generally—on college campuses. I'd like to add a few things about football specifically. An interview would be fine. Face-to-face or a talking head?"

"Let's try for face-to-face."

"Great!"

Melissa thought a moment. "I've got to float this past Hobbs. He's the boss. But I think he'll go for it."

Melissa left the office and crossed the newsroom.

Ford turned slightly. "How's it going?"

"Tip top," Royce said.

"I mean about Melissa. Any idea who killed Danny?"

"Not yet. We're working on it."

"I'm concerned. Somebody's after her."

"It does look that way," Royce conceded.

"She's a TV star. And pretty. Those are the women these nutty fans go after." Ford was watching Royce.

"So I've heard," Royce said evenly. "You know," he went on

before Ford could speak, "you don't owe the University of Seattle anything. Why are you doing this interview to help Dr. Stark?"

Ford hesitated. "I think he's being pushed around by that basketball bunch. I understand Melissa used to go out with their coach."

Royce nodded. "So I hear. And?"

"You make Stark look bad, and O'Hara comes out the Golden Boy."

"From one Golden Boy to the other," Royce noted.

"Me? Not according to Melissa. She sees tarnish in the cracks." Royce smiled.

"How did they part?" Ford asked. "I mean Melissa and Scott O'Hara."

"Amicably," Royce responded.

"A nothing word that could mean anything," Ford scoffed.

"You suspect O'Hara of something?" Royce asked with interest.

Ford shrugged. At that moment Melissa strode into the room, beaming. "Hobbs thinks it'll be the greatest thing since the Hula Hoop." She sank down at her desk and looked over at Ford. "You all set for tonight's six-o'-clock news?"

"Sure," he said, leaning back in his chair.

She was smiling now. "Maybe this will make up for that open letter I addressed to you. And the Jack Adams interview."

Ford smiled. "I'd forgotten all about them."

"Oh, sure! Come on, let's get to work."

Forty

"Let the Games Begin!"

The actual interview that night on the six-o'-clock news was reminiscent of the original argument between Barry Ford and Channel 8's Melissa Bonner, although of course it was held in a much friendlier spirit.

Melissa first introduced Barry Ford as the quarterback for the Seattle Sea Lions and gave a brief background sketch of his previous experience. Then she reprised her own recent interview with Dr. Jonathan Stark.

"Although we thought the statement by Dr. Stark was remarkably balanced and fair, we learn that many pro-football fans are upset over any talk whatsoever about dropping any kind of sports. Let's hear what a working quarterback has to say about the move here to ban football from the campuses."

MELISSA: Mr. Ford, what is your feeling about the proposal of the academic group to shut down football at the University of Seattle?

FORD: I'm against it.

MELISSA: What bothers you most about the banning of football?

FORD: Banning football from the university would in effect cause the University of Seattle to vanish from the sports scene in America.

MELISSA: Don't you think men could train for professional football careers without going to college? Isn't one of the problems that the men who play football really don't get a college education anyway?

FORD: Untrue. I'll admit that many men drop out before they've gotten their degrees. But, on the other hand, many do graduate.

MELISSA: Do you feel college sports help some athletes to get into a profession where they can thrive after college?

FORD: Absolutely. America is full of kids who normally would never get a chance at a college education, were it not for sports scholarships.

MELISSA: But hasn't the sports scene been cheapened recently by all kinds of illegal activities? Hasn't recruitment itself been subjected to probes of all kinds? Aren't some schools on probation or suspension because of illegal practices?

FORD: True. But the sport itself hasn't suffered. Only the public's view of it.

MELISSA: What about Tonya Harding and Nancy Kerrigan? Now there was a case of an act that affected an international sport.

FORD: The media built that up into a spectacle.

MELISSA: Didn't the need for money on the part of one of those skaters bring on the act?

FORD: It did not ruin the sport of skating, however.

MELISSA: But even the Olympic Games, which started out as amateur events, have become professionalized over the years. Doesn't that dilute the "sportsmanship" of "sportspeople"?

FORD: Not those who do not indulge in gambling or in endorsing products.

MELISSA: What do the universities gain by producing sports spectacles for the public?

FORD: Many schools would be forced to close down if it were not for the amount of money they make in running a good sports program.

MELISSA: And you support the idea that advertising beer, for example, is a healthy inducement to men and women to become a part of the sports scene in this country?

FORD: No one has to drink beer. No one has to smoke.

MELISSA: What is your message to those at the University of Seattle who want to shut down sports?

FORD: Don't destroy the educational system just to root out a system of athletics that you personally don't like. Let the games begin!

When it was all over, and they were back in the office watching a tape of the show, Melissa smiled. "Hey, I liked that last bit! The Olympic Games thing."

Ford grinned. "Me too."

And, in spite of the ever-present Andrew Royce, he gathered Melissa in his arms, held her tightly, and kissed her long and thoroughly.

The games, Melissa thought, had definitely begun.

Forty-one

In the Cards

His shoulder holster hung over the back of his kitchenette chair, with the Colt .45 carefully laid out on the table in front of him. In his hands Andrew Royce held a sheaf of three-by-five file cards covered over with writing.

He was close, he knew that. Somewhere in this garbled trash can of data was the one essential clue that would identify the stalker, the dog food dispenser and dog killer, the distributor of sick stories from the rip-and-read, the break-and-enter perpetrator, the red Taurus driver—in short, the person who intended to do bodily harm to Melissa Bonner.

And perhaps to Denise Bonner as well.

Since his arrival on the scene a week ago, Royce had been visited a number of times by Augie Simms. He and his liaison in the Seattle Police Department had exchanged a great deal of information about the people written up so carefully on his cards. And, of course, Royce had done all this without telling Melissa Bonner about it. She was one of the main subjects on his card—a subject he hoped somehow and in some way might help provide a proper motivation for a would-be killer to act.

He went through the list once again, laying the cards carefully down as he read through each one, trying to think beyond the bare details that stared up at him, etched in his precise, carefully scripted draftsman's capital letters.

The first card was that devoted to Melissa Bonner. It looked like this:

NAME: BONNER, MELISSA.
BORN: 1969.
PLACE OF BIRTH: SIOUX CITY, IOWA.
EDUC: SIOUX CITY, IOWA & CHICAGO, ILLINOIS.

EDUC: UNIVERSITY OF SEATTLE. 1986–90.
EMPL: CHANNEL 8. SPORTSWRITER. 1990–92.
EMPL: CHANNEL 8. SPORTSCASTER. 1992–94.

Royce had obtained this information from associates of Melissa Bonner—at least, what he couldn't get from printed records. Her parents had both died in 1988; there was no reason to write out cards for the two of them.

The second card read:

NAME: BONNER, DENISE.
BORN: 1964.
PLACE OF BIRTH: SIOUX CITY, IOWA.
EDUC: SIOUX CITY, IOWA & CHICAGO, ILLINOIS.
EDUC: NORTHWESTERN UNIVERSITY, ILLINOIS. 1981–85.
MARRIED: MARK ENRIGHT. 1985.
DIVORCED: 1987.
EMPL: ADMISSIONS, UNIVERSITY OF SEATTLE. 1990– 94.
EMPL: PRESIDENT'S SECY, U. OF SEATTLE. 1994–

The story, as Royce had gotten it from some of the people in the newsroom, was that Denise came to the Coast after her marriage broke up in Iowa. She was trying to overcome the trauma of the divorce—the first in her family's history. While she was living with Melissa in Seattle, and while Melissa was still in college, their parents had been killed in a household accident. Their place had been blown apart by a natural gas explosion.

Then Denise finally obtained a lead on a job at the University in Admissions, and had taken it. Later she became President Stark's private secretary. Since Melissa had known Stark, it seemed obvious that she might have been helpful in getting her eventually placed with him.

Still, there was one slightly twisted personality quirk in Denise Bonner that Royce had spotted almost instantly. The woman was older and more experienced than Melissa, experienced in life's little problems, like marriage, for example. But she had nowhere near the personality or natural beauty that Melissa, her kid sister, possessed.

There was envy there, all the time, simmering just below the surface. She controlled it; she diverted it into other channels; but it was there. Of that Royce was positive. Yes. Jealousy was a possibility in the case of Denise Bonner. And the opportunity to act was easy to seize because of her proximity to Melissa.

It had also occurred to Royce that Denise could have faked her own burglary in order to confuse the issue. That is, with Melissa as target, Denise was suspect. With Denise also as target, she was not.

There was another point. Was envy actually a strong enough motivation to kill for? In opera. In novels. But this was real life. Royce might be wrong, but his experience told him that there just wasn't enough to be envious about to drive Denise to murder.

NAME: O'HARA, SCOTT.
BORN: 1962.
PLACE OF BIRTH: BREMERTON, WASHINGTON.
EDUC: BREMERTON.
EDUC: UNIVERSITY OF SEATTLE. 1980–84.
EMPL: SAME. BASKETBALL COACH. 1986–94.
FRIENDS: BONNER, MELISSA. 1993–94.
  BONNER, DENISE. 1994.

Royce bent over the cards on the table and studied this one carefully. In Royce's conversation with Barry Ford, he had detected a suspicion about the basketball coach. Was Ford justified in being suspicious, or was it simply an overlap of his own interest in Melissa, who had certainly had an affair with O'Hara?

On the face of it, Scott O'Hara presented himself as a straightforward, outgoing person. He had become a success because of his basketball team's victorious season. There was no reason, Royce felt, to look at him twice. And yet Barry Ford had looked twice. Again—probably because of his own interest in Melissa Bonner.

Royce flipped to the next card.

NAME: STARK, JONATHAN.
BORN: 1951.
PLACE OF BIRTH: BOSTON, MASSACHUSETTS.
EDUC: BOSTON.
EDUC: AMHERST. 1968–72.
EDUC: HARVARD. 1972–75.
EMPL: RUTGERS, NEW JERSEY. 1975–85.
EMPL: UNIVERSITY OF SEATTLE. ENGLISH. 1985–90.
EMPL: SAME. PRESIDENT OF UNIVERSITY. 1990–.
MARRIED: BASCOMB, CORNELIA. 1977.
DIVORCED: 1992.

Stark did not concern Royce. He had seen him in action. The man was no hypocrite. He was exactly what he presented himself to be: an elegant, aristocratic man with impeccable credentials. Royce would bet the farm on him. He would not kill someone's dog, follow her in a red Taurus, send her stories in the office mail. And he was very fond of Melissa Bonner.

Next card was Barry Ford's. Royce tapped the three-by-five on the table and pondered. There was something vaguely primeval about Ford. It was a masculinity that did not bother Royce, but he knew that Ford could be a problem once he was aroused about something. He had a way with him that simply did not brook argument. That was what made him a superior quarterback.

He was bright—no question about that. He was virile—no one would question that facet of his persona either. He was in charge, wherever he went, whatever he did. This was the kind of man that most women would swoon over—if he so much as looked at them.

Still, there was nothing dubious about his past. He had women in every city, Royce was sure about that. But it was obvious that he had so far managed to avoid commitment to anyone. Now he was very close to Melissa Bonner. Royce felt that Melissa was under his sway.

Melissa was a lovely woman. But she was exactly the kind who would fall for Barry Ford and never be missed when Ford moved on to someone a little more luminescent, a little more sleek, a little more sophisticated.

Melissa was getting to him. He knew that. He couldn't afford to let that happen. He picked up the card and studied it carefully.

NAME: FORD, BARRY.
BORN: 1966.
PLACE OF BIRTH: FRESNO, CALIFORNIA.
EDUC: FRESNO.
EDUC: STANFORD. 1982–86.
EMPL: MIAMI DOLPHINS. 1987–94.
EMPL: SEATTLE SEA LIONS. 1994.
FRIENDS: ANNE WHITTAKER. ACTRESS. L.A.

Nothing there, really. Royce lifted the last card. It read:

NAME: DOTY, LUANNE.
BORN: 1971.
PLACE OF BIRTH: VANCOUVER, B.C.
EDUC: U.C. BERKELEY. 1987–91
EMPL: SEATTLE TIMES. 1991–92.
EMPL: CHANNEL 8. 1992–94.

He had studied Luanne Doty only because she seemed always to be underfoot in the newsroom. She had come on to Royce his first day there, hardly thirty minutes after he had put in an appearance in the Channel 8 office.

He knew instantly that she wanted to ingratiate herself with him. Knew it, and fought it. But somehow she had managed to get closer to him than he had realized. It was obvious from the first ten minutes with her that she was simply aching to become Melissa II, to wear her clothes, to do her thing, to be as popular on the air.

She was a conniver, a plotter, and a manipulator. And tough as nails. But she was not the kind to follow Melissa or to kill her dog.

It was motivation that was the missing element in the case of Melissa Bonner. There was a plethora of opportunities. A weapon was no problem—anyone could come by *something*. But there was absolutely no motivation visible. To carry the problem to its logical conclusion, how could anyone profit from the death of Melissa Bonner?

He ticked off other possible motivations.

Revenge. But she had never done anything really bad to anyone. Sure, she had broken off with Scott O'Hara. And O'Hara was a question mark. But Royce could not see O'Hara in the role of a conniving stalker or destroyer.

Political advantage? How could Melissa Bonner help or hurt anyone politically?

Blackmail? Royce almost laughed. Melissa was in no way the kind of woman who would dream up a scheme to blackmail anyone—for whatever reason.

There was always the problem of big money moving things mysteriously about in the background: that is, mob money betting on sports. Mob money that had profited by the Sea Lions when they were losing. That would provide motivation to turn a winning team led by Barry Ford into a losing team by getting at and controlling Ford through Melissa.

The scenario was too Byzantine for Seattle.

Royce flipped through the cards once more. He looked at his watch. Christ! Three o'clock!

He'd have to crawl in, or he wouldn't be able to get up in the morning. His eyes were closing already as he made his way to bed.

Then, as he reached up to turn off the light, a random thought struck him. He instantly hopped over to the kitchenette table and picked up the cards. He flipped through them. And there it was. How had he missed it? By not connecting obvious connectable points.

Still, there were other details to be nailed down. Every problem solved involved another problem to be solved in turn. Even at this time in the morning.

He reached for the phone.

Forty-two

Campus Demonstration

Thursday dawned gray, with the sky overcast and threatening. Melissa Bonner shivered as she made her way along her jogging route, with the Range Rover following close behind her. She had awakened in the middle of the night to tiptoe out into the living room. There were no sounds coming from across the corridor, but when she opened her door and peeked out she could see a tiny sliver of light under the door.

What was Royce up to? It simply wasn't like him to pace about so late at night. He was the coolest customer she had ever seen. But something had him ruffled. He had been up and down throughout their brief acquaintance, but Melissa sensed that something big was bothering him now.

She had crawled back in bed and fell immediately to sleep. Then, in the morning, she had invited him in for breakfast, but he said little.

After jogging, they made their usual shopping tour in silence. Melissa watched Royce as he constantly looked around him. She knew him well enough to understand that he was keeping a very close surveillance on everyone he could see—including all strangers male and female.

"What's eating you?" Melissa finally asked as she drove the four-wheeler through town to the television station.

He looked at her with blank eyes. "Nothing."

"There's something," Melissa said decisively. "You've been as prickly as a warthog all morning long."

He shrugged. "I'm just prepared."

She shook her head. If he wouldn't alert her, so be it.

They settled down in her office and had been there forty-five minutes when the phone rang for Melissa. "Hello?"

"Scott O'Hara, Melissa."

She was nonplussed. "Hello, Scotty. How are you?"

"This isn't a social call." He laughed. "I've got news for you."

"Let me have it."

"We've got campus action," he said.

"Action?" Melissa noticed that Royce had turned around and was looking at her, obviously trying to eavesdrop on the phone call.

"Yeah. You know about the group that's trying to make the administration drop football."

"I sure do."

"They're demonstrating today. I've called Dr. Stark. But I don't think he's going to be able to roll them up. Anyway, I've got some of my people interested."

"In what?"

"In a kind of counterdemonstration." There was a silence, as if he had put his hand over the handset. "Hey, I've got to go. Just thought I'd tip you off."

"Thanks, Scotty," she said, but he had already hung up.

Royce was on his feet, leaning on Melissa's desk. "Demonstration?"

"Yeah. The anti-football faculty at the University of Seattle."

"How many marchers?" Royce asked, his voice tense.

"I don't know," Melissa admitted. "I've got to tell Hobbs. We'll be getting over there as quick as we can." Then, as an afterthought: "They're planning a counterdemonstration."

Royce's eyes widened and he straightened up quickly.

Hobbs returned with Melissa to find Royce sticking his weapon in its holster after checking its action.

"Be careful over there," Hobbs told Royce.

"You bet your life I will. This is only a preliminary move, you know. The demonstration. The next move is up to the basketball jocks. Their counterdemonstration. This is all standard operational procedure. I've worked demonstrations before. It's going to be a busy day today."

Hobbs spoke to Melissa. "By the time you get there, I'll bet the jocks will be in full force. Just to be sure, I think I'll alert Barry Ford. Maybe he can help."

Melissa reached for the phone and called Kubo and Griswold. In ten minutes they were in the van and on their way to the campus.

When they arrived, they discovered the anti-football demonstrators confined by sawhorse barricades to an area in front of the Administration Building. Campus security had roped off the front steps of the building, leaving a pathway open for people who had to use the building.

A group of about twenty students and professors were patrolling the area in front of the Administration Building, marching around in a ragged circle. Most of them were carrying signs. One said, "A pox on football jocks!" Another read, "Support your local book dealer."

Melissa looked over the marchers deliberately. It was not hard to spot the leader. He was a middle-aged man with hair just a little longer than normal. He was in a suit and tie. He did not march in the general line of marchers, but kept moving around and talking briefly to his fellow demonstrators.

Although she did not recognize him, she quickly joined him and asked his name.

"I'm James Morris," he said. "I teach zoology."

Channel 8 had already had Barry Ford on camera. And Jonathan Stark. Now it was James Morris's turn.

"Over here!" Melissa ordered him, pointing to a cleared spot of grass next to the Administration Building. "We'll have the crowd in the background."

"Thank you."

She got Griswold and Kubo set up and motioned Morris over. Then she spoke directly to the camera. "James Morris is a member of the science department at the University of Seattle," she said, facing him so that the camera had a two-shot of them in profile. "What is the purpose of today's demonstration?"

"The administration has turned down our petition to throw out the football program. We're demonstrating for attention in order to put an end to football participation at the University of Seattle."

"Now that the administration has turned down your petition, what is the next step, Mr. Morris?"

"We are prepared to call a faculty strike if our aims are not met.

And we have already gotten the impression that no one wants any change here—except for the students and most of the faculty."

"Do you think you have the chance to win such a strike?" Melissa asked.

"Absolutely!"

"Thank you, James Morris."

Melissa turned aside. "That's a wrap on Morris," she told Griswold. He panned the camera around at the crowd, which was visibly growing. Morris thanked Melissa and ran back to his group. As she glanced back at the Administration Building's entrance she was surprised to see Jonathan Stark standing there, surveying the crowd.

"Dr. Stark!" she shouted, waving at him.

He nodded and quickly joined her. "I heard all that," he told Melissa. "Could I have a few words of rebuttal?"

Melissa smiled. She waved to Griswold and Kubo. "Come here, guys!" In a moment she had set up another interview, this time directly in front of the stylized Gothic doorway.

"Dr. Jonathan Stark, president of the University of Seattle," she said as the two of them stood in profile to the camera. "Have you anything to say in response to Mr. Morris's statements?"

"Indeed I have," said Stark slowly. "I'm not going to label Mr. Morris's statements a tissue of lies, which I could rightly do, but instead I would like to correct a few erroneous implications. In the first place, the administration did *not* turn down his petition; we set it aside for further study. We have *not* denied anything."

Melissa then asked, "And yet it seems to me that you might be trying to ignore the movement that seems to be gaining force in your faculty to do away with sports."

"In no way are we ignoring his request," Stark replied. "But such a move would cause massive changes in our fiscal status. Our public image would change drastically."

"Are you *for* the sports program or *against* it, Dr. Stark?"

"I am for it as it exists today, in spite of the fact that I would be in favor of some alterations and improvements. But I do *not* subscribe to the idea of abolishing football."

"Thank you, Dr. Stark."

As Griswold moved to another position to film the crowd, Jonathan shook Melissa's hand and thanked her. "I've got to run," he said and immediately entered the Administration Building again.

"Hi, Melissa!" She turned quickly. It was Barry Ford. She remembered that Hobbs had said something about calling Barry Ford.

"What are you doing here?" she asked him in pleasant surprise.

"We heard the college jocks under Scott O'Hara were going to try to pull a counterdemonstration. I just wanted to get over here to be sure you're all right."

"You stay right here," Melissa ordered him. She yelled for Kubo and Griswold. Griswold came over and saw Ford. He began filming an establishing shot before Melissa got through telling her crew what she wanted, which was, of course, a front-on interview with Barry Ford. It was set up in seconds.

"Barry Ford, quarterback for the Seattle Sea Lions. Mr. Ford, what is your interest in college football?"

"The ancients used sports to prepare their soldiers for battle. In England, the whole idea of the marriage between sports and education was started on the playing fields of Eton. The sports scene on the campuses of America is a direct offshoot of the British system."

"You are obviously *for* sports on campus," Melissa said.

"Oh, yes. Learning and training are part of the same thing. I believe in training the mind and in training the body. Each without the other is incomplete."

"A healthy mind in a healthy body, Mr. Ford?" Melissa couldn't help smiling.

"Exactly! Couldn't have said it better!"

"Actually, Juvenal said it better too—and he said it in Latin. Thank you, Barry Ford. And good luck Sunday!"

"Thank you."

There was a sudden cry of excitement in the distance, and then, as the anti-football demonstrators continued in their clockwise march in front of the Administration Building, a number of casually dressed students came running out of the parking lot toward them, led by the very high-profile Scott O'Hara.

Melissa shouted to Griswold and Kubo, waving them toward the oncoming rush, focusing them on O'Hara. Griswold turned quickly and began filming this new threat. Kubo was waving the microphone stick around in the air, adjusting his earphones. Now Melissa saw Royce. He was glued to a pair of binoculars, watching intently as the crowd surged down the walkway.

And then, as Melissa stood by Griswold, watching the oncomers coming in to mix it up with the demonstrators, she saw a lone individual running in from the side, looking directly at her. She *seemed* to recognize him, although she could not be sure where she had seen him before. He looked familiar—and yet—unfamiliar.

Then she had it. What made recognition easy this time was the fact that he did not have his biker's reflecting shades on.

He was running now. She looked at him more carefully. He was coming directly toward her. And he held a handgun of some kind. Royce could tell her what kind it was. Where *was* Royce when she so desperately needed him?

Forty-three

Hero of the Day

Andrew Royce had spotted the would-be killer of Melissa Bonner the moment the jocks started their rush down the slope toward the anti-sports demonstrators. He was surrounded by a lot of people bigger than he was, but he blended in perfectly with the rest of them—sports shirt, ballooning slacks, heavy red Reeboks.

Royce had memorized the face. Narrow chin, sloping down from knife-sharp cheekbones. Thin eyes, very close together, brown and shifty. The nose was long, and broken in the middle. The hair was thick and dark, growing low over the forehead.

Augie Simms had delivered the picture he had requested from the Seattle Police Department the night before. It took only a moment of his time to memorize the face. The image would be unmistakably etched on Royce's memory forever.

Royce had employed traditional detective methods to identify the man who meant to hurt Melissa. He had to stop the son of a bitch before he carried out his vendetta.

Then he saw the gun.

Royce started up the slope toward the advancing of jocks. His man was lost to sight for just a moment, and then Royce spotted him again. He had moved to the side of the walkway, probably to get a better angle on Melissa. He was out in the open now, with a nine millimeter in his hand, a clean shot for Royce. The man began to run toward Melissa, keeping the weapon pointed at her.

Royce had guessed right: the man was intending to use the divisive action of the demonstrators to cover his planned murder of Melissa Bonner.

Royce drew his Colt and crouched, gripping the weapon with both hands, sighting it at the extended right hand of the running man. He fired once. There was a shout of pain. The targeted man plunged forward into the crowd. There was a sound of metal skidding along the walkway. Suddenly a woman screamed. Bystanders nearby scattered.

Royce saw his target again, this time climbing slowly to his feet, shaking his right hand and cursing. Royce could make out the nine-millimeter clearly. It had been shot out of his hand and had cartwheeled into the grass. It was lying now in plain sight.

Royce ran now, as fast as he could, shoving people aside. The would-be murderer had seen the weapon. He frantically tried to retrieve it.

"Get down!" Royce shouted. He raised his Colt again, aiming at the man. Someone was in the way. He couldn't fire. The man stooped to pick up the weapon. Royce saw him quite plainly now. Shoot him in the head!

There were too many people around. He pushed through the wall of people and was face-to-face with the would-be killer. The killer had the weapon in his hand, but his hand was bleeding. He looked down. Royce lifted the Colt and pointed it at the man's face.

"Freeze," he said.

The man shifted the gun painfully to his left hand and fired.

The shot went astray. Royce jumped and karate-chopped the man's left wrist. The nine millimeter arced over into the grass again.

Royce had the Colt's barrel pressed in the man's neck. "Don't move a damned inch," he told him. Royce reached around in back of him and removed the handcuffs from his belt. He clicked one on the man's left hand and propelled him toward one of the campus security men, who took charge of him.

Royce looked for Melissa. She was standing right beside him. "I know who he is," she exclaimed. "It's Mark Enright! Denise's ex!"

And as Royce reholstered his Colt, he realized that he was right in the eye of Griswold's camera. Behind him he spotted Kubo, waving the stick mike and grinning.

"Mr. Andrew Royce, security," Melissa said in her announcer's voice as she stood aside and watched him intently. "You're a hero, you know that, don't you?" she said, holding out the hand mike to him.

Royce shrugged. "I had to disarm the man. He seemed intent on creating a disturbance."

"What did he want?" Melissa asked, almost playfully.

"Disturbed people want to be noticed. This was a textbook example."

Melissa watched Royce's face. There was no indication that he was telling a deadpan lie. He seemed as calm and as cool as he always did.

"Well, he failed in his purpose, thanks to you," Melissa went on.

She signaled a wrap to Griswold. He panned the camera on the group that was beginning to dissipate, now that the excitement was all over.

"How did you *know* it was Enright?" Melissa whispered to Royce.

"I'll tell you later."

She smiled. "Prediction. You'll be a hero on national television."

"So will you." He let his eyes remain on her face just a trifle longer than they should have. "I never saw anyone as cool as you under fire."

"From you, that sounds mighty like a compliment."

"It is."

Barry Ford was there, looking at Royce with slightly narrowed eyes. "You ever think of taking up sports? You've got the moves."

Royce grinned.

Ford kissed Melissa on the cheek. "Great news bite. You'll be famous for it!"

She turned away and immediately almost ran into Dr. Stark.

"Melissa!" he said anxiously. "I heard the commotion from my office and came down to make sure you were all right."

He was holding her by the upper arms and she could feel him trembling.

"I'm fine, Dr. Stark," she told him with a wide smile. "I think everything is finally going to be all right."

Forty-four

The Avenger

Andrew Royce's explanation to Melissa took place that night after the ten-o'-clock news at Ada's across the street from Channel 8. Melissa Bonner was, of course, one of the stars of the confrontation on the University of Seattle campus. But the real hero was Andrew Royce, as Griswold's film showed.

Channel 8's exclusive was the talk of the town—with the other stations lining up for bits and pieces of Melissa's exclusive coverage to broadcast on their own stations with attribution to Channel 8. The story became an instant and nationwide sensation.

Melissa's main question was "how"—how had Andrew Royce *guessed* what was going to happen? How had he managed to isolate and identify the person who had been stalking her?

"Experience," Royce told her that night. "It's an old trick of the hit-man trade to use a demonstration to camouflage a contract killing. I knew we might be approaching a situation of exactly that kind, and I knew that I had to find out who would be trying to kill you."

"*How* did you do it?"

"I've been building a file on you ever since I've been covering you. That is, I've found out everything I possibly could about *anyone* you have contact with. And it finally paid off last night."

"*Tell* me."

"Three specifics are necessary in the accomplishment of a successful killing. You need motivation, opportunity, and the proper weapon. I already had figured out that the demonstration would be the *opportunity*. The weapon could be anything. The most puzzling aspect was motivation. Why would anyone want to kill you, Melissa? For gain? I couldn't see that. You're not rich. You don't have anything someone else would want—except for your job, maybe. I thought of Luanne, but I dismissed her."

Melissa was astonished. "Luanne? You *can't* be serious."

He shrugged. "Vengeance? That is, to pay back someone for something done to an injured party? I had to think about that. I kept going through my cards one by one—and then, last night, I spotted it."

"What?"

"The proper motivation."

"Which was—?"

"Your sister was divorced from her husband, Mark Enright, in 1987. You told me your father had sent him back to Arkansas. But then in 1988 your parents were killed in a gas explosion in their home in Sioux City."

"Yes."

He spread out his hands. "I didn't know what kind of a man Enright was. But I don't like coincidences. My mind took a fanciful leap. What if your parents' deaths and your father's treatment of Enright were linked? Vengeance, Melissa. Enright hated your father for shaming him. We later found out that it was probably Enright who killed your parents by making a rigged gas explosion look like an accident. At least the Sioux City detectives had suspected someone might have set off the explosion."

"I see!"

"Once I'd made that connection, everything fell into place. Enright's got a rap sheet a mile long in Little Rock. You didn't know it. Denise didn't know it. He's a bad apple—always was. That's why he left home for Chicago, where he met your sister. It only took a little investigation for me to get at the truth."

"I had no idea he was out here on the Coast."

"Nor did anyone else. But once I got his picture faxed in from the Little Rock Police Department, I knew what he looked like."

"Why was he after *me?*"

"You're the visible Bonner now. He started with your father. He had to get back at *all* of you. You all knew his shame. After your father, it was you. You are well known out here on the Coast. He found out when he came here. We don't know why he came here initially. Possibly it was to try to fix things up between Denise and himself. But when he got here, he figured he'd score on you rather than tackle Denise. Besides, if he hit you, *he'd* be a celebrity. He wanted media attention. And so he went right after you. Step by step. A stalker by instinct."

"How did he kill Danny?"

"Broke in through the front door, made friends with Danny by feeding him. You know the rest. It was Enright who instructed Alita Sanchez to start sending you those stories. He faked his I.D. and got a job at Channel 8—on the graveyard shift. He'd shaved off the mustache he had when you knew him, along with the long hillbilly sideburns. He looked different. And he made sure to keep out of your way."

"Did he break into Denise's apartment?"

"Oh, yes! He had killed Danny and he had upset you both. His mind was obsessed with doing in all the Bonners. He was preparing for the final acts. Kill you. Then get Denise."

At that moment there was a commotion at the doorway of Ada's. Then Darryl Hobbs came walking in, followed by Barry Ford, Takeo Kubo, Al Griswold, Luanne Doty, Jill Jamison, Ian Chambers—even Tim Harrison—and most all of the gang in the news department, including the co-anchors.

They spotted Melissa Bonner and Andrew Royce at their table, and swarmed forward.

"Just a little impromptu celebration," Ford announced, taking over in the same way he did on the football field. "All together now? In honor of Melissa Bonner, who gave one of the most exciting sportscasts of her career tonight!"

The group began singing. "For she's a jolly good fellow."

When they were through Hobbs waved them quiet. "But now for the real hero of the day. In honor of Andrew Royce, who saved her life!"

And the group went on. There was clapping and shouting afterward, and laughter. The newcomers all sat down and ordered drinks.

First to come up and lean over Melissa Bonner was Tim Harrison.

"I'm usually right," Harrison said. "I pride myself on being right." He smiled wanly. "This time I was wrong."

He held out his hand.

"Congratulations, Ms. Bonner. You're not in the *wrong* business. You're in the *right* business. You handled that confrontation in the coolest manner I've ever seen. In the future, if anyone tells you you've blown it—send them to me!"

He gripped her hand in an honest handshake and saluted her with his drink.

"Oh, and by the way, I'm doing a bit of rewriting on my assessment of Channel 8. I've changed my final recommendation. Cheers!"

Melissa was about to ask him what his recommendation would be, but he had slipped away in the crowd and she could not find him.

Barry Ford slid into the chair on the other side of Melissa from Royce and ordered a round of drinks for the three of them. Before the drinks came, he took an envelope out of his shirt pocket and opened it.

"What is that?"

"I thought you'd never ask." Ford grinned. He removed a newspaper clipping from it. It had been cut out of the *Los Angeles Times*. He handed it over to her.

It said, quite briefly, that starlet Anne Whittaker had recently announced her engagement to Steve Doran, a young actor who had just signed a six-figure contract with Universal Pictures for a new drama series to be shown on the Fox network.

"That's why I saw her in Los Angeles," Ford reminded Melissa. "To break it off with her." He leaned forward to kiss her.

She felt herself blushing. But she didn't push away his face. Or his hand. Or his thigh. Or his knee.

Forty-five

The Gioconda Smile

The moon was full. She could see it through the bedroom window of her apartment. Beside her on the nightstand she saw the digital clock radio blinking away. It was some time after 3:00 A.M. She wondered why she had come awake so suddenly.

Then she saw him standing beside the bed. She sat up, pulling the bedclothes around her.

"What are you doing here?"

Andrew Royce snapped on the light. "I never got a chance to finish my story the other day."

"What story?"

"The story of my life."

She could not help but feel his eyes on her nightgown. Yet somehow the feeling did not seem amiss, nor did it disturb her in the least. Rather, she gloried in it. "Come on," she said, headed for the kitchenette.

She watched him put on water to boil for the instant coffee he had already put in the cups. "Now, what's this all about?"

"My tour of duty is officially over. At exactly three o'clock, as Mr. Hobbs told me."

"So? I have only to say that you did a grand job."

"I never enjoyed a case so much before."

She studied him with guarded eyes. "You never showed it at all."

"Of course not. I was on duty."

Her tongue traced the inside of her upper lip. "Ah."

"Now that obligation is out of the way."

"And?"

"I now intend to appear to you in my own persona."

"And is there to be a great change?"

"Perhaps."

The teakettle began to whistle and she rose to its summons. As she moved past him his arms reached out and encircled her waist.

"Oh," she said, turning sideways and slipping gracefully down onto his lap.

His lips were on hers, touching them softly and warmly. Then, as she moved against him for a moment, his arms tightened, and his mouth continued to move against hers. She could feel his tongue moving into her mouth.

Deep within her there was a loosening of muscles, a warming of flesh, a tingle of anticipation in her spine. She was breathing faster now, more deeply, more surely. She probed his own mouth with her tongue, and he tightened his grip on her body.

When he had released her, she said one word. "My."

And he grinned and took her in his arms again. Her mind was a blank now. She had no thoughts other than to relax and enjoy his presence so close to her. The flimsy nightgown could have been nonexistent. His hands moved against her, and then slid the delicate straps of the gown off her shoulders.

Almost immediately he was shifting his position to plant his tongue on her nipple, which had become erect and hard. Then his teeth were nibbling it tenderly and sensuously and she squirmed against him, feeling his hardness against her thigh.

His hands slid up under her nightgown and gripped the silken smoothness of her buttocks. She seemed to float away as he moved with her toward the bedroom door, his arm holding her to him under her frivolous outer wrappings.

At the door he paused. "Good night," he whispered.

She turned to him, startled. "Good night?"

"You have established a relationship with Barry Ford. And you have, unless I am mistaken, established a relationship with Dr. Jonathan Stark. I am now in the process of announcing my own intentions toward you. But I do not like to encroach on what others consider as their exclusive property without having my intentions thoroughly understood and consented to by you."

"God," she breathed, kissing him on the ear. "You're such a *stickler* for rules and regs."

"As you know, I could not state my intentions when I was under contract to do a job, of which you were an integral part."

"I know," she said. She turned to him, slid her arms around his neck, and kissed him deeply. Then she let him go and moved over to her still warm bed.

"P.S.," he said. "I've made up my mind."

"About what?"

"About my life. I'm getting out of security. I'm switching to what I always wanted to be in." He laughed. "The law."

"Bravo," she said.

"Good night, Melissa."

"Good night, Andy."

She lay against the pillow with a smile on her face. The last thing Royce saw before he walked out of the bedroom was the moonlight shimmering through the curtains and onto her face and neck and breast. And onto her lips, curved slightly in a Gioconda smile.

Forty-six

A Question of Identity

First of all there was an almost blinding flash of dead white—an explosion that spread out from the middle of her consciousness to the outer ends of her vision. Then, gradually, she was aware of the fact that she was not focusing on individual objects of any kind. In fact, she seemed to be enveloped in a misty universe that stretched to eternity and back.

She was walking. She looked down. A sidewalk, familiar as the sight of her feet in their running shoes was—except that she did not recognize it as any special sidewalk or any special street.

Where was she?

She felt a tiny spark of panic. It grew instantly and seemed to explode inside her. The mist swirled about her body but she could not tell where she was. Another question immediately replaced the one concerning her whereabouts. What was she doing here? Somehow the misty environment was familiar.

She tried to retrace her path.

She had come out—

Her shoes stopped their movement ahead. She simply stood there, dazed and unbelieving. Where had she been? Where was she now?

She frowned. To get back to basics, she thought, I must concentrate. She closed her eyes, and all that did was shut out the mist. Here she was, walking along a street in the fog, unable to remember where she was going.

Concentrate!

And then the horrible truth suddenly began to roil up inside her to envelop her and to freeze her into terror.

She couldn't even think of her own name!

She fumbled instantly with her jogging clothes. But she knew before she began to look that she would not have her identification with her. There was no sign of who she was anywhere on her body. No locket. No service person's dog tags. No I.D., as the police might put it. Only the key to her apartment.

And how did she know that?

What she did *not* know was where the apartment was located.

If only the mist would rise, part its curtains, and show her the way she should go. Yet now she knew it would not happen. She had lost her memory. Amnesia. That was what it was called by physicians and scientists. That was what it was called on the television soaps and in mainstream novels.

It did her no good to think *around* the problem. She had to think *within* it! She had to dredge up the facts of her persona. And that was proving not only difficult, but impossible. She began walking again, in the direction she had been going when she had suddenly surfaced from what seemed to be a deep dive into the bottom of the ocean.

Three.

It now occurred to her that the number three she was thinking about was a Roman numeral three, and not an Arabic three. Three straight vertical lines. Three forms. Aha. Three people! And these three—men.

As she stared into the fog the Roman numeral three changed into a Roman numeral one—it was as if the three sticks had been merged into one stick.

Something within her was urging her on to action. She was to change the three into one. How could she do that? For the first time, she was frightened. She *must* do it, or something dreadful would happen.

Without thinking, she had started to walk, continuing in the direction in which she had been going. She would turn right at the park, pass the college campus, turn at the playing field, and then she'd be on her way home.

That was it. That was where she was going? On her jogging route. She stepped up her pace.

Of course. Now she had it. She was Melissa Bonner. Had there ever been any question about that? And she was trying to figure out which one of three men she should be married to: Barry Ford, Dr. Jonathan Stark, or Andrew Royce?

She came suddenly awake. She was lying in her own bed, safe and sound. She had simply dreamed. She wasn't out on her jogging course. She was in a nightmare.

She was obviously overstressed by the choice she had to make. She *had* to decide sooner or later. Her conflicted psyche was screaming out a warning to her.

Help! she thought.

She couldn't think about it tomorrow, like Scarlett O'Hara. She had to make up her mind today.

Forty-seven

Which Man?

In the history of their meeting one another at the Tavern in the Town, Melissa Bonner and her sister, Denise, had never had their heads so close together before. Even the waiters who knew them had never seen them so intent on any discussion.

Denise Bonner could tell that her sister was on the verge of a very real crisis. But it was a crisis that a lot of people love to face. And Denise herself did not feel one whit of pity or sympathy for her sister. As for Melissa, she could hardly believe what she was going through.

It was a very simple matter. Three of the most eligible men in town were each demanding a primary place in her life.

As soon as she heard about Melissa's dream the night before, Denise had outlined a scheme for getting to the bottom of the problem. She had written down a number of key points that the two of them should consider, subjecting each of the three prospects to the scrutiny of their eagle eyes.

"Mom used to thank God she had married a good provider," Denise said. "I think we've got to consider *that* even today."

"But I'm working," Melissa argued. "I don't *need* a provider. I provide for myself."

"You might not always," Denise said sternly. "Think about kids."

"I'm not going to think about kids!" Melissa said. "Just because you're a wife, you don't have to be a mother."

Denise lifted her eyes to heaven. "What about Barry Ford? It's obvious he'd be a good provider."

"Even after he's out of football he'll be some kind of company president or super salesman."

"Okay. Check one plus for Barry Ford on provider." Denise frowned. "What about Dr. Stark?"

"No problem," Melissa answered. "I think he's virtually loaded, with stocks and bonds in reserve."

"So that's a plus for Dr. Stark."

"Right." Melissa made a face. "I don't know about Andy. But I have the feeling he's a survivor. I'm sure he could provide."

"You're one in a million." Denise sighed. "Three yeses on one of the most important things in married life."

There was a pause as they both went at their wine.

"Now," said Denise, her face lighting up. "The *important* thing. How is he in bed?"

Melissa threw up her hands. "I knew it by the look on your face. If you miss sex that much, why don't you—"

"Who says I'm missing it?" Denise asked.

"Scott O'Hara? Why didn't you *tell* me?"

"You never asked!"

Denise cut right in on Melissa's comment. "Barry Ford," she said. "I gather that's a definite yes."

"Oh, indeed yes! Two thumbs up, as those two television movie critics have it."

Denise stared at the table between them. "Dr. Stark?"

"I'm willing to take a chance there."

"There's the *age* thing working against him," Denise observed cautiously.

"I doubt that would make much difference. He wouldn't be one to overcompensate—turn into a Mark Enright, I mean—would he?"

"Good God, no!" Denise shrugged. "Let's let it pass then with a plus."

"You can just check off Andy Royce. He knows when to move in and when not to do so." Her face had betrayed her, turning a lovely pink.

"You've gone to bed with him?" Denise asked. Her surprise was genuine.

"Close to it," Melissa said. "He's very sensitive to a woman's feelings. I think he could teach even Barry Ford a thing or two about—women."

"Well, I'll be damned," Denise said. "The things you learn over a glass of wine."

Melissa laughed. "What's next?"

"I've got to bring up a most important thing, and I don't know how to word it. I'm talking about the way a man treats a woman. I mean, my first husband was a beast. He beat me up. Physically."

"I know," Melissa said.

"But there are various degrees of beating. You have men who treat you like some kind of worm that just crawled out of a hole in the ground. Who lash out at you with their tongues. Who beat you up psychologically. Emotionally."

"I understand. Barry Ford." She thought a moment. "This'll surprise you. I simply don't know. He's a question mark."

"Why?" Denise asked.

"His whole life is devoted to being the boss. I don't really know how he'd treat me. I mean, how he'd treat a woman he's married to. He's marvelous on a date. But life isn't a date."

"Question mark," said Denise firmly. "Leaders of men are tough to fathom."

"Just as Jonathan is," Melissa said. "I'd put a question mark down there, too."

"Right. Royce?"

There was a long pause. "I wouldn't want to put a yes there if it's really a no. I simply couldn't guess."

"Question mark," Denise said. "Interesting." She looked up. "I didn't know it, Ellie, but it looks like we're a lot more feminist-oriented than we thought we were. Don't you see what we're saying? That men don't know how to treat women!"

"Well, let's say they don't know about sharing."

"How about a man's ability to be a friend and companion, as well as a husband?"

"Plus for Ford. Plus for Stark." Melissa squinted. "Plus for Royce."

"Easy stuff," Denise said. "There's more to a marriage than

friendship. What about being able to support a woman in the crises of her life?"

"Important," Melissa said. "In Barry we have a big ego. In Jonathan we have a big ego, even if he does keep it well hidden. In Andy there's some of that. He has never let it show. This is something it's hard to judge ahead of time."

Denise shrugged. "Three blanks. You would want a man to give his wife as much of a career boost as possible. I mean, this is going against the profile of the supportive housewife, but it's what we want now, isn't it?"

"Absolutely." Melissa straightened up. "Jonathan has offered to give me the most important professional chance of my lifetime. I certainly cannot ignore that. Neither Barry nor Andy can do what Jonathan can do. I'd have to give Jonathan a ten on that, with the other a five apiece."

"There's one last thing. You've got to give me the dates of their birthdays."

Melissa looked at Denise slantedly. "You're going to do horoscopes?"

"I know yours. I'd like to see how the men fit in."

"My birthday, you know, is June 23."

"You're a Cancer."

"I know Barry Ford's. It's October 11."

"He's a Libra. How come you know the date?"

"Publicity releases. I keep a birthday book for cards. As for Jonathan, it's May 10."

"That's Taurus."

"Royce's is April 3. See how nosy I am?"

"An Aries."

"Of course," Melissa said, "you know most people think astrology is hooey."

"I still want to take a look at this. I'll let you know the first thing."

"Maybe *I* think it's hooey," Melissa said.

"But you're open-minded."

"I don't know what to think. These three men are dreamboats—

every one of them. And here I am, trying to make up my mind which one to spend my life with."

"I remember Mom always had an answer about being in love. She'd ask you the same thing right now. I know it."

"What's that?"

"Which one do you love?" Denise giggled.

"But how do you know who you really love?" Melissa wondered.

"Mom had an answer to that, too."

"I don't know that I ever heard her answer. In fact, I'm sure I never asked her the question. It simply didn't come up for me."

Denise smiled. "She said, 'When you do fall in love, you'll know it.'"

LIVE LIKE *You're* BLESSED

DR. SUZAN JOHNSON COOK

LIVE LIKE
You're
BLESSED

Simple Steps for Making

Balance, Love,

Energy, Spirit,

Success, Encouragement,

and Devotion

Part of Your Life

Doubleday

New York London Toronto Sydney Auckland

PUBLISHED BY DOUBLEDAY
a division of Random House, Inc.

DOUBLEDAY and the portrayal of an anchor with a dolphin
are registered trademarks of Random House, Inc.

Book design by Michael Collica

Cataloging-in-Publication Data is on file with the Library of Congress

ISBN-13: 978-0-385-51719-5
ISBN-10: 0-385-51719-X

PRINTED IN THE UNITED STATES OF AMERICA

June 2006

5   7   9   10   8   6   4

In loving memory of my parents, Dorothy C. and
Wilbert T. Johnson, who lived the blessed life

CONTENTS

ACKNOWLEDGMENTS

In Luke's Gospel, the angel tells Mary, "Rejoice, highly favored one; . . . *blessed* are you among women." With the wonderful opportunity to publish this work, I have substituted Mary's name with my own. God still amazes me with His goodness and mercy that have followed me all the days of my life. How awesome it is to work with Trace Murphy and the Random House/Doubleday family, who understand how to allow me to express and share my blessings in print. Special thanks to Lois de la Haba, my literary agent, who has compassion and wit; to my husband, Ron, and sons, Samuel David and Christopher Daniel, whom God gave to me as gifts; and to the Believers Christian Fellowship Church (BCF), a blessed people, who allow me to lead them. Finally, this work would not have been possible without Brenda Lane Richardson, author and former seminarian, who joined me in prayer, inspired me, and served as a second pair of hands and eyes throughout the writing of this book, whose "gift truly makes room for her" (Proverbs 17), and who has the combination of literary and spiritual genius to bring real stories to life.

LIVE LIKE *You're* BLESSED

How I Learned to Feel B-L-E-S-S-E-D

W hen I was growing up in Harlem during the fifties, my parents attended different churches, and that made Sundays busy for me and my brother, Charles. First we'd accompany Mom to 137th Street's Rendall Memorial, with its Presbyterian, traditional style of worship, led by our dynamic and handsome pastor, the Reverend Doctor Eugene Houston. He was loved and respected by congregants, and perhaps especially by the children. We'd run to him when we could, bestowing hugs, and reveling in his murmured blessings. Somehow, he managed to deliver inspiring sermons in twenty minutes or less. Closing my eyes, I can still taste Mrs. Bowman's famous strawberry shortcake after Sunday morning service.

An hour later, we were back outside, walking along Lenox Avenue, bound for 145th Street, where Dad ushered at Union Baptist. We knew that once we arrived, we would receive an equally warm embrace from the men and women of the congregation. One of the particular blessings of Union Baptist was its strong male presence. Several of these men became members of our extended family. During the week, many of the men and women worked in uniforms. Sundays were their shine times, when they dressed in sharp suits and freshly pressed shirts, with ties and cufflinks; the women's elegant dresses and suits accessorized with hats and jewelry and gloves. Blessings continued as Dad's pastor, the Reverend Leonard Terrell, delivered stirring charismatic gospel sermons.

Attending two churches was simply what we did in our family, and our full days of worship weren't all that unusual in Harlem. Both of the churches offered different ways of worshipping, but I didn't prefer one place to the other any more than I loved one parent more than the other. We never felt we had to choose. We always knew we had the support of both congregations. We were embraced by two wonderful communities of faith, which are still in my life and ministry today. They truly embody what it means to have church families.

During the walk to Union Baptist, even on cold days, when the wind was like a taunting younger cousin that we had to abide, we might start out with our heads bent, but we knew we couldn't look down for long, not with so many people to greet. I don't mean just giving people a passing nod. Lots of these folks were from the rural south, and had come north during the Great Migration, squeezing into the former neighborhoods of Italian and Irish immigrants. One custom they maintained was getting to know their neighbors. Of course, no matter how familiar with one another, people were addressed as *Mr.* or *Mrs.* or *Miss* by children and adults alike; the titles *Aunt* and *Uncle* being reserved for close family friends.

Because of their long workdays, we didn't see most of these people during the week, but when it became necessary to find someone, these streets were a good place to start. Come Sunday mornings,

Harlem transformed into Church City, with music emanating from run-down storefronts as well as hundred-year-old architectural wonders with towering spires.

Spilling out of residential buildings, spiffed-up adults set out on foot, along with neatly dressed children. This was Manhattan, where parking was scarce and owning a car was more common among the well-to-do. The adults probably felt more relaxed on Sundays than they had been the day before or would be the next. Their jobs, where they were often called by their first names, were still twenty-four hours away. For now their hair was done, apartments cleaned, chickens, and at least two other meats, were salted and readied for cooking. Throughout my mother's lifetime our Sunday dinners were feasts. This was the day to thank the Lord for the week's safe journey.

I've often reflected on the alluring mix of that Sunday Harlem crowd: Baptists, Methodists, Episcopalians, African Methodist Episcopalians and Zionists, Presbyterians, Lutherans, Catholics, Pentecostals, and Holiness. The holiness women were easy to spot by their tambourines, lack of makeup, and long black skirts worn even on the hottest summer days. And Pentecostals had a special way of returning a greeting. When you said hello and asked how they were feeling, they often responded, "I'm blessed." As a child, I heard that phrase so often it became like any other greeting. Many years passed until it changed my life, before I could offer it to others who wanted to change theirs.

With so much church in our lives, you'd have thought that I would drag my feet on the way to Union Baptist. But I didn't, because I knew that Daddy's nephew, Uncle Bob, would be standing out front waiting for us. Uncle Bob had a special connection to our family. Years earlier, when Dad was fifteen, he'd left Prince Edward County, Virginia, because he was anxious to escape sharecropping, an existence he found uncomfortably close to slavery. Two years later, when he was still scrambling to earn a living in New York City, he would send part of his earnings to his older sister, to help raise her three children. With Dad's assistance, one of his nieces, Katherine Cyrus, graduated with a teaching degree from St. Paul's College in Lawrence, Virginia. His two nephews enlisted in the service. When World War II ended, one of the nephews, our Uncle Bob, moved to New York and began attending Union Baptist, which partially explains why he waited for us outside the church.

Uncle Bob and his friends would always hand me and my brother dollars, more than enough to buy two cones of homemade ice cream. Since Dad had provided for Uncle Bob years before, this was his nephew's way of "sowing into us." Before we could finish that last lick of ice cream, we knew Uncle Bob and everyone else would ask, "Where you going to college?" School was a ticket to a more secure life, of course, and he was letting us know that we were expected to attend college. He hadn't had the opportunity himself, and neither had most of the grown-ups in our neighborhood.

My mom, Dorothy Johnson, was different from many of our neighbors when it came to her education. Like her mother, she was college educated. Immediately after graduation from Fayetteville State Teachers College, she'd taught twelve grades in a three-room segregated school in Monroe, North Carolina. Many of the pupils were her cousins. Before long though, she developed an insatiable desire to move to New York. This had a lot to do with meeting my dad, Wilbert T. Johnson.

Years later, I found letters that she'd written to him, with references to the money she'd saved up from a few weeks' worth of wages, sent for deposit in his credit union, minimal sums like $1.47. The two of them were building a nest egg, waiting for the day when they could be together. Meanwhile, Dad worked on his GED. Mom, always the schoolteacher, encouraged his progress, and in one letter, wrote: "Your penmanship is so much better, dear."

Finally, they married and she moved to New York. By then, Dad had become one of New York City's first black trolley drivers, and a few years later, he was trained as a subway motorman. A few blocks from our home, on 144th Street, Mom (along with a dynamic group of black and Jewish educators), began teaching the first of three generations of black children, at P.S. 194, which was called the Countee Cullen School, after the black poet who was educated in New York City public schools before attending Harvard.

Like many members of the emerging black middle class, our family moved to another part of the city as we became first-time home-owners. When I was five, my parents purchased a house in Northeast Bronx, but we didn't get disconnected from our roots. Every few days I paid fifteen cents to hop on the bus and then catch the D train to Harlem, for piano lessons with Ms. Shep, French fries with the girls and the corner store, and to meet mom and her colleagues at P.S. 194.

Disembarking from the train, I often ran into Mr. Tex, a numbers runner, his smooth brown head topped with a tall cowboy hat as he smoked a cigar. Business must have been profitable; he often gave me five dollars, simply because I was Mrs. Johnson's kid. In fact, most of the people on the street recognized or referred to me as Mrs. Johnson's daughter. I'd sit in the back of the room as Mom finished her class, but after a while, Mrs. Carroll, the kindergarten teacher, would ask me to sit in her class too, saying I was a role model for her students. She and other teachers, most of them women, became another branch of our extended family tree. Their graciousness, and that which I received from others, imparted a sense of privilege and protection that made me feel like royalty.

Imagine my shock then, when, after the sixth grade—when I longed to attend the local public school in my neighborhood—my parents insisted on enrolling me in the private Riverdale Country Day school, located in a highly affluent bastion in the Bronx. The $4,000-a-year tuition was a great sacrifice. But, concerned about the cutbacks on services in city schools, my parents grew determined to offer me something more. I got off to a rough start in Riverdale, where I had my first real encounters with racism. For all their mansions and extensive travel, a surprising number of my white, wealthy classmates were culturally ignorant, like the girl who touched my Afro and said it felt like Brillo.

Before long, my parents joined with other black couples, whose children attended predominantly white private schools nearby, and formed a black families association that provided a new group of friends, and eventually dates. I also had a chance to hang out with kids in my neighborhood when I joined a local girls' basketball team.

The alienation I felt at Riverdale continued, however. I only performed marginally well. Then I learned that I'd have to be tutored in English over the summer, because I'd failed to turn in most of the homework. This meant missing out on my regular summer trip to Monroe, North Carolina, where I spent time with my mother's mother, enraptured with her stories about the family and the old days. My grandmother always ended one of her narratives with a parable for life. For instance, she would say, "Suzan, you go back to Riverdale and paint that school black." She was telling me to stand out and make an impression, show my classmates that I came from a family of worthy people.

My school failure was all the more of a disgrace when I realized that my summer tutor was a white Riverdale student, just a few grades ahead of me. I promised myself I'd never be in that situation again. Returning to school that fall, I started earning As and Bs, and in the ninth grade I became the school's first black junior school representative.

That elevated status didn't stop a racist guidance counselor from insisting that I was not "mature enough" to spend my junior year abroad with several of my white classmates in a school exchange program in Spain. When my parents realized they couldn't win that battle for me, they paid for a school course in Valencia, Spain, and sent me over there for the summer. That next year our family traveled together to Puerto Rico, a trip that allowed me to hone my Spanish skills. Two years later, at sixteen, I graduated from Riverdale, and eventually from Boston's Emerson College, at the age of nineteen.

College was great but so was the experience of attending a black charismatic church, St. Paul's AME in Cambridge. Under the leadership of Pastor John Bryant, with the assistance of his wife, Mrs. Cecelia Bryant, St. Paul's became one of the most dynamic churches in Cambridge. There was standing room only on Sunday mornings, as black college students from around Boston swelled the congregation. We were drawn by the holistic ministry that encouraged us to share our gifts while expressing our faith. One young member, who was working on a doctoral degree in physics from the Massachusetts

Institute of Technology, was Ron McNair. Later, he became an astronaut, and sadly, died in the 1986 *Challenger* explosion. Long before that, however, Ron was St. Paul's karate instructor. He'd earned a black belt, and with encouragement from Pastor and Mrs. Bryant, shared his gift with us. As for my contribution, I used my background as a drama and speech major to direct and produce plays involving parishioners.

After years of coping with racism in predominantly white environments, we students appreciated that St. Paul's encouraged us to feel brilliant and black and Christian without apology. Passion can be powerful, especially when people work together in God's name. With an eye on world events, the St. Paul's congregation organized a telethon, WATER, and raised $60,000 for building wells in the famine-plagued African Sahel.

After that, it was no longer sufficient to simply read about the Motherland. Eager to see the continent up close, I volunteered for Operation Crossroads Africa, a program that served as a model for the Peace Corps and that was started by a black Presbyterian minister, the Reverend James Robinson, whom I met through my mother's church connections. I solicited the required participation fees and, immediately after graduation, spent the summer months volunteering in Ghana. It was life-changing to see the land from which my ancestors were kidnapped and brought to America in chains. And something else significant came out of the trip. With no televisions or radios to distract me, I heard God call me to serve through the ministry.

Sadly, my father wasn't there to talk with me about my new endeavor. He died in 1975, during my senior year of college. But heeding God's call, I asked the new pastor at Union Baptist, the Reverend Ollie B. Wells, who was my pastor, to recommend me to the deacons as a candidate for the ministry. I didn't attend their next meeting, but the atmosphere must have been charged with tension. A number of the deacons were in their sixties and seventies, and this was the first time they'd had to decide whether a woman should be allowed to preach. What I do know, is how it ended. I'm told that Reverend Wells reminded the others, "Now, this is Wilbert Johnson's daughter." Partially on the strength of Dad's good name and forty years of service as one of Union's gatekeepers, the deacons scheduled me for a trial sermon. I considered it Dad's last gift to me.

So there I stood in 1980, all of twenty-three years old, the person who used to be that girl out front taking a few last licks of ice cream before the service. The church was packed with regular congregants and my large, encouraging extended family. They waited to hear the young woman who'd gone off to study drama and speech, and in the intervening years had earned a master's degree in teaching from Columbia, and worked as a producer at television stations in Washington, D.C., and in Boston. Now I wanted to preach.

My sermon message was from Paul's letter to the Church at Rome. It's interesting to note that Paul's conversion occurred shortly after he'd finished stoning a Christian and was struck blind. Ironically, the people who nursed him back to health were Christians, and this witness to their faith compelled Paul to change his life. He gave himself over to the ministry. This story suggests that even when we want to resist it, truth can confront us. I knew personally that his call to the ministry must have been humbling, for it required a turning around in an entirely new direction.

My sermon seemed to win over the diehards. I was given a license to preach, and soon afterward, began working on my master's of divinity from Union Theological Seminary in Manhattan, and eventually earned a doctorate of ministry from United Theological Seminary in Dayton, Ohio.

My first parish was an assignment at the Mariners' Temple, a black congregation of fifteen on Manhattan's Lower East Side. Over the course of my thirteen years there, Mariners' grew into two congregations of five hundred each. By the seventh year of pastoring, my life was out of kilter. I'd spent most of my time tending to the needs of my congregation, while leaving none for myself. My efforts to balance my needs with those of others were reflected in two books, *Sister to Sister: Devotions from African American Women* (Judson Press, American Baptist Churches of the USA, 1993) and *Too Blessed to Be Stressed: Words of Wisdom for Women on the Move.*

Following the principles described in the body of my work, thanks be to God, I can say that blessings have continued to flow. In 1991, I married Ronald Cook, who works as an administrator at the Convent Avenue Baptist Church. For him I reserve the highest of compliments: He's a good Christian man. In addition to being a wonderful husband, who takes me dancing and cooks most of the meals, Ronald is a gifted father. Together, we're raising our two sons, thirteen-year-old Samuel and ten-year-old Christopher.

Blessings have continued to flow, including my new church planting position at Believers Christian Fellowship in the Bronx, located a short drive from our home. Ron and I organized Believers in 1996 with twenty-seven founding members, which has grown to include three hundred families. Six years later, in 2002, I was named to a four-year term as president of the Hampton Ministers' Conference, the largest interdenominational clergy conference, representing ten thousand ministers and three million parishioners. Opportunities for public speaking have also multiplied, particularly after I began traveling and speaking with the well-known Bishop T. D. Jakes.

Keeping so many balls in the air has proven to be a challenge. For this reason, I started looking back to my parents' life, wondering what I could salvage from their lessons that would help me serve God, while living my life to the fullest. They were no longer alive when I began this work, but fortunately, I continue to feel their encouraging spirit.

My genesis for illustrating spiritual concepts through storytelling began with my participation, with other African American women from all walks of life, in a group founded in 1998 named Isis, for the Egyptian goddess of fertility and motherhood. Gathering throughout the year, we share stories from our lives that we don't share with others. For that reason, we call it "our safe space" and, thanks to God's grace, we come away feeling emotionally healed.

I pray that you too will find a refuge in these stories. In some cases, the early lives of the people in these stories are marked by what seems a complete absence of hope. In a reflection of the life of our Lord Jesus Christ, they too struggled from the darkness into the light. Their narratives make true that old saying: There is no testimony without a test, no triumph without a trial. Their victories are reminders of the Lord's ability to redeem and restore; His power to help us all lived blessed lives.

With that in mind, I've returned to those Sunday morning crossroads in Harlem, when my family and neighbors remained mindful that no matter how difficult the outside world might be, a deep spiritual reserve could protect us by helping us feel our blessings. With my parents as models, I have learned to live as if I'm blessed. This is not simply something to be mouthed; I've put it into action.

For starters, the word "blessed" is comprised of seven letters, a number that has powerful biblical significance. There were, of course, seven days of creation, and God rested on the seventh day. Seven therefore represents the process of creation as well as completeness in terms of perfection and achieving a goal. Seven is also the number used throughout the Book of Revelation, with its predictions of God's return.

Just as importantly in terms of this book, each of the seven letters in "blessed" offers a suggestion for how to break through the most difficult situations. For that reason, this work is divided into seven parts, with each chapter exploring various aspects about how we can live as if we're blessed.

The *B*—for balance—is a continuation of the messages in my earlier works, which focus on the importance of maintaining emotional equilibrium. My parents, for example, were hardworking people who also knew how to play hard and make time for worship. They also understood the *L* in blessed, which stands for love. This includes accepting the love that flows from God, and extending it to partners, children, and family. *E* for energy is the physical stamina that powers our dreams and helps us to keep on keeping on by nurturing our physical bodies and minding our emotions.

S as in "spirit," is the Creator's power within us, which allows us to serve as God's hands. This reminds me of my father when he was a seventeen year old, sending money back home to help raise his nieces and nephews, and my mother showing up at the end of the day with various children from school, urging them to view our home as a refuge from difficult circumstances. After my mother's death in 2003, I heard from a woman who explained that my parents had helped her pay her law school tuition, and I've since learned of other acts of generosity they extended.

My parents were far from wealthy, but that brings me to the second *S* in blessed, which stands for success. Their wise spending and respect for what they earned allowed them to reach a comfortable level of financial success. To me, success goes beyond an individual's earning power. Financial success empowers us to help others as well.

Thus, it makes sense that the next letter, *E*, stands for encouragement, which my parents certainly practiced. Finally, the *D* in blessed is for devotion to God, which shaped my parents' lives and mine.

I couldn't be more grateful for my parents and for what they gave me, and so I dedicate this book to their rock-solid partnership. To them I say: Dearest Mom and Dad, who are buried together in New York and live together with our Lord in Heaven, I am honoring you through my daily words and deeds. Because of you, I know that I'm blessed. I promise to live as if I am and to help others follow in that path.

PART I

BALANCE

LESSED

CHAPTER 1

Steadying the Seesaw

I heard a story recently about a woman who was proud that she was able to push herself beyond the limits of endurance. And she did manage to get a lot done in the course of the day. But then again, her "day" didn't really end at sundown, or even close to it. In fact, this graphics designer found herself working until 2:30 one morning, and only stopped when she could no longer hold her eyes open. Wanting to have plenty of time the next morning—there was so much to do—she set her alarm for 4:30 a.m. This way, she could finish the work project, get her son off to school, run errands, and take care of household chores.

Just as she'd planned, she was up two hours later, waking herself with a cool shower and mug of steaming coffee. She read her son's homework and convinced him to redo certain sections, while she made him a special breakfast of pancakes. Soon she was waving goodbye to him at the bus stop. Knowing that two hours of sleep hadn't been nearly enough, she scheduled another two at mid-morning and fell into a deep sleep.

When she awoke, she figured that some kind of gooey mucus or something had dried over her eyes, because her vision was out of focus. When a warm water rinse failed to do the trick, she started panicking, thinking about all the reasons she needed her eyes, wondering for instance, "How will I see what I want to draw for work? How will I see how to get down the street to pick up my son?"

She started praying, begging God to help her get her sight back. "Forgive me for bothering you," she started. "God I know there are people who have it worse than me ... people who can't see and can't hear. But please, if it's your will, let me see again."

That calmed her down a little bit, and sometime in the next hour, her vision began improving, but still wasn't back to where it had been. She phoned her physician, scheduled an emergency appointment, but almost pulled a no-show, because she began seeing with complete clarity again. Still, puzzled over why the loss of vision had occurred, and terrified that the episode was the first sign of some terrible illness, she kept the appointment and submitted to a complete physical.

After a full exam, her doctor said he couldn't offer any explanation for her loss of eyesight. The doctor told her she was healthy: great blood pressure, cholesterol, blood sugar. And the temporary loss of vision, he assured her, was not a symptom of degenerating nerves, brain tumors, etc. He added, "I have to admit that I'm stumped."

Grateful and eager to get on with her busy schedule, she thanked the young doctor and was about to say goodbye, when he turned and asked, "By the way, before this occurred were you involved in anything that might have caused you a lot of stress?"

She laughed, and at least that felt good, now that she knew death wasn't imminent. "Doctor, I'm always doing something stressful. Last night, for instance, I was on a deadline, so I only slept for two hours . . . But don't look so surprised. I took another two hours this morning as soon as I sent off the completed job." When he failed to look impressed, she said, "I try to catch up on my sleep on the weekends."

She'd have to do more than that, he told her, if she didn't want to suffer another vision loss. "I think your body was telling you something," he added, and he asked her to sit at a desk and write down everything she'd done in the last twenty-four hours.

After reading over her notes and totaling the number of hours, he shook his head. "If what you're telling me is correct, you worked fourteen and a half of the last twenty-four hours; slept for four; showered, dressed, and made-up in one; four hours were spent running errands and finishing chores, one hour helping your son with homework, and thirty minutes walking here."

He paused, and looked at the woman with a puzzled expression. "Your life is completely out of balance. You'll have to make changes immediately. Your body just told you that, and I don't think it's in the mood to negotiate."

She left, promising him and herself that she'd change her schedule right that moment, that there was nothing that was worth the loss of her eyesight. Walking home, she noticed the trees and people around her. It was late spring in New York City, the rains appeared to be over, and all around her trees were sporting their new warm-weather outfits, bursting with green new life. She even appreciated the people rushing around her, because only hours ago, she'd experienced what it would be like to not see them.

So she thanked God for her vision, and kept taking in the sights, speaking in her head to God, promising that this renewed vision was enough and that she'd never again take her life for granted. "This was gift enough," she finished the prayer. "Lord, I'm not going to ask for another thing, not anytime soon anyway."

With that said, she stepped into the bank to use the automated teller, wanting to buy flowers from the vendor on the corner. But lo and behold, she discovered that her bank balance was zero. What had happened? Had someone gotten into her account and ripped her off? She got out her cell phone and called the bank operator, but got no relief there. It was no mistake, the operator told her. A big check had just cleared, and she gave the woman the number. Yes, she remembered writing that one, but she'd thought she had enough left over to meet her needs. The bank operator advised: "Go home and check your deposits and withdrawals and call us back if you need to. We're here for you twenty-four hours a day."

The woman's steps dragged on the way home, and she certainly didn't feel any better after looking through her bank records, because she couldn't come up with any answer about why the balance she thought was supposed to be there wasn't. "All the other checks I've written will bounce," she thought, and her mind began to fill with ominous thoughts about how maybe this would never be cleared up and how it could be turned into a financial catastrophe . . . The mind works overtime in these situations.

Suddenly, she made a connection: out of balance. Hadn't the doctor used similar words, about being out of balance? This time when she prayed, she dropped her to knees. "God, I just finished saying I wasn't going to ask for anything else, so I'm sorry about panicking like this, but please help me work this out. I can't figure out the message, but I know it's got something to do with balance."

She didn't hear any divine words in her ear, and hadn't expected to, but taking a few deep breaths, she phoned the bank again, and this time she wound up with a bank employee who went out of her way to help. The two of them discovered the problem together. During one of her errands, when this woman was rushing through her busy day, she'd hit the wrong buttons in making a deposit. Rather than $2,400, she'd left off a zero, and credited her account with only $240. The situation was rectified; money was transferred from her savings account to cover today's incoming checks, and she was told that within the next twenty-four hours, the correct balance would show.

Rather than feeling relieved this time, the woman held a finger to her lips, striking a pose of deep concentration as she wondered about the day's theme and what God expected her to learn from it. *Twenty-four hours* and *out of balance*: The words had repeatedly popped up.

"God," she prayed again, "I'm going to figure it out, I promise." Her prayer was interrupted by a call from her daughter, who was attending an expensive private school out in California. The young woman's voice seemed hoarse. "Mom, I'm afraid I have some bad news. I've been in bed for the last few days with a terrible cold. And you know I'm like you, I never get sick. But . . . and don't say I told you so. I've been playing Frisbee. I know you told me I needed to spend any spare time earning good grades, and not waste it with something silly like Frisbee, but I did. And there's this girl on my Frisbee team who always forgets to bring her water bottle, so I've been letting her drink out of mine . . . Yesterday, she told me that she wasn't going to be able to take the finals at the end the quarter, because she has a bad case of mononucleosis: She's exhausted from severe cold symptoms. The upshot is that I think I have mono too, and that means my whole semester may be wasted."

She sounded as if she was waiting for her mother to fly into a rage, but the woman didn't. True, her heart was beating faster at the prospect of her daughter suffering through a long-term illness and falling behind in school. But what she said to her daughter didn't reflect that concern. She said, "I don't blame you for offering your teammate a drink of water after a workout. And if you haven't gone to the doctor yet, you have no way of knowing if you're really sick. If it is mono, we'll deal with it. Now, call me back as soon as you're finished at the infirmary."

While the woman waited for the phone to ring again, she considered calling a client to tell her that she wouldn't be able to make tomorrow's agreed-upon impossible deadline, but she didn't do it, not that moment anyway.

She got back down on her knees and she spoke to God. "I get the message, Lord. I'm not going to start out by apologizing for turning to you. I'm not going to allow myself to feel ashamed for being needy. Things happen in the course of a day and you aren't an eight-hour God, you're there always and at all times. And you're a lot better than a twenty-four-hour teller, because you have my best interests at heart. I'm going to keep coming back to talk to you, praising you for being with me and I'll trust that you'll help me bring my life into balance. The next time I total up my hours, there's going to be more praying. I'm literally going to stop and smell the flowers and do what I need for my body so it can continue to function smoothly. Thank you for blessing my daughter and making her a generous soul. Thank you for the skills of the doctors that are examining my daughter. Bless that woman at the bank who handled my panicky call."

When she'd finished praying, her daughter phoned to say that the doctor diagnosed her as suffering from a bad cold. The young woman would be back on her feet and playing Frisbee in no time. She paused, as if that part, about Frisbee, had slipped out. She knew her mother didn't approve of "time-wasters."

Her mother read her mind. "Honey, I was wrong to tell you not to play Frisbee. I'm so glad you're taking time to enjoy your life. I'm going to start doing the same. In fact, I heard about dance classes at a local gym, and you know . . . your dad and I used to love to dance. Maybe I'll even turn on some music tonight and see if the two of us can remember some of our old moves."

That's right, this woman had a husband, but you wouldn't have known it by her schedule, right? What about you, what are you leaving out of your life?

If you had to write down the ways in which you've spent your last twenty-four hours, how would it look? Try it. Pull out a paper and pen and jot it down. Does your day look balanced? Is there time allotted for resting the body and the mind? Some people need more sleep than others. I call myself an eight-hour woman, and I make it a point to let my friends know. I'm generally in bed by nine and up by five. I've had to learn to make time for all that's important in my life.

When I was a girl, my parents either gave or attended a party every weekend. Doesn't sound like people who sometimes held two or three jobs at a time, but they managed to do the work, raise us, party with friends, save their money and invest it, and attend church. At one point in my life, I lost sight of maintaining that kind of balance. Even my soul was weary.

Since then, the many strategies I employed for alleviating my spiritual, emotional, and physical lethargy have been shared with thousands of men and women, from all walks of life. I have traveled the country talking with those who are seeking hands-on practical advice for managing their lives and tools that will help them create a measurable difference. I've spent more than a decade helping others pursue their passions and dreams. Often, in assessing our lives, we realize we have not devoted enough time or thought to our own passions, plans, and pursuits.

As the Balance Doctor, I am always trying to find ways to help people realize their dreams and live the lives they truly want. They begin by learning to balance their lives by holding on to a mental image of the seesaw. I use this familiar childhood playground favorite, the seesaw, because everyone can relate to it.

Often, a picture of scales is used to connote balance. But I believe that down time, recreation, and play are important aspects of the "dream life." In the park, the seesaw is more than a piece of wood that goes up and down. It teaches children that if a balance isn't struck, they will not have a smooth and successful ride. Too much weight on either side causes one end to go up and the other down. This is true in life as well. Too much weight in life causes our stress indicators to go up, our health to go down; our blood pressure up, our spirits down. Our lives require balance.

I have learned to borrow a page from my parents' lives. Recently, in fact, Ron and I hired a sitter and danced the night away to our favorite seventies songs. And because life is so circular, decades earlier and a few blocks from where we were clapping our hands and moving to the melodies, Ron had been a teenage member of the Afro Gents dance group, helping to get more than a few parties started. He's still a smooth operator. More than that, he's my play-mate; the partner who helps keep my seesaw balanced. We all need that kind of lover, or friend, or relative, or perhaps a spiritual advisor, someone to depend on who will be there for us during life's many ups and downs. Remember the seesaw ride when the ride was going smoothly until the other person suddenly leaped or fell off? You went slamming to the hard ground and that felt pretty miserable. That's why you need to seek reliable, prayerful support.

Can you recall a recent time in your life when perhaps a physical symptom, financial loss, or alarming phone call sent you crashing to the ground? Of course, life happens, but there's a way to spend more of your time maintaining an even keel.

I can just hear the protests. "I've got work to do," or "Who's supposed to bring in the money while I'm playing on that seesaw?" I understand the skepticism. Let me assure you, I believe in the benefits of hard work. And no matter what kind of work you may be doing, including volunteering, it's good for the soul. We should all work and contribute our gifts. As Big Mama, one of the characters in Brenda Lane Richardson's *Chesapeake Song*, points out: "Everybody's got to work. Even a broke clock give the right time twice a day." The catch is that you'll work more efficiently if your life is balanced.

I've included tips on how to move beyond the guilt that's churned up as we make time to create balance in Chapter 2. For now, try the following visualization.

Sitting in a comfortable position in a quiet spot, where you can breathe easily and deeply, imagine waking up on Christmas morning. See yourself descending a wide marble stairway and hearing a loving, joy-filled voice greeting you: "Good morning. Oh, just wait until you see what I have for you. There's so much I want to give you."

You exchange warm hugs and kisses and, as you sit, you're handed your first brightly wrapped package. You pull off the wrapping, and the figure eight drifts out, which makes you ecstatic. "Eight hours," you say. "I have eight hours."

You're imagining what you can accomplish in all that time, and like almost everybody at Christmas, in the back of your mind, you're wishing there was another gift to open. And there is: The next package actually contains another eight hours. The eight floats up, undulating in the air and you laugh at its playfulness, assured that now there's time to add fun to your list. You feel rich in time. And you are.

And because God always gives us more than we ask for, there is still another box under the tree. And, you guessed it, it contains eight more hours!

As you continue visualizing, you hear your favorite music playing. You jump up, the shining eights bouncing and twirling as you dance. What a day of gifts! You embrace your time and promise your gift-giver, who is the Holy Spirit, that from this point on you'll spend the gifts wisely. With a deep, cleansing breath, open your eyes.

Using your favorite pen and taking your time, write a list of what you want to "purchase" with your gifts of time. Work at changing your perspective by remembering the wise words of poet and Nobel laureate Rabindranath Tagore: "The butterfly counts not months but moments and has time enough."

Since you're not rushing, take the time to write in a penmanship that reflects you at your best. Write your list as if you were communicating with someone of great importance, because you are: This list is for you. If you start by listing rest, recuperation, sleep, exercise, and meditation you may find that these set just the right tone for change in your life. Then there's work, of course. (Hopefully you're engaged in a career you love. If not, I'll discuss that in detail, later in this book.) What else is added to your list? How about chores? Regular responsibilities, like cooking dinner, shopping, helping the kids with homework. Remember to leave time for spontaneous events—like calling a best buddy and asking her to meet you for dinner and a laugh-filled conversation.

As you compile your list, whenever you find yourself panicking about how you'll get it all done, go back to that place at the foot of the Christmas tree . . . feel the gift. Thank the Creator and remember to keep your spiritual account balanced.

Prayer for the Day: *Dear Heavenly Father, you have given me so very much that I am wealthy beyond measure. Thank you for the hours of the day and the sense of purpose I carry that has been passed on from my ancestors. Dear Lord, help me to remember that your wristwatch doesn't necessarily run at the same speed as mine, and that your time is the highest authority. With your help I'll keep an even keel, sailing my ship of life. Above all, I will remember that right at this moment I am exactly where I'm supposed to be. All things in your name, Amen.*

CHAPTER 2

Eliminating Guilt

T he young woman had made an appointment and as soon as she was seated in front of my desk, and the door closed behind her, she collapsed into sobs. It took awhile to ferret out the reason for her distress as she continued by moaning about having to pay for her selfishness. With gentle probing, I learned the cause of her anguish. Her husband of two years was having an affair, and he blamed her. "He's tired of coming home to an empty home and empty bed," she explained.

This twenty-something, childless parishioner was an up-and-coming business executive and during the previous year had spent a lot of time on the road developing her career. As her tears subsided and we continued talking, I learned more about her so-called "selfishness."

Every Friday, even when it might mean the loss of a potential client, she flew back into town early enough to prepare dinner for her husband, so they could start the weekends off right. And she kept Saturdays sacrosanct, always reserving the day to join him for his favorite sports events, even when she would have preferred to take some down time or get her hair done at a favorite beauty salon. During her weeklong absences, she often phoned him and sent him romantic notes and occasional gifts.

Maybe you're thinking (as I was) that she sounded like an exemplary wife, so I wondered why her husband was blaming her. And how had he managed to turn the tables and make her feel guilty? The truth is that no one can *make* us feel guilty. They might attempt to, but their manipulations won't work unless life's experiences have made us prone to feeling guilt.

Exploring the issue of guilt is of particular importance here, because it can get us off balance and keep us there. If the goal is to maintain a state of equilibrium—remember the image of the seesaw and the laughter it evokes—then guilt could well be described as dead weight. This young woman didn't have any children who needed her time and attention. She'd been intentional about building her career before having children, hoping that later, when and if she became a parent, she could have more flexibility and travel less. And she was clearly making an effort to shower her husband with love. Why should she feel guilty about having to be out of town for work or ignore her own needs?

Don't get me wrong. A modicum of guilt can be healthy. There aren't many pastors who won't agree. Righteous guilt is an inner alarm that God designed in humans to tamp down our arrogance and help make us moral beings. Those feelings of unease and that flush of discomfort remind us that there are some things that we really should—or should not—do. It's not necessary to enumerate those "shoulds" and "should nots": They were written in stone and can be found today in Exodus 20. Of course I'm referring to the Ten Commandments.

As a pastor, I've found that women tend to experience generalized feelings of guilt that have to do with societal expectations about the female role; about nature and nurture, and the fact that during childhood most girls are given dolls to rock and tend to—early training in how to devote ourselves to the needs of others.

The most damaging form of guilt is that which is passed on in families, when parental figures harshly scold children for making mistakes and blame them for their misfortunes. I'm thinking about a well-meaning single father who took on an extra job to pay for his son's Catholic school tuition. Unfortunately, when the boy brought home a failing grade, his dad angrily listed the sacrifices he was making so the son could get a good education. Although the boy hardly listened when his father said, "I'm proud to be your father and blessed to be able to give you a good education," he did feel profound guilt during his dad's scolding lectures. In fact, he started hating that he was enrolled in a school that was so expensive that his dad was exhausted and broke trying to keep him there.

The guilt the boy felt interfered with his learning. He was disappointed in himself, and finally admitted during one heated family session that he spent all his extra time playing computer games and talking on the phone, rather than doing homework. Furious with his dad for humiliating him when he failed, the boy was unintentionally trying to get back at him by failing. It was a clear example of guilt standing as an obstacle to a balanced life. The boy taking time for play and socializing was great, but his life could have been more balanced if his guilt and anger hadn't caused him to fail.

A lot of adults struggle with guilt long after childhood, especially when it stems from memories of parents favoring one child over another. Some of these favored children suffer with "survivor's guilt." One woman from Kansas, I'll call her Paula, has a life that many would envy. She's an active Christian, happens to be physically beautiful and healthy with a sunny disposition and, after a first marriage that ended in an amicable divorce, Paula became independently rich.

Despite her comfortable life, Paula struggles with survivor's guilt. Her two sisters have lived through great misfortune, and whenever they call for loans—which is often—they constantly remind her that their parents didn't love them as much as Paula. Not for a minute am I discounting the grief these women feel. In too many families, especially in the past when there was less information available about the emotional needs of children, parents often showed favoritism. The grief these sisters felt was probably genuine.

But here's the catch. Guilty feelings are out of control when we feel responsible for the happiness, comfort, safety, and peace of mind of those we love. It's an impossible task, and yet, when we don't live up to it, guilt leaves us feeling helpless, remorseful, and powerless. Time after time, Paula has flown to different cities to bail her oldest sister out of legal troubles stemming from her drug use, and she has footed the bill for her to enroll in several rehab programs, which have proved unsuccessful. The youngest sister has her share of troubles in choosing the wrong men. Paula has rushed in trying to save her, too.

Paula is a perfect example of someone struggling with what I call the Savior Complex. Of course people like her don't think they can handle supernatural tasks, but they do feel they can make everything better for those they love. But allowing loved ones to work through their own problems, saving themselves, actually gives them opportunities to mature and feel more confident. When we insist on trying to alleviate a loved one's suffering, that loved one may take us for granted or treat us with contempt.

A few years ago, for example, Paula was ill, but when she called to ask for support, her sisters didn't return her phone call. Paula recognized the connection between her deteriorating health and the guilt she felt about her sisters and turned to a therapist for help. In creating a balanced life she has learned to say no to her sisters. Not surprisingly, they were furious with her. In fact, one of them called her a selfish bitch.

When you try to bring your life into balance and make your needs a priority, don't be surprised if some of the people who are closest to you respond in a negative manner. Children and siblings, friends, husbands, boyfriends, parents—the list can be endless—won't want you to pull back in providing for them. As theologian H. Richard Niebuhr has pointed out, the first law of humanity is self-preservation. No matter how much we may pride ourselves on our independence, in our hearts we all want to have someone who will place our needs above their own.

In creating balance, we focus on that which helps us feel nurtured, while maintaining clear boundaries: understanding about where our responsibilities end and where a loved one's responsibility for himself begins. And we learn to decipher the difference between *feeling* selfish and actually behaving in a selfish manner.

My female biblical role model is Deborah, who I consider the first real multitasker. A wife, prophetess, and judge, Deborah was a woman with clear boundaries and high self-regard. She took pride in her respected position in the community—one of the other people who rose to her level was Moses. And talk about intriguing work! As a judge, she got to make decisions; as a prophetess, she remained attuned to God's desires.

It was an enormous job, but rather than running here and there to hold court with the Israelites who turned to her for help in settling their disputes, she sat beneath a tree that was named for her— the Palm of Deborah—and people came to her.

At some point, Deborah told a man named Barak that God commanded him to assemble ten thousand warriors and confront their enemy. When he responded by saying he wouldn't go unless she did, she agreed to accompany him, but first she reminded him that he wouldn't get all the credit for her work. She said there would be no glory for him in victory, because the Lord would be delivering the Canaanites into a woman's hands.

Deborah was right: They won the battle in an overwhelming victory. And today, Deborah is known as the Mother of Israel. Something tells me she didn't spend a whole lot of time feeling guilty about reaping her well-deserved glory.

Another of my role models, my mom, did feel somewhat guilty about not always being around when I needed her. After we moved to the Bronx, Mom had to manage the household on a fairly rigid schedule. Dad left for work on weekdays at 4:30 a.m., long before we awoke. About an hour later, Mom rose and got dressed and was in the car by 7:15 for her drive to Harlem. The infrequent mornings when she was still around and I was attending a neighborhood elementary school, she walked me about a block, kissed me goodbye, and prayed that I'd arrive safely. Most afternoons, when I wasn't taking the train to Harlem to meet her, I was a latch-key kid and went home to an empty house.

Several of the homes of our Italian-American neighbors were more traditional. Many of the mothers stayed to home to cook, clean, and care for younger children. There were times when I wished for a similar lifestyle, and years later, I told my mother, "I wish you'd been around to brush my hair."

My mother responded without bitterness, "Honey, I did the best I could do."

How gracious of her not to snap at me and remind me of how much she'd done for me. Any sadness I felt about not having more of her in my young life was mitigated by a life-changing experience. I became a mother.

I remember waking up that first day, at the hospital. I'd slept deeply, following an epidural. Ron had left the room temporarily and Mom was standing over me.

My first words were, "Did you see my baby?"

"I saw your baby and he's healthy, beautiful, and fine."

Before the day was over, she was cradling Baby Boy Samuel and showing me how to feed him, hold his head, and change his diaper. She kept kissing and kissing him, wanting him to know that he'd been born into a loving family.

I have two sons now, and know what it's like to have to balance their needs and mine, without letting my guilt take over. We all do the best we can.

During a recent speaking engagement in Atlanta, someone offered me a luscious dessert, and although I would have enjoyed it, I turned it down, and confided to a friend that my favorite desserts were my husband's still warm, fresh-from-the-oven banana pudding and my son Samuel's yellow cake with chocolate frosting. Hours

later, when I returned home late in the evening, I found a note taped
to the front door.

"Hi Mom, please go to the kitchen. There's something you like
in there."

As if he'd read my mind, Samuel had baked a yellow cake with
chocolate frosting. Savoring a healthy slice, I sat in our sleep-hushed
home, feeling too blessed to feel guilty.

Battling Guilt

- If you're a parent, start a purse-sized notebook for each of
  your children, and when work requires you to be away,
  write a short entry. It might be something as short as,
  "Oakland, Calif., Jan. 16th, here for consultation. Wish
  you were here to laugh with me about the nasty pancakes
  room service delivered. Miss you, Mom." Let your child
  read the notebook when you return home, and continue
  writing. Over the years, this will become a valued keepsake.

- It is also important to plan great vacations when you're
  away a lot. For example, when I recently returned from
  leading the Hampton Minister's Conference, I had planned
  a family vacation—an eight-day family retreat in the
  Bahamas—so we could have uninterrupted time together.
  Since the boys heard that I'd stayed in a "Royal Suite" it
  was important to them for them to have similar
  accommodations.

- Parents also find that it helps to relieve guilt if they make
  it a point to praise children for skills they may have learned
  as a result of them not being there. Maybe a child learned

to do laundry because a parent didn't have the time to handle that chore. When you praise your child for a job well done, point out that he is making it easier for you to support him.

- E-mail is a great connector for parents who are often away from home. If you subscribe to a service with parental controls, you'll have more peace of mind when you encourage your child to IM or e-mail you.

- If you know you're going to miss a lot of your child's school events—plays, games, recitals—find a parent that does attend regularly and offer to share photo processing expenses if he or she takes pictures of your child as well as his or her own. Be sure to display photos of your child in action—on a refrigerator, office desk, as your computer's wallpaper.

- If you have to break an engagement with a loved one, send them an IOU. Say "This is good for one_____" and fill in the blank: basketball game, concert, lunch out. Make sure you honor your heartfelt debt sometime in the near future.

- Stave off feelings of guilt concerning a romantic interest by finding creative times together during the day. One woman used to meet her husband in the lingerie section of an exclusive department store, and after they purchased something he wanted her to wear, she made it a point to find a time when she could model it for her. Another couple takes "poetry breaks": via telephone, by reading lines from Rita Dove, Langston Hughes, or excerpts from other favorite poets. Another variation on this is the share-a-joke calls.

• If you have a friend who often feels guilty about being away from a child or spouse, host a "praise party" for her. Invite her closest friends and family and take turns telling her why you think she's wonderful and why she's important to you.

Devotion: *Lord, thank you for giving me this day my daily bread. I have not accomplished all that I wanted to, but for what I have accomplished, I give you thanks and glory. I praise you for the spirit that kept me going. I've done my best today. Please let me sleep peacefully and begin tomorrow fresh and ready for that which awaits me.*

CHAPTER 3

Spiritual Balancing

Given New York City's outrageous traffic, with cars moving in fits and starts, creeping along and then picking up speed, cabs veering into different lanes and jaywalkers darting between cars, a lot of residents refuse to drive. I'm not one of them. I don't like taking cabs or letting someone drive me. When I'm alone in the car, I'm in control. I know back streets, and there's always the challenge of creating new routes. I'm an aggressive New York driver, and when I'm alone in my car, I'm working out my stuff. By the time I get to where I'm going I've chilled out.

This doesn't work for me when the tires on my car need balancing. After a winter of bumping over gaping potholes, the steering wheel begins to vibrate, and after awhile I have to take the car in to have the tires balanced. The technician mounts a tire on the balancing machine and spins the wheel to locate the heavier part. By the time he's finished and I'm on the road again, I'm pleasantly surprised at how much smoother my car rides, and then I'm back in control, behind the wheel.

There's a parallel between feeling in control behind the wheel and feeling in control in life. Just as I'm intentional about taking my car in to have the tires balanced, I have to approach life with the same sense of purpose.

Moving through life is the issue. We are powered by God, who is within us. Yet, he has blessed us with free will. He doesn't move us around like puppets. He gives us the freedom to love and obey him. The goal, then, is to keep our lives balanced so we can discern God's purpose and distinguish between what we want and what He wants for us: God's perfect will.

I have four different approaches to spiritual balancing that you might find helpful, all of them involving prayer. When it comes to praying, the equation is this: much prayer, much power; little prayer, little power; no prayer, no power.

Fasting

For me, personally, prayer in conjunction with fasting has proven to be a powerful combination. Some people think of fasting as a modern fad, but of course it dates back thousands of years. Perhaps one of the most memorable fasts in the Bible is undertaken by Jesus when he was in the desert for forty days. "He ate nothing during those days, and at the end of them he was hungry" (Luke 4:2). To Satan, who tried to tempt him, Jesus responded: "Man does not live by bread alone, but on every word that comes from the mouth of God" (Matthew 4:4).

Jesus's single-mindedness and focus was enhanced by the spiritual discipline of fasting, for it serves a number of functions. As a ritual, it has a humbling effect, reminding us of our neediness. It is also an act of devotion that subjects our will to the will and wisdom of the Holy Father. His will and wisdom are more easily discerned because fasting gives us more time for praying and listening, when we might otherwise be taking time for meal preparation and eating. And finally, fasting is an act of emulation, showing God that we too are willing to suffer for the greater good.

In 1991, after ending a disappointing relationship, I wondered about my future. I'd pastored a church for eleven years and had discovered that since leading a church was such a new role for women, a lot of men viewed me as holy, unapproachable, and untouchable. Not many men were comfortable in the role of the pastor's boyfriend or husband. That meant I had an additional challenge because I would have to be in an unusual holy alliance. I felt that if it was God's will for me to remain single, I was certainly willing to accept that. If it wasn't, I'd already had enough of heartbreak and heartache, and I didn't want to move into another relationship blindly. I wanted help in finding the right mate and felt that fasting would help me discern God's perfect will.

There are no rules or standards for fasting. Dietary approaches always work best when they're based upon an individual's specific health. In my case, after getting medical clearance, I began a forty-day fast, ingesting liquids during the day and having one meal in the evening. During that time, I prayed to God, asking for clarity and focus concerning my romantic life. My fast began in January and lasted into February. This wasn't the first time I'd utilized this tool, and as before I found that cutting down on food became easier with each passing day. As excess weight dropped from my body and my cells were cleansed of toxins, I began to feel energized.

A month later, on the Monday of Holy week—which that year began in February—I attended a conference at Convent Avenue

Baptist Church in Harlem. At the end of the day I was greeting one of the pastors, the Reverend Fran Manning, when out of the corner of my eye, I noticed a handsome African American man in a well-tailored suit.

I asked Fran if she knew who he was. Raising an eyebrow she watched him for a minute and then turned back toward me with a smile. "That's Ronald Cook, our church administrator, and I think he's single."

I'm not generally very assertive when it comes to meeting men, but this time I practically insisted that she invite him to join us for dessert at Copeland's Restaurant, where we planned to dine, and he quickly accepted.

The entire time the three of us sat in that busy Harlem eatery, Ron and I kept making eye contact, and as soon as Fran went to the bathroom, it seemed he and I couldn't stop staring at each other. So I was pleased when he said, "I've always wanted to meet you." He admitted that he'd always thought of me as unapproachable.

I was thinking, "I've always wanted to meet you too." I'd seen him before from a distance, but this was our first time talking. What I'd heard so far impressed me. His job as Convent's administrator required him to understand the rigors of a pastor's duties. He was also religious, intellectually curious, and a good listener, and he had a great sense of humor—and did I mention he was good-looking?

Later that evening, it was just the two of us, sitting in his parked car on 125th Street, hurriedly exchanging biographical details. Ron had been raised on 144th, the same street where I was born, and, like my parents, his hailed from Virginia and North Carolina. All of that could have been written off as coincidence, until he added, "I've just finished a fast."

I almost gasped when he said this, and grew more astonished as he continued. "I asked God whether I was ready for marriage. If you are the woman God sent to me, I promise to be a good steward over this gift."

Enclosed in his car and hearing these words, I felt I was about to embark on a holy alliance. I was deeply moved as he added, "Let's leave it to God to confirm. Why don't we fast again for another forty-eight hours and then talk?"

I know now that it was love at first sight. From the time I saw Ron at church, it was as if I had always known him. We saw each other that next Wednesday and then practically every day thereafter. By June we wanted to get engaged. First, though, Ron wanted to ask some special people in my life for permission to take my hand in marriage: my mother and my favorite aunt, Katherine—one of the nieces from Virginia that my dad had helped support and put through college.

My mother had already grilled him on several occasions, and as far as she was concerned he'd already passed her stringent test. Aunt Katherine gave an enthusiastic response, and pulling me aside, she whispered in my ear, "He's a good man. Be good to him. Don't chase this man away." Only weeks later, she died and I never again saw her alive. My mother, however, lived for many more years and took Ron to her heart, like a mother to son.

The moral of this story is not that fasting will lead you to the life you desire. Jesus's life certainly wasn't a bed of roses after he returned from the desert. But fasting did prepare me to become more engaged with my spiritual life. And for all I know, submitting myself completely to God's will softened my body language or added luster to my skin, thus making me more attractive to my future husband. You'll remember me saying that before our meeting Ron had viewed me as unapproachable, but this time he hadn't. And this I know for sure: The discipline of fasting prepared me to be more open and trusting and reawakened my bruised heart. Like the saying goes, chance favors the well-prepared.

Visualization

There's another romantic story I'd like to share, about a woman who prayed and asked for discernment, utilizing a slightly different approach. Lee's two-year marriage had disintegrated and she was troubled at having to raise a son without an involved father. She became very intentional about the kind of balanced life she hoped to create.

"Maya Angelou has said that if you want to know about a person, you only have to listen and he'll tell you all about himself," Lee says. "That couldn't have been truer about my husband. When we met, he told me he was a Christian, but that he didn't go to church. I didn't challenge him because I was happy to have someone who loved me. I settled for less.

"Once we were married," Lee continues, "serious problems surfaced. He kept a mistress, stayed out plenty of nights, spent lots of time in bars, and beat me if I dared to complain. That was when I realized that just saying you're a Christian doesn't mean much. I could say I'm a bumble bee, but I can't fly or collect nectar from flowers because I'm not a bee. I wanted to live in a home and be part of a team of two Christian parents whose faith could be seen through their actions. But I could never appeal to my husband on moral grounds, because he felt whatever he did was acceptable, as long as it didn't land him in prison. He had no moral basement. He just kept getting lower and lower. I knew that this was a long way from the life I wanted, and I made him leave."

Distraught, every weekday morning Lee began going to a chapel located in the church building where she dropped her son off for preschool. "I went faithfully, and spent about a half hour each time on my knees, praying and visualizing the kind of man I needed. I wanted someone who could be a good father for my son and a faithful husband to me. I didn't picture any physical characteristics, but I merely asked God to send me someone who walks his faith. I kept visualizing a man who was literally walking, bathed in God's light. I wanted a Christian marriage."

Worried about Lee's sanity, her friends asked her about her long prayer sessions in the chapel, and she assured them that she was growing stronger by the day. About a year later, she took a business trip to New York with a coworker. When she was rushing from her hotel room for a meeting, her coworker admitted that he was attracted to her and she grew outraged. "I don't know why his confession infuriated me, but he had a creepy personality." She went to the meeting as scheduled, but midway through, began feeling terrible about the way she'd spoken to this coworker. Leaving abruptly, she sought him out and apologized.

"He accepted my apology, and knowing I was familiar with the city, he asked me to take him to Grand Central Station, where he was meeting a former roommate for lunch. I didn't want to go, but I'd acted so ugly earlier that I wanted to make it up to him and I consented."

They stood in the middle of busy Grand Central Station, and Lee turned her gaze toward the flow of busy tourists and commuters, rushing toward trains and subways. "At some point, I saw the face of a tall, handsome man. I got only a glimpse, but that nanosecond was long enough for me to notice that he was wearing a clerical collar. I thought, 'Okay God, that's the kind of man I've been praying for, someone who walks his faith.' At that point Lee says the man looked toward her and her coworker. "He began waving at us, and the closer he moved in our direction the faster he walked."

The friend her coworker was meeting was an Episcopal minister. They exchanged numbers, and after a few years of dating, he and Lee eventually married. Over the next fifteen years Lee's husband and her son had a turbulent relationship, but today her husband and son are close.

"When things got rough between the two of them, my husband could have thrown up his hands, said 'He's not my son,' and walked out, but he didn't. He stayed because he's a good man with a conscience and when we took our vows he knew the deal included my son. Staying was the right thing to do. My son got the message from watching him that a real man doesn't walk away from obligations. Now he has grown into a man who honors his promises."

There are no scientific explanations for the events in Lee's story. It's true that researchers have found many instances in which people have focused on an image, and given it lots of positive energy until it became an objective reality. But there's no need for a scientific explanation. Through the frequency of her prayer Lee aligned herself with He who governs the principles of the universe, our Great Creator, the Lord God.

Writing Letters to God

Few things can make parents feel more desperate than out-of-control teenagers. When children are little and don't follow orders it's easy enough to just lift them up and carry them to wherever you want them to be. But if they act out when they grow up, life gets more complicated. The rage and fury generated between parents and children can throw every member of the household off balance.

John, the father of a teenage son, had always said that if his son didn't obey him he was either going to put him into the street or kill him. Fortunately, he didn't overreact when his son was fourteen and was arrested for shoplifting.

"When the call came, I was like one of those parents on TV: 'Sorry, officer, you must have the wrong number. My son is upstairs doing his homework.'"

But there was no mistake; it was in fact John's son. John gave him a stern warning and grounded him for a month. "He started sneaking out at night, after my wife and I went to bed."

More arrests followed, as did angry confrontations and attempts to handle the situation with "Tough Love."

"When we received another call from the police station and heard that my son and his friends had stolen someone's car keys, I told them they could keep him in lockup." John's wife begged him to let their son return home, and for a while things seemed to be improving, especially after the young man went into therapy. "I was willing to try pretty much anything," John says. "I felt shell shocked. The two of us had once been very close. Things cooled down around my house."

Not for long. The young man quit therapy, stopped going to classes, and his parents found marijuana in his room. "He heard I was looking for him, and he didn't come home for three days. In the middle of the second night, I was combing the streets for him when

I ran into one of his youth pastors. She advised me to go home and start writing letters to God. What else was there left for me to do?"

John wrote long impassioned letters to God, pouring out his grief, asking how things had come to such a sorry state. At the end of each letter, he thanked God for keeping his son safe and asked him to help him calm the anger between the two of them.

"I have a box full of those letters. For the next year my son was in and out of the house, but I didn't ask him to leave and I kept writing."

Years passed and the box was put away, and then one afternoon John ran across it at the top of a closet. "I reread the letters and was dumbfounded at how bad things used to be between us. I suppose I forgot because we lived through his rebellion. He served in the Marines and he's over here all the time now, with his wife and children."

I've found that often when we ask God to intervene in a difficult situation, if the change doesn't occur very quickly, we forget to acknowledge the blessing. John's letters may have had a hidden benefit, providing him with an emotional release that mitigated some of his anger and made it easier for his son to approach him. If you decide to write letters to God, you may enjoy entering them in your journal.

Assembling a Prayer Group

The woman, a writer, had been working on a particular manuscript for three years, and time and time again she met with disappointment. She received rejection letters from thirty agents, but whenever one of these communications contained helpful advice, she incorporated changes into the manuscript and then sent it out to different agents. After two years, she found an agent who liked her writing enough to submit the manuscript to editors at major publishing houses. Two weeks before the submissions, she wrote to twenty of her most prayerful friends and asked them to pray for her.

"I didn't ask them to help me get a lot of money," the writer explains. "I asked them to pray for my peace of mind, because I knew I would be sitting on the edge of my seat while the editors were looking over my manuscript, and I asked them to bless the editors who would be reading it." Her friends wrote back with assurances of prayer.

Five editors received copies of the manuscript. "It didn't take long for my agent to call and tell me about the first rejection from an editor, who said I didn't write well. Of course, I was disappointed." The second, third, and fourth rejections caught her by surprise. "One claimed it moved too slowly. Another thought I should cut out references to faith. Another said he was sure I'd sell it, but not to him." News of the fifth and final rejection was swift in coming.

"I heard my agent's voice on the phone and I said, 'Don't tell me. She's not going to buy it.' My agent agreed that I was right, but added, 'There's some good news. She says you're very talented. She loved the book and just wants you to make some minor changes.' "

The writer is now back at work, making revisions in the manuscript. At this point, she still doesn't know whether the editor will buy it. But she says of her prayer group, "Their encouragement and support has allowed me to rewrite with a renewed vigor. I've pursued this dream for a long time, and I was exhausted. Those rejections from editors, especially comments about me not being able to write well, might have put me out of business, but I'm at it again. My friends continue to send me encouraging notes that I treasure. Their prayers are keeping my battery charged."

Remember that image of taking a car in for servicing, when the technician mounts it on a rack so he can balance the tires? Well, this is the human version of balancing. Good news or bad, the writer will emerge from this experience with a community of friends willing to stand as his or her partners in Christ. If you're facing a difficult situation, you might consider asking friends and family for support. They'll keep you lifted up through prayer. What a positive way to develop a sense of balance.

CHAPTER 4

Coming to Ourselves

s we continue to explore the *B* in Blessed, under the subject of spiritual balancing, it's important to consider the story of the Prodigal Son (Luke 15). In this narrative, the son takes his inheritance from his father and goes off to enjoy a dissolute life, squandering his money. When he realizes his mistakes, he returns home and is welcomed by the father. This symbolizes our relationship with God, who offers unconditional love. He is always willing to forgive us, no matter what our sins.

For the purpose of completing our discussion on creating balance in our lives, it is important to home in on one particular verse in the Prodigal Son's story. It is the passage in which the son seems to awaken from a drunken stupor: "And when he came to himself, he said, How many hired servants of my father's have bread enough and to spare, and I perish with hunger" (Luke 15:17). The hunger of which he speaks is the need for something substantive in his life. Now, ordinarily, I wouldn't think it was wrong for a son to ask for his inheritance and strike out on his own. I encourage people to seek out new experiences. But this is not just any Father and child, this passage is about breaking away from God. A second offense is the son's squandering of his inheritance. An inheritance isn't something that we earn; it is a gift, and thus, this story is about not misusing the gifts that God has given us. The son makes mistakes, as most of us do, but more importantly he eventually "came to himself."

Let's look closely at that phrase and the meaning behind it. It seems he finally recognized his own nobler attributes, which were his greatest inheritances and which could not be accounted for in a bank ledger, aspects like self-respect, love, gratitude for family, and obedience to God.

After a time of drunkenness, coming to oneself represents a moment of great sobriety. The prodigal repented. And repentance is a decision followed by appropriate action. He realized he would prefer to be with his father as a slave than alone amid the fleshpots of the city, and he returned home.

This moment in Luke is tremendously important for those of us striving for balance. In Part I of this book, we have learned why striking a balance is important, moved through the guilt that might prevent us from attaining it, and learned how to utilize tools that can help us enjoy balanced lives. But it's impossible to move on to the next step, if, like the Prodigal Son, we are not spiritually ready. If we are not ready, we will allow our gifts to be squandered. If we are not ready, it won't be necessary for a robber to take our gifts away from us by force—we will hand them over of our own accord.

This is a lesson played out repeatedly in the media. Consider all the Hollywood celebrities who supposedly have "everything," including talent, good looks, fame, mansions, and multimillion-dollar bank balances. All this allows them to acquire anything they want, when they want it. And yet, so many of these celebrities appear on television talk shows, or in courtrooms, or write tell-all memoirs detailing their squandered lives. They aren't the only ones. Think of the many political leaders and corporate executives who seemed to have it all, but come to admit they have so little. They are glitzy reminders that we must come to ourselves before we can savor the taste of the fruits on our Father's vines.

Whatever happened to the Prodigal Son? Once the party his father threw to welcome him back had ended, did he spend the rest of his days making up for his lost time? Did he strike it rich or forget what he'd learned and once again head for greener pastures? It doesn't say, and there's reason for that. It's not what Luke wanted us to focus on. In writing this story, he was pointing out that as long as we breathe, our future, like that of the Prodigal Son, remains open to possibilities.

When I consider possibilities, I think of a young woman, who, for the sake of anonymity, I will call Linda. Unlike the Prodigal Son, Linda was not born into prosperous circumstances. In fact, Linda was raised in Miami by a teenaged mother. "She was only fifteen when she met my father," Linda says. "He was twenty and had just arrived from the Dominican Republic. He reeled my mother in. I was her first child and I have five siblings under me." Her father eventually went to prison on drug charges and she saw little of him.

"When I was little, I used to wonder why my mother exuded such anger toward her mother. My grandmother was young too. After she moved to Miami from Georgia, she started having children at fourteen, and she had eleven of them—five from her husband, who was sent to jail and then never returned home, and six kids from a boyfriend. My grandmother was the type that hung out, partied, and drank with her kids. She liked having a good time.

"I later learned that her boyfriend had raped my mother, and when my mother explained what happened, my grandmother called her a liar. She must have believed her though, because she stabbed her boyfriend with a knife. He stayed around after that for many years until he died. Fortunately, no pregnancy resulted from the rape."

Linda's mother, a victim of this man's violent behavior, became angry and overwhelmed with the responsibilities of raising her own children and turned to drugs. "When I was eight or nine years old, my mother would take me to her friends' broken down rooms and I was her protector. I'd have twenty dollars tucked down in my panties to make sure we had money to get home after her drug spree. I'd watch her shoot heroin into her veins. She got money from welfare. When she had four kids and was pregnant with twins, I started begging her to let me go along when she cashed the checks. She'd say, 'No, bitch, I'm the grown-up here, I'll take care of it.' I knew if she didn't take me along to the check cashing place, she would go off with her friends and get high, then we'd have another month with barely anything to eat."

With so much turmoil at home, attending school regularly was difficult for Linda. "Especially because my mother was physically abusive," Linda continued. After an angry argument with a boyfriend, when Linda was about nine, her mother called her and a younger brother into her bedroom and asked whether they thought she loved them. Before they could respond, "She beat the hell out of us," Linda said. "I thought she was going to kill us. She hit us with her fists and with any objects she could grab. She punched and scratched my face. I'd fall and she'd say, 'Get the fuck up, bitch.' She ripped my brother's T-shirt and started on him. I grabbed him and ran and we hid under a bed."

When Linda showed up at school the next day, one of the neighbor's daughters, Emma Jean, invited her to their home. Once there, Linda confided in her classmate about her mother's abuse. "I didn't realize that Emma Jean's mother, Mrs. West, was listening outside the door. Mrs. West scolded Linda's mother about the abuse and took Linda to church, where the young girl found comfort in the idea of a loving Father.

Life only grew harsher for Linda and her siblings. "My mother died from AIDS when I was sixteen. My grandmother had already raised eleven kids and she was resentful about having to take us in, but there wasn't anyone else." The grandmother pressured Linda to drop out of high school and get a job. Linda did quit, but she ran off with a man who was ten years her senior. He rented a furnished room for them in Delaware. "I figured now I could create a better life for myself and then help my brothers and sisters."

That better life never materialized. As psychologists often point out, a lot of people re-create situations in their new lives that are reminiscent of the ones they left behind. In Linda's case, that meant drugs and physical abuse. Her new boyfriend free-based cocaine and he beat her. When Linda tried to leave him, he doused her with gasoline and tried to set her on fire. Her life was spared when his cigarette lighter failed to work.

Returning to Miami to escape him, Linda discovered that her oldest brother was selling drugs. She moved in with her grandmother, determined to help support her other siblings, and found a job as a manager at McDonald's. Before long, she met Alfonso, a police detective, the man of her dreams. "Talk about awesome!" Linda enthuses, and adds, "try fantastic, wholesome, the epitome of a good man. I kept waiting for the other shoe to drop. I was sure he'd tell me he was gay or he'd turn on me and beat me."

Five years her senior, Alfonso turned out to be protective and gentle. "He was the youngest child in a middle-class family. His parents worked for the city. They're stable people who spend holidays and birthdays together, enjoying each other. My experience with family gatherings had been people getting drunk, fights breaking out, and seeing blood. Alfonso's family showered him with affection. He'd had some trouble in his past. When he was younger, someone offered him coke and he took it and got hooked. But his parents hung in there, made sure he got treatment, and he joined a twelve-step program."

After two months of dating, Alfonso took Linda to meet his family. She watched with awe when he spotted his mother returning home from a shopping trip and rolled down the car window and called, "Hey Mama, where you going, beautiful?" Alfonso parked, hugged his mom, and insisted on pulling her grocery cart. "When I saw that show of love, I was blown away. That was the day I thought, Oh, God, I love this man."

Like many people who have experienced childhood trauma, Linda unconsciously tried to drive Alfonso away. "By 1991, we lived together. One day I came out of the shower with a towel around me, thinking Alfonso was gone. But he was at the desk paying bills. I thought my body was too heavy and ugly to be seen, so I asked him to leave the room so I could get dressed. When he resisted, I said, 'Get the fuck out.'"

Instead of leaving in a rage, Alfonso told her, "'I'm not leaving. I don't know where you're coming from, but I won't entertain it.' I was still in fighting mode, so very gently, he pulled me to the mirror. He said, 'Have you looked at yourself? You are so beautiful. Anybody would want to look at you.' I repeated, 'Get the fuck out of the room.' He told me, 'I love you, but you still don't trust me.' He pulled the towel away from me, and oh, my God, my worst fear was feeling vulnerable. But he made me look in the mirror. He said, 'Do you see that woman? I love everything about her. You're beautiful. Even if you had five stomachs I'd love you. I want you to be my wife. I know we have many enemies out here, but I'm not the enemy. Stop trying to ruin our relationship.' From that point on, I felt I could fly. I thought, 'This is it. I'm covered. I'm protected. He loves me for me, fat or thin, stupid or smart, progressing or digressing. He simply loves this person.'"

The two married soon afterward, started a successful security business, and purchased a five-bedroom home. But by Christmas of 2001, three months after September 11, 2001, Alfonso was struggling with the sense of helplessness that plagued so many officers in the wake of the attacks, a situation that was compounded by recent arguments with his ex-wife over seeing his eight-year-old son for the holidays. To Linda's great dismay, Alfonso began using drugs again.

"I got hold of him at work. I was livid. He'd stayed away all night, and I said, 'Alfonso, what are you doing? We've got a lot going for us.' He talked to me about the drugs, how they were like a demon. 'I can't seem to fight them,' he said. That night, when he didn't come home, I knew I'd never see him again."

She was visiting Alfonso's sister when the police arrived. They said he was sitting in a parked car and had died from a single gunshot wound to the head. "It was suicide. I felt like somebody had robbed me."

There was a $100,000 insurance settlement, but Linda ran right through that. The business she'd built with Alfonso failed and she was unable to maintain the mortgage payments on their home. "I moved to Philadelphia, wanting to get away from the memories. I started asking God, 'Why did you let this happen to me? I'm scared and I'm standing in this world all alone.' For years I was like a zombie. I worked as a receptionist and lived a quiet life. I didn't have anybody. I didn't think I had God either. I wasn't getting any answers and I was just about ready to give up on Him."

At some point a niece phoned Linda and convinced her to accompany her to a church service in suburban Philadelphia. When they arrived, Linda learned that the guest speaker was Bishop T. D. Jakes. Linda had read about him and was moved by his powerful sermon.

When he finished preaching, Reverend Jakes looked out at the congregation, and announced: 'I came all the way from Dallas, Texas, because there's someone out there that God wants me to talk to. I know you think you're here by accident, but God knows you're on the brink of giving up. He said to tell you, don't give up, that he has a plan for your life. Whoever that person is out there, all you have to do is stand and come to this altar. But first you have to believe that your new life is getting ready to happen."

I and a few others went down to the altar. Reverend Jakes looked me in the eyes and said, 'Don't give up. God is at your door. Don't you even think about giving up.' "

Linda said that moment marked a turning point. "From that point on, I decided to live my life on purpose. I thanked God for seeking me out, and I am so grateful that there is still breath in me. I do have a protector, someone I can rely on. And that person is not a man or woman. All that can pass away. God's love is forever." She says her new attitude made her work more enjoyable and she stopped dragging through the days.

I've shared Linda's story because her moment of realization, when she came to herself, is an important one. Many of us may have different details to our stories, but we have also experienced pain and disappointment, and I want you to know that God has not forgotten you. God, who only acts for the good, has a better life awaiting you.

Finally, there's a last important point I'd like to make about the Prodigal Son. When he returned home, his father didn't just look out the window and say, "Well, he's coming back. I knew it." No, he made no attempt to hide his joy at the son's return. In fact the father ran outside to greet him. That is God's grace. As in the story, our Father says: "What happened before no longer matters."

If, like Linda, you feel lost and weary, take comfort in knowing that God seeks you and awaits your return. The Holy Ghost is relentless and will never stop seeking you out.

If you don't belong to a church now, I urge you to join one, attend, and confess your faith. As Linda learned, if you haven't invited God in, make room, because He is just outside your door; He is simply waiting for you to come to yourself.

PART II

Blessed

Love

CHAPTER 5

Loving God Back

In the preceding chapter we were reminded of how blessed the Prodigal Son was to have a father who offered forgiving and restoring love. By extension, we too are blessed because that loving Father is our God, as known to us through Jesus Christ. Hallelujah! Glory be to the Father, and to the Son, and to the Holy Ghost. Amen, Amen. Amen. If you think I'm smiling, you're right. Moving on to the *L* for love in "blessed" makes me think about the Lord's love, and that makes me happy. It puts me in the mood for a party or two and gets me chanting: Ain't no party like the Holy Ghost party, and the Holy Ghost party don't stop.

I've got to stop myself right now—no easy task, because I'm blown away by the power of God's love. After all, it was from the abundance of divine love that creation spilled out. That's right. God didn't *have* to create us. He didn't create us out of *necessity*. We are the products of the overflow of God's love, and we love God back. Don't we?

Well, let's think about that. What does it mean to *say* we love

God? That's an important question when you consider that we often say what we don't mean. If someone greets us in the morning and asks, "How are you?" even if we're dragging in the depths of our soul, we usually respond, "I'm fine, thank you." We might not mean it, but we want to be civil.

And our polite but perhaps not genuine kind of responses don't necessarily end with salutations. Think about a job interview. Maybe someone has grilled you, and left you feeling a bit inadequate and unsure about whether you'll get a hoped-for position. When it's time to go, you might extend a hand and say, "It was good to meet you." No big deal, a mere utterance. Sometimes these kinds of words reflect our true spirit and other times they are merely polite ways of communicating with a new acquaintance.

Some words, however, are reserved for the most intimate of relationships, and "I love you," is one of them. Those three words are serious. They raise the stakes. If we say "I love you" and don't mean it and our actions contradict it, the listener might feel betrayed, and rightly so. We hear the word "love" quite often in songs and read it on greeting cards and hear actors on television and in films say it aloud.

These are expressions of love between human beings. That's different from the love we accept from and offer to God, according to my spiritual advisor, Dad Mason. To much of the world, this vibrant eighty-three-year-old is the Reverend Doctor Elliott James Mason, Sr., a former Fulbright fellow who served for twenty-three years as the pastor of the three-thousand-strong Trinity Baptist Church in Los Angeles.

"When people fall in love with one another, whether they admit it or not, they're usually expecting something in return," says Dad Mason. "Unlike humans, God doesn't deal in percentages. God doesn't ask for fifty percent. God's love for us never diminishes. He loves us even when we don't give anything back. It's unconditional love."

But when we say, "I love you too, God," we're talking to someone who, whether we live or die, we shall not be separated from. That's why loving God back calls for a personal and total commitment, the kind that's discussed in Luke 10:27: "You shall love the Lord your God with all your heart, and with all your soul, and with all your strength, and with all your mind; and your neighbor as yourself."

Just in case we missed the part about the neighbor, Jesus continues by explaining the story of the Good Samaritan, who showed extreme compassion to a stranger. Jesus isn't a halfway kind of savior. What he was saying is that action speaks louder than words. If you want to show me how much you love me, then love your neighbor.

You might remember Lee, whose stories are woven throughout this book. When she and her family moved to New York City, she thought she'd prepared her children for every kind of contingency. They'd lived in California, in an exclusive suburb outside Oakland, where doors were left unlocked and, from their front door, her children walked barefoot if they liked, down to a pristine playground where, at the end of the day, fathers were rolling up their shirtsleeves and teaching their sons how to hold baseball bats. The weather was often so perfect year-round, they called it Garden of Eden weather; the streets were safe, the houses luxurious. They lived in that neighborhood through God's graciousness. Someone from church owned the property and kept the rent low so Lee and her family could afford it. Lee's family thought they'd be there forever, where the neighbors were pretty easy to love.

But Lee's husband, a minister, was called to a new job, teaching seminarians in Manhattan, and the family left the easy life behind. After the pristine, homogenous environment they'd known in California, New York City was a little intimidating, to say the least. But they were prayerful people. Lee figured that if she taught her children to be street smart, the rough edges of their new life could be smoothed out.

Determined to teach their children to love the Lord with all their heart and soul and strength, the couple made time for their family each morning before heading out to work and school. They huddled in a circle, their arms around one another's shoulders as they thanked God for their blessings and asked Him to help the children get over the grief they felt about leaving behind friends and comfortable lives.

As had become their practice, once the last amen was said, Lee's husband took their twelve-year-old son uptown by subway. In the afternoon, the boy rode home with classmates. One morning, before walking out of the door with his dad, the boy looked over at Lee. "Mom, when I'm on the subway without a grown-up, all these homeless people come over to me and ask for money and . . . well, they're so dirty and . . . they smell so bad. I don't know what to do. They scare me."

Getting ready for work and not wanting to hold the boy and his father up, Lee said the first thing that came to mind: "Whatever you do, if one of those men asks you for something, don't answer, don't make eye contact, and walk away."

The door was almost closed when the boy poked his head back inside. "But Mom, what if one of them is Jesus?"

The question haunted her the whole day long. She couldn't risk her son's safety. He couldn't give money to any stranger that came along. But the boy was right. How did her message jibe with what she'd taught him about the Good Samaritan and about loving our neighbors as ourselves? If it was true that God was in every one of us, those men on the train were no different. But she'd told her son to turn his back on God.

By evening, she'd worked out an answer. She apologized to her son for brushing him off that morning and told him that his question had been a good one, the kind she needed to hear. "I'm not backing off on the warnings. Don't take unnecessary chances. It's not a good idea to speak to strangers. But how about this: Once a month we'll have bake sales in the lobby. You and I can bake on Friday evening, and on Saturday morning, we'll set out a table and sell the goods so we can give the money to the homeless."

The boy loved the idea. That was five-and-a-half years ago. He's seventeen now, but they're still hosting bake sales. Year in, year out, calling out to passersby, "Cinnamon rolls and blueberry muffins; red velvet, coconut, carrot and lemon cakes; chocolate cookies and banana bread." The two of them—mother and son—have become quite a fixture with their folding card table. And the hundreds of dollars they've raised over the years have been donated to a local men's shelter, buying food and blankets, and one year, a Christmas tree.

As is true of all volunteer work, it's not just the recipients of the charity that profit. Lee and her son have remained close even during the typically difficult adolescent and teenage years. In fact, in that same spirit, that boy—now a young man—is preparing to go to

Kenya for the summer as a member of a relief team that will help construct a school for children whose parents have died of AIDS. That young man will spread word of God's love through example. As Dad Mason says, "The only way we know we're returning God's love is when that love flows through us to others."

He is so right. Loving God can change your life. The more love we give Him, the more He gives back. It's the gift that keeps on giving.

Loving God back is not something we can do by following the numbers. God is always challenging us to do more. Coming to know and accept Jesus is for us the very essence of discipleship. It's about undergoing a radical transformation. Consider the story of the rich young man who obeyed God's commandments, but who was told by Jesus: "Go, sell what you have, and give to the poor, and you will have treasure in heaven; and come, follow me." When the young man heard this, "his countenance fell, and he went away sorrowful; for he had great possessions."

This passage is often invoked by me and my fellow pastors to remind Christians of the importance of tithing as a religious duty, but as is always the case with our Good Book, there's more beneath the surface. That story is about submitting to God's will. That means allowing the Holy Spirit to guide our prayers, hearts, tongues, minds. That passage is about total commitment, moving beyond self-centeredness to being God centered.

This deep level of commitment requires more than weekly devotions. Some people think that going to church on Sundays is sufficient. They may think, "I sinned this week, but I'm going to church, and I'll ask God to forgive me." God is always ready to receive us, and although He does appreciate our efforts, He by far prefers steadfast love over sacrifice.

Loving God back is a twenty-four-hour-a-day commitment; it doesn't end because we're busy or feeling stressed. That's what a woman I know reminded herself after a long workday. Before going home, she rushed into a supermarket, grabbed a chicken and, with growing impatience, stood on a slow-moving line and listened in outrage as a surly cashier lashed out at customers. "I couldn't believe the way people allowed her to intimidate them. She snatched money from them, sucked her teeth if someone asked a question about a price, and she tossed their change on the counter. People were shaking their heads and commiserating through eye contact, but no one stopped her. By the time she got to me, I figured she deserved a good scolding. When my turn came, and she gave me one of her nasty looks, I said in a voice that carried: 'Oh, I've got it. You're pretending to be the world's rudest cashier, because there's a hidden camera under there. This is some kind of reality show, right?' "

The cashier blushed beet red, and her eyes grew moist as she said in a tremulous voice, "I'm sorry. I've had a terrible day."

The customer later said, "I felt terrible for her and I regretted allowing myself to react like a bully. People like that cashier are almost always miserable."

Maybe you're thinking, That girl deserved that and more. No matter what her problems, she should have left them at home. On one level I agree. We can usually find an excuse for un-Christian responses. And perhaps for women of color who have an ancestry that involved servitude, humbling yourself in the face of withering contempt is not an easy discipline to master. The next time you're in a similar situation, it might help to envision yourself towering over the rude salesclerk, or whoever seems determined to ruin your day, and seeing yourself as having been made larger by God, who's lifting you up. This can help you walk away without the nasty verbal payback, still your tongue, and allow you to respond to who this person truly is—probably someone hurt and broken.

Seeing differently is part of the radical transformation that we undergo in giving love back to God. If you were raised to envision God as a shaming, hectoring, angry, and disapproving father figure, know that this is more of an outgrowth of your childhood experiences than the reality. A lot of people believe that God punishes people by allowing terrible calamities to befall them. But as Dad Mason reminds us, "We can't blame anything bad on God. Humans may commit evil, but the very nature of God's movement is to rescue us. God is nothing but goodness."

One of the most important passages that supports Dad Mason's point can be found in Romans 8:28: "In everything God works for good with those who love Him."

Because we are among those who love Him, let's conclude by thinking of someone we've known, whom we loved quite deeply, but who is no longer with us. Maybe it's a mother or father or grandmother. Whoever this person might be, concentrate on someone who worked hard and didn't receive the glory he or she deserved.

Now imagine getting a phone call and hearing that this person has actually come back to life and is going to be celebrated for his contributions. You've been invited to join the crowd and wave and cheer when he passes by. At that point, you arrive at a ticker-tape parade, just in time to see the person you love passing in a car, with the convertible top down. You're so grateful to this person for all he has done for you, and your cheers mingle with those of the others in the crowd. You wave your hands and call out, "I love you. Thank you for all you've done."

When it's over, you think, "Isn't it funny, the crowd was so large and yet I felt that he saw me. But even if he didn't, I was just glad to be there to say thanks."

A little later, when you run into a neighbor and she asks you where you've been, you explain that you've just left church. Because that's what church is, joining with others, taking part in the thanking and praising when He is in our midst. Because we know that actions speak louder than words, attending church is one more way to express: "I love you too, God." You're loving God back.

CHAPTER 6

Healing Shame

We're still exploring the *L* for love in "blessed," so let's consider what might happen to make us stop loving ourselves. You've heard of all-purpose cleansers. Well, toxic shame is an all-purpose blocker. Like a high wall that keeps sunlight from penetrating into a room, toxic shame blocks out self-love because it keeps us unaware of the various gifts God has given us. Toxic shame is so powerful and packs such an industrial-strength wallop, that even if our lives are filled with abundance—including God's love, good health, a rewarding career, and a comfortable income—toxic shame will block us from living like we're blessed.

Guilt, which was examined in Chapter 2, is very different from shame. Both are painful, but guilt is connected to behavior. The discomforting flush of guilt is caused when we have not lived up to our own standards or values, or have hurt someone we care about. Adam and Eve almost surely and deservedly experienced terrible pangs of guilt. Their sin wasn't about biting into an apple, explains the retired New Testament professor William J. Richardson: "Their sin was that they sought to establish their lives on their own terms apart from God, while using the gifts God had given them. They were trying to be like God." Fortunately, God allows us to atone for our sins. As such, guilt can be mitigated by changing our behaviors or attitudes.

Shame, on the other hand, is personal and insidious. It makes us feel that *we* are wrong and that no matter the extent of our achievements, we aren't good enough and never will be. Though we might be the honored guest at a posh celebration, shame can make us feel as if we're dressed in rags and that we're inadequate, phony, failures.

Everyone experiences shame; it's only human. But shame can build up in some people until it reaches toxic levels and becomes corrosive, eating away at a person's healthy self-image. People suffering with toxic shame are so busy trying to hide their sense of inadequacy that their behavior becomes exaggerated. Instead of radiating self-confidence, they are contemptuous of others. Instead of offering helpful advice, they are controlling or self-righteous. Instead of enjoying one drink they may have many—often *way* too many. Compulsive behavior usually shows up in one form or another, including eating and indebtedness. Instead of buying a nice outfit, for instance, this person may buy a closet full of clothes and overspend until there's no money left to pay the mortgage on a much-cherished house. Another image that pops up for me, as I think of squandering God's gifts, is of inmates in long-term confinement who didn't become great mathematicians, or lawyers, teachers, doctors, artists, historians, or whatever because—just as someone can be "high" on a drug—they were "low" with toxic shame and made terrible choices.

Acknowledging shame and asking God for help are certainly important first steps in healing. Unfortunately, too many people have had their faith derailed by self-righteous people who used religion as an excuse for abusing them. All of us know people who were "whupped in the name of the Lord." Their parents might have whaled away at them, reminding them on each down stroke that "God don't like ugly."

I'm not talking about a mild spanking, but physical or verbal abuse, which is degrading and dehumanizing. These children may grow up filled with toxic shame and feel estranged from God, if the parent claimed that he or she was acting on God's behalf. Although the parent or guardian may have whipped a child under the guise of making him or her "walk right with God" this treatment can actually have the opposite affect, estranging the individual from God. And once the covenant is broken, an individual can begin to feel numb inside and act shamelessly.

One of my closest friends, who for the sake of privacy, I will call Frank, is a pastor at a thriving Baptist Church in Tennessee. Frank grew up in Atlanta, with five siblings, in a home headed by two hardworking parents. His mother was a registered nurse, and his father was employed by the city.

"My father was co-owner of a liquor store," adds Frank. "And unfortunately, he was his own best customer. He was what you call a functional alcoholic because he kept a job and earned a good living, despite his abuse of alcohol."

What his father couldn't control was rage, and some of Frank's earliest memories are of his father beating his mother. "My sisters and brothers were fearful when they saw this occurring, but I was the child that my father said had 'too much mouth,' and I didn't remain silent. I'd try to protect my mother, and my father would turn on me. One time he pistol-whipped her and I beat him with a hammer."

Frank was too young to overpower his father. "I took the brunt of the beatings, and these went beyond the norm. Once a belt was deemed insufficient, I was beaten with boards, broom handles, whatever was in reaching distance."

Although friends and relatives advised Frank's mother to leave her husband, she refused, on the grounds that marriage was a sacred bond that should not be broken. "It was clear from observing my parents that there were two ways to go in life: the way of the light or of darkness. My mother was the epitome of a saved person. She prayed for my father and believed her prayers would save him. And she knew that when sober, he was among the best of men. Unfortunately, he was rarely sober during my childhood and he often came home in a drunken stupor."

Despite the father's misbehavior, he demanded that his children follow the highest moral standards. "I was a little bugger," Frank recalls. "I'd lie about something, nothing catastrophic, but my father couldn't stand for me not to be truthful. When I was about nine or ten, I bullied a little boy and took his money, and lied to my father when he asked me about it. My father went through my coat pockets and found the money. He felt beating me wasn't getting him anywhere, so he tried psychological abuse."

His father picked up the phone and pretended to call the police, saying that he wanted his son taken away. He packed the boy's clothes and told him to get ready to go. His sisters and brothers sobbed and begged their father, "Please don't let them take Frankie away." At this, Frank says, he broke down and began crying. "My father discovered he could torment me with psychological abuse."

School became a refuge for Frank, and he excelled academically, skipping two grades. At the age of fourteen, during his sophomore year, he was called by God to preach. "I was pretty focused about becoming a preacher and serious about school. The worse things became for me at home, the more it drove me to prove that I could be better than my father. I was undaunted."

By sixteen, during his senior year, when his father threatened him with another beating, Frank moved away and rented an apartment. After high school graduation, he worked full time at a local factory, while attending college full time, striving for an undergraduate degree. "On the afternoon work shift I had a certain quota to meet, and for the first hour and a half I'd get ahead of schedule, then I'd go into the bathroom. I'd hidden my textbooks in the garbage can when I first arrived, and that's how I got my studying and homework done, sitting on the toilet, my feet propped up, hiding in a stall." One of Frank's supervisors noticed his long bathroom breaks and asked him if he had a problem. "I told him yes, I did. I'm lucky he didn't ask me to elaborate."

Through graduate school and while working on his doctoral degree, Frank continued supporting himself, proud that "I didn't have to ask my father to buy me as much as a pencil." Over the years the two men have reconciled. Frank's father has stopped drinking and apologized for his past cruelties, but some pain isn't easily diminished.

Frank's academic life continued full tilt, but at heart he was still that little boy who'd been beaten like a mistreated farm animal. Desperate to numb himself from his shame, he became a womanizer. "I looked mature for my age, and I was about thirteen or fourteen when women began exploiting me sexually; some were from church. I thought their special attention meant that I was special. I started believing that sex was just a way of expressing myself. From my perspective it made me more of a man. In this society, the guy with the charisma that gets the girls is seen as the one with machismo."

His sexual promiscuity occasionally got him into trouble, and caused at least one near-death encounter. A Vietnam vet, disappointed upon returning home to hear that his girlfriend had been unfaithful, "phoned me at my mother's house, and said, 'Listen, man, I was right outside your church today. You didn't see me because I was across the street with a rifle. I saw your head through the scope . . .'"

Frank now says, "That definitely encouraged me to give the woman up, but she kept pursuing me."

Frank knew that he was hurting the women that he slept with and then casually discarded, but he now realizes that he wasn't the only one acting out his shame. Many of the women seemed drawn to him because of his misbehavior. He continued using sex like a drug. His shame made him believe he would remain that way forever.

Despite the changing faces in the lineup, Frank maintained a relationship with a longtime steady girlfriend, Anne. "She was so innocent, my mother loved her. I occasionally brought different women home to meet my parents, and a lot of them were very impressive, but my mother would tell them, 'You're a wonderful girl, but do you know my daughter, Anne?'"

His mother insisted that Anne was the woman he'd marry. "It was true that I always loved her, and somehow, even though she knew I was acting up, Anne remained supportive and prayerful. She never ranted and raved, and she never had another man in her life. Anne believed that God would change me."

One demonstration of her faith in him was that Anne quit college after two years so she could help him continue, and she gave him most of her $3,500 savings. "I realize now that I was re-creating my parents' relationship of light and darkness."

When he was twenty-six, Frank married Anne. "With God's help, I put that womanizing life behind me," he says. Knowing that shame only festers when you try to bury it, he opened up to his wife and others about his childhood abuse and his own adult wantonness. One of his favorite sayings is, "By reconnecting with who you are, you can redirect who you are; it's connection with direction." He adds, "When you get right with God, you're right for everyone else."

A few years later, he was leading a church, building membership from eighty to eight hundred. He and Anne have two teenage daughters and two grown sons who are enrolled in law school. He and his wife also own a thriving restaurant.

Frank's past still weighs on him. When asked to imagine what he'd say to the women he slept with and then deserted, Frank's rich baritone voice faltered. "I would certainly say that I'm sorry, sorry for corrupting and reducing the value of your worth. I treated you like objects. What I did was not worthy of you or God. I'm sorry that I made you part of my ugly reality. And I urge you not to settle for anybody who will make you feel less than you're worth."

Frank encourages people with similar childhood experiences to speak out about what they suffered. "Don't hide your past, don't act as if terrible things haven't happened," he tells the young people of his church. "Use your past honestly and let God help you redeem it."

Listening to Frank's story reminded me of men that I've known who hurt me. When I emerged from a relationship feeling mistreated, I felt shame. In seminary, I dated a fellow student and we were talking about getting engaged. When I started pastoring at Mariners'

Church, parishioners grew accustomed to seeing us together. But the relationship ended abruptly, because that was his wish. It left me reeling. I felt vulnerable and exposed, because I was the one who had to keep explaining our breakup, even though I didn't really understand the reasons myself. Maybe you're going through something like that now, and if so, I'm sorry. I remember how much it hurts.

That was one reason I shared Frank's story. I hoped by understanding his past you would see how many people—men and women—bring their own brokenness to their relationships with others. Even when you can eke out a little sympathy for the person who hurt you, you may wish he could offer you an explanation.

That's what happened to Brenda Lane Richardson. "James was my first boyfriend," she says. "I was fourteen, and I still have a faded photograph of me sitting with him on the grass, during our first and only date. It's obvious from the way I'm staring at him that I adored him. I can remember our first kiss and that he told me he loved me. A few days later, when I called him, he hung up the phone. I dialed again, and for the second time he hung up. I couldn't fool myself anymore. He'd dropped me like a sack of dirty laundry. When someone does that, you're so embarrassed; it's as if your body lights up and everyone's staring right through your clothes."

Thirty years later, James and Brenda reconnected. "I was speaking at the National Association of Black Journalists, in Atlanta, and was surrounded by a group of people when a man approached and said, 'You probably don't remember me.' Without missing a beat, I said, 'Sure I do. Your name is James, and you broke my heart.' He was astounded that I remembered him." When Brenda explained that she was happily married with three children, James seemed pleased. He said he'd heard she was speaking and that he'd driven from Florida to see her.

He said, "I'm in Alcoholics Anonymous and I'm making amends to the people I hurt. When I hung up on you that day, it was partially out of cruelty, but it was also to protect you. Our house was insane. It made me reckless and angry and I knew I was bound to hurt you. But I hurt you anyway, and I'm sorry."

I commend James and Frank for their honesty and for their willingness to change. How about you? Have any of your childhood experiences led you to hurt others or yourself? In your journal, write a letter to an adult who hurt you when you were a child. The idea isn't to blame that person for your troubles nor does the person have to see the letter, but naming him or her and detailing the experiences are a good start toward healing the shame.

When you have finished writing, close your eyes and visualize yourself unearthing a treasure chest. You open it to reveal precious jewels and glistening gold coins, which upon closer examination are the gifts God has given you. Take a deep breath and describe those gifts aloud.

When you have finished speaking, open your eyes, and know with perfect assurance that the harder you work to uncover the experiences that caused you to feel shame, the closer you come to recognizing and utilizing your gifts from the Creator. In coming weeks, continue to write in your journal, join a support group, or seek out therapeutic help if necessary.

As you repeat the buried-treasure visualization you will find that your list of gifts continues to grow. Like a flower sprouting and then bursting open in sunlight that recognition is your growing self-love. I'm tempted to close by saying God bless you, but He already has. Your task is learning to give expression to those blessings.

CHAPTER 7

Learning to Love Yourself and Others

I n the preceding chapter, I explored the ways shame blocks self-love, but now we need to consider why self-love is so important. When I was growing up, loving yourself wasn't something that was considered positive. Back then it had a different connotation. If someone said, "He's in love with himself," that suggested the self-ishness and self-absorption of a narcissist. You know the kind of person I'm talking about. He or she might inquire about some problem you're going through and instead of sympathizing or coming up with a solution starts thinking about how he or she will be impacted by your troubles. They won't want to be inconvenienced. Bet you know someone like that. Believe me, I've been there.

Another belief system that contradicted the need for self-love was the notion of agape, self-sacrificing love, as practiced by God. Of course He demonstrated His love for us through the death of his son, Jesus Christ, which allowed us to be reconciled to Him: This is the most important message of the Bible.

The question then becomes, how do we as Christians *dare* to love ourselves? But it also stands to reason that if we believe that we are created by God and in His image, then it is our responsibility to love ourselves. This is not simply a fuzzy, feel-good idea. Loving ourselves as God loves us allows us to sustain ourselves through hard times. Our inner well of love is created by serving God—and by that I mean loving God back—and benefiting from positive childhood experiences.

So many times in my life, my heart has swelled with gratitude at the memory of my parents sitting spellbound as I read to them aloud in Spanish. They understood that the world was growing into a global village and they worked extra jobs to earn enough to send me to Spain and take our family to Puerto Rico, so I could master the language.

Those parental looks of admiration and other experiences, like my Uncle Bob waiting outside Union Baptist to remind me that I was smart and had to go to college because I was representing the family, those infusions of love and confidence filled me with self-regard. When the hard times came—for instance, that almost-fiancé of mine, calling it quits and leaving me to explain to others why he was gone—I had to tap into my inner well for reassurance. That, and knowing that God was with me, helped me get through it.

But what happens when the well is dry? Maybe you had hardworking parents who were so focused on the necessities of your survival that there was little time or energy for demonstrating the kind of love we all require. Toni Morrison, one of America's greatest living writers, brings home that point in her novel *Sula*. In one scene, Hannah asks her mother Eva—who literally sacrificed a foot to support her children—whether she ever loved her. Eva's response is bone-chillingly to the point.

You settin' here with your healthy-ass self and ax me did I
love you? Them big old eyes in your head would a been two
holes full of maggots if I hadn't . . . Wasn't nobody playin' in
1895. Just cause you got it good now, you think it was always
this good? 1895 was a killer, girl. Things was bad. Niggers was
dying like flies . . . What you talkin' bout did I love you, girl.
I stayed alive for you, can't you get that through your thick
head.

This scene makes clear how love can be viewed from two completely different perspectives. Eva felt that keeping her children fed
and housed was a sufficient show of love. But Morrison demon-
strates that Eva's inability to show motherly affection didn't preclude
Hannah from needing it. For that reason, Hannah doesn't survive
long after this conversation. It is as if Morrison is reminding us that
we don't live by bread alone. We need love, and that includes self-
love.

Taking a look at the quality of your relationships may be the best
way to gage self-love. In the last chapter's discussion of toxic shame,
we looked at the exaggerated behaviors that can be adopted as defenses against shame. Consider how contemptuous behavior, for instance, can drive people away. It is the same for angry outbursts,
self-righteousness, and a host of other negative behaviors. That's
why toxic shame and self-love can't coexist within our psyches.
Working to lower toxic shame is an important first step in learning
to love yourself.

Journal writing and prayers continue to be of critical importance.
Men may feel more comfortable with a spiritual guide (ask your
pastor for recommendations). As you write or speak about painful

memories, which may include abandonment and abuse, your soul will begin to feel lighter.

Then comes the important job of learning to take care of yourself. If you have a history of mistreatment, of course you have learned to devalue yourself. So it's important to begin providing for yourself the way you would your own beloved child. That may sound strange, but the truth is it's often easier to care for others than it is to care for ourselves.

For instance, there are certain things that you might want to keep your daughter from experiencing. Maybe she has a boyfriend that neglects her and runs around with other women. You would almost surely counsel her to move on, and tell her that she deserves better. To treat yourself lovingly, you may have to follow some of your own good advice.

Developing a nurturing internal voice is a challenge, but an important one. To illustrate that point, I want you to stop a moment and think about what you need right now for the rest of your day to feel more balanced. I asked that of one woman, who said, "I just want to take a shower. I've been so busy getting this house clean that I was afraid to stop. The kids will wake up in a few minutes and I need to have my work finished."

When I pointed out that her actions suggested that it was more important to mop a kitchen floor than to give herself a few minutes relief under a warm and soothing shower, she realized what I meant. She added that she'd fire a babysitter if she neglected her daughter that way. This is why acting as our own good mothers is so vital in learning to treat ourselves lovingly. The more we act on our own behalf, the more we love the person we're fighting for.

What do you need to do for yourself right now? Maybe the an-

swer is to continue reading this book. And if that's true, let's connect in this moment through God, friend-to-friend style, with a
prayer.

> Dear Lord, I always want to start off praising you. You give me
> so much and you fill me up. Until now, I didn't stop to ask why
> I deserved to have you breathe life into me. I didn't wonder why
> you gave me a brain that helps me do so many tasks I take for
> granted, like deciphering the symbols on this page, as I read
> and learn something new about you and myself. But now I'm
> stopping for a moment. I'm breathing deeply, enjoying each
> breath, and I hope you don't mind me saying this, but I think
> you've given me breath and kept me alive because the world
> needs me. Dear Lord, this world is waiting for my next contri-
> bution. That's why you gave me gifts. And because I am impor-
> tant, I'm going to ask that you allow me to get better at taking
> care of myself, at loving myself, better at keeping my heart
> open and filled with your love. Thank you, Jesus, and praise be
> your name. Amen.

How was that for you? Be sure to keep an ear out for the soothing quality of your internal maternal voice. If you were brought up
in harsh circumstances, you may find that you speak to yourself
with sarcasm, or even insults. You might look at something you've
accomplished and think: "Oh, come on, you can do better than
this?" Or you might think, "The world is waiting for your contribution, hah!" Or at some point, when you need to rouse your tired
body, you might hear yourself thinking, "Get with it, girl."

There's a way to change the timbre of your internal voice. If you have a photo of yourself as a child or infant, pull it out. Make quiet time for yourself, lighting a few candles if possible. Sit comfortably and breathe deeply. Look at the picture and speak to yourself. Lee has a photo of herself as an infant, and although her beloved mother has passed away years earlier and she can't confirm her idea, Lee's convinced that this photo was taken when she was eight months old, a few days before her mother took her down south and left Lee and her sister with their grandparents.

"The smile on my face is so tentative," Lee says, "as if my mom was standing in the background at the photographer's studio, encouraging me to smile. I was wearing a pretty little cotton dress and the corners of my mouth are turned up, but my eyes look so unhappy, as if I sense that I'll be separated from my mom for a long time. I don't blame my mother for leaving me. She did what she had to. My father had deserted us and she needed to get a full-time job to support us. But pain is pain. If someone steps on your foot and breaks your toe, it may be an accident, but that doesn't mean your toe won't throb. That's what I feel when I look at the picture. I think about a hurt, abandoned girl."

Lee has learned to talk to the photo, and in this manner she has developed a strong and soothing internal voice. "I might say something like, 'Hello, you beautiful darling girl. I love you so much. You are so precious. I thank God for you. You don't have to smile if you don't want to. Let me just hold you and stroke your lovely head.' "

Sometimes that supportive voice can come from caring others. Not too long ago I received a beautifully framed photograph as a gift, and I was about to take it to my church, thinking my parishioners would enjoy it, when my assistant stopped me and said, "Pastor, you love that picture and you're always giving to others. Why not put it in your office?" She was right, and that's just what I did. I love looking up and seeing the photo and remembering her kind words. This is the tone you're striving for, one that's complimentary and supportive.

For some of us, developing an internal mothering voice will be close to rewriting our own history. And let me tell you, it can transform your life. Because when your heart softens, so will your demeanor. Your eyes, your skin, everything about you will reflect your self-regard. When we love ourselves, we become capable of visualizing ourselves with someone who holds us in high regard.

Maybe you've given up on romance. Perhaps you've told yourself that there are no good men around. Think about what you're really saying. If low self-regard had led you to become involved in relationships that were abusive or demeaning, no wonder you believed that. You may have looked at men who did care for you as boring losers. Do you get the connection? When you don't love yourself, you assume that anyone that does love you mustn't be worth much.

But a new day is dawning and you want to open yourself to new possibilities. Keep in mind that it is written in I John 4:8, "He that loveth not knoweth not God; for God is love." Don't limit yourself to a life without love because you're tied to old beliefs. Here's a new belief to replace the old one: God, who is love, wants you to have love.

And that's the gospel truth.

PART III

BLESSED ENERGY

CHAPTER 8

Revving Up Your Emotional Energy

If you've read Parts I and II, for the letters *B* and *L* in "blessed," and you're wondering how you'll drum up motivation to follow through on suggested ideas and actions, you've turned to the right page. This chapter is designed to help you figure out what you'll need to do to generate more get-up-and-go.

Right off the bat, I can tell you that boosting your emotional energy level can make a major difference in the quality of your life and future achievements. With that said, you're probably wondering what I mean by emotional energy. Rather than explaining what that is or how to boost it, I encourage you to take the Emotional Energy Quotient (EEQ) Test, which I've designed for those who want to learn how to live like they're blessed. It will provide a reasonably accurate analysis of your motivational level and help you understand why you need high reserves of emotional energy.

You'll want to choose answers that best reflect your responses. If you reach a situation that doesn't apply to your life, think about what you would do. You will find three possible responses. If two or more answers seem to fit your response, choose the one closest to your situation. Try to answer spontaneously. No one is looking over your shoulder judging you. It would be a waste of your time and even misleading if you choose the answer you thought you should pick or that sounded "right." There is no right or wrong here. Your goal is to live like you're blessed.

You'll need a sheet of paper and pen or pencil to keep score. Fold the sheet lengthwise into fourths. In the far-left column write "Red" at the top; in the next column, "Yellow"; then "Blue" in the next; and in the final column, write "Green" at the top. Please put the paper aside for now and concentrate on responding to the situations in the EEQ.

The Emotional Energy Quotient Test

1. You wake up and wonder how you'll ever get everything done.

    Ⓐ Never   Ⓑ Occasionally   Ⓒ Frequently

2. You feel angry.

    Ⓐ Never   Ⓑ Occasionally   Ⓒ Frequently

3. You're in a physically or emotionally abusive relationship.

    Ⓐ Never   Ⓑ Occasionally   Ⓒ Frequently

4. At day's end, you're satisfied with what you've accomplished.

    Ⓐ Never   Ⓑ Occasionally   Ⓒ Frequently

5. Your dresser drawers and bedroom closets are neat.

    Ⓐ Never   Ⓑ Occasionally   Ⓒ Frequently

6. You love swimming and often engage in this sport.

    Ⓐ Never   Ⓑ Occasionally   Ⓒ Frequently

7. When it comes to least-favorite tasks—such as filing taxes, filling out expense reports, or getting your teeth cleaned—you procrastinate until it's almost too late.

    Ⓐ Never   Ⓑ Occasionally   Ⓒ Frequently

8. You make time to see supportive friends and relatives.

    Ⓐ Never   Ⓑ Occasionally   Ⓒ Frequently

9. You attend church and tithe.

    Ⓐ Never   Ⓑ Occasionally   Ⓒ Frequently

10. You often express creativity through drawing, singing, writing, or other endeavors.

    Ⓐ Never   Ⓑ Occasionally   Ⓒ Frequently

11. You balance your checkbook.

    Ⓐ Never   Ⓑ Occasionally   Ⓒ Frequently

12. You remain in an unfulfilling job.

    Ⓐ Never   Ⓑ Occasionally   Ⓒ Frequently

13. You smoke, overeat, drink too much alcohol, or engage in another unhealthy addiction.

    Ⓐ Never   Ⓑ Occasionally   Ⓒ Frequently

14. You make New Year's resolutions that you keep.

    Ⓐ Never   Ⓑ Occasionally   Ⓒ Frequently

15. You want to give a party but you're too busy.

    Ⓐ Never   Ⓑ Occasionally   Ⓒ Frequently

16. When an individual says or does something that makes you uncomfortable, you speak up for yourself in an appropriate manner.

    Ⓐ Never   Ⓑ Occasionally   Ⓒ Frequently

17. You use the Internet.

    Ⓐ Never   Ⓑ Occasionally   Ⓒ Frequently

18. When you're not working, you're usually alone or on the phone.

    Ⓐ Never   Ⓑ Occasionally   Ⓒ Frequently

19. You exercise regularly.

    Ⓐ Never   Ⓑ Occasionally   Ⓒ Frequently

20. You pray regularly.

    Ⓐ Never   Ⓑ Occasionally   Ⓒ Frequently

21. You worry about someone you care about.

    Ⓐ Never   Ⓑ Occasionally   Ⓒ Frequently

22. You get sick with colds, the flu, or other infections.

    Ⓐ Never   Ⓑ Occasionally   Ⓒ Frequently

23. You get a good night's sleep.

    Ⓐ Never   Ⓑ Occasionally   Ⓒ Frequently

24. You have someone in your life with whom you share affection.

    Ⓐ Never   Ⓑ Occasionally   Ⓒ Frequently

25. You perform volunteer work.

    Ⓐ Never   Ⓑ Occasionally   Ⓒ Frequently

Now pull out that sheet of paper with the four columns. Every response below is followed by a color: red, yellow, blue, or green. If your response to situation 1 corresponds with red, write the number 1 in the red column. If your response to situation 2 corresponds with green, write the number 2 in the green column, and so on. When you finish, you'll have twenty-five different numbers dispersed among the four columns.

Responses to Situation 1

  A. If you awake and *never* wonder how you'll get everything done, you're laid back to the point of being blasé or you may not feel sufficiently challenged. If that's so, you'll want to look for meaningful opportunities to use your many God-given talents. You'll also want to consider whether this lack of concern is an indication that life's trials have robbed you of passion. **Green**

  B. If you *occasionally* wonder how you'll get everything done, you may have a fairly balanced schedule. Unforeseen

events do interrupt plans, and if we live creative and
dynamic lives we're able to roll with the punches. **Green**

C. If you *frequently* wonder how you'll get everything done,
you're overextended and this is a major energy drain. I
feel this way at times, and often say that I don't just have
a lot on my plate, I have a lot on my platter. Moving
from restful sleep to instant alert is hard on your body. If
you're doing too much for others, insist that they help. As
you find ways to pare down your schedule, use your
nurturing inner voice to remind yourself that you deserve
to make time for your own needs. You are important to
God. **Yellow**

Put a 1 in the appropriate column.

Responses to Situation 2

A. If you imagine that you *never* feel angry, you may be
in denial about this very natural response. If you think
it's un-Christian to get angry, remember Jesus cleansing
the temple of the money changers (John 2:15). He
was righteously angry about God's values being
violated. He lost his temper because he was human.
Everybody has some anger, and if you're denying and
suppressing it, you're experiencing a serious energy drain.
Yellow

B. If you *occasionally* feel angry, you may be good at reading
your own emotions. Remember, this question is about
how you feel, not how you behave. Seething after your
supervisor scolds you is a natural response. Blowing up at
him might get you fired, but a healthy alternative might

be lunching with a supportive coworker and letting off steam. Like real steam, anger can build up, and when it comes to bodies, this emotional pressure can create health problems. If you're aware of times when you're angry and find healthy ways to express it, you're conserving emotional energy. **Green**

C. If you're *frequently* angry, good for you for recognizing that. That kind of anger often stems from long-term issues, and you may want to use your journal to explore unresolved pain from hurtful childhood experiences. Anger doesn't simply go away, it remains in your body and can affect your energy level and damage your health. **Red**

Put a 2 in the appropriate column.

Responses to Situation 3

A. If you would *never* remain in an abusive relationship, you know how to treat yourself lovingly. **Green**

B. If you're *occasionally* abused by a partner, you may be convinced that you're staying in the relationship to keep up appearances or for the sake of your children. Couldn't that just be an excuse? Children are never a good reason for staying in a hurtful relationship. Children or no children, if you're being treated in an inhumane fashion, you are getting by on the dregs of your emotional energy reserve. **Red**

C. If you're *frequently* abused, you may have grown up in a home in which you witnessed violence between your parents or you may have been abused. If you are in an abusive relationship, I urge you not to wait until it's too late to leave. God gave us a sense of pain as a sudden and startling way of reminding ourselves what we should avoid, and that includes avoiding people who hurt us. You probably feel terrified, and fear can deplete your emotional energy. **Red**

Put a 3 in the appropriate column.

Responses to Situation 4

A. If you *never* feel satisfied with what you've accomplished, you may be overscheduled or might be holding yourself to impossible standards. **Yellow**

B. If you *occasionally* feel satisfied with what you've accomplished, you'll want to look closer at your life. Try writing in your journal to consider what you can do to better appreciate your contributions, and follow your own good advice. **Blue**

C. If you *frequently* feel satisfied with what you've accomplished, then you view your contributions as worthwhile. You place great value in your day-to-day endeavors, and your emotional energy level may be helping you maintain a balanced schedule. **Green**

Put a 4 in the appropriate column.

Responses to Situation 5

A. If your dresser drawers and bedroom closets are *never* neat, you probably aren't making time to care for yourself. This is not about the quality of your housekeeping.

Dresser drawers and bedroom closets are repositories for your personal items. On busy days, if they're messy, you'll be left scrambling. **Yellow**

B. If your dresser drawers and closets are *occasionally* neat, it sounds like you sometimes take the time to straighten them up. Even if your life isn't as balanced as you'd like, you sense the need to take care of yourself. **Blue**

C. If your dresser drawers and closets are *frequently* neat, that doesn't mean you're a housekeeping perfectionist. Dressers and bedroom closets are the repositories of items that help you make your way through the world. While they may not reflect the most fashionable or expensive of tastes, they enhance your sense of self. **Green**

Put a 5 in the appropriate column.

Responses to Situation 6

A. If you *never* swim because you hate getting your hair wet, keep in mind that people with balanced lives are flexible and open to experiencing the world. Maintaining a hairstyle with every strand in place doesn't allow for spontaneity. And if it is fear that is keeping you from taking the plunge, consider taking a class for the water-shy. My mom learned to swim as an adult, after she realized that my brother and I, who had become avid swimmers, were going to spend a lot of time in pools. Like so many others before her, she found that swimming reduces stress and offers a low-impact aerobic workout. And consider this: Two-thirds of God's earth is covered in water. Swimming imparts a sense of physical mastery over the world, while fear zaps emotional energy. **Yellow**

B. If you *occasionally* swim, that means you've learned how and you understand the pleasures of moving through the water. If keeping your do in place is keeping you from taking the plunge more often, try scheduling swims before the beauty salon. Swimming implies certain flexibility in one's lifestyle. Good for you. **Blue**

C. If you *frequently* swim you've learned to feel at one with the earth. I've just started swimming three to four times a week, early mornings, and I love it. After all, humans come to life and are sustained in the fluids in our mothers' wombs, so it should not be surprising that swimming has a calming effect. **Green**

Put a 6 in the appropriate column.

Responses to Situation 7

A. If you *never* put off least-favorite tasks until the last minute you are in a rarefied minority, and I can only take my cap off to you. It sounds as if you've fashioned a well-honed schedule. With the less pleasurable aspects out of the way, you've made time for fun and spontaneity. **Green**

B. If you *occasionally* put off least-favorite tasks until the last minute you're likely to run into me on the waiting line, and we'll have plenty of company. Life is rushed and busy and although we're working at making it run like a well-oiled machine, we haven't gotten there yet. **Blue**

C. If you *frequently* put off least-favorite tasks you may often feel out of control and nervous. Anxiety is right up there at the top of the list for energy drains. **Yellow**

Put a 7 in the appropriate column.

Responses to Situation 8

A. If you *never* make time to see supportive family and friends, you're socially isolating yourself, and that's punishing. Supportive family and friends are a blessing. Just recently, my Aunt Bertha, who was one of my mother's best friends and godmother to my sons, advised me about what to wear for my annual sermon as president of the Hampton Ministers' Conference. When Aunt Bertha deemed a suit "just right," "too matronly," or "in need of tapering," I appreciated every word. We all deserve the sense of relaxation that is imparted when we spend time with friends. Supportive family is an additional plus because they're the ones who keep us in touch with where we came from. They are truly our roots and keep us grounded. **Yellow**

B. If you *occasionally* make time to see family and friends, you're headed in the right direction. Since these individuals can sustain you during hard times, you'll want to boost those connections by figuring out how you can see them more often. **Blue**

C. If you *frequently* make time to see family and friends, you feel their blessing. They let you vent when you need to, give you sound advice when you need it, and offer opportunities to exchange hugs and deep belly laughs. They boost your energy level. **Green**

Put an 8 in the appropriate column.

Responses to Situation 9

A. If you *never* attend church or tithe, that's akin to pulling the plug out of your radio and wondering why you can't hear the music. You'll know you've found the right church if you return home feeling as if your batteries have been recharged. I'm not saying this because I'm a minister. Just praising Jesus makes me feel energized. Hallelujah and get thee to the church, sista! **Yellow**

B. If you *occasionally* attend church and tithe, you already understand why you need to, but you haven't fully committed yourself to the Lord. If you find the right services, you won't use being tired as an excuse not to attend; you'll want to attend so you won't feel tired anymore. **Blue**

C. If you *frequently* attend church and tithe you may have found one that gives you back as much as you give, and you know that's a blessing. With the right spiritual boost, you'll find that all during the week when you encounter difficulties, you can keep on keeping on. **Green**

Put a 9 in the appropriate column.

Responses to Situation 10

A. If you *never* express your creativity, your highest self is trapped within you. Since we're made in God's image, we're filled with the power of creativity. One woman,

Yvonne, used to complain that she had no creative talent, but after praying on it she began designing gift baskets of flowers and baked goods that she delivered to the sick and shut-ins. Ask God to help you develop your creativity, and then after listing what you enjoy doing, your gifts will be revealed. **Yellow**

B. If you *occasionally* express your creativity, ask yourself what you can do to make this a more dominant aspect of your life. The world is waiting for you. **Blue**

C. If you *frequently* express your creativity, you may be earning your living by utilizing one of your talents. If so, rev up your engine by tapping into another outlet for your creativity. If you don't earn your living with a creative talent, consider how you might and go for it. **Green**

Put a 10 in the appropriate column.

Responses to Situation 11

A. If you *never* balance your checkbook, face it, you've given control of your money to a bank clerk who may make mistakes—but always in the bank's favor. Few people enjoy setting aside time to balance a checkbook, but those who master the discipline are people who take care of their finances. You deserve to have all the money you earn, while those who live in a state of financial chaos have unbalanced statements and unbalanced lives. **Yellow**

B. You *occasionally* balance your checkbook, which means you know it's a good habit to develop. Some people follow a can't balance; can't spend rule. What that means is that once a month, after payday, they don't allow themselves to spend any money on anything pleasurable—ice cream, videos, dinner out—until the checkbook is balanced. Try that. **Blue**

C. If *frequently* balance your checkbook you're developing the kind of habits that will lead you to financial abundance, which sure makes it easier to sleep deeply. **Green**

Put an 11 in the appropriate column.

Responses to Situation 12

A. You *never* stay in an unfulfilling job? If that means you skip from job to job, try hanging in there a bit longer and giving yourself time to rise to the challenge. That will help you develop a discipline that will aid you in your next endeavor. But if it means you'd never stay in a dead-end job without marshalling your efforts to find something better, then you're prepared to fight for the quality of your life. Congratulations. The effort alone will add to your emotional energy score. **Green**

B. If you *occasionally* remain in unfulfilling jobs, you're doing what you can to keep the money flowing, and hats off to you. You will also want to work at shutting down any ill will you may feel once you're in the workplace, or you'll wind up hurting yourself by getting fired. In the meantime, cultivate new skills so you can move on to something better. **Blue**

C. If you *frequently* remain in unfulfilling jobs, then take a look at your work history and ask yourself what you've learned from each one. That's right, even that 7-Eleven

convenience store job, where the owner's agitated
Doberman watched your every move, offered a lesson.
Maybe you learned a particular life lesson. Now, here's
the next question: What can you do with all those
lessons so you can find more fulfilling work? **Yellow**

Put a 12 in the appropriate column.

Responses to Situation 13

A. If you *never* smoke, overeat, drink too much alcohol or
engage in any behavior harmful to your health, you treat
your body as the temple that it is. And you're probably
looking and feeling pretty good, which is its own reward.
Green

B. If you *occasionally* smoke, overeat, drink too much, or
engage in any harmful behavior, you act like the majority
of the people in the world. But remember that *trying* isn't
good enough. Overdoing any behavior is a sign that your
life is out of balance. **Blue**

C. If you *frequently* smoke, overeat, drink too much alcohol,
or overdo anything else harmful to your health, this is
addictive behavior. It may have already interfered with
your intimate relationships. Compulsive behavior is a
defense for childhood experiences in which people were
made to feel shame. Your emotional energy reserve is
almost on empty. But the news isn't all bad; be assured
that there's a professional out there waiting for you to
call, wanting to serve God by helping you heal. Please
make that call. **Red**

Put a 13 in the appropriate column.

Responses to Situation 14

A. You make New Year's resolutions that you *never* keep. My response to that one is a big "So what?" Making New Year's resolutions is a game. While the tradition may boost profits at health clubs, after people who want to start exercising regularly sign up and then stop attending a month later, there's no stipulation that says you're supposed to feel guilty about not following them. Make a list of some of the resolutions you've never followed and use it as a reminder of what you really want to change in your life and then take it to the Lord in prayer. Now that's a resolution you'll want to keep. While you're at it, thank God for your sense of humor, because smiling and laughing can certainly boost your emotional energy reserve. **Blue**

B. If you *occasionally* keep New Year's Resolutions, you have benefited from this game—and it *is* a game. But if you're better off as a result of keeping those resolutions, who would complain? Make a list of the resolutions you've adhered to and pat yourself on the back. As for those you haven't followed, ask God for help in changing. You're more likely to stick to the plan when prayer is involved. **Blue**

C. If you *frequently* keep New Year's Resolutions, you really view this first-of-the-year game as a promise that you've made to yourself. That's admirable, and it's also a sign that your emotional energy is helping you function at a high level. Be sure to thank God for your discipline. **Green**

Put a 14 in the appropriate column.

Responses to Situation 15

A. If you *never* have time to give parties, you may be using a busy schedule as an excuse for not celebrating your life. Even busy people make time for parties. Parties allow us to make our houses homes. When the event is in full swing, you'll see people who care about you coming together, enjoying one another and you. Parties help us feel restored and renewed. **Yellow**

B. If you *occasionally* give parties, then you know how to enjoy your friends and good times. Parties require emotional and physical energy: sending out the invitations, preparing the food, and cleaning the house. There's usually anxiety leading up to the event, but boy, will you experience a natural high once things are in full swing. **Green**

C. If you *frequently* give parties, you either have paid staff (aren't you fortunate—and I hope you're treating them with respect) or you're extremely spontaneous. Spontaneity certainly signifies a life well lived. **Green**

Put a 15 in the appropriate column.

Responses to Situation 16

A. If you *never* speak up when people do or say something that makes you uncomfortable, frustration may be tamping down your emotional energy. One woman couldn't bring herself to scold the maintenance man who always rubbed her back when she passed him in the hallway of her apartment building. She was annoyed with herself for not speaking up sooner, especially after he used the building key to enter her apartment—without ringing! At that point she told him off. Her outburst, and the energy it wasted, could have been avoided if she'd reminded him early on that some boundaries should never be crossed. **Yellow**

B. If you *occasionally* speak up when people do or say something that makes you uncomfortable, that's a start, but it's not enough when it comes to your well-being. People struggling with this issue have to practice speaking up. They have the disease to please, and they haven't developed their own emotional voices. The next time you run into an uncomfortable situation, think of a way of expressing yourself that will leave you with your dignity intact. If this proves to be difficult for you, learn to use a blanket statement. You might say, "That's not okay with me." **Blue**

C. If you *frequently* speak up in an appropriate manner (which means not "going off" on the person) when people say or do something that makes you uncomfortable, you've learned to care for yourself. If you feel an embarrassed flush after speaking up, use your internal nurturing voice and assure yourself that you've done what was necessary. **Green**

Put a 16 in the appropriate column.

Responses to Situation 17

A. If you *never* use the Internet you're cutting yourself off from a world filled with information. Sure there's some inappropriate stuff to be found online, but the technology is now so advanced that most of the uglier aspects of the Internet can be blocked from view. If you're not using the Internet and insist on communicating with everyone through snail mail, you're wasting time and energy that could be better spent, and you're giving into fears that lead you to believe it's too difficult for you to learn. I understand that kind of hesitancy. After decades of typing on a manual Royal typewriter I had to talk myself into taking that big step, and started signing up for computer classes during our family cruises. I couldn't even pretend I was too old to learn. My mother learned at seventy, so she could keep apprised of operations in the security company she owned and supervised. If you can't afford a computer, use one at the library and get a free e-mail address. **Yellow**

B. If you *occasionally* use the Internet then you've learned to use a tool that will only continue to be expanded upon. Now's the time to take that next step and get comfortable enough to navigate the Web. You can click into everything from biblical verses, to information on how to find favorite recipes, to finding whatever item you're searching for in your neighborhood. It brings the world in close, and by utilizing this time saver you'll have energy left over for good works. **Green**

C. If you *frequently* use the Internet, this may imply a fearlessness that helps you navigate through the world. **Green**

Put a 17 in the appropriate column.

Responses to Situation 18

A. If you're *never* alone during nonworking hours, you may
   be longing for solitude. Time alone offers opportunities
   for regrouping and introspection, and it suggests that you
   enjoy your own company. But if you're never alone
   because you can't stand solitude, there may be aspects of
   your life that you're afraid of confronting. If that's the
   case, journaling is the perfect opportunity for you to be
   with yourself and explore any uneasiness you feel about
   being solo. **Yellow**

B. If you're *occasionally* alone, explore through journal writing
   whether you prefer your own company or spending time
   with others. If you prefer being alone, you may have
   grown up hearing a parent or significant adult express
   similar feelings. How would you describe that individual's
   emotional life? Was it one that you'd like to emulate?
   Also write about how you felt if that individual didn't
   want to spend time with you. If you aren't usually alone,
   these periods of solitude will offer opportunities for
   replenishing your emotional energy. **Green**

C. If you are *frequently* alone you may have cut yourself off
   from vital connections. You may argue that you're alone
   by choice, but the question is why do you choose an
   isolated life? That's a topic to explore in your journal.
   Yellow

Put an 18 in the appropriate column.

Responses to Situation 19

A. If you *never* exercise, you're doing your body a great disservice. Regular exercise promotes good health, and it will certainly boost your emotional energy level. **Yellow**

B. If you *occasionally* exercise you're getting on the good foot, but try to talk yourself beyond this halfway commitment. The best way to exercise regularly is to ask a friend or colleague to join you. You can keep one another motivated. **Blue**

C. If you *frequently* exercise, folks have probably commented on how good you're looking, and that can only make you feel better. Regular exercise is energizing. **Green**

Put a 19 in the appropriate column.

Responses to Situation 20

A. If you've *never* developed the discipline of regular prayer, then ask yourself why. God is waiting for you to communicate through prayer. Go ahead, stop reading and speak to the Almighty. You'll be all the better for it. **Yellow**

B. If you *occasionally* pray, there's nothing to stop you from establishing a more permanent connection. As a matter of fact, there's no better time than right now. **Blue**

C. If you *frequently* pray, unlike the guy in the commercial, you don't have to ask: "Can you hear me now?" You know God is listening. When it comes to loving God and filling your emotional energy reservoir, there's no such thing as too much prayer. **Green**

Put a 20 in the appropriate column.

Responses to Situation 21

A. If you *never* worry about someone you care about, you are absolutely awesome. You've reached a point of nirvana. Worrying is an emotional energy drain. **Green**

B. If you *occasionally* worry about someone you love you have developed a close working relationship with the Almighty. Lee tells the story of how, two hours after walking her son to the school bus stop, she received a phone call from his headmaster asking why the boy wasn't in school. She asked the headmaster to call back as soon as he had any news, and immediately bent her head in prayer: "Lord, please hold me in your arms while I wait to hear good news." The phone rang minutes later and the headmaster apologized over an attendance error. Her son was in class. She thanked him for calling and then she turned back to the Lord and thanked him for soothing her anxieties. **Green**

C. If you *frequently* worry about someone you love, enlist your friends and family members as prayer warriors. Write them (hopefully via e-mail), tell them your concerns, and ask them to pray with you for a positive outcome. Worry feels like acid eating away at your stomach lining and will surely deplete your emotional energy. **Yellow**

Put a 21 in the appropriate column.

Responses to Situation 22

A. If you *never* come down with colds, viral infections, or the flu, your efforts to create balance in your life are paying off. Researchers have established a direct connection between a low immune system and high levels of stress and anxiety. **Green**

B. If you *occasionally* get colds, viral infections or the flu, your immune system seems to be functioning well. According to researchers, our immune systems work best when we work through anger, stress, and anxiety, rather than trying to suppress these emotions. **Green**

C. If you *frequently* get colds, viral infections or the flu, read *You Can Heal Your Life* by Louise L. Hay or *Emotional Intelligence* by Daniel Goleman, so you understand how you can improve your health by clearing away emotional energy blocks. Frequent ailments can leave you feeling drained. **Yellow**

Put a 22 in the appropriate column.

Responses to Situation 23

A. If you *never* get a good night's sleep I urge you to advocate on your own behalf. Sleep is absolutely necessary for boosting your emotional energy. Sleep-deprived people are less likely to exercise, they become depressed and irritable, and their responses are slowed. Sleep deficits can put you at a higher risk for accidents, and you're more likely to put on extra, unwanted weight. Consult your doctor and if necessary try alternative holistic approaches. **Yellow**

B. If you *occasionally* get a good night's sleep, you're settling for less than you require for good health. After three or four weeks of sleep loss, a weakened immune system will make you more susceptible to colds, flu, and other infectious diseases. Sleep helps us rebuild energy, so find a way to make it happen. **Blue**

C. If you *frequently* get a good night's sleep, you awake feeling refreshed and restored. This is one of the best gifts you can give your body and it will put you in the mood to get up and get going. Since I need eight hours of sleep, most people know not to call me after 9:30 p.m., except for emergencies. You too might want to pass the word around about your sleep needs. **Green**

Put a 23 in the appropriate column.

Responses to Situation 24

A. If you *never* receive and give affection you may be feeling the loss. Affection is rejuvenating. I'm reminded of this when I conduct "Wonderful Wall Street Wednesdays," at St. John United Methodist Church, in Manhattan's financial district, from Memorial Day through Labor Day. People of various Christian denominations, races and ethnicities walk in looking burdened by the tensions of the stock market. After they turn to one another (at my suggestion) and offer each other hugs and encouragement, their faces glow and they leave smiling. **Yellow**

B. If you *occasionally* receive and give affection, you remember how good it feels. After World War II, doctors visiting European orphanages found that some babies had stopped growing. The infants had been fed and clothed, but because the orphanages were understaffed, the children had not received affection. Doctors call this syndrome "failure to thrive." From the day we're born until the day we die, we need love and affection. **Blue**

C. If you *frequently* receive and give affection, you're taking it in, allowing it to fill you up. God gave us sensitive skin and fingertips because we were meant to touch loved ones, so enjoy. **Green**

Put a 24 in the appropriate column.

Responses to Situation 25

A. If you *never* engage in volunteer work, you're suggesting by your inaction that you're too tired or too busy to serve as God's hands. You don't have to sign up at an organization. Lee made it a point to greet strangers at the cooperative apartment complex where she lives. She baked items to welcome newcomers and introduced them to other neighbors. One of these people turned out to be a wealthy woman who put up a substantial sum of money so Lee and her family could move to a larger apartment. Lee didn't greet strangers to get something back, but that's the nature of doing for others. You put that energy out into the world and one way or another it comes back and enriches your life. **Yellow**

B. If you *occasionally* engage in volunteer work you know the enriching experience of serving as God's hands. If you can't schedule time to perform a regular service, ask God to show you how you can make more of an impact with your time and your gifts. **Green**

C. If you *frequently* engage in volunteer work you serve as a force for good and this replenishes your emotional energy reserve. You allow your contributions to take your mind off your own problems. And your efforts make you grateful for all that you have. **Green**

Put a 25 in the appropriate column.

Now you can tally your score. Twenty-eight different figures are dispersed throughout the color columns. Tally up the numbers in each column. For instance, you may have two numbers in the red column, nine in the yellow, eight in blue, and six in green. Figure out which column has the most numbers, which column has the second highest number of figures, which comes in third, and which last.

Here's how to read your emotional energy level. Red is the column for emotional baggage. By that, I mean the issues that may stem from childhood and that are weighing you down, like toxic shame and long-term anger. If you have any numbers in the red column, you are more likely to feel dragged down. If you are high functioning despite all this baggage, you may still feel emotionally drained.

If you scored high in the yellow level, your emotional energy reserve is medium-low. It's like having the gas gauge on your car slightly above the empty mark. You know that if you don't fill up soon you'll likely run out of gas and wind up in trouble. If you have most of your scores in the red and yellow area, you are running on fumes.

A high score in the blue range indicates a medium-to-high emotional energy range. You're close to creating the balanced life you desire.

And last, but definitely not least in the scoring is the green range. Green represents spring, when Jesus rose from the dead, and it symbolizes new life. If most of your scores divided between the blue and green areas, you have a high emotional reserve. No matter what your score, you'll want to note thoughts and feelings that came to you. By working through this Emotional Energy Test, you know which areas of your life need a boost.

Finally, here's a color coding system that might help you in your scheduling. I use colored markers to help me keep my schedule balanced. In my calendar, I fill in out-of-town trips in yellow; pink means I'm making a speech; blue days are for times when I've scheduled rest periods; and green indicates family time. As I look over my schedule, I keep an eye out for blue (rest) dates, and if I don't have enough, that is a sign that my schedule is out of balance. If I see too many yellow (out-of-town) days, I know to cut back on upcoming engagements. And no matter how important an engagement may sound, I never budge if I have an invitation for a blue (family) day. Using this system, I was able to attend my son Samuel's middle school basketball games (the team made it to the championships!).

It took me awhile to learn to use this system efficiently, but it seems everyone in our family has caught on. When Ron and I were young parents and had overscheduled our sons' weekend, Christopher, who was five at the time, said, "Next Saturday I want to stay home, get up late, watch television, and have a Me day." It was a great idea. All of us could use a few Me days to keep ourselves from feeling drained. In the next chapter you'll meet a woman who was running on empty and was confronted with religious issues that might have kept her from creating the balance she needed in her life.

CHAPTER 9

Healing Depression

As we continue to explore the *E* for emotional energy in "blessed," this is a good time to introduce the vivacious and pretty Marilyn, who was usually the life of the party. Quick to smile and with a luminous intelligence apparent in her big brown eyes, she has a gift for getting the most uptight sort of folks to relax. Her charisma is a real plus in her work as an investigative reporter on TV. On one morning that she recalled, her smile seemed washed away by her tears, and the emotional energy that had kept her going for forty-three years seemed to have dissolved from her body. "I was shattered. I kept telling myself to get out of bed, but I kept laying there."

Marilyn reminded herself that women in her family didn't act like this. But the pride that was usually generated when she thought of the strong, independent black women that had come before her wasn't doing the trick that day. "I couldn't understand why it had affected me so deeply."

The "it" she referred to was the breakup of her second marriage. After a year together, her husband had moved out on the first day of December, and eleven days later, the divorce papers arrived. Reading the words that signaled an official end to their union probably shouldn't have been such a surprise. After all, she and Benjamin had certainly engaged in their share of disagreements, especially when it came to his teenage daughter, who along with Benjamin, had moved into Marilyn's comfortable Detroit home.

"His daughter was seventeen and completely out of control, staying out all night, but he wouldn't say anything to her. And he got angry with me when I caught her in a lie. I think he felt guilty because her mom was a heavy drinker, so this girl hadn't had a great mother. He was trying to make it up to her."

Despite the couple's differences, Marilyn had expected that she and Benjamin would work them out, especially through prayer. After all, their mutual faith was what brought them together in the first place. Benjamin was an assistant minister at her Baptist church, and as someone who was "new to the Lord" Marilyn found his biblical interpretations spellbinding. "He was a biblical scholar. I thought he could really teach me something, and he also fit my quote-unquote checklist. He was handsome, and intelligent, and before working for the church he'd earned a law degree and served as a judge. On top of all that, he was divorced and raising a daughter. I found the whole package appealing."

Benjamin seemed to admire her too and gave her every impression of being deeply in love with her. As a new arrival to Detroit, Benjamin had put on a full-court press as he pursued Marilyn. "He swept me off my feet: brought me flowers at work. And once when I went out of town, he showed up at the airport wearing a tuxedo to celebrate my return. I pictured us settling down together and studying the Bible."

But that was not to be. One morning Benjamin announced that he was leaving her—that day. "It was the beginning of the Christmas season, and a few weeks later, when one of my friends dropped by, he said he'd just seen Benjamin and his daughter at another woman's house. They'd moved in with her and they were decorating a tree."

Four days after being served with the divorce papers, Marilyn dragged herself to the office. "My boss took one look at me and said, 'You're falling apart. You can't work like this.' I thought, 'Oh God, I'm going to lose my job.' "

She didn't need a specialist to know she was depressed. Everyone gets the blues now and then, she told herself, and besides, her grief was normal. She'd have worried about herself if she hadn't felt depressed. She resumed her work schedule, but as she continued dragging through her days, feeling weak and disinterested in life, she knew that she was suffering from something a lot bigger than disappointment.

In fact Marilyn was clinically depressed. According to Dr. Brenda Wade, coauthor with Brenda Lane Richardson of *What Mama Couldn't Tell Us About Love*, symptoms of depression include, "hopelessness, fatigue, loss of interest in sex and other normally enjoyable activities." Also, according to Dr. Wade, depressed people tend to think pessimistically and are highly critical of others and themselves. Additionally, they may feel lethargic, cry frequently, over- or undereat, oversleep or suffer from insomnia, and mask symptoms with irritability and excessive worry. With all those negatives, depression could easily be called the major emotional energy drain.

As you learn the details of Marilyn's story, you'll discover the events that led up to her depressive episode. Her husband walking out on her was far from her first loss, but that did put her in touch with the abandonment she experienced in childhood. Like many successful people, Marilyn employed a combination of grit, determination, and talent to fight her way to the top, while trying to convince herself that she could ignore hurtful memories. But as we learned in the last chapter, emotions are energy. In fact, they are energy in motion. To function at our best, our energy needs to flow and move. Emotional baggage from childhood presses our energy down. That's what depression means, pressed down energy.

Also like many of us, one of Marilyn's greatest blessings was her faith in God. And throughout her ordeal, her relationship with God remained firmly intact. For some people their faith collides with the question of how to deal with depression or other emotional maladies, which they feel they should be able to "snap out of." Maybe you or someone you know questions whether these maladies can be dealt with through reliance on God. Some people point to the biblical story of Paul pleading for a cure from his pain, when God told him in (2 Corinthians 12:9), "My grace is sufficient for you, for my strength is made perfect in weakness."

What a blessed gift. By the grace of God, He promises to be with us even in adversity. He urges us to use our struggles as an opportunity to increase our faith. A lot of us make the mistake of judging God's love through providence. What I mean by that is that when our lives are going well—maybe we got the raise we'd hoped for or a relationship is progressing smoothly—we might think, God really loves me. And we would be right, He does. But He loves us just as much when we're experiencing hardship. The test for us is whether we can love him just as much in our pain as in our happiness.

During those days in bed without food, Marilyn, like Paul, was fasting and praying, asking God to make it better. What do you think she should have done to relieve her symptoms? Did her lack of improvement suggest that God wanted her to remain in pain? Should she have allowed her supervisor to become more concerned about her condition, perhaps even fire her?

I can tell you that Marilyn has a good life today, and rather than launching into an explanation about how that occurred, it's important for you to know the events that predated the collapse of her second marriage.

Marilyn was born in a rundown section of Portland, Oregon, not in a bed of roses. "My mother was a teenager when she got pregnant with me. She'd been living with her mom, who was divorced, and she'd never really known her dad. She was just about to finish high school, and really smart. Her dream was to escape from home and the life she had there."

But pregnancy put an end to her mother's dreams. "My mother viewed me as the one who tied her down. She had to get a job to support me."

For the first eight years of her life, Marilyn remained happily ensconced in the home of her maternal grandmother, who was fun-loving and generous. "I have memories of her bundling me up on chilly days and taking me out to play." Marilyn's mother would visit occasionally, and she also has vague memories of her father, who was forced by his parents to marry Marilyn's mother. "I remember him and my mother taking me to a pool. He carried me on his shoulders, and I was just above the water, kicking and playing. My mother was calling from the edge of the pool, telling him to bring me back to her. It's one of my fondest childhood memories."

When her parents divorced, Marilyn's mother remarried, and one day, her mother stopped by accompanied by the new stepfather. "That was the first time I met him. He was big, six-foot-nine, and he earned a good living as a contractor's assistant." Through the years, they had five children together. "My mother didn't have a lot of patience. My sister once told me a story about a time after I left home when Mom got really angry and locked all the rest of the kids in the garage. She told them, 'I never wanted to have children. I don't want you and I didn't want you.' " Marilyn once asked her mother why she'd had so many kids, and her mother told her that her husband wanted a large family. "She didn't stop having kids until birth control came out. My sisters and brothers are like stair steps. The only gap is when Mom had a backroom abortion."

During the younger years when Marilyn lived with her grandmother, she saw her mother during occasional visits, and learned quickly not to ask about her biological father. "She didn't like him, and she'd remind me that he never sent any money for my support, to put clothes on my back or food in my stomach."

When her beloved grandmother died, Marilyn went to live with her mother, and she praises her attributes. "My mother is a voracious reader, so we always had newspapers and magazines around the house. And she watched the news every night. She was an information addict, and that's certainly what led to my love of news. We were also one of the only families on the block to have a set of encyclopedias. People would come to our house when they wanted to look something up."

In her new home, living with her mother, there was a great deal expected of Marilyn, and she was eager to please. "It was my responsibility to keep an eye on the other children. My mother worked evenings at the post office, and she trusted me to keep meals on the table, and I did the laundry."

Although young, she wasn't overwhelmed by her responsibilities; young Marilyn saw it as a matter of being trusted rather than burdened. "The brother closest to me is five years younger and the next one is ten years younger, so I had to be a responsible adult from a young age. I was entrusted to teach them their alphabets, names, phone number, and address before they started school. My sister actually went the wrong way once, and based on what she'd learned, she rang a neighborhood bell, said she was lost, and gave her name, address, and phone number."

One privilege of being the oldest sibling was getting her own bedroom. Marilyn was ten when her stepfather first started coming in at night, while her mother was at work. "He was huge and I was a toothpick. I had no experience of dealing with men, and he was the father of my sisters and brothers. But he threatened to kill me if I told anyone. I didn't even feel like telling my mother. She loved him, and I was afraid of him. All of us were terrified of him. He could get loud and he spanked us and would get very dramatic, rolling the belt around his fist. My whole goal was not to get hurt, and to keep my siblings from getting hurt. Sometimes, if I knew that one of them might get beaten, I'd lie and take the blame and get beaten in their place. . . . So I didn't fight my stepfather when he forced himself on me. It wasn't until I was in my twenties that my sister told me he'd molested her too. She was damaged by it. She ran away and had drug issues."

Marilyn connects her own survival to God's grace, which included spending her first eight years with her loving grandmother. Marilyn also excelled at school, earning high grades and praise from her mother, whom she deeply loved and wanted to impress. "I was the hero in the family, the academic achiever. My mother told me I would never be pretty and that she wanted me to focus on getting good grades."

Meanwhile, her stepfather's sexual abuse continued for six years. "I'm convinced that my mother must have known, but she wasn't willing to give up her middle-class lifestyle for me." Marilyn told a classmate about her troubles, and the police were notified. Without warning, uniformed officers showed up at her predominantly white school and took Marilyn out, as if she were under arrest.

"They'd called my mother about the abuse, and she told them I was lying. She claimed I made it all up because my stepfather refused to let me date and that she would not keep a liar in her house. Back then the police didn't know how to deal with a situation like this." The officers took Marilyn to juvenile hall, where she remained for months. "My mother came to visit me once. She said I would have to stay until I told the authorities I was lying. I refused to take back what I'd said."

With her mother refusing to allow her to come home, Marilyn was sent to foster care, where she was again sexually abused. She was removed from that home, sent to another, and was again abused.

Feeling unloved and abandoned, Marilyn was drawn to the first man who complimented her. "I was sixteen, and fell for the oldest line in the book: 'Hey baby, you sure are fine.' Nobody had ever said that to me before. . . . Percy's full-time job was hanging outside the high school. He asked me for my phone number and said he wanted me to be his girlfriend. When I learned that he played a saxophone I was in love—musical talent, in addition to saying I was fine! I had sex with him. And wouldn't you know? One time and I was pregnant."

It was 1968, a time of social upheaval, but the circumstances were similar to when her mother had become pregnant at almost the same age: both of them smart women, lacking in self-love, tied to men who didn't want them.

"Percy's mother and grandmother insisted that he marry me," Marilyn says. "At first, we lived on welfare, but when my son was two years old I aced a test for a county job and they hired me." Arguments between the young couple often ended with Percy beating Marilyn. His grandmother convinced them that the baby would be better off living with her. Marilyn was too weary to argue otherwise and allowed the grandmother to take the baby. The situation was eerily reminiscent of what had occurred with Marilyn's own mother. When people carry around unhealed scars they often repeat their own parents' damaging patterns.

With no full-time child-rearing responsibilities, Marilyn took a friend's advice and enrolled in junior college. A few months later, when her husband blackened her eye and chipped her tooth, she decided to leave him, despite the fact that she was six months pregnant with their second child. This time Marilyn gave birth to a daughter. Struggling to work full time and attend college, she allowed Percy's grandmother to take this child too—the situation was supposed to be temporary.

Through the next few years, she spent time with her children on weekends and during vacations, and continued excelling at school. "One of my teachers at community college convinced me to apply for a scholarship to a four-year school." She was able to attend the University of Michigan, all expenses paid. While attending college, she reintroduced herself to her father and found him smart and charming, and she continued to thrive academically. After graduation, she was hired by a local television station.

A larger income helped her to continue supporting her children and to purchase a home so they could visit more frequently. "I'd tried getting them back when they were younger, but their grandmother fought it. Still, they were never out of my life; they'd come for summers and holidays. But they'd heard all this negative stuff about me from their father's family. My son believed I didn't love him because I hadn't raised him. And when he was fourteen, he announced to the family that he was gay. I have to admit that we put him put down for it. His grandmother beat him over the head with a Bible."

As for her private life, Marilyn admits she was sexually promiscuous. "I later learned that some people who are abused use sex as a conquering tool. When I was little, I couldn't control what was happening with my stepfather. As I grew older, being promiscuous made me feel I was in charge of the sex." She enjoyed drinking too, and was driving home from a bar when her car was hit by a drunk driver. "My car rolled over an embankment. I hadn't been religious, but at that moment, I said, 'Jesus, help me.' A voice in my head told me to be calm." The car was totaled, the convertible top smashed as flat as a pancake, but she crawled from the car, unscathed. The next day, after sharing details of the crash with a minister, she was led to Christ.

Her deepening faith didn't mean that life progressed smoothly, but it helped her through a terrible ordeal. Her son died at twenty-two from an undiagnosed heart condition. "He had lived with me for a little while and I thanked God that we had a chance to get close. A friend had told me about a gay man who died and how no one in his family came to his funeral. That scared me to death. A lot of gay people have to make their own family because they get rejected. I didn't want that for my son. When he was twenty-one, I'd called him for his birthday. I said, 'I want you to know that you're my son and I love you.' He said it was the best gift he'd ever had for his birthday."

Not long after Marilyn buried her son, her daughter announced that she wanted nothing to do with her and refused to speak to her. She accused her mother of abandoning her. Years passed before the two were reconciled.

So, as you can see, Marilyn had experienced many losses by the time her second husband walked out. And although she'd excelled at school and work, she was still struggling with her past as a victim of sexual abuse. In one of the best books to address the subject, *No Secrets, No Lies: How Black Families Can Heal from Sexual Abuse*, author Robin D. Stone writes of women like Marilyn. "We have buried sexual abuse so deep into our psyches that we would never connect it to today's physical illness and pain, our depression or addiction, our inability to hold a job, get out of debt, find satisfaction in a relationship, nurture our children, or simply say no to people or situations that do us harm."

Marilyn considered herself pretty tough, but, after her husband's abandonment, "If I'd ever had a period of depression that was it." She didn't have qualms about turning to a psychologist. As she points out, "God sent Luke the physician to help Paul."

I agree with her decision to seek professional help. God does give some people gifts that can help us heal. From my point of view, not seeking a release from pain and waiting for God to heal it is akin to emptying a bag of corn kernels on an open field and asking God to make it grow. *We* are God's hands. Marilyn found an African American woman, a licensed psychotherapist, to help her restore her life. Talk therapy has been found to be tremendously effective in relieving the symptoms of depression.

Marilyn says, "This woman said something really important to me. I was crying about losing my husband, and told her, 'I thought he was really different.' She said, 'You thought he was different, but from what you've told me, they were all the same men with different faces. They were all physically or emotionally abusive.' "

During months of therapy Marilyn worked on the issues of sexual violation and her heart-wrenching guilt concerning her children. After a year and a half, she decided to sell her house and attend graduate school in Boston. She has since relocated to Philadelphia, and has found a church home. "I was driving by looking for an apartment and I passed a Baptist Church. It turned out to be the best place for me."

That's also where she met her current husband, a business executive. She credits her therapy with helping her attract a man who truly loves her back. If you phone their home, he answers in a deep baritone and offers a warm greeting. Handing the phone to Marilyn, he says, "It's for you, honey." They're simple words, but for a woman who once thirsted for kind words, they're like balm from Gilead.

He and Marilyn were friends for a few years, but their relationship deepened when he insisted on accompanying her to visit an ailing aunt. "My aunt eventually regained her speech and began telling me that he was wonderful. He and I began studying the Bible together. We still do. And we spend a lot of time praying together." It would not be a matter of putting words in her mouth to say that Marilyn feels blessed. She is, and she lives like it.

It you're struggling with depression, I urge you to seek help, particularly if you have entertained any suicidal thoughts. If you do see a therapist, ask God to bless your actions. Dr. Wade says emotional energy is directly tied to our spirituality. "A therapist can help you clear up places that have been siphoning off energy. Therapy can help you create a space for energy to flow through. Once that energy is no longer pressed down, there's room for an even deeper connection to God."

Resources

- Dr. Brenda Wade, who practices in San Francisco, California, can be reached via e-mail at Docwade@docwade.com.
- Voices in Action. This organization provides referrals for therapeutic help and support groups: (800) 786-4238, www.voices-action.org.
- Survivors of Incest Anonymous. This referral line can offer information on twelve-step recovery programs in your vicinity: (410) 893-3322, www.siawso.org.

In the next chapter, you'll find suggestions that will help you continue to take positive steps toward living your blessings.

CHAPTER 10

Naming the Blessings

One of my most vivid childhood memories is of my father, Wilbert T. Johnson, setting aside time each and every evening to thank our Lord and Savior for the many blessings in his life. There I was, a little girl, seeing this beloved man, so big and strong and powerful, in a position of supplication: on his knees, head bent, and palms pressed together as he elucidated his many and varied blessings. This nightly devotion served as a powerful lesson to me about the importance of praising the Lord, of naming the blessings as a way of recharging one's emotional energy, so that we can become a force to be reckoned with.

As the years passed, my father seemed to have more and more to be grateful for, and one business venture in particular prospered. In 1962, with $1,000 in savings, he and my mother founded the Johnson Security Bureau. Almost from the start, business skyrocketed as he supplied security personnel to local concerns—everything from supermarkets to Catholic bazaars and weekly bingo games. The family-owned business gave me an opportunity to see firsthand the tremendous self-sacrifice that was required, and how it could eat away at a person's time. Dad was never too busy to pray, however. (Let me pause to point out that my mother was also prayerfully powerful, often praising God as the source from whom all blessings flow.)

My father's daily prayers were a way of acting on what he believed to be a spiritual obligation: "In everything give thanks, for this is the will of God in Christ Jesus for you" (I Thessalonians 5:18). Of course I wasn't privy to exactly what Dad was saying, but I'm sure that among many things, he praised God for the opportunity to start the business, for the contracts that kept it afloat, and for each and every worker and their families. Today the Johnson Security Bureau employs as many as three hundred individuals and was recently cited as the longest running black-owned family business in the Bronx.

I'm not suggesting that the enterprise prospered solely because of my father's gratitude. There are proprietors and professionals of every stripe who wouldn't consider thanking anyone but themselves for their success, but who still manage to turn impressive profits. We've all heard the expression, "God helps those who help themselves." It's important to remind people that God also helps those who can't help themselves.

Here's the trick about praising God: We don't do it just *for* God; He wants us to do it for ourselves. Learning to praise the Lord is a spiritual discipline that reaps rewards, according to Robert Emmons, Ph.D., a psychologist who pioneered a study of gratitude and coauthored *Words of Gratitude: For Mind, Body, and Soul.* Dr. Emmons writes, "The more grateful we are, the more reasons we have to be grateful. This knowledge can create a shift from gratitude as a response to gratitude as an attitude, as a receptive state that allows blessings to flow in . . . this attitude brings about a relationship with the Divine, the source from which all good comes."

Studying gratitude in the psychology department of the University of California, Davis, Dr. Emmons and his colleagues found that people who tend to express gratitude report high levels of alertness and energy and are likely to be engaged in social behaviors that involve helping others. "Not only do they feel good, they also did good," he writes. Compared to those who seldom express gratitude, he found that grateful people tend to be better at coping with problems, enjoy better health, and are more socially adaptable.

Dr. Emmons's research confirmed what so many people have long sensed: that praising God makes us feel better by revving up our energy level. That's all the more reason to follow the call to: "Bless the Lord, O My soul, and forget not all his benefits" (Psalm 103:2). Praising God makes the colors of spring seem brighter. Praising God makes food tastier and more satisfying. Praising God, even on the chilliest nights, makes us feel warmer, more comforted. Gratitude helps us feel the fullness and joy of life.

The healed leper in Luke understood the joy of gratitude. After Jesus had healed ten lepers, only one returned to thank Him. "And one of them, when he saw that he was healed, turned back, and with a loud voice, glorified God, and fell down on his face at his feet, giving him thanks; and he was a Samaritan. And Jesus answering said, 'Were there not ten cleansed? But where are the nine?' " (Luke 17:15–17).

Let's get this straight from the start. Jesus wasn't asking for praise and gratitude for himself. He wasn't an insecure gift-giver who got puffed up with self-concern when people kneeled at his feet. The Lord is perfect and self-contained. He can't be manipulated into giving us what we feel we need because we praise Him. He fills our lives with gifts because He loves us. He sacrificed His life for us because He loves us.

If there was ever proof that the Lord wants us to learn gratitude for our own sakes, consider the celebrities and multimillionaires plastered on the front pages of newspapers and magazines and featured on television shows. These are people who drive the biggest cars, live in posh neighborhoods, and carry credit cards that seem to have no limit, and yet, we can tell by their actions that despite their wealth, they often feel spiritually destitute, empty, null, and void. Some will take drugs, hoping to fill up the spaces. Others will drink to drown out their troubles. They may shop 'til they drop, and isn't that the truth, because the only thing going down is them: They feel more deprived, more resentful, more negative and gloomy.

Lee's oldest son, Paul, twenty-seven, learned about gratitude from the other way around. An internship at a restaurant was one of his graduation requirements at the California-based culinary school he attended. He moved to New York and landed an unpaid job that allowed him to train under one of the most highly recognized chefs in the city. As the low man on the totem pole, Paul was often subjected to this chef's selfish, angry tirades. Despite this atmosphere of ingratitude, Paul worked hard. At the end of the three-month internship, when the chef asked Paul to continue working for free, the young man, somewhat embittered, refused, and moved back to California. Paul found a good job at a restaurant, but after a year of working for a contentious manager, Paul was fired.

Out of the blue, the very next day, Paul's mother ran into the chef from the New York restaurant, and this chef began singing Paul's praises and asking her to tell her son if he ever wanted to come back, there was always a paid position waiting at his restaurant. Paul didn't want to move back to the Big Apple, but he did want to capitalize on the chance meeting by writing a letter to the chef asking for a letter of reference that would help him secure another job. As Paul wrote to the chef, something strange happened. He knew that if he was going to ask the man for a favor, he'd better start out by praising the chef, and he did. He wrote about how much he'd learned working under him, and as he began to list what he'd learned in detail, Paul felt himself relaxing. Any residual resentment he'd felt about this chef's mistreatment began to fade away. He also found himself shaking off the anxiety he'd felt about finding another job. By praising the chef, Paul realized how blessed he'd been to work under this man. And *then*, he asked for the letter of reference. And so it is with God. Gratitude prepares us for a relationship with the Almighty.

Showing gratitude is a beautiful thing. It builds energy, gathers momentum, stirs people up and makes them want to start something, do something good. We who are grateful to the Lord know we couldn't exist without Him. But simply knowing is not sufficient, not if we want to keep a positive balance. At least one major corporation seems aware of this fact. Witness the advertising campaign of an international bank whose slogan states: "We don't say thank you, we *do* thank you."

The decision makers at the top of that megabank recognized that the only way to keep ahead of the competition and boost profits was to generate energy from within by reminding their employees that without their customers they would cease to exist. The marketing managers knew they could create more employee loyalty, more customer satisfaction with their newest slogan: "Let the thanking begin."

I say hallelujah to that idea, and I'm going to say it again, "Let the thanking begin." That's what we do at Believers Christian Fellowship, the church I pastor that relocated in 2004 to Harlem. And maybe it's the same at your parish. Several minutes before the service begins, a Praise Team comes out. This team is comprised of five to seven people blessed with musical and singing talent, and they get the energy rolling among the early attendees by proclaiming the good news about our crucified, risen, and soon returning King. They're like an advance team that warms up a crowd before a politician comes out to speak, gets them cheering and clapping, energized and ready to hear the Lord's word.

I am grateful and say many prayers of thanks for our Praise Team, for once they've performed, by the time I come out, I can feel a force of energy in that sanctuary. Minutes earlier, people might have walked in feeling burdened by their cares. They may have walked in intending to ask God's help in getting their marriages straight, or calming wild teenagers, or coming up with rent money, or passing the next big exam. And there's not a thing wrong with them asking.

God never grows weary of our cries for help. He encouraged his disciples to always pray and never give up (Luke 18:1). He urges us to devote ourselves to prayer (Colossians 4:2). He promises to bring about justice for those who cry out to him day and night (Luke 18:7–8). And even when we're too weary to utter the words, He promises that the spirit will intercede with groans that words cannot express (Romans 8:26). But before we ask for help, He asks for something from us. Before our prayers and petitions, He asks for words of thanksgiving (Philippians 4:6).

And this is how the ministry of the Praise Team works at Believers Christian Fellowship. Their words and songs of praise, the gratitude they generate among the congregation puts people in a state that makes them more receptive to the blessings. Suddenly it's no longer a building housing individual minds that are focused on their own problems, but a congregation focused on the glory of God. The worshippers are no longer just an assembly of individuals but one church, built on one foundation of Jesus Christ our Lord.

These parishioners have found that gratitude and praise help generate the energy that can help us live like we're blessed. It will help create the aspects of blessed that we have covered in Parts I, II, and III: the balance, the love, and the energy that is necessary to bring about radical change. Expressing gratitude gets us down on our knees, even if only mentally, with our heads bent and hands pressed together.

Some people prefer to wait until they're in pastoral settings, perhaps sitting by a beautiful body of water or looking out on a springtime field of flowers. As for me, I don't want to wait for a beautiful environment. I thank the Lord whether I'm sitting in my car stuck in traffic, amid blaring horns, or at the doctor's office waiting to hear about the results of my mammogram. Like any form of prayer, I know that the more I praise God the better I'll feel.

Katherine, a thirty-year-old historian, knows about praising the Lord even during difficult times. She smiles with pleasure as she recalls finally reaching a point in her fifteen-year marriage when she and her husband were both earning more and could finally start saving. When they had a tidy sum put away, they were hit with a problem that caused them to spend every penny of their savings, a problem that eventually put them into debt and zapped their future earnings for the next several years. The family was shocked by their sudden change of circumstances. They'd always been a praying family and during this period they prayed even more. But there was some resistance when Katherine said at one of their family prayer sessions, "I want to thank God for our financial hardships."

She later explained that she wasn't suggesting that God had caused their troubles. She understood that God only brings about good, never adversity. But she reminded her family of the promise that "All things work together for good to them that love God, to them who are the called according to His purpose" (Romans 8:28). She told them that she trusted God enough to believe that with His help, they could make something good of their troubles. Five years later, she knows just what that good was.

"For years, the biggest obstacle for me and my husband was our different attitudes about money. It wasn't as simple as he hated spending and I spent everything, but we were definitely a contrast in styles, and this caused many conflicts between us, and our kids knew this because we argued, loudly. But I believe our prayers and love of God helped us make something good out of those years on a financial edge. By necessity, I had to start cutting back drastically. I came up with all kinds of cost-saving measures. We had to watch every cent. It took about two years into our financial troubles before I noticed that my husband and I had stopped arguing over money. I will always trust God to comfort me when something terrible occurs and to work through me for the good. I'll always praise His name."

A few other people were asked to share their thoughts on developing attitudes of gratitude. Jane G. Ravarra, eighty-four, who worked as a receptionist for thirty-three years in the prosecutor's division of the Wayne County, Michigan, criminal justice system, praises God dozens of times in a given day.

Ravarra says, "As soon as my eyes fly open and my tail lifts up, I say 'Thank you, Lord.' I had surgery recently and my niece was with me, but it was frightening to know that I was going through a door and didn't know what was waiting for me on the other side. Praising God made a difference. I thanked Him for guiding me through every step of my life. People like to think they deserve what they get. But there's a difference between having a talent and having a gift. If you take sewing class and get good at making clothes, that's a talent. If you sit down in front of a piano for the first time and you touch the keys and make a musical sound, that's a gift and that's from God. He's waiting for us to discover our gifts. He gives them graciously. I am grateful for the gifts that I've identified and those which have not yet been revealed. And for that, I thank Him."

Closer to home, my husband, Ronald Cook, responded to a question about what he felt grateful for in the moment. He said, "I thank God for my family. God is good. At the moment, many of the people I care about are enjoying a reasonable portion of health and strength. Thank you, Lord. I'm grateful that I can contribute to this world we live in. I'm grateful for my wife. I praise God for leading me to someone with whom every day is an adventure. I'm grateful that she can travel all over the country to spread the word and no danger or harm has come to her. Thank you, Lord. I'm grateful that I have a job, working at Convent Avenue church as an administrator. I'd do this for free if I could, and so I praise you for my position. If there is loss in my future, I intend to keep my head high, praising God and telling Him that I'm willing to receive whatever He has for me."

It's no coincidence that this chapter began with an image of my father praising God and then closing with my husband's words of gratitude. They are two of those strong and wonderful black men that statistics tell us no longer exist. I thank God for helping me to ignore the naysayers and for giving me vision that helps us see the divine reality. God's creation is bountiful, and in this moment, for this I praise Him.

Ten Ways to Cultivate an Attitude of Gratitude

I.   Morning devotions. Get in the habit of praying every morning before you walk out the door. Whether you are single, are married, or have children, use these moments to lower your head and thank the Lord (in advance) for taking you through the day. Thank the Lord for the job you are about to perform. Thank God for allowing you to make a positive difference in the world. If you're praying with schoolchildren, thank God for their teachers and their school.

2.   Praise book. Carry a small notebook and throughout the day make a list of all you're grateful for and praise God for each of these.

3.   Listen to yourself. As you converse with others notice whether most of your comments are laced with complaints. Don't scold yourself if you hear yourself complaining, but do explore whether there is anything good that might come out of a difficult situation.

4.   The right words. Get in the habit of thanking people for even the smallest services. Remember that we're all made in God's image. When we're kind to others, we are thanking God for the human creation. And saying thank you to those who assist us is a way of acknowledging their worth.

5.   Volunteer time. I know that I mentioned this in the last chapter, but it bears repeating: Find some way to utilize those God-given gifts by sharing with others.

6. Little things. Know those beat-up slippers that you slide into at the end of the day? That's right, they're almost worn to a nub, but don't they feel good? Learn to thank God for the small things and you'll start seeing the world through new eyes.

7. Posting a quote. Copy this quote and tape it to your mirror or on your dashboard or refrigerator as a reminder to praise the Lord: "It is a good thing to give thanks unto the Lord, to sing praises unto thy name, O most High: to show forth thy loving kindness in the morning and thy faithfulness every night. Upon an instrument of ten strings, and upon the psaltery; upon the harp with a solemn sound. For thou, Lord, has made me glad through thy work: I will triumph in the works of thy hands. O Lord, how great are thy works! And thy thoughts are very deep" (Psalm 92:1–5).

8. Check energy drops. When you are feeling low, your energy level is dipping. Rev it up by praising the Lord. The more energy you invest in the moment, the more empowered you will feel.

9. Elder care. Develop a relationship with a sick or shut-in elderly person. Even if you can only find time to send occasional greeting cards or phone on weekends, know that these are precious moments for the lonely, and you're sure to hear a thank you. Accept the gratitude on behalf of the Lord.

10. Evening devotions. The end of the day is a good time to praise God for all He has done. If you're not doing this, it's a great habit to start. If you do it already, keep it up!

PART IV

B
L
E
S   SPIRIT
S
E
D

CHAPTER 11

Forgiving Seventy Times Seven

Although sometimes confused with energy, the emotions that motivate us to live fully, spirit—the first *S* in "blessed"—is God's awesome power. This life force, which surrounds us and lives within us, is a vital requirement for those of us who want to live as if we're blessed. The presence of the Holy Spirit within us is one of our greatest gifts, for we are promised that "the fruit of the Spirit is love, joy, peace, longsuffering, kindness, goodness, faithfulness, gentleness, self-control" (Galatians 5:22–23). These qualities can empower us to achieve the unimaginable, and thus, compel us to learn about the care and handling of our inner spirit.

Maintaining a relationship with our inner spirit requires that we never neglect it or allow it to grow cold. If you think I sound as if I'm referring to keeping a fire stoked, you're right. Paul compared God's spirit to an ember in a fire and urged Timothy to stir it up and fan it into flames. Of course prayer and expressions of gratitude, along with other suggestions offered in this work, will help maintain your spiritual relationship. Tapping into your highest self, however, requires bringing this work up a notch.

Just as the buildup of clutter in your home signals that it's time for a spring cleaning, and just as that rumble in the car's engine indicates that it's time for a tune-up, there's a way of knowing when you're in need of a spiritual cleansing. The key sign is whether you've been able to forgive those who have hurt you. Don't shrug off the idea. Simply saying you've forgiven someone is not the same as actually forgiving. Holding on to resentments is human. That's why Jesus taught us to pray: "Forgive us our sins as we forgive those who sin against us." He was reminding us of our contract with God. He will forgive us for hurting Him by sinning, if we can forgive those who have hurt us. It's not like he minced words on the subject. When Peter asked him how often he should forgive, Jesus replied, "Seventy times seven" (Matthew 18:21–22). He meant that our forgiveness should be boundless.

I urge you to fight your way through denial about forgiving past transgressions. Remaining spiritually strong requires letting go of past grievances. I know it's not easy, and in fact, I've found forgiveness to be among the most challenging of spiritual disciplines. It helps to remember that lack of forgiveness is so powerful it can destroy love. Hatred and resentment are so consuming they can douse the flames of the most fiery inner spirits. Unforgiveness manifests itself in our bodies and can make us ill.

Many of my parishioners know this, and in their determination to be good Christians, they often turn to me for help in learning to forgive. They can be tough on themselves because they want to be able to forgive and forget. So they're surprised when I tell them that forgiving is recommended, but that they should never forget. They may be stunned to hear this from their pastor because they recall God's own sterling example: "For I will forgive their iniquity, and their sin I will remember no more" (Jeremiah 31:34).

I thank God with all my heart for His perfection. He is able to forgive and forget my sins. And that poses a dilemma. We humans do sin, and we are imperfect, which is why we can't afford to forget who injured us and how. Forgetting could mean leaving ourselves or loves ones open to more pain. The only way we can protect ourselves or others is to remember how we were hurt, so we can avoid future injury.

Rather than forgetting, we can keep the fires of our inner spirit burning by learning to forgive. At the end of this chapter I offer specific steps for entering into the forgiveness process. You'll know that you've reached your goal when you can remember the experience without triggering past hurts. Ridding your life of resentments can lighten your load.

Madison De La Burre of New Orleans learned at an early age that anger and resentment have real consequences in our lives. At twenty-nine she still possesses the long, lean body that made her a successful model. But what's most surprising about her is not that she's so lovely, but that her experiences have not left her with a hardened heart. "A lot of people grow up without their fathers," Madison points out. "My mother had me at sixteen, and then my father abandoned us. When it was just me and Mom it was great. We'd go to the movies and to the park. We had fun."

Her family's troubles began after Madison's mother married, had three more children, and was subsequently abandoned by this man. "My mother is Haitian and speaks French; she never learned to speak English. And she stayed home to care for me and my siblings, so she didn't have any job experience. After my stepfather left her with four kids to feed, she was in trouble. Then she met this woman across the street from us, who introduced her to drugs. My mother started partying with her and left me to take care of the kids."

Ten years older than her youngest sibling, Madison dropped out of school to care for them. Somehow they managed to get by for a few years, barely surviving on the minimum wage that her mother earned through infrequent jobs. "My mother came up with an idea about moving into a women's shelter and putting us up for temporary custody. I told her that we should all go to a shelter together or that maybe she could go into rehab and I would continue taking care of the kids. I was afraid of our family getting split up. My little sister and brothers were like my own kids, but my mother wouldn't listen to me." By that time, when Madison was fourteen, her mother was using heroin and crack cocaine. "I begged her to change her mind about the shelter. I was afraid we'd never see her again, but she'd called a social worker, who told her to bring us down."

Madison remembers the cold sterility of the social services office. "My mom was in one office talking to the social worker, the kids were outside playing, and I was waiting out in the hall. All of a sudden something told me to go and check on the kids. I was still pretty short, but I stood on my toes and looked through this tiny glass window. I saw a man taking the kids by the hand and leading them toward a car. I ran back to the office for help, pounded at the door, yelling at my mom: 'Someone's taking the kids.' This social worker started telling me how this was for the best, and that since I was older, they couldn't place me with my siblings; that I had to be sent someplace for older children, even though they'd promised to keep us together."

Madison raced after the car that was transporting her siblings from her life. "Their little faces were pressed against the back window. I didn't get a chance to say goodbye." Her eyes filled with tears as she remembers that day, and then she recalls her anger.

Back in the office, after demanding that the children be returned, Madison exploded. She threw chairs and broke windows. "I bit that lady. I hit her. I kicked her in the shin. I made a big mess. They had to restrain me and they gave me sedatives."

She awoke in a group home, several miles outside of New Orleans. "I didn't know where my family was. I stayed there for a couple of months, but I was small and there were so many bullies. One day I stole some money from the office, grabbed the photograph I had of my siblings, and I ran away."

Unaccustomed to traveling on her own, Madison took several days to return to the city. "I slept in train stations and alleyways, on rooftops, and one time beside a pigeon coop. I only had a few dollars, so I'd watch people coming out of fast food restaurants, and ate what they threw away. I begged a man at a restaurant for food but he told me to get the fuck away from him. Another time, I walked through a tunnel at night and these boys chased me. One of them grabbed the chain around my neck, but I pulled away." Determined to locate her family, Madison eventually returned to her old neighborhood, but was unable to learn anything about their whereabouts.

For a teenage girl living on her own life was not easy. She checked herself into a group home, but was sexually abused. So she took to sleeping at a bus station. She continued to search for her siblings while the social worker refused to divulge their location. During her frenzied search, Madison did learn the whereabouts of her biological father, but it turned out that after a disagreement with his new wife he had moved to another state.

Finally, when Madison was eighteen, a sympathetic social worker heard about her plight and arranged a reunion with her mother. "Mom was in a shelter. I don't think I would have recognized her. She was so thin from doing drugs. Her face was scarred and she'd had syphilis and had been raped. She was glad to see me, but she wasn't really there. She started crying, begging me to take her home with me."

By then Madison was starting to earn enough from modeling to support her mother, and she acceded to her request. "I was able to forgive her, because I told myself it was the drugs that led her to make bad choices. I blamed the drugs, not her. She went into rehab and stopped using."

With her mother back in her life, Madison was able to track down her siblings. Four years had passed, but Madison found that they were still together, living in foster care. "They hadn't forgiven us for abandoning them," Madison says. "The youngest one asked my mom, 'Why did you take so long to come and get us?' I was glad to see them and proud. They were so beautiful."

Madison's mom still had visitation rights and slowly the family started on the delicate path of getting to know one another again. Their relationship seemed to be moving in the right direction until Madison's mother relapsed and began using drugs again. "We had a court hearing coming up about the kids, but I had to work. I told Mom to get it postponed. She didn't do it. She went to see the social worker on her own. This woman probably realized she was high. She got Mom to sign some papers."

A week later, when Madison and her mother showed up for their weekly visitation, they learned disappointing news. "My mother had signed away her rights to the kids. They'd been adopted and taken away. We went to court to get them back, but we lost. I've never seen them again."

Bitter and disappointed, Madison moved away. Her life didn't progress as she'd planned. One night at a party, someone offered her drugs and she tried them. Before long she was addicted. "I sniffed heroin and then I got into freebasing. I eventually went to jail, where I was raped and beaten. I was stabbed and shot."

After her release, she met a man who'd also done time, and like her, had become a devoted Christian and was determined to never go back to prison. They started a life together, but not before Madison did the one thing she needed to do to thrive: She forgave her mother.

"I don't believe in judging anyone. I'll leave that to God. If I'm still in this world after so much has happened to me, I know God's looking out for me. My mom loves my fiancé. We live together and have a good life. If I hadn't forgiven her, I could never have rested in peace."

Madison forgave her mother because that was the only route to true salvation. She knew that her mother was precious to the Lord and that when Jesus died for our sins, He wasn't excluding anyone from that list. He died for all of us. She knew that as long as her heart remained hardened toward her mother, she was living out her grief over her lost siblings and the loss of her own childhood.

By taking drugs, she realized, she'd been shackled to her mother's

past. Drugs were Madison's way of trying to forget rather than forgive. When we forgive it helps us, not necessarily the other person.
By forgiving, Madison freed herself and was able to move on. That
was why after all her terrible experiences she still seems so alive. One
look at her radiant smile and it becomes obvious that she is in possession of the fruits of God's forgiveness: love, tenderness, compassion, and humility.

Madison says of her life today: "I love going home to my mom
and my fiancé. We're very close." In fact, the three of them make
that family she'd always wanted.

As Madison's story suggests, the closer we are to someone the more
they have the power to wound us. Sometimes the hurt inflicted occurs over a long period of time, causing resentment to build up.
That's what happened with Carol Reed of Chicago, who met her
husband, Al, in 1941, when she was all of nineteen, a slip of a girl,
standing on State Street, bemoaning the fact that her sister's car had
broken down.

"I can't remember if it was engine trouble or a flat tire, but I do
remember Al walking up to us. He was so tall and handsome in his
Marine uniform. He offered to assist us. We fell in love right away."

They married right away too, and moved to North Carolina. Al
was one of the first African American men accepted into the segregated branch of the Marines, and was subject to racist belittling
from the white officers. Al remained civil but demanded that they
show him respect. "He was a very proud man, and when he felt he
was being treated unjustly he spoke up," Carol says. Although this
kind of attitude is not generally acceptable in the military, it didn't

harm Al's career. He served with distinction during World War II, and for another two decades in the military.

In the sixties, the family, which eventually included three sons, resettled in Chicago, and Al was hired as one of the first black managers of a major plant. "It was a great job, but Al drew the line at being misused by anyone. The workers respected him. He was proud that he'd been a Marine. He didn't wear his uniform anymore, of course, but it was hanging in the closet, intact. His workers called him Sarge. At home he was a role model for our sons. He was so involved with them."

Ten years into the job, however, a white truck driver punched Al, and when Al struck back, a supervisor told him that he should have "done a Martin Luther King and turned the other cheek." Just like that, Al was fired.

"It tore him apart," Carol says. Determined to keep working, he accepted menial jobs. But he was unable to get over what had happened to him, and he was unable to forgive and move on. "Our lives changed from the day he was fired," Carol says. "I prayed for change, but he became depressed, started drinking. He became a different man."

He also became more possessive of Carol. "His pride was hurt and he was feeling insecure. I'd started working at a grocery store and my new manager, a young man, became good friends with my husband. This man really looked up to him. Al would barbecue and he'd come by with his girlfriends, and he really enjoyed our boys."

When her manager was promoted and moved across the state to a district job, Carol hoped the father-and-son relationship would

continue between this man and her husband, but Al's growing inse-
curities caused a permanent rift between them.

"I got a phone call from this young man at work. I was excited to
hear from him, until he started to ask me what I'd told my husband.
I didn't know what he was talking about until I learned that Al had
somehow gotten the idea that this man had some interest in me
other than friendship. He'd accused this man and then suggested
that I'd admitted to it. Of course I hadn't. Nothing had happened
between us. It was damaging. This young man had gotten married
and Al had spread the rumor so that his wife heard about it. This
young man was furious, and I was hurt and humiliated."

Al's inability to forgive those who had hurt him had changed
their life for the worse. Carol was at a point of no return. She had
tolerated Al's heavy drinking, intensifying jealousy, boisterous and
angry temper tantrums, but she was unwilling to take further humiliation. "We still had one son left at home, but I told Al I wanted
our marriage to end. When he refused to move from the house, I
took our son and moved into an apartment. I left everything else behind. The only thing I took was clothes and one pot. The boys were
all very upset and I was brokenhearted."

Though she had moved out, Carol encouraged her sons to honor
their father. "I told them, 'If you're short of time and you have to
choose who you'll visit, go to him.' I wanted them to remember that
he'd been a good father."

Over the years, heavy drinking took a toll on Al's health, and di-
abetes and a failing heart left him confined to a wheelchair. Carol
consulted with the Lord and then knew just what to do.

"I started stopping by the house every day to see if there was anything Al wanted. I cleaned his house and drove him to doctor's ap-

pointments, made sure he was all right. One day he told me he wanted to borrow money on the house, but that the woman at the bank said that a loan would require my signature. I went to the bank with him to sign, and once we explained that we were separated, the bank manager couldn't believe it. She warned Al that this would make it easier for me to get the house from him if he didn't pay the note. He looked at me and told her, 'Carol would never do anything to hurt me.' I knew that was his way of apologizing for wrecking our marriage."

One day, Al asked Carol why she was so good to him. "I told him, 'Because you need me.' " Days later, one of her sons phoned to say that Al had died in his sleep. Al was laid to rest in a military funeral, with full honors. Carol was grateful to God that she hadn't let her resentment cause a rift in the family.

She stood at Al's grave and knew that she'd forgiven him. "I stopped picturing him as someone who was angry and loud, and reminded myself of what he'd been like on that first day when I saw him, when he came to my rescue, that tall, handsome Marine. That's how you forgive people, by remembering who they were at their best."

Here are some more suggestions that can help you remain in the spirit, working your way through to a point of forgiveness.

1. Write it down. On a slip of paper, write about how you were hurt and your fantasies of revenge, and include thoughts on how you'd like to even the score. Don't try to be polite. Write fast and furiously and let it rip. Now release the anger. When you've finished writing, burn this

slip of paper or tear it into tiny pieces and flush it away. Tell yourself that it's over. Remember Paul saying in Philippians 3:13–14, "Forgetting the things which are behind, . . . I press on toward the goal unto the prize of the high calling of God." In other words, release it, and look to God in prayer.

2. Write in your journal. Ask yourself whether you have ever denied the seriousness of the offense or blamed yourself. If you have, use your soothing internal voice to comfort yourself.

3. Decide to forgive. This is a choice that you get to make.

4. Pray. Ask God for assistance in forgiving and allow the Holy Spirit to work through you. You'll know you're closing in on your goal when you can comfortably ask the Heavenly Father to lift this person in prayer.

5. Check in with yourself. If you are struggling with forgiving, continue to take time out for journal writing, exploring the ways your resentment has hurt you and others.

CHAPTER 12

Maximizing Your Creative Spirit

I'm going to start this chapter in an unusual way . . . by asking you to put this book down, for the moment at least. Before you do, however, let me explain. I'd like you to open your Bible to the beginning, to Genesis, and take your time reading aloud if possible the first and second accounts of creation, ending with 2:24. Please start now.

If you have just finished your reading of Genesis, perhaps those last words, "and they were not ashamed" linger in your memory. To me, those five words help me imagine Adam and Eve as trusting, childlike, and jubilant over the beauty of God's creation. Those words "and they were not ashamed" go directly to my inner core, to that place where I feel no need to be perfect, no need to strike a certain pose or speak in the right tones; a place where I feel no judgment from myself or others, an emotionally safe place. Some describe this kind of euphoria as "getting happy," and that's all right with me, because when I read the creation stories I *am* happy and childlike, and thrilled by the mighty power of the Lord, our God and Savior.

In fact, I hope you will allow yourself to step into this same space, right beside me, where someone might truthfully say of you, "and she was not ashamed." Go on, take God's hand and step down without fear of failing or falling. Shake off feelings of self-consciousness and allow the words "Thank you, Lord" to burst from your lips.

In this space, you can experience God's creative power by picturing the miracle of His creation. From a formless void He created the heavens and the earth, hallelujah. He separated the light from the darkness and the waters from dry land, hallelujah. He covered the earth with vegetation: "Herbs yielding seed after their kind, and trees bearing fruit" (Genesis 1:12). And He saw that it was good, but He didn't rest there. By the end of the fourth day He had created the great lights of the sun and the moon, and as the week continued, birds and fish and "everything that creeps upon the ground of every kind." Hallelujah! Isn't God good. I didn't forget the question mark on that sentence. I *know* He's good. And I know *you know* He's good.

He's so good that He could have stopped right then and there with the miracle of His creation. But He didn't. He created man and woman. He created humankind. He created us and connected our life to His with His breath. That's why I asked you to read both creation accounts, because the second story fills in the details about our uniqueness. "God formed man from the dust of the ground, and breathed into his nostrils the breath of life; and the man became a living being" (Genesis 2:7).

I want to pause momentarily to examine something of tremendous importance pertaining to the creativity theme of this chapter, as a continuation of the exploration of spirit, the first *S* in "blessed." Our bodies are, of course, the temples of God's spirit. After molding our forms, He blessed us with the "breath of life." But just what does that mean? We know that long ago, whether people were writing in Hebrew, Greek, or Latin, they used the same word for "breath," "wind," and "spirit." They knew that like the wind, God's spirit is an invisible, mighty force.

Picture God shaping Adam from the dust, and when you imagine Him breathing into that lifeless form, erase the image of one of those white-jacketed doctors administering oxygen from *ER*. Don't compare the scene to someone giving mouth-to-mouth resuscitation on one of those beach patrol shows. Those shows portray actors pretending to keep someone from dying. Genesis is about life, not death. It's the real deal here, and we're talking about the Almighty, the Everlasting, the Lord God, the Great Creator. He wasn't just keeping someone alive, he was *making* someone come alive, bringing someone to life. God was infusing Adam with His spirit, with His invisible, powerful creative force.

We aren't self-centered enough to forget that we weren't the only living, breathing beings that He created. We know from Genesis that God loves the animals he created. That's reason enough to cherish them and treat them with kindness and respect. As it says of the animals in Genesis 1:22, "God blessed them."

In that same book though, you'll also find another significant truth. God made humankind unique in all of nature. We know this not simply because he gave us dominion over the animals, and not even solely because he breathed his life force into us. We know of our creative uniqueness because among all living things, He gave us the power to name: "And whatever the man called every living creature, that was its name" (2:19).

The fact that a human being could name the other animals helps us understand that God intended for us to share elements of His creative spirit. Adam was able to name things because God gave us the gift of language, a way of communicating thoughts and ideas. Language is the basis for creation. Let me explain what I mean. Of course we aren't the only animals that communicate with one another. Take the groundhog for example. For the sake of survival, a groundhog may grunt and bend its head to indicate to a mate that it has found eatable buried roots in a particular spot. We humans, on the other hand, blessed with the capacity for language, might simply call to a mate, "Honey, I found roots here, and the soil is moist, so if we look around we might find a riverbed, and this might be a good spot to build a house." Through language, we expand the power of knowledge in a condensed form.

As a result, while other animals must adapt to their natural habitats to survive, we alone have the language skills to pass on information so we can make things from nature—create—in essence adjusting nature to ourselves. Thanks to our gift of language and because we house God's creative spirit, humans have invented wheels to traverse long distances. Because of the gift of language, humans have learned to pass on information about the usefulness of fire—which is from nature—and rather than having to wait for lightning to strike, we've created a technology that makes fire available when we need it.

We don't simply use our creative gifts to communicate the vast amounts of information required for our survival. We look around at the beauty and plentitude and notice that the river sparkles with the radiance of the sun. We dance in joy, mimicking the movement of the leafy boughs stirred by the invisible force of the wind. We create music and art and poetry as a reflection of the beauty of God's creation and to enhance our environment. And when we live blessed lives we use our creativity to enhance God's creation in the knowledge that using our creativity is a way of returning the favor to God. Our creative output may be seen in everything from the preparation of an appealing and delicious meal to the sewing of a quilt or needlepoint to the design and construction of a lovely home by the water's edge.

As you read about ways to utilize your creativity, I hope you are not thinking of reasons why you can't express your creativity. You wouldn't be the only one. Here's a list of responses from people who were asked whether they take the time to express their creativity.

I'm too busy.

I don't have the money.

I have to work.

I'm not talented at anything.

I'm not the creative type.

I don't want to look foolish.

I've got to be the grown-up in the family.

I used up all my ideas.

I will, when I get through this divorce (or other distraction or obligation such as weddings, moves, term papers, work deadlines, etc.).

I'm creatively blocked.

If you have devised a rationale about why you can't express your creativity, say it aloud. And then picture yourself back in the Garden of Eden. Remember to leave your defenses at the gate. As you stroll past meadows and flowering trees, listen to God's voice: " 'See, I have given you every plant yielding seed that is upon the face of all the earth, and every tree with seed in its fruit; you shall have them for food. And to every beast of the earth, and to every bird of the air, and to everything that creeps on the earth, everything that has the breath of life, I have given every green plant for food.' And it was so" (Genesis 1:29–30).

It's true that you may be in the middle of a busy city or squeezed into a subway car, or in any number of scenarios that seem far from the Garden of Eden, but none of that negates God's offer. Your imagination, your ability to read these words and picture that beautiful scene, means that your creativity, God's spirit, His breath of life, resides within you.

That variety of life in the garden, that creative force infusing every leaf and animal represents the multiplicity of creative possibilities in your life. There is endless abundance in that garden—not just one green, but hundreds of shades and hundreds of hues of green—all reminders that contained within you is God's creative spirit, more than enough to power hundreds and hundreds of projects.

Standing right there in the middle of the garden, what happens when you try to repeat your excuse out loud? Maybe you want to say, "I'm not talented," but the droning of the bees making honey seems to drown out your words. Perhaps you're saying that you don't have the time, but there's a big inviting rock by the water and you can't resist sitting down and relaxing your mind and body. Your excuse doesn't work in here, does it? Denying your creativity is like turning your back on God's generosity. Do you see now how infinite possibilities can be born of faith?

If you can't imagine something creative that you'd be good at, don't be hard on yourself. But do take out your journal and write about experiences that stifled your creativity. Mark, a pastor from Oregon, recalled just how much he loved drawing when he was a child, and how that was stifled when his third-grade art teacher gave him a D on one project and an F for a crayon drawing. For decades afterward, he refused to draw even a doodle, and as an adult he insisted that his duties as a minister kept him too busy for "such nonsense." His wife encouraged him to start drawing again when their children were very young by giving him and their toddler a set of crayons and a coloring book. It took a while before he stopped worrying about whether he was "coloring outside the lines," but Mark eventually began enjoying the art time he shared with his daughter. As a matter of fact, his daughter has grown up to be a wonderful artist and Mark hasn't given up on his artistic bent. Last year he crafted a beautiful table for his wife, and in the fall he plans to design and build a loft bed with his daughter.

Mark's reluctance to engage in any creative endeavors stemmed directly from his childhood shaming experience. There is no greater barrier to creative energy than shame, and, happily, the opposite is also true. If we can move past shaming experiences—identifying them and telling others about them—our creativity will flow. Following are some suggestions for maximizing your creative energy.

- Prayer. Thank God for the abundance of His creation and ask Him to allow you to give back by identifying a talent and using it to the greater good or to earn a living.
- Self-encouragement. Use your nurturing inner voice to try various creative endeavors until you find one that you

literally feel you can't live without. Speak sweetly to yourself and avoid negatives, such as, "You could have done better." Instead try something along the order of, "Good for you for trying. You are so courageous."

- Sign up for a class. I've recently registered for a drama course. Acting and producing were my loves and I'm determined to keep my life in balance by paying attention to that aspect of my personality. What did you used to enjoy doing? Go for it.

- Visit a museum off the beaten track. If you live near a large city or university town, read up on unusual exhibits and museums until you find something that strikes your fancy. That doll museum in the next town or rose garden might be just what your soul is craving.

- Jot down these words from Genesis. Write the words, "And they were not ashamed" on a slip of paper and repeat them to yourself when you take a creative plunge. These words will help you remember the importance of nurturing that innocent, trusting child within you—that's where your creativity lies.

- Read *The Artist's Way: A Spiritual Path to Higher Creativity.* This workbook by Julia Cameron sets the gold standard for books that help you become more creative in any enterprise. After working through the book, you may want to start an Artist's Way group, with members supporting one another in various endeavors.

B
L
E
S

SUCCESS

E
D

CHAPTER 13

Discerning the Path to Success

Something tells me that a number of readers who've worked their way through to this second *S* for success, in "blessed," will be disappointed by this chapter. But I pray that you'll keep reading as you learn an essential truth about my spiritual leadership: Unlike many in my profession, I don't equate faith with financial success.

I feel the need to state this since there are ministers seen on national television each week who point to their mansions, fashionable clothing, and even their jets and yachts as if suggesting that their flamboyant lifestyles were provided by God because of their devotion to Him.

I often find myself mentally wrestling with their messages, wondering, if what they claim is true, how these ministers explain poor people. Are they actually suggesting that some folks aren't rich because they don't know how to relate to God? That, of course, would be impossible to swallow, since our faith is based on Jesus Christ our Lord and Savior, who as the King of Kings might have worn silk

165

robes and jeweled crowns, but who instead lived the modest and simple life of the son of a carpenter and as a Palestinian, a people oppressed under the Roman system.

I'm not condemning financial wealth. An ample supply of money can assist us in living blessed lives. My complaints are with those who extol unlimited earnings. Keep in mind that the B in "blessed" is for balance. You've heard the expression "Too much of a good thing." Well, an unlimited quest for money can throw life out of balance. God wants us to love Him and one another, and we're counseled to keep our "lives free from the love of money" (Hebrews 13:5). The fate of those who fall in love with money is exemplified by people who dominate the headlines with scandals, because they are willing to do whatever it takes to grow rich beyond measure. They're proof that life on a material plane is uneven.

To me, success means living in alignment with my deepest convictions and values. No bank can take away those assets, because my head cashier is the Holy Ghost and my deposits are acts of obedience to His will. It's the least I can do, and it's what He expects of me. Paul wrote in Philippians 2:13, "For it is God who is at work in you, enabling you, both to will and to work for His good pleasure." That message suggests that if we cooperate with divine purposes, God will work through us to accomplish His will.

The retired New Testament professor William J. Richardson, Ph.D., illustrates the working relationship that God offers by describing three fathers who are teaching their sons how to ride a two-wheeler across a street to reach home: "The first father, doubting his son's ability, keeps a steady grip on the bike as the boy pedals across," Dr. Richardson says. "The second dad is lackadaisical, leaning against a fence and watching as the boy pedals unsteadily across the street. The third father is God. As the boy takes off, He runs beside him saying, 'I won't hold on, but I'll be right beside you to offer assistance when you need me.' "

If that was one of my sons, I'd certainly want him to travel with the Lord's guidance. I'd tell my sons that if they're aiming for success, they can tap into God's wisdom by learning spiritual discernment, the spiritual way to make decisions. Spiritual discernment is a process in which we ask the Holy Spirit to lead or give direction in our lives, as we practice hearing, seeing, or feeling God's answer.

Since the onus is on us to receive the information, some people might view discernment as a test. According to this misplaced logic, if we experience failure then that means we didn't work hard enough to understand God's message, or we must be bad Christians for not following His advice. Let me assure you that God would never set us up like that. There are no hard and fast rights and wrongs in the discernment process. Sometimes the decisions we make after a long and prayerful period lead us to hard times. The way I see it, that means we're in the middle of a situation that offers an opportunity to acquire wisdom.

You know what wisdom is, don't you? Some people are confused by the word. We live at a time when many folks understandably feel compelled to get as much education as possible, perhaps earning several degrees or enrolling in one training program after another. If they work hard they might graduate with a great deal of knowledge, and I salute their efforts. Knowledge is the kind of power that can help us advance at a swifter rate on the road to success. As helpful as knowledge may be, though, it would be a mistake to confuse it with wisdom. I agree wholeheartedly with the pundit who said, "Knowledge can help you make a living; wisdom can help you make a life."

While knowledge can be gained from attending schools and reading books, wisdom comes from God. James wrote, "But if any of you lacks wisdom, let him ask of God, who gives to all generously and without reproach, and it will be given to him" (James 1:5). Did you hear that one? It's the deal of a lifetime, and let me explain why. Day after day you can turn on the television and hear cell phone companies offer free long distance service. Many of us are hesitant to sign up because we know there are hidden charges and that by the end of the month we'll end up owing more than we can afford. But think of our loving Father in Heaven, who is always willing to offer guidance. I call that long distance without hidden charges. His service is not only free but highly reliable. With God, we don't have to ask, "Can you hear me?" We know He can. Can I get a witness!

I don't want to make the process of discernment sound easy. Since we're only human, it's easy to misunderstand God's will. I'm thinking here of people like the young woman who assured me that God had sent her a sign she was marrying the right man, because after weeks of rain, the sun shone on her wedding day. A lot of people mistake acts of providence for God's answers. They might get a raise, win the lottery, marry the right guy, and think, "God's telling me I'm on the right track." Unfortunately, discerning God's will isn't like following the easy-to-read signs posted along a highway.

One helpful way to understand what God wants is to read the Bible and attend a church where you can be enlightened about scripture. Knowledge of scripture is certainly helpful when it comes to making a choice. You might be lonely, for instance, when a handsome and charming man enters your life and courts you until you fall in love with him. But later, when you discover he's married, your choice might seem pretty clear. Although he may beg you to remain with him in an adulterous relationship, you recall that adultery is the subject of the Seventh Commandment (Exodus 20:14) and you remember another passage that instructs that "marriage is honorable in all, and the bed undefiled; but fornicators and adulterers God will judge" (Hebrews 13:4). Because God gave us the gift of free will, we're sometimes caught in the struggle between right and wrong. Thanks to scripture, I've never been wishy-washy about what kind of behavior I'd expect from myself. By my standard of success—to live in alignment with my deepest convictions and values—adultery would make me feel like a failure.

As I have said, however, God's will is not always clearly discernible, but there are others who seem to keep up a running conversation with God. I'm thinking now about Bonnie Guiton Hill, Ed.D., who, at sixty-three, is one of the most notable women in America. She is a former assistant education secretary under President Ronald Reagan, served as consumer advisor to the first President Bush, was dean at the University of Virginia's McIntire School of Commerce, was president and chief executive officer of the Times Mirror Foundation, and was senior vice president of communications and public affairs for the *Los Angeles Times*. Dr. Hill is currently president of B. Hill Enterprises LLC, a consulting firm, sits on several prominent corporate boards, and is cofounder, with her husband, Walter Hill, of Icon Blue, a brand marketing firm that serves major corporations such as Honda, Toyota, and the Hilton Hotels.

This highly accomplished woman doesn't define her success by her career highlights. She is proud to say that she has a strong relationship with the Almighty and that she regularly turns to Him for guidance. She's also happily married to a man of faith, serves those who are less fortunate, enjoys loving relationships with her daughter, stepdaughters, and grandchildren, and could fill a room with people who count her as a trusted and loyal friend.

Dr. Hill's road to success wasn't paved with smooth stones, but thanks to the influence of her maternal grandmother, who was with her during much of her early childhood in Springfield, Illinois, Dr. Hill learned early on to trust God. "My grandmother gave me my spiritual foundation. She took me to church, and I can remember that when I had the chicken pox, she read the Bible aloud and talked to me about God."

Sometimes her faith seemed to compound the difficulties of her life. She didn't grow up with her biological father in the house, and she was raised hearing the details of his one and only visit to see her. Although she doesn't remember all the details of this particular event, she says, "I was about two or three and since I was preparing to eat, I began saying my blessings. My father apparently grabbed a butcher knife, stuck it in the table and told me not to say prayers with my mother." Dr. Hill would never get a chance to ask him about his actions. "When I was seven, he was stabbed and killed by one of his girlfriends."

Despite difficult circumstances, little Bonnie—the future Dr. Hill—learned to present a positive face to the world. Her mother was an alcoholic, and Bonnie learned early on to think of her as two women. "When Mom was inebriated, she was not herself. She could curse like a sailor, but somehow she always made it home. Then there was the other mom, who was sober and worked as a domestic."

Her mother's rich, white employers marveled at little Bonnie's manners, and often gave her hand-me-down clothes and shoes. To this day, Dr. Hill has trouble with her feet from those days of walking in ill-fitting shoes. Despite this and other difficulties, she has warm memories of growing up with the sober side of her mother. "She taught me to take pride in myself. And she was so proper that she wouldn't take the garbage out without taking the rollers out of her hair. Her motto was that even if you're dressed in rags, they should be clean and your hair should be neat and your shoes shined."

People familiar with Dr. Hill know that this maternal message stuck with her. She is known for her elegant appearance. One of her longtime friends swears that she saw her at an indoor parking lot, and that although the wind outside was whipping umbrellas from pedestrians' hands, Dr. Hill glided inside on designer heels, carrying a beautiful umbrella matching a raincoat that fit her slender frame like the proverbial glove. "And not a hair on her well-groomed head was out of place," the friend adds.

Long before she grew into that perfectly coiffed businesswoman, she was little Bonnie with hell to pay. Her mother continued to attract violent men, and as a result, "She was a battered woman," Dr. Hill recalls. "One night when I was ten, I was sitting on the stairs of our house. Mom wasn't home, but somehow I knew that wherever she was she was being beaten. I started praying to God, asking for His protection and asking what I could do to protect her. As I watched the moon, a dove flew out of the clouds and landed on my shoulder." Dr. Hill says the bird felt real to her.

A dove is generally a sign of peace, but the evening did not prove to be tranquil. Shortly afterward, Bonnie's mother and stepfather returned from their evening out. "Mom was black and blue from another beating." Little Bonnie decided to take matters into her own hands. "After they fell asleep, I got a butcher knife from the kitchen and stood over my mother's husband." The intoxicated adults were sleeping deeply, but, as if sensing that his life was in peril, the man's eyes flew open. "He saw me, and he started screaming and woke my mother."

That next morning, when her stepfather left for work, little Bonnie, as if interpreting the dove as a message to "fly away," packed her clothes and her mother's and, grasping the money she'd saved from a small allowance, convinced her mother to flee with her. They took a train to a nearby town and lived for a short while with her father's mother, before eventually moving to Milwaukee, then to Oakland, California.

Without family to lend emotional support, Dr. Hill's mother increasingly depended on alcohol. "She stopped working and went on welfare. It was humiliating. Social workers would go through my closets, checking to see whether my mother had any men hiding in there." Dr. Hill had arrived in Oakland in time to start the seventh grade. "It seemed a lot of the kids knew who was on welfare and they teased me about it." Her clothes may have helped give away her situation. A preteen by then, Dr. Hill dressed in borrowed clothes, and the outfits were often too large for her slender frame.

With all these difficulties, she didn't excel in school, although some teachers thought she could. "One of the teachers saw I was academically advanced and offered to promote me, but Mom wanted me to stay with my age group. I was so bored in class that I started sleeping." By her junior year of high school she'd fallen behind her classmates. "Two teachers pulled me aside and said, 'We know you're better than Ds and Fs.' I told them that I didn't have an appreciation for Socrates and Plato, because I wanted to develop a skill that would help me land a job, so Mom and I could get off welfare. They enrolled me in a vocational course." She proceeded to learn secretarial skills, and after graduation passed a civil service exam. With her first paycheck from her clerk's job, Dr. Hill moved herself and her mother off welfare.

Dr. Hill's life only looked easy from the outside. She'd been attending a local church for several years, and from the time she was fifteen, the pastor had been sexually abusing her. "I was a very young teenager, not worldly at all. And he said that if I told anyone, he could make my mother die. I believed him because I'd seen him heal people, and he had a way of pointing out his enemies to me. When any of those people happened to get sick or die or some tragedy befell them, this reverend claimed it happened because of his power. I was terrified of him. I never told anyone what he was doing to me, and I kept it a secret. It lasted for four years." Money from her new job gave her a little leverage. When Dr. Hill was nineteen, she moved away in the middle of the night, insisting that her mother not pass on her new address if the minister sought her out.

Her relationship with this minister didn't destroy her faith. "Thank God, I could see that there were other good people in the church. But I did learn a year later that he'd also been abusing another girl." The full impact of this minister's harm didn't quite register, until after Dr. Hill's first marriage, at twenty-four.

She and her husband, Harvey Guiton, an Oakland businessman, tried to conceive a child, but a doctor explained that this would be impossible. "He told me that I had a displaced uterus. I knew how that had happened. When I was still very young and this minister was abusing me, I missed my period and he was so terrified that I was pregnant and people would discover what he was doing that he paid a dentist to perform a C-section on me. The procedure was brutal, and it turned out that I wasn't even pregnant."

Years later, the doctor's advice to the contrary, Dr. Hill and her husband did conceive, and she gave birth to a beautiful baby son. Unfortunately, the infant lived only four days, due to birth complications connected to her uterine difficulties. This time the doctor was certain that Dr. Hill would never conceive again.

Through prayer and meditation, she emerged from the situation knowing just what she should do. "I went back to my old pastor and told him I'd lost my son, due to complications he'd caused. I said that I'd never forget what he'd done, but that I forgave him. With God's help, I knew that I would never be all right if I didn't let my anger go. When I forgave that man, the weight of the world seemed to drop off of me." Two weeks later, she and her husband had conceived again, and this child lived. Nichele, now a college graduate, a business executive, and a wife and mother of two, lives within driving distance of Dr. Hill's home in southern California.

Over the years, Dr. Hill has continued to face her challenges by asking the Lord for guidance. Her husband, Harvey, succumbed to heart disease, but not before he saw his young wife develop into a force to be reckoned with. She eventually took classes at Mills College, where she was employed as a secretary, and in the evenings attended two different community colleges. In two and a half years, she earned a bachelor of science degree, majoring in psychology, and followed that up with a master's degree in educational psychology from California State University, Hayward. Years later, she earned a doctorate in education from the University of California, Berkeley.

When questioned about how she was able to accomplish so much, Dr. Hill insists that she still prays over decisions and then listens for a still small voice. "I tell my daughter and my stepdaughters not to be afraid to ask God for a sign. When I've had job offers, I've visualized myself in the job and then prayed over it. There are quite a few things I've turned down on the basis of these responses."

One need only meet Dr. Hill to understand that one of her most persistent prayers has been answered. "I wanted God to help me move on from the old. I've prayed that I'd learn from each harsh experience but not make those experiences part of my present. You can't hold on to hostility and at the same time move on."

Her story provides answers about how the process of discernment works. Consider the quote that I mentioned earlier in this chapter: "If any of you lack wisdom, ask of God, who gives to all generously and ungrudgingly, and it will be given you" (James 1:5). Now that you're familiar with Dr. Hill's story, you may better appreciate the words that follow in the next verse. "But ask in faith, never doubting, for the one who doubts is like a wave of the sea, driven and tossed by the winds; for the doubter, being double-minded and unstable in every way, must not expect to receive anything from the Lord" (James 1:6–8).

As you digest those words, please remember that this is not the time to blame yourself for wrong turns on your path or for moments of doubt. James 1:6–8 offers a loving promise. If you have a strong, unwavering faith in the Lord, He will guide you. Don't forget to continue thanking God for all that He has given you and for working through you in the most difficult situations. True faith requires the understanding that He loves you just as much when you're in doubt or when you're suffering so greatly that even His voice seems to be drowned out. After World War II, as more Nazi atrocities came to light, a message was found on the wall of a concentration camp: "I believe, even when He is silent." Yes, even when God seems silent, He is with you.

And be assured that as you continue to work through this book, you are demonstrating your faith in Him, not in me or my words. I believe in my deepest heart of hearts that He is blessing me by allowing me to offer you words to live by. God, I thank you God, for this opportunity, and in all ways and all things, I will remain your humble, grateful, and loyal servant.

CHAPTER 14

Finding Your Holy Mission

A s we continue forging new definitions of success, while exploring the second S in "blessed," you may want to set aside time to compose a mission statement. Just in case you're wondering what a mission statement might be, let's look closer at that term. *Webster's Dictionary* defines "mission" as "the special duty or errand that a person or group is sent out to do." Most of us have heard of Christian missionaries who devote their lives to the mission of converting souls to Christ. And as you probably know, a statement is something that you tell or declare in a formal or definite way that serves as a record or report.

When it comes to composing your mission statement, just forget the word "formal," or even "report" for that matter, both of which make the process sound intimidating; something akin to an assignment that might be marked, corrected, and graded by a teacher. Composing your mission statement can actually turn out to be fun, and may well prove to be one of the best things you've ever done for yourself.

You probably have a hard time believing that claim if you've ever worked for a corporation or nonprofit center where there were long and exhaustive meetings, with folks debating lofty goals and insisting on including phrases that reflect their areas of expertise. Writing your personal mission statement will be more like soul work, as enjoyable as sitting around with a group of favorite friends to discuss *your* dreams and hopes and aspirations.

Simply put, a mission statement is a clearly written note—you can write it in your journal or on a separate sheet of paper—that might run anywhere from five sentences to a couple of pages, declaring your goals and objectives in life. It can begin with a vision of your future and continue by stating who you want to be. Despite its simplicity, it's absolutely necessary for those of us who hope to experience success. Because if we don't know where we're going, we might wind up taking so many detours that we never reach a meaningful destination.

Hopefully your soothing internal voice has kicked in, and if not, you may be using this as another opportunity to put yourself down. Maybe you're thinking that you've probably wasted time because you should have written a personal mission statement long ago. Let me assure you that your past experiences do count, no matter how unfocused they may seem. Your mission statement, just like this book, is all about faith, faith that God loves you and created you with a purpose. And because He brings all things to completion, you can trust that no matter what your past may include or what is occurring now, all will be well and will work for the good.

I certainly traveled alternate routes in my lifetime. After my postgraduation experience in Ghana, I returned to Africa a few years later, backpacking through the continent with Yolanda King, the daughter of Dr. Martin Luther King, Jr. She and I had not known one another until we embarked on our journey. Mutual friends had set up the introduction for the purpose of the trip. Yolanda and I only had a few hours together before our departure from New York's Kennedy Airport, but we bonded during our trip.

As for my career, I wasn't quite sure which direction to take. At nineteen, after earning a bachelor's degree at Emerson College, majoring in mass communications and speech with a minor in theater, I applied at my home church for a license to preach. While waiting for a date for my first sermon, with my mother's urging, I applied and was accepted at the Teachers College of Columbia University to study education technology. Between classes, I traveled to various states and performed with *Voices Incorporated: Journey to Blackness*, taking theater into classrooms and teaching through drama. Two years later, armed with a master of arts and teaching experience, I was prepared for a career in the educational field, but I moved in a different direction.

Relocating to the nation's capital, I lived with my Aunt Katherine—one of the nieces my dad had helped raise—while I trained to be a producer at WJLA-TV. At the end of the training program, I accepted a job with the station as a floor manager and was quickly promoted up the ladder to assistant producer. But something was interfering with my peace of mind, and I believe it was God's call. Despite opportunities for advancement in the broadcasting field, I was growing convinced that God wanted me to step from behind the scene into the somewhat uncomfortable preaching limelight. Keep in mind that in the late seventies, women preachers were an even rarer breed than they are today.

Testing the waters, I enrolled in night classes at Howard University's seminary, but my television career was taking off, and I joined the staffs at WBZ-TV in Boston, and then WPLG in Miami. My salary more than doubled during those five years, but the Lord seemed to be guiding me back home to New York.

I sent out a few feelers, and job opportunities in the Big Apple began to present themselves, including one possibility with the CBS news program *Sixty Minutes* and another with ABC's *Good Morning America*. Strangely enough, I grew interested in a public relations position at Bronx Lebanon Hospital.

When people asked me why I left the lucrative and exciting broadcast industry, I could only explain that I was following a call. I'm also a strong believer in the notion that to everything there is a season. With God's guidance we know when a season is over. That doesn't necessarily mean, though, that we always take His blessed advice. God may be saying one thing, while your mind suggests another course of action and your heart says something completely different. In my case, my best friends in the world live in Washington, D.C. To this day, I still take the train to Union Station so we can meet for laugh-filled, intimate lunches. Although my heart was telling me to move to D.C., no job presented itself in that area during this time in my life.

The hospital job in New York was still available, and I accepted. The salary and benefits were good, but more importantly, I wouldn't be required to work the crazy schedule often expected of a television producer. I believe God was getting me positioned in just the right place, at the right time. Not long after returning to New York, I applied for and was accepted at Union Theological Seminary and attended classes during my lunch hours and after work. Even with a more moderate work schedule, though, I often found myself torn between my duties to work and school.

The turning point in my career occurred on one particularly high-stress day, when I'd rushed from an exam given by the Reverend Doctor James Forbes. Union Seminary has a plethora of gifted teachers, but even among these illustrious scholars, Dr. Forbes is a standout. In 1989, he was installed as the senior pastor of Manhattan's Riverside Church, with its international, interracial, interdenominational congregation of 2,400. Often called the "preacher of preachers," Reverend Forbes was named by *Ebony* magazine as one of America's greatest black preachers and recognized by *Newsweek* as one of the most effective preachers in the English language. This gifted man was my preaching teacher. I'd rushed from his final exam, trying to get to Bronx Lebanon Hospital, where a major news event was unfolding. As the head of publicity, I was expected to address journalists.

Wouldn't you know then that I'd get caught in a major traffic jam just as I was driving across the 155th Street Bridge? Sitting there with my stomach in knots, I felt I was letting everyone down, including myself. I finally looked skyward and said, "God, I can't do this anymore. I'm going to devote my life to preaching your word." No sooner had the words departed from my lips than the traffic opened up, like the Red Sea. As soon as possible, I phoned the hospital and explained that they wouldn't see me that afternoon, and then I went back to my exam. That evening, I turned in my resignation at the hospital. I've never looked back. A month from the day I made the decision, Pastor Wells phoned and told me it was time to be ordained.

My first opportunity to serve as a pastor was a tough inner-city assignment, Mariners' Temple, a predominantly black parish on

Manhattan's Lower East Side, in the heart of Chinatown. I made it a point to keep the conversation going with God as I introduced myself to the fifteen senior citizens who made up the congregation. Over the course of several months, with God's guidance, membership at Mariners' grew to 150 souls. Most were struggling members of the working poor or people barely getting by on welfare, and they had numerous problems that required a pastor's support. I was twenty-three and single, and I gave them everything I had, putting in long days—an effort of 200 percent.

But there's a cost for moving at a frantic pace without direction. After seven years I was totally burned out. A year earlier, I'd met the dean of Harvard's Divinity School, so when he called in August 1990, to offer me a Presidential Administration Fellowship, I wanted to accept, but I worried that my parishioners might not agree to me taking a year's leave from work. Calling a congregational meeting, I addressed a hushed room and was soon surprised by the response of my parishioners. People stood up and applauded. They'd assumed I'd called them together to quit and seemed genuinely happy to learn that I only wanted to be away a year.

The only difficulty I encountered from that point was from other pastors, warning that if I left the church under interim leadership, I wouldn't have a congregation to return to. Black churches didn't have a tradition of their pastors taking time off. As it turned out, my leave set up a paradigm for black churches allowing their pastors to take sabbaticals.

My time at Harvard was undoubtedly a gift from God. The college is like a little city, with every resource imaginable. Thanks to the fellowship, I was given money, enjoyed the benefits of an officer of Harvard, and was housed in a charming apartment on the Charles

River. Mom was with me when I first entered the campus. We were mindful that our ancestors had picked cotton, and it was like an out-of-body experience for both of us.

The Harvard program allowed me to set my schedule, and many times I sat by the Charles River, feeling gratitude at the deepest and most immediate level. The experience was beautiful and spiritual, but religious reflection without a connection to real life is like a carefully preserved house of cards: If the two are disconnected, sooner or later, a difficult moment or question will expose its fragile or tentative state. Not all of us can stop and sit by a river to ponder the direction that we dream of taking, but I urge you to take a weekend, day, or an afternoon to engage in the discernment process and, with God's guidance, write about your future.

You might begin by writing a letter to God. I did, expressing my hopes and dreams for the next decade, intentionally omitting goals that weren't in keeping with His plans for me. At first it was difficult to think purely of my dreams, because I'd spent the last several years focused on the needs of my parishioners. After awhile though, the ideas began to flow. I wanted to find a venue for spreading the good news of the gospel to a larger audience. And because I had spent time in schools, working with the poor and disenfranchised, I added that I wanted to use my convictions to shape national policy decisions. On a more personal level, I hoped to fall and love and be loved, and to start a family, instilling in my children the values that had been passed on to me. I described a home filled with love and laughter, and above all, obedience to God. There was one specific feature I wanted concerning our home: that it be located near a body of water, where I could feel my soul restored.

I'd written down my objectives, and now another and important aspect of this work was figuring out how I could achieve the desired results. I realized then that I needed to return to school and begin working on a doctoral degree. As the first female American Baptist pastor, I had to be as prepared as possible. As for the marriage prospects, I promised myself that I'd give it awhile and then begin a conversation with God on that very subject.

After describing my personal vision and making some practical decisions, I continued through prayer and through discernment to seek God's advice about my mission in life. I heard the Lord through the voice of Isaiah: "Learn to do good, seek justice, rescue the oppressed, defend the orphans; plead for the windows." For someone weary at the soul, the idea of finding relief for the oppressed seemed monumental. The more I thought about it, though, the clearer the vision grew of me speaking out on behalf of those who could not speak for themselves. The widows and orphans of biblical days could easily be viewed as my congregants at Missionary Baptist, as well as people of every race and socio-economic background who desired fuller lives in Christ. This renewed my determination to return to my parish and inspire my congregants to improve their lives.

I also began writing my third book, *Too Blessed to Be Stressed: Words of Wisdom for Women on the Move*, offering advice on recovering from burnout. The book was widely received and helped me find that larger audience I'd written about in my vision. My first two books, *Wise Women Bearing Gifts: Joys and Struggles of Their Faith* and *Sister to Sister: Devotions for and from African American Women*, had been published by a small press.

Once the sabbatical ended, I joyfully returned to Mariners' Temple, where I stayed for five more years. In that time I commuted to Dayton, Ohio, where I earned my doctorate of ministry at the

United Theological Seminary. A few years later, I met and married my wonderful husband.

Although there were pitstops and detours along the way, my vision for my life continued to unfold much in the way that I had hoped. But let's face it; life often occurs in overdrive. In 1991, I resigned from my job with the full intention of devoting time to starting and raising the family I'd described in my mission vision. The year before, I'd applied for a White House fellowship—remember that dream that called for influencing public policy on a national level—and as life would have it, both the fellowship and the baby arrived at virtually the same time. I'd applied with slim hopes. After all, two thousand people applied for this yearlong paid fellowship, which allowed winners to work in the offices of the president, vice president, or a cabinet member. I was accepted in July of 1993, and was expected to report at the White House by September.

Ron encouraged me to accept the fellowship, even though he thought it best to remain at his Manhattan job. I took off for the capital with our infant Samuel, and initially felt discouraged when I couldn't locate a suitable nursery for him. But persistence paid off. I called the White House program for kids a second time and learned that a slot had miraculously opened up.

Securing a position at the White House didn't go as smoothly. No one seemed to have an idea about how they could use my skills, and I was required to interview at different offices, hoping someone would offer me a job. In the last few months, I'd immersed myself in policy issues, preparing myself for the tough issues I thought might be pertinent to President Clinton's welfare reform. To my surprise, none of the people interviewing me asked me about policy; they wanted to know about my ministry. At that point, the only real hitch as I saw it was that my potential employers would expect me to work long days, without regard to my baby's needs.

I should have relaxed and reminded myself that God always prepares a way. In one interview, one of my sweet little baby's photos caught the eye of Carol H. Rasco, White House Advisor for Domestic Policy. Rasco, a mother of two, is a former middle school counselor, volunteer, disability advocate, and policy counselor at the state and national level. To say we have many interests in common is an understatement.

Carol Rasco looked at Samuel's photo and said, "You're going to have offers to work in various departments, but keep in mind that the most important thing for you to do is pick up your baby every day at five." Before the day ended, I had seven job offers, including the Domestic Policy Council, headed by Carol Rasco. I accepted her offer and became her domestic policy analyst. Her office oversaw all of the issues related to children and family. The knowledge I'd accumulated in teachers' college and as a classroom drama teacher added to my value as an analyst—so that "detour" in my life had not been a wasted effort.

During the year I worked at the White House, President Clinton spoke at many churches. It wasn't long before his speechwriter was sending the president's speeches over to me, asking for feedback. After a while, the president began to see me and began referring to me as "the Baptist preacher from the Bronx." At times the two of us would walk down the hall together discussing various issues. On a few occasions he stopped at my office, stuck his head through the doorway, and asked, "May I come in for a minute?" I could see Secret Service agents gathering outside as he entered.

Looking back, I realize that this was the point at which I became convinced that God not only opens doors for us, He also helps us step through the doorway. That means that no matter how detailed our mission statement might be, He's likely to give us far more than we asked for. I was blessed by the unfolding opportunities around me. Sometimes during that year at the White House it was difficult to imagine that what I was experiencing was real. And there was Ron, offering encouraging words over the phone most weeknights and in person on Friday nights and Saturdays, when he joined me and our first son in D.C.

There's another lesson here: When you visualize your future, don't be ashamed to tell God what you truly want. It's not as if you want Him to wave a magic wand and deliver the goods. You'll recall that I asked for a home by the water. My family and I have one, but that doesn't mean we don't have to work hard to pay the mortgage.

I hope you've learned from my story that no matter where you might be at this time in your life—a young student, middle-aged career person, parent with young children, minister leading a large urban parish, just getting off of welfare—it doesn't matter. From the vantage point of writing your mission, it's as if your life will start from this day forward. If that sounds like a line from a marriage ceremony, that's not surprising: A personal mission statement merges the person you are today with the person you want to become. Here are some pointers on shaping your mission statement. As you read through them, you might want to jot down ideas in your journal.

- Make it holy. Use the letters BLESSED to remind yourself
  of what you want your life to be like. Remember that *B* is
  for balance. Ask yourself how you might achieve a balance

among your work, spiritual, and personal needs. The *L* for love is also important to factor into your dream. God, who is love, wants us to have love in our lives. And you'll also need the energy in *E* for a healthy emotional state; the *S*, which is, of course, the Lord's Holy Spirit, and another *S* for success at realizing your dreams. In upcoming chapters, we'll explore the second *E* for encouragement and *D*, offering suggestions on becoming even more devoted to the Lord. Visualize it all, asking God to guide your way.

- Stress the positive. You certainly know who you don't want to be. When Lee was asked about how she saw herself in the future, she said she didn't want to become someone who stopped growing. When asked to turn that around into a positive statement, she realized that she wanted to spend a lot of time traveling after her retirement, learning about new cultures. She also realized that she wants to learn how to swim. Ask yourself what you want to be like.

- Recognize your gifts. You've worked through "blessed" sufficiently to no longer feel the need to "hide your light under a bushel." By now you may have recognized and thanked God for your special gifts. These may range from being welcoming to strangers or being good with kids to being a good public speaker or artist or singer. Ask yourself which of these gifts you'd like to continue developing and consider how you might use them to accomplish your mission, and perhaps, to earn additional income, if necessary.

- Picture someone you love and/or admire. Some people mention celebrities with admirable traits, such as Maya

Angelou, who always seems to speak with authority and wisdom, because they want to emulate these individuals. Others mention a favorite aunt or recall a parent who was especially generous. Ask yourself what characteristics you'd like to be remembered for by loved ones.

- Give it a timeline. When you write your mission and visualize your future, give yourself from two to five years for events to unfold. Check with your vision every six months to ensure that you don't stray too far from your chosen path.

- Don't get too serious. Remember that this is not a contract that someone will sue you over if you don't live up to your end of the agreement. These statements are more like welcoming signs posted on the boundaries of your new neighborhood. That's the tone you'd like to establish: "Hi. We're so glad you're here. You're just the sort of person we've been waiting for, someone who is _____." Fill in the characteristics you hope to develop.

- Use quotes. I remind myself of who I want to become by carrying around a small notebook filled with quotations from people I admire. During difficult moments, these quotations help me remain focused on my dreams.

CHAPTER 15

Creating Financial Health and Wealth

The young parishioners were working hard to hold it together. After ten years of marriage, Sean and Louisa were going through a crisis. Sean, a forty-one-year-old shipping clerk, had applied for a credit card and was shocked when the company denied his application, citing a poor credit record. "I thought we had a great credit rating," he told me. Since Louisa hadn't been home to offer an explanation, Sean searched through their monthly statements and discovered a secret that seemed powerful enough to tear them apart: "We're $37,000 in debt," Sean said angrily, and he slipped a stack of frayed envelopes onto my desk. "Louisa has been lying to me all this time."

Louisa, thirty-six, who manages a law office, balled up a tissue and swiped at her tears. "I haven't been lying, Reverend Cook." She gave her husband a sorrowful look. "Baby, me not telling you about those debts was my way of protecting you. It's not like I went out and bought clothes or new shoes with that money. The two of us don't earn enough to pay our bills. When I started getting those blank checks in the mail they seemed like money from heaven. I used it for the kids' school fees . . . that time my mother got sick, car repairs, and that time when we needed the work on the roof . . . those kind of things." When her husband refused to make eye contact with her, she shrugged and turned back toward me. "I got behind in the payments, and I didn't want Sean staying awake nights, like me, worrying every time the phone rang, thinking it's gonna be a collection agency. I've been through hell worrying."

It would be difficult to find a pastor that hasn't encountered a similar scene with parishioners stressed out over bills and desperate to find a way out of their financial entanglements. Like Sean and Louisa, many are hardworking people who have had to put their dreams of success on hold simply to pay attention to the details of surviving. It's no secret that it's harder to get ahead than ever before, what with high prices on basics such as medicine and housing and the soaring gasoline prices, and companies cutting back on employee health care and retirement benefits. As a result, increasing numbers of people are caught in financial binds. Throughout the years, I have talked with a number of people struggling with financial issues, and they often fall into one of several categories.

- Recent college graduates. Although saddled with
  educational loans, many are so relieved to have finished
  college that they want to start their adult lives off with a
  bang, and that often means a new car. But then they're
  faced with the heavy toll of supporting themselves, making
  payments on their school debts and their car, and meeting
  other expenses, such as the cost of building a professional
  wardrobe.

- Single mother. Those who can't count on generous child-support payments from former spouses are burdened by the need to pay for child care and a host of other expenses that two people should be sharing. As the sole breadwinners, they feel their finances derailed by unanticipated expenses.

- Divorced fathers. They're trying to do the right thing and support those they've left behind, plus they're trying to keep roofs over their own heads, and they too are caught in a bind.

- The working elderly. Many have retired from long-held jobs and now work one or two part-time jobs. Sometimes they're forced to choose between medicine and food, both of which they need for life.

- Couples. Sean and Louisa are typical of many families trying to live the American Dream. For too many people, the dream has become a nightmare.

- Shopaholics. They seem to get more of a thrill out of buying new clothes, shoes, or things than they do in actually wearing or using them. Many shopaholics have closets filled with clothes with tags attached to them. What's generally most surprising about people with this problem is that even when their income increases, they find a way to keep spending more than they make.

- Addicted to debt. These individuals get in the habit of handling crises by running up charges on their credit cards or cashing those blank checks that banks mail out. Like Louisa, people addicted to debt can often justify why they need the money, but the more of that seemingly "free" money that they spend, the deeper a hole they dig for themselves. After a while they may feel like modern-day sharecroppers, working solely to keep up the payments on their debts, so they just can't seem to get ahead.

The kind of money pressures these people are struggling with would appear to be beyond the realm of my spiritual guidance. And while it's true that I do often recommend seeking expert advice, I couldn't possibly turn away folks like Sean and Louisa who are in desperate need of shoring up their spiritual resources. Yes, money problems absolutely impinge upon spiritual issues.

After all, money represents a portion of our time, talent, and energy in a form that can be negotiated. The Divine doesn't expect us to simply be good stewards over our tithed portion of income. He wants us to honor the other 90 percent of what we earn. Since our time, talent, and energy come from God, we honor Him by demonstrating good stewardship over all our gifts. Underscoring that point, Obie McKenzie, a managing director for Merrill Lynch, who also leads a Bible study group at Manhattan's Canaan Baptist Church of Christ, refers to I Corinthians 10:26: "For the earth is the Lord's, and the fullness thereof." McKenzie says, "The earth and everything on it belongs to the Lord. We come into the world naked and we will leave naked. We're just here on a lease plan. God gives us the authority to utilize his resources and expects us to use them to help others. If we don't obey, we'll derive no satisfaction from our money."

That being the case, why should we use our God-given talents to fill the coffers of a credit card company? Wouldn't we be far better off if we followed God's word and used our money to help those individuals who could really use our help? And that brings me to another point about the nexus of money and the spirit. Financial troubles can keep us from fulfilling our holy mission in life. Louisa, for example, who believes her life's mission is to help educate young people, was studying to become an elementary school teacher. But her desperate financial straits derailed her plans when she had to stop taking classes at a local college.

Financial problems also press down on our emotional energy, which can keep us from feeling and living as if we're blessed. As discussed earlier, we need to be able to draw from our emotional reserve to be at our best, whether we're launching or maintaining a new creative endeavor or relationship. One self-employed woman whose house was in foreclosure was surprised at how quickly she was able to start generating more cash once she took action to shore up her finances. Robbing Peter to pay Paul is emotionally exhausting.

Failed finances can also distance us from our inner spirit. As we are asked in Isaiah 55:2, "Why do you spend your money for that which is not bread and your labor for that which does not satisfy?" The question posited is a good one: Why spend money on that which has no intrinsic value? So what about that new designer bag that you may have charged on your credit card or that unplanned trip to the islands? While creating a momentary thrill, what do they mean for you in the long run? Don't misunderstand me. I enjoy spontaneity and certainly have an appreciation for the perfect pair of heels, but not at the cost of throwing my finances out of whack. Besides, even the hottest pair of heels can't fill my spiritual hunger. What I need is available for the asking. It was Jesus who told us, "I am the bread of life" (John 6:48).

And let's not forget the subject of success, in this final exploration of the second *S* in "blessed." In today's computer age, taking a look at someone's credit record is as easy as a potential employer pushing a few buttons. A poor credit history can leave you stuck in the slow track, far away from the mission you've discerned with God's help.

Financial recovery expert Glinda Bridgforth counseled one woman who left her high-level management job in the human resources department of an insurance company. This woman was humiliated when a head hunter confided that the reason she wasn't getting many job offers was that corporations were frightened off when they saw she was late in paying some of her bills. Bridgforth says, "It's no longer unusual for companies to use your credit rating as a criterion for judging you when you're applying for a job." She points out that a poor credit score can also translate into paying higher interest rates on a mortgage, which will leave you with a lot less money for doing the right thing. It might also mean being denied that apartment you want to rent, which can certainly dim your sense of abundance.

The point is, even if you aren't in a financial hole, if you're not where you want to be, start now to work toward financial health. And set an ultimate goal of creating wealth. Notice I didn't suggest that you should aim to grow rich. "Rich" pertains solely to money. As financial wizard and Bible teacher Obie McKenzie reminds us: "Wealth is not measured by how much you have but how little you need. Wealth is rooted in contentment and satisfaction. A real sense of abundance is created by the gift of presence; the ability to stay in the moment, not in the past or in the future."

That may sound like a strange mouthful coming from a man whose job requires him to put together pools of money, as in a recent $4-billion investment deal. But McKenzie says his spiritual roots help him see beyond that which money can buy. "The Christian faith is grounded in the word 'giving,' as in God *gave* his only begotten son." McKenzie says that we don't need to be rich to give, not if we follow his golden monetary rules: Don't borrow money (unless it's for something like buying property); get rid of credit card debt, which can be ruinous; and don't spend more than you have.

Glinda Bridgforth agrees, and offers another word of advice: "Even if things seem out of control, take action. Don't bury your head in the sand. There are steps you can take to get started on the road to financial recovery." She should know. Bridgforth, a former bank executive and author of a series of best-selling financial advice books, was mired in debt following a painful divorce. Today she has not only rebuilt her finances, but started a holistic financial management agency that counsels clients throughout the United States, and is a frequent guest on television and radio shows. Bridgforth is also a joyful newlywed. Her husband, by the way, is a good Christian man—and as far as I'm concerned, there can be no higher endorsement. Bridgforth, who took action steps to recover her finances, never faltered in her daily habit of thanking God for His gifts, and asking for His continued guidance. In fact, she readily credits God for helping to bring her right to where He wants her to be. She is indeed a woman of wealth and wisdom.

Here are some action steps to help you shore up shaky finances or save or invest more cash so you can carry out your mission in life.

Taking Charge of Your Financial Future with God's Help

1. Ask God for help. As you speak to God through prayer, continue to thank Him for showering you with gifts and

for continuing to keep you strong and focused as you bring yourself to financial health and wealth.

2. Forgive yourself. If your finances are not where they need to be, take responsibility by taking action, but don't waste emotional energy blaming yourself. Corporations spend millions of dollars devising advertising campaigns that make their products and services seem irresistible, so it should not be surprising that you have been lured by their messages. Use your internalized nurturing voice to soothe and comfort yourself. Focusing on your God-given mission in life will build up your resistance.

3. Keep tithing. This may sound self-serving coming from a minister, but not if you keep in mind that you don't tithe to your pastor. You tithe to the glory of God. You tithe because you're blessed. You tithe because God wants you to. The practice of tithing dates back to the Old Testament, when those who learned of God's glory began setting aside one tenth of their earnings for God, and lived on the other 90 percent. (After you have set aside 10 percent for God, try to save the same amount for your future goals.) I can personally testify that when you honor God first, He truly blesses your life. Scripture tells us that if we tithe, the Lord will open the windows of heaven and pour down overflowing blessings on us (Malachi 3:10). In other words, God will give us more than we'd ever hoped for. If you're struggling to keep your bills paid and wondering how you can possibly pay 10 percent of your income to the church, try writing the check at the start of each month (or record the amount

on a slip of paper). During the next few weeks, thank God for money-generating ideas and revitalized energy as you go about earning the amount you have recorded. You'll get there. Giving money will boost your emotional and physical energy levels.

4. Balance your checkbook. Sure it's one of those pain-in-the-neck chores, but if you're not already doing it, this is an important first step in taking charge of your finances. Returned bank checks are costly and embarrassing. And we aren't the only ones who make accounting mistakes—bank employees do too, because they're only human. You shouldn't have to pay for their mistakes, or your own. Banks make it easy today to check your balance online, but you'll still want to balance your account at the end of each month.

5. Learn about compound interest. Remember the scenes in horror movies when someone got stuck in quicksand, and as they struggled, seemed to get pulled in deeper? The reason it's so important for you to pay off any credit card debt that you might owe is that these companies charge you compound interest. According to the Internet site moneyinstructor.com: "Compound interest means that the interest will include interest calculated on the interest." For example, if $5,000 is invested for two years and the interest rate is 10 percent compounded, at the end of the first year the interest would be $5,000 × 0.10, or $500. In the second year, the interest rate of 10 percent will be applied not only to the $5,000 but also to the $500 interest of the first

year. Thus, in the second year the interest would be $5,500 × 0.10, or $550. So pay off your credit card debts as soon as possible, doubling up payments when you can.

6. Get rid of extraneous credit cards. You can probably get by using just one for emergencies or for charges that you can afford to pay off by the end of every month. One woman I know follows up every charge by mailing a check for that amount to her credit card company. This way, she doesn't find any forgotten charges when her statement arrives. If you've abused credit cards in the past, cut up all but one and seal that one in a zip-top plastic bag and store it in your freezer. Use it only for emergencies.

7. Attend debt-elimination seminars. My church's development corporation sponsors financial literacy or debt elimination seminars, led by financial experts. Parishioners who attend and eventually pay off their debts often comment on the sense of freedom they experience at being debt-free for the first time in years. Debt is an embarrassing and oppressive force. If your church sponsors one of these seminars, I urge you to attend these goal-oriented meetings. If your church does not sponsor these seminars, organize other folks to get one started.

8. Seek outside help for debt emergencies. If you need help now and there are no debt elimination seminars being held through your church, contact the National Foundation for Credit Counseling on the Web at

www.nfcc.org, or phone the organization in Silver Springs, Maryland, at (301) 589-5600, to locate low-cost financial counseling in your area.

9. Slow down on ATM withdrawals. If your money is shaky, limit yourself to one ATM withdrawal a week, and then be sure to record all transactions in your checkbook. Frequently withdrawing money from an ATM adds to the illusion of picking it off trees. Before you start spending, thank God for the money you do have, and then list the ways you need to spend that money. When you stick to your plan and resist impulse buys, congratulate yourself.

10. Handle your money with care. Smooth out those dollar bills in your wallet and arrange them by denomination—fives with fives, tens with tens, etc. This is another way of showing respect to that which represents your time, talent, and energy in a negotiable form. You work hard for your money and, from this point on, promise to treat it and yourself with respect.

11. Substitute a spending plan for a budget. Rather than writing an impossible-to-follow budget, record every cent you spend for a month. This will give you an accurate picture of what you're spending, and allow you to figure out ways to bring in extra money, if necessary, and find areas where you can cut costs. Glinda Bridgforth's *Money Mastery Book*, for recording twelve months of spending, can be ordered online at www.bridgforthfinancial.com. Remember to celebrate your spending cuts as you trim "fat." For example, if you spend four bucks a day on

gourmet coffee drinks, start brewing it yourself at home, or do your hair yourself between salon visits.

12. Save something. No matter how much you may have to dole out to creditors, put some aside in a savings account on a regular basis. You work hard and you deserve to pay yourself.

13. Read all about it. One of the best books that can help you is *How to Get Out of Debt, Stay Out of Debt and Live Prosperously*, by Jerrold Mundis. In addition to offering practical solutions, this book forces readers to confront their emotional money issues. Two other excellent books that also delve into the emotional realm and offer nuts and bolts advice are Bridgforth's "Girl" series—*Girl, Get Your Money Straight!* and *Girl, Get Your Credit Straight!*, which is scheduled to be published in 2007. All of Bridgforth's books can be ordered through her website, www.bridgforthfinancial.com.

14. Tear up blank checks that come in the mail. Louisa found an effective way to stop putting aside these blank checks to use on rainy days, a practice that later came back to haunt her in the form of out-of-control debts. She says, "I started picturing them as a syringe filled with drugs, and me plunging a needle into my arm." While it was true that the checks could ease her through emergencies, she came to realize that they were dangerous for her financial and emotional health.

15. Pay your bills on time. Record payment due dates on your calendar and mail your payments out, allowing extra days for them to be delivered and credited to your

account. The companies are not necessarily anxious for you to pay your bills on time because they profit from late charges, but being late can mar your credit report. One woman who used a Discover card simply to pay for the company's travel accident insurance—only $7.95 a month—was late with one payment. She was stunned to learn that this was recorded as a "30-day late" to the credit bureau and that her credit score was lowered a number of points.

16. Study your financial roots. Look back at your family history and consider the messages that were passed on to you about money. Perhaps there was a lot of drama and anger concerning money during your childhood. Could you be acting out what you learned? If so, figure out ways to break the family patterns. *What Mama Couldn't Tell Us About Love*, by Brenda Lane Richardson and Dr. Brenda Wade, is an excellent resource for breaking damaging family dynamics.

17. Invest money. Investments are like worker bees that keep going around the clock while you sleep and play. Talk to an investment counselor for help in making your money grow, and read Bridgforth's *Girl, Make Your Money Grow!* Her coauthor on this investment guide, Gail Perry Mason, whose story is included in the next chapter, helps clients choose stocks and other investments that reflect their values. Perry Mason can be contacted at gpmason2000@aol.com.

18. Generate extra cash. Consider your many God-given gifts and consider how you might use them to generate extra

cash. One of Glinda Bridgforth's clients used her strong organizational skills to help people organize their closets, garages, and offices. She used the extra money to pay off bills. Another used her cooking skills to sell homemade dinners to her fellow tenants. Other ideas for earning extra cash include: sewing and selling made-to-order quilts; restoring old furniture and selling the pieces; buying books from friends and associates and reselling them at a profit.

19. Enjoy your own reality show. It's easy to get caught up in the fantasy lives portrayed in television and film stories. Even when playing lowly paid workers, some stars inhabit the roomiest, most well-decorated apartments and wear the most fashionable clothing. On the other hand, characters driving older cars and wearing bargain clothing are portrayed as "losers." In truth, real losers are people who know better, but who waste their money anyway. Don't allow Hollywood images to ruin your relationship with the Almighty by constantly complaining to Him about what you don't have. By developing an attitude of gratitude you can learn to focus on the here and now. Thank God for gifts you might take for granted, including the vision that allows you to read these words and the chair you may be seated on, which offers physical support. As artist Henri Matisse once said, "There are flowers everywhere for those who bother to look."

20. Get thee to the library. Cancel your book club membership and visit your local library. If you don't see

books by your favorite authors, ask your librarian to do an interlibrary loan or order them. A free public library system is a blessing offered by few other countries. You may also want to buy more used paperbacks to cut back on spending. (Many used books are available at Amazon.com.) Another option is to start a book club at your church and offer to share or swap books with other avid readers.

PART VI

B
L
E
S
S
ENCOURAGEMENT
D

CHAPTER 16

Encouraging Others

I don't know about you, but when I see a film, I don't want to leave the theater dragging my feet and feeling hopeless. I like stories that leave me feeling hopeful. My favorite books are also the ones that leave me feeling hopeful. That's why I love reading scripture, and it's one more reason that I love the Lord. He is the bearer of good news about the Kingdom, offering us hope in salvation. In fact, the word "gospel" means good news. He encourages us through a method called "reframing."

That word means pretty much what it sounds like. Imagine a picture of something that's so dreary, every time you glance at it, your spirits plummet. But take the picture off the wall, pull away the worn, dusty border, encase it in a beautiful frame, and suddenly you see the picture quite differently as you notice details that you missed earlier: The gilt frame shines and makes the colors appear more vivid. And now you can see that the objects in the picture symbolize treasures that seem within reach.

Jesus was a masterful teacher who used reframing to convey His message. In reminding us not to get caught up in day-to-day worries, he suggested that we see with new eyes, everyday, ordinary aspects of nature: "Look at the birds of the air; they neither sow nor reap nor gather into barns, and yet your heavenly Father feeds them. Are you of not more value than they?" (Matthew 6:26), and, He added: "Consider the lilies of the field, how they grow; they neither toil nor spin, yet I tell you, even Solomon in all his glory was not clothed like one of these" (Matthew 6:28–29).

The human mind is too complex, of course, to simply dismiss worries with a false sense of closure, and so God blessed us with the ability to encourage ourselves. During worrisome times it helps to find a quiet spot and sit comfortably, close your eyes, and breathe deeply. Even in a city as big and as busy as New York, I often find quiet spots. One of my favorites is a park behind the mayor's mansion, where I often sit beside the water to watch the waves dance and remind me how to get back into my flow and natural rhythm of life. Rather than trying to push your worries away, line them up like toy soldiers and let them pass through your consciousness. With God's help you are in control of those worries, and that means they can't crowd into your head and create a sense of panic, not if you remember the words of our Savior. Picture the birds and the lilies. Notice the details. See the birds swooping and playing and feeding their young. Remember that God provides. Watch as the lilies sway in the breeze, hundreds upon hundreds of them, representing God's abundance. After each vision, as you continue to breathe deeply and evenly, allow another concern to enter, followed by the bird and flower images. As you continue this meditation, your concerns subside, especially as you thank God for your many gifts, and ask Him to help you see your concerns in a new light. He will show you a way. Like the birds, your concerns will take flight. Like the lilies, your problems will be buried beneath the soil.

I hope this exercise allows you to tackle your problems with renewed courage. "Encouragement" means to arm with courage. God works through us to help us encourage one another, and I thank God for any opportunities He gives me to imitate and make visible signs of His Kingdom. It is the spirit of encouragement and hope that binds the Church together as we practice the ways of Jesus, who modeled the peaceable Kingdom.

As we continue exploring "blessed," through the final *E*, for encouragement, I urge you to look closely at the people whom you turn to for advice, and ask yourself whether they reflect the kind of encouragement all of us need. People are sometimes surprised to learn that four of my closest friends are seventy or older. I've always been drawn to older people, but perhaps especially since my mother's death, because I appreciate their wisdom and life experience. And I'm not talking dropping by to pay my respects a few times a year. No, these vibrant, brilliant, and wise folks could be considered my girlfriends. Well, that's not completely true, since one of them is male.

You may recall me mentioning earlier my spiritual advisor, the Reverend Doctor Elliott James Mason, Sr., who is eighty-three. He is such a gift in my life that sometimes, after a hard day, I return home and check my telephone messages, only to discover that he has called and left a prayer for me, my family, and my ministry. I often turn to him for advice and feel so blessed to even know this pious, God-fearing man.

My prayer partner—we meet at designated times throughout the week to pray for each other's concerns—is Mercedes Nesfield, who, at seventy-three, is a ball of energy. In 2002, I convinced her to start working with a personal exercise trainer, so she now does weight training, in addition to tennis and power walking.

Shortly after my mother's funeral, I grew much closer to Dr. Thelma C. Davidson Adair, eighty-five, a longtime and dear friend of my mother's. She and Mom, both of whom worked in the field of education and were natives of North Carolina, met in the 1940s, as two of a handful of African Americans in the predominantly white Presbyterian Church. And just as my mother had dedicated her life to encouraging others, so too had Dr. Adair.

Some people refer to her as the "Mother of Harlem." She and her husband, the Reverend Arthur Eugene Davidson, organized the Mount Morris Ascension Presbyterian Church, and she helped establish Mount Morris New Life, which operates a children's day-care center that today serves more than two hundred Harlem families. When the federal Head Start program began in 1965, Dr. Adair organized the programs now offered at five Harlem locations.

And just as Oprah has asked Maya Angelou to serve as village mother, because she appreciates her sage advice, I and several other women look to Dr. Adelaide L. Sanford, the New York State vice chancellor for the Board of Regents, the state's educational governing body. As the unofficial leader of our group, Isis, she is one of the most astounding speakers of our time. Because of her encouraging nature, she knows just how to get us talking, but she has a story of her own that needs to be told.

Decades ago, in the Bedford Stuyvesant area of Brooklyn, as the principal of P.S. 21, she helped build this failing public elementary school into one of the city's most high achieving. Her methods included teaching the parents and their children—most who lived in a nearby public housing project—about the glory of their African and African American ancestors. Dr. Sanford says, "We took down illustrations of our nation's leaders, such as those of George Washington and Benjamin Franklin from the walls, and replaced them with pictures of black people of achievement, who looked like the students." Plants and vases of flowers were set up in hallways, and in addition to instituting a more rigorous academic curriculum, she insisted that the children study black history and literature. "And I taught the parents that although they might not have much education, they had an inherited genius and they knew how to raise gifted children."

Twenty years after leaving her principal's post, Dr. Sanford is still stopped and thanked for her work, by graduates of P.S. 21, many of whom have gone into banking, education, and numerous other professional fields. The student she may have most impacted never attended her school, however. She met him a few years ago, after making a speech. "A tall, solidly built young man asked if he could speak to me, and when we were alone, he said, 'You saved my life.' I asked, 'Do I know you?' And he said I didn't know him, but that he knew me." He went on to say that several years earlier, he was a prisoner in solitary confinement. He said, 'I didn't care whether I lived or died, and didn't love anyone, including myself.' " Someone had given him a tape recorder and a tape of one of Dr. Sanford's speeches in which she spoke about the history of the African people, and she encouraged their descendants to honor those achievements by making the best of their lives. Hearing the tape changed him, he said. While still in prison, he worked hard to get his general equivalency diploma, and after his release attended college. He concluded with the news, "Now I'm getting a master's degree from Temple University."

A little bit of encouragement can go a long way. It's not something we do as Christians to be nice, it's what Christians are expected to do. On that note, I'd like to share the stories of two young women whose lives were saved by God through encouraging adults. Both are equally impressive human beings.

Gail Perry Mason, first vice president of investments for Oppenheimer, in Grosse Point, Michigan, is a wife as well as a mother of three sons. Most Tuesday evenings, she works with children at an orphanage, teaching them that it's practically sinful to not use the gifts God has given them. "When I first started working with these children, I asked them each to name the gifts that God had given them, and for them to tell me the ways in which they'd been blessed. They remained silent."

One older boy, attempting to speak for the other children, acknowledged that they all had gifts, but he said he didn't believe that they came from God. He demanded of Perry Mason, "If there's a God, why would he allow us to be here? If there's a God, why did some of us come from homes where our parents beat us or burned us or cut us?" When Perry Mason pointed out that there are lots of good people, the boy revealed a deep level of cynicism. He said, "Sure, there are corporations that contribute to places like this, but they only doing it for the tax write-offs. So where's the God that makes them good?" She was stunned by his words. "I wanted to answer him, but I was crying and didn't know what to say."

The next week, when Perry Mason returned, she asked the children to tell her what they wanted to be when they grew up. They had big dreams, and she enjoyed listening to them. After they'd finished, she challenged the children, asking, "If God forgot about you, where did you get the ability to sing...and you, the ability to draw..." and she went around the room, having memorized their dreams and respective talents. The children remained subdued, even the boy who'd spoken for the others.

One little girl concluded, "I guess He didn't forget us, Ms. Mason." From there, her classes began. Through the years she has helped these young people identify their talents and plan on using them. If one wants to be a mechanic, for instance, Perry Mason researches a range of salaries for mechanics, and then helps the individual see what that salary would afford. "We break it down. If they want a certain car, then the child has to figure out how much that will cost a month. If he wants to live in a certain place, we look at the rents." Once expenses are added up, the child begins to grow more realistic, perhaps deciding that an inexpensive Saturn might be a safer bet than a sports car, until money is saved and invested. Through the years she has worked with hundreds of children.

Her interest in the orphanage is personal. A few months after her birth, Perry Mason, now forty-two, was given up for adoption—in this place where she volunteers—by her white biological mother, whose relatives were furious that she'd become pregnant by a black man. There's a good chance that Perry Mason might have spent her entire childhood in this place. She certainly wasn't considered most likely to be adopted.

"I had hip dysplasia; my hip was deteriorating, and I couldn't walk. I also couldn't talk by the age of three, and I was baldheaded." Perry Mason thinks she was withering away, from lack of love. "The staff was stretched thin and there was little time for each child. I was picked up and played with for fifteen minutes a day, according to a schedule that was listed on a chart over my crib."

Despite a less than promising start, Perry Mason was adopted by a woman with meager financial resources, whose love and encouragement worked wonders. By the age of five, Perry Mason was not only walking, but running, and talking—in fact, her ability to speak is one of her gifts, along with a head for numbers and knack for making money for her clients.

By working with young people, Perry Mason hopes to return the investment her adopted mother made in her, and she works hard at it. She hasn't had a vacation in seventeen years, in part because she sponsors a summer camp for sixty African American children, many of them from extremely difficult circumstances. She pays for the endeavor out of her own pocket, and it costs her thousands of dollars, as she hires teachers who instruct them on everything from table manners to investing, and buys the children eyeglasses and pays for dental work—whatever is needed to help them return to school ready to learn.

Mason launches the first session of the summer camp by holding up a hundred dollar bill and asking if anyone wants it. This quickly gets the attention of the participants. Then she invites them to come up and stomp all over the bill. Once the frenzy ends, and Ben Franklin's face is scuffed and the bill frayed around the edges, Perry Mason asks if there's anyone out there who'd still like to have it. As the kids yell and shout and wave their hands, vying for the bill, she makes her message known: "Even though this bill has been through some hard times, it hasn't lost its value. Some of you in this room have been through hard times too, but you're still worthy. Your gifts are intact. Don't let anything stop you from performing at your highest level."

Perry Mason is inspirational, but so is Toni Daniels, whose story begins in Meridian, Mississippi, during the Jim Crow era, a time marked by the rigid enforcement of segregation. The early fifties were also a time when the dreaded polio epidemic killed and paralyzed thousands of Americans, many of them infants and children. By 1956, the disease was on the wane. A polio vaccine, introduced the year before, exposed children to a small dose of the virus that was designed to trigger their immune systems to produce chemicals that resisted the disease. In some cases, however, the inoculation actually gave people the disease. That's what may have happened to Toni Daniels, who at the time was a healthy three-year-old, living with her grandmother in Meridian while her parents worked to put money aside, hoping to give her and her brother a comfortable life.

Twenty-four hours after Toni's inoculation, the usually active child was bedridden, and her grandmother phoned the local physician and reported that the child was suffering with a sore throat, fever, and headache, early symptoms of the disease. "There were no black doctors practicing in the area," Toni recalls. Some white physicians treated their black patients scornfully, and the man her grandmother contacted was no different. "He dismissed her concerns, and insisted that I'd only come down with a cold." A few hours later, when her grandmother called again, reporting that Toni was showing signs of muscle weakness, another symptom of polio, the doctor told her not to call again.

"About two hours later, when she tried to wake me up, I was like a rag doll. I couldn't lift my head or sit up. She called my uncle, my mother's brother."

The two adults rushed her to the closest hospital, despite its policy of not treating black people. According to Daniels, "This white nurse took one look at me, and said, 'We don't know what she has, but we're not taking her.' "

Knowing that the polio virus spreads through the body like poison, attacking nerve cells and eventually an individual's nervous system, Daniels's grandmother and uncle drove fifty miles, to another hospital. The head nurse was just turning them away when proof was offered that God's spirit can overcome the most hateful circumstances. A white doctor intervened, telling the nurse, "You can't send her away. This child is in respiratory failure."

He was new at the job and young, but when the nurse warned him that he might get fired for treating Toni, he followed the example of Jesus, traveling through Galilee: "healing all manner of sickness and disease among the people" (Matthew 4:23).

Polio is not curable, and it had already marked little Toni's body. She was placed in an iron lung that helped her breathe, and once she was out, she wore a full body-brace until she was six years old. Today, however, thanks to ten surgeries and physical therapy, she can stand and walk and uses a scooter for traveling through hallways and streets.

Toni's grandmother reframed the story of what had happened in that emergency room, shaping the type of person she would become. "She didn't want to teach me to hate white people, and she didn't believe in hanging on to bitterness." Instead, they shared the good news. "They told me about a doctor risking his job to do what he knew was right, and how I'd been blessed."

This sense of being saved through God's grace later helped Daniels survive at the University of California, Los Angeles. While many of the school's 25,000 students have received exceptional levels of academic preparation, Daniels attended a school for handicapped children, which had not provided a challenging education. "I read only one book all the way through high school," Daniels says.

The university's admissions committee, realizing her great intelligence, did accept her, however. And she chose one of the most challenging majors: science, with classes that included calculus— which she failed. "I must have cried every day of my freshman year," she recalls. Help arrived in the form of another young black woman, Kathy Brown, who has since become a physician. "She'd noticed that I was often in the library, working really hard, and she asked me if I needed help." In the days and weeks to come, Kathy Brown would tutor Daniels and share her notes. If she didn't know a subject, she'd find someone who did. "Several of the other black students rallied around and helped me out." Through the years, Dr. Brown and Daniels have maintained a close friendship.

Daniels did graduate from UCLA, and later, in 1996, she earned a master's in business administration from Baruch College in New York, and she has since read enough books to make up for the lost years of reading. Her close involvement in the church has continued and led to her accepting a job as the executive director of enrollment at the General Theological Seminary in Manhattan, a postgraduate institution. Daniels is single, financially secure, and fit and independent. In fact, she's considering taking up the sport of hand-powered bicycling.

During the summer of 2005, Daniels attended the Billy Graham Crusade, along with hundreds of thousands of others. Reverend

Graham prayed for every facet of God's community to be transformed as the Gospel is proclaimed. Daniels looked around through the crowd and saw faces of every human shade—some heads were bowed, others lifted skyward, hands clasped, arms raised in joy—and she knew that she was alive and had been blessed with the ability to encourage others because the light of God is so mighty, it shines through the darkest of nights. To that I say, amen and hallelujah. Glory be to God, the highest.

PART VII

B
L
E
S
S
E

DEVOTION

CHAPTER 17

Devotion During Hard Times

As you turn to this last chapter and explore *D*, for devoted, in "blessed," you may wonder about the process that was used for selecting people with this final characteristic. The individuals whose stories appear in the preceding chapters have exemplified *Balance, Love, Energy, Spirit, Success,* and *Encouragement.* But this last characteristic, devotion to God, requires steadfast love and loyalty to God.

So how could I find people of such faith? The truth is you've already met them through their stories in this book. In some cases, there were stories of neglect, suffering, loss, and abuse, and yet these people kept loving God back, praising His name.

As testimony to the power of the Lord's message, those people were only a few among many. In fact, when planning this book, there was never even a need to draw up a list of those whose stories *had* to be included. Suddenly a name would happen to come up in a conversation or a usually difficult-to-reach individual would call out of the blue or suddenly become available at just the right moment. I can only surmise that God's grace was involved in the process. And I thank Him for His devotion to us.

I have to admit that I was sometimes puzzled about the composite picture of those who generously shared their stories. For instance, I happen to know many people who live blessed lives, and that includes many singles. It turned out, however, that most of the individuals that were interviewed are happily married. I mention this to caution you against misinterpreting this as a sign that living a blessed life requires marriage. Instead, I view these numbers as a direct challenge to the widely held notion that there are no good men out there. You've probably heard this before, for it's a claim that's often made loudly and unabashedly.

In fact, when Brenda Lane Richardson was ready to mail off the manuscript for *What Mama Couldn't Tell Us About Love*—which includes suggestions for attracting "good" men—a postal clerk who'd asked about the subject of her work insisted that anyone who bought that book would be wasting money, because there are no good men. "They're all dogs," she added.

An elderly woman, who'd listened to the postal worker's tirade, said what everyone else within hearing distance seemed to be thinking. She told the young woman, "If that's what you believe, dear, is it any wonder you haven't found someone to love?"

I didn't share that story about how an individual's beliefs can shape her reality to suggest that all single people need attitude adjustments. But the old saying that "chance favors the well prepared" does often hold true. If the unexpected happens, we want to be at our very best. And God does offer us opportunities to grow and transform through even the most horrific experiences. Through discernment we move toward particular goals as Christians, so there's a good chance we'll encounter others who are seeking similar paths. If we don't get what we'd hoped and prayed for, however, it's certainly not because God favors one person more than another.

None of that seems to stop many of us from trying to explain God's intentions, but that is scarcely surprising. We live in a society in which answers are easy to come by, and this is, after all, the Information Age. Want to know how to take the salt out of a ham? We can get online and get an answer. Want to know how to take off ten pounds of unwanted weight? There are shelves full of "proven" weight-loss methods at the local Barnes and Noble. And thanks to an explosion in scientific knowledge, researchers know more about the human body and the mysteries of the universe than ever before. With so many answers a short reach away, it's no wonder that we try to devise easy answers even to the toughest questions, including those that are related to God.

The question regarding why some of us have love in our lives and why others do not seems almost easy in the face of what I call the Big One. Think back on some of those stories you've read, and you may wonder why God would allow such terrible things to occur. It's the most sensitive question of all, perhaps especially because the "wrong" answer can easily offend people of faith. But I believe devotion to God requires us to explore difficult questions, rather than accepting pat and easy answers. This helps us to serve Him better and deepens our faith. For that reason, I'd like to explore some popular fallacies of why bad things happen to good people.

I. We're all born sinners and have to suffer the consequences.
   The notion of original sin is that Adam and Eve's failures
   in the Garden of Eden damaged human nature, and as

such we are all innately predisposed to be sinful and can't overcome this without God's intervention. Simply put, Adam's fall sent human beings into eternal damnation. Well, I do think we're all innately sinful, in our thoughts if not our behaviors, and that as human beings we can't possibly live up to God's perfection. But I take comfort in the image of God as the forgiving Father who welcomes us home. It is only by an act of grace on the cross that we are saved. And I thank and praise Him for giving His only begotten Son, Jesus Christ, Our Lord, who died for our sins. So it doesn't make sense that God would continue to punish us through eternity for our inborn imperfections.

2. God punishes us for our individual sins, and a child's suffering is payment for the sins of the parents. I've often visited parishioners in the wake of tragedies and heard them blame themselves. Someone will say that the sudden death of a child, for instance, is God's way of punishing parents for not keeping up tithe payments or having an abortion long ago. Their need to blame, to put the onus on someone is understandable, but I hasten to assure them that God would never punish them in this manner.

In fact, this subject is discussed in John 9:3, when Jesus is questioned about whether a man who is blind from birth is suffering from his own sins or those of his parents. The Lord refutes the notion that human tragedy is God's punishment for sin. I have no reason to doubt the Lord, and would never believe that our Heavenly Father would ever make innocent children pay the price for their parents' sins.

The idea that if we're evil we'll be punished by God,

and if we're good we'll be blessed by Him is an example of cause-and-effect theory. And there is scripture to support it. "Tell the innocent how fortunate they are, for they shall eat the fruit of their labors. Woe to the guilty! How unfortunate they are, for what their hands have done shall be done to them" (Isaiah 3:10–11). And, according to a proverb, "No harm befalls to the righteous, but the wicked have their fill of trouble" (Proverbs 12:21). Agnostics contrast passages such as these with Jesus's condemnation of the idea that human tragedy is punishment for sin and describe them as contradictory statements. They seem to have missed the point that these would only be contradictory if they had been written by one person. As we know, one of the reasons the Bible is so powerful is that it was recorded by various people who were faithful to their understanding of God.

The cause-and-effect theory of why people suffer is not easily sustained because, as we've often seen, evil doesn't discriminate between good and bad. Time and time again, we see instances in which good people, including innocent children, suffer. For that matter, a lot of evil people suffer too. In the Sermon on the Mount, Jesus points out that God causes the sun "to rise on the evil and on the good, and sends rain on the righteous and on the unrighteous" (Matthew 5:45). One indication of this truth is that some people, who boast of having turned their backs on God, enjoy comfortable lives that include everything from good health to loving families to financial prosperity. I pity these people. They lack a close relationship with the Almighty. But this is a choice the individual has made.

3. God gives us pain so we can become better people. Paul does say that we are made worthy for the kingdom of God through suffering. "We suffer with Him, that we may be also glorified together" (Romans 8:17). And we are told, "through many tribulations we must enter the kingdom of God" (Acts 14:22). This does not mean that God causes us to suffer, but that we have the chance to become closer to Him in our suffering. One example of this is the suffering that slaves endured in the United States. For more than two hundred years, African Americans were beaten and reviled, the women raped, and families sold away. Their response to this suffering was to turn to God in song and words of praise. Millions came away from the experience with so many gifts, such as faith, creativity, and sense of humor. Their faith sustained them and brought out their absolute best.

Given my beliefs about human tragedies, I cannot blame God for our grief and misery. These seem to be more likely explanations for why humankind suffers.

- Free processes in the world. In nature, one act sets off another. For instance, lightning might strike and cause a forest fire, which wipes out thousands of trees. God doesn't stage-manage every natural event, and the same goes for His involvement in our behavior. We too have been given the power to act freely, and those who choose to do evil may negatively affect others. As a result we all absorb the weight of other people's choices. If someone drinks and drives, he or she might strike a child with a car and kill him. God's not causing the suffering of the child or those who love him—it is the act of an individual.

- Effects of nature. Genetics may be the cause of death or suffering. A genetic mutation, such as a bad heart, may be passed on from a parent to child. Also, environmental conditions, like a polluted stream, might cause disease, suffering, and death. And random events such as an accident might occur. In one instance, during an informal school meeting, a young man was sitting on a classroom window ledge. Another student asked to sit beside him, and he reached down and extended a hand to help lift her up. His hand slipped out of hers, and he fell backward out of the window. He died from the impact of hitting the pavement. No alcohol or drugs were found in his system. No one and nothing was to blame for his death. It was purely a random accident.

You may disagree with me about why we suffer. I certainly don't claim to have all the answers. It might be helpful, though, to remember that when Job was crying out about his losses, God challenged him in the same way he challenges us, asking, "Where were you when I laid the foundation of the earth?" (Job 38:4). He was reminding us that we will never understand all of His mysteries. What He wants us to do is to love and trust him despite our lack of understanding. This is true devotion. In the end, it doesn't really matter why He allows us to suffer. What counts is our response to the pain. We must forever continue to praise and thank Him for being the welcoming Father, the confident Father, who runs alongside us, promising that He will be there whenever we need Him. Breaking away from that loving Father is a terrible loss indeed.

We end on a high note, for we are filled with the hope of all that awaits those of us who remain devoted, those of us who take His advice. The answer can be found in a psalm that happened to be a favorite of my parents. Throughout my childhood, I heard them repeat it so many times, that I can still hear their voices as they repeat it together. I invite you to say it along with me, picturing all that we can expect from the Lord when we remain in relationship with Him and enjoy the blessed life.

The 23rd Psalm

The Lord is my Shepherd; I shall not want.
He maketh me to lie down in green pastures:
He leadeth me beside the still waters.
He restoreth my soul:
He leadeth me in the paths of righteousness for His name's sake.

Yea, though I walk through the valley of the shadow of death,
I will fear no evil:
For thou art with me;
Thy rod and thy staff, they comfort me.
Thou preparest a table before me in the presence of mine enemies;
Thou annointest my head with oil;
My cup runneth over.

Surely goodness and mercy shall follow me all the days of my life,
and I will dwell in the House of the Lord forever.